REDEMPTION
The Dhamon Saga • Volume Three

Jean Rabe

REDEMPTION

©2002 Wizards of the Coast, Inc.

Distributed in the United States by Holtzbrinck Publishing. Distributed in Canada by Fenn Ltd.

Distributed to the hobby, toy, and comic trade in the United States and Canada by regional distributors.

Distributed worldwide by Wizards of the Coast, Inc. and regional distributors.

Printed in the U.S.A.

Cover art by Jerry Vander Stelt
Cartography by Dennis Kauth
First Printing: July 2002
Library of Congress Catalog Card Number: 2001092212

9 8 7 6 5 4 3 2

UK ISBN: 0-7869-3007-1
US ISBN: 0-7869-3006-3
620-17984-001-EN

U.S., CANADA,
ASIA, PACIFIC, & LATIN AMERICA
Wizards of the Coast, Inc.
P.O. Box 707
Renton, WA 98057-0707
+1-800-324-6496

EUROPEAN HEADQUARTERS
Wizards of the Coast, Belgium
T Hofveld 6d
1702 Groot-Bijgaarden
Belgium
+322-467-3360

Visit our web site at **www.wizards.com**

DEDICATION

This one's for Janet—

Cat-fancier and coffee connoisseur.

You order the chocolate-raspberry next time,

and I'll get us the table by

the front window.

CHAPTER ONE
WIND AND SCALES

T he creature's leathery wings beat strong and steady as it climbed into the night sky and cut its course against a violent wind. The full moon illuminated a manticore easily the size of a hatchling dragon. It had the body and coloration of a lion, a disconcertingly human-looking visage, and a long, ropy tail ending in a clump of deadly spikes. Without warning the manticore threw back its head and roared, an eerie sound that sliced through the howling wind and sent shivers down its three passengers' spines.

Dhamon Grimwulf sat just behind the head of the manticore, wedged with Fiona between two of the spikes that ran the length of the creature's back. He leaned as far to his right as safe and practical, avoiding the manticore's flailing mane, but the wind stung his eyes and caused the ragged garment's sleeves to billow and snap like a sail. He thought the wind oddly warm, despite it being early fall and so late at night, and despite their flying at least forty feet above the tallest trees of the black dragon's swamp. Fiona's breath was warmer still, and gentler, against his neck. The Solamnic Knight's arms were wrapped around his waist, her chest pressed tight against his back. She spoke into his ear.

"I must buy a fine gown for my wedding, Dhamon. When we reach a city . . . it won't be long until we reach a city, will it?"

Never mind, Fiona, that you haven't a single steel piece in your pocket, Dhamon thought, or that there will be no wedding. Your beloved Rig is dead, and you are mad. You and I saw him die an arm's length away.

"My mother always told me I look best in blue," she added.

"Colors don't matter, lady. Only thing that matters right now is that this damnable beast is flying too fast." The grumbling came from Ragh, the sivak draconian who was perched precariously behind the Knight. "Much too fast in this strong of a wind."

He repeated his complaint twice more, getting no reply—either because Dhamon or Fiona didn't care or couldn't hear his whispery-hoarse voice above the wind and the beast's noisily flapping wings. The draconian was clearly distraught, and his legs were growing numb because he had them clenched so tight around the manticore's haunches. Ragh dug his stubby claws in for good measure, feeling the manticore's coarse hide ripple in protest. The creature roared again.

"And we're too damnably high."

Though most sivaks could fly—they were the only draconians who could naturally do so—Ragh had lost his wings to a cruel punishment and had no desire to see if he could survive a fall from this lofty position.

He kept his eyes trained on the back of Dhamon's head, sucked in a deep breath, and tried to calm himself—fighting the sensation that his stomach was rising into his throat. After nearly an hour had passed and the air had cooled a little, the draconian indeed managed to relax—if only slightly. He decided to chance a brief look below. Peering at the darkness underneath that marked the weave of cypress branches, Ragh spotted a gap in the foliage and through this caught a glimpse of a silver ribbon, which was the moon reflecting off a river tributary. There wasn't much more of the swamp to clear now.

Training his eyes to the west—the direction in which they were headed—Ragh spotted what looked like a pane of black glass, which was the New Sea. Beyond it, barely visible, stretched the wrinkled landscape of the Eastwall Mountains of Abanasinia. A bank of pale gray clouds hung above the peaks like a mantle, and yellow threads of lightning flickered inside the clouds.

Far beneath them, Ragh sensed something worse than a storm brewing. There'd been a prickling at the back of his scaly neck ever since they had left the ground, his uneasiness growing worse by the minute. He'd told Dhamon right away, but Dhamon said he didn't detect anything. That was better than an hour ago now. They certainly seemed to be all alone up here, high in the sky. Nothing was around to bother them.

Still, Ragh took another glance down, this time after several minutes spotting . . . *something* . . . his eyes were far too keen to play tricks on him. There was something there, something definite paralleling their movement, a black shape amidst the darkness of the tree tops. No, two shapes. Maybe three.

Definitely three. But everything was too murky, and they were moving too fast to make out details, save that the "somethings" had wings and were sizeable.

Perhaps he should shout to Dhamon Grimwulf and Fiona that he'd seen . . . *something*. Shout that *something* definitely didn't look right about the shapes following them. He was certain he could be heard above the wind and the wings if he truly wanted to be heard. Perhaps the manticore should dive and hide in the uppermost canopy of the swamp rather than cut through the open sky where there was no cover.

"Fiona," he growled. "We might have company. Fiona?"

No reply.

"Dhamon?" Ragh persisted. Perhaps the shapes were nothing more than a few giant owls, coincidentally headed in the same direction. Or perhaps the strong wind might be tossing the branches a certain way to create shadowy illusions. He craned his neck around Fiona's slender shoulders. Dhamon had his head thrown back and was letting the wind rush across his face, enjoying the ride in the way Ragh used to enjoy flying when he had wings. If Dhamon—with all of his preternaturally sharp senses—was not at all concerned, the draconian told himself, then he needn't be concerned either. But . . . he did see *something*.

Or did he? Ragh squinted and blinked away the tears caused by the wind, stared downward, trying to again find the shapes. There was nothing there now. He stared for several minutes. Nothing but treetops. So ... no reason to alert Dhamon after all. No reason to be dismissed as a worrier, chided about his nerves. The sivak sighed and withdrew his claws from the manticore's hide, placing them lightly around Fiona's waist. Then, like Dhamon, he canted his head back, closed his eyes, and let the wind stream across his angular, silver face.

Dhamon had heard the draconian, had also heard Fiona say something about Rig. He ignored them both. He was trusting that the manticore knew the way to Southern Ergoth, to the Solamnic outpost on its western shore where he wanted to deposit Fiona. The female Knight had slipped into madness following Rig's recent death in the black dragon's city, and Dhamon realized she needed someone to tend to her. He considered himself neither qualified nor obligated to do so. Still, he knew that no matter how insensitive he'd been to people lately he couldn't simply abandon her. And so, this aerial voyage.

"Rig's dead, Fiona," he said, as much to himself as to her. Dead and likely filling the bellies of the foul creatures on display in the city. He doubted the black dragon's lackeys went to the trouble of burying anyone. Dhamon had never truly considered Rig a friend, at least not a close one, but he had respected the mariner and he had, in grudging fashion, admired him, at times envied him. The mariner's death sat uneasily on his conscience, as if there was something he could have done to prevent it. One more departed companion to add to Dhamon's list. To know me is to risk death, he grimly mused.

Dhamon sighed and breathed deep of the air, which was cooling as they flew farther and rose higher away from the heart of the black dragon's realm. He realized some part of him was relishing this crazy ride. It reminded him of the times he was paired with a blue dragon in the Dark Knights' army. He rode that swift dragon at every opportunity, reveling in flying high above the world, feeling cocooned by the air, the wind, the clouds, and the sky.

A myriad of smells filled Dhamon's keen senses: the muskiness of the manticore that bore them; the fetidness of the damp land below; and now the pleasant and salty scent of the New Sea, signaling they were finally beyond the swamp and over the water. There was also the faint sulfurous smell of a blacksmith's shop, which he attributed to Ragh—all sivaks seemed to carry that odor like a brand. Too, Dhamon could smell his own rankness, clothes covered with dried blood and sweat, skin and hair coated with days of grime. He wrinkled his nose in disgust.

Beyond the New Sea lay the mountains that were their destination. He let his thoughts drift and the wind consume him. There would be time enough to address his worries when his feet were again on the ground and when Fiona was in other hands.

Suddenly Dhamon felt the manticore tense beneath him. He opened his eyes and looked over the great beast's side. Through the beating wings he spotted three black shapes rising from the blackness of the New Sea. The shapes were difficult to discern, and if the moon was not out, their coloration would have rendered them effectively invisible.

"Spawn!" Dhamon cursed. He drew his sword with his right hand and firmly twisted his left in the manticore's mane. Fiona's sword was already out, though she kept one hand hooked in Dhamon's belt.

The manticore tucked its wings against its sides, turned, and dived on the lead creature. Ragh again dug his claws into the manticore and swore inwardly for not warning Dhamon about the *some-things* he'd seen a while ago.

They were particularly large spawn, each at least eight feet tall, broadly shouldered, and vaguely man-shaped. Glossy black against the blackness of the New Sea, their scales caught the moonlight and made them shimmer like oil. Through the wind Dhamon heard their scalloped wings beating, faintly heard their almost-in-unison intake of breath, their jaws opening wide. He braced himself.

The lead spawn was the first to release its spray of acid. Under the right circumstances, it would have drenched the manticore and its riders, seriously injuring them all and probably causing them to fall to their deaths. But the manticore had angled itself with the wind, cutting the force of the acid-spray. Only the manticore and Dhamon were hit, and only lightly.

"Aye, but you are a smart beast!" Dhamon called to the manticore. "You use the wind to our favor!"

The spawn hovered, keeping their distance and hurriedly communicating in a collection of hisses and grunts. Dhamon strained to catch the few intelligible words, but even his uncanny hearing couldn't entirely cut through the shrieking wind and the loud, insistent flapping of the manticore's wings. All he managed to pick up were the words "attack" and "ssslay," both of which seemed staples in spawn vocabulary.

Suddenly the middle creature raised its claws, and the other two flew off to either side, attempting to circle the manticore and its riders. Dhamon stretched as far as he dared, leading with his sword and swinging, but he couldn't quite reach the nearest spawn—it was just beyond his range. That meant it was also too far away to claw at him but close enough to breathe on him—and this time the spawn was on the quiet side of the wind. The spawn released a gout of acid that splashed against Dhamon's tunic and burned through to his skin. Most of the spray caught Fiona, however.

"Come closer!" Dhamon shouted at it in frustration. "Fight me, you scaly demon!"

Behind him, he felt Fiona lurch in pain, nearly dislodging him because she was holding fast to his belt. Somehow she held on and was swinging at the spawn on the other side. She shouted in triumph as she landed what felt like a solid blow.

"Fight me!" Dhamon shouted at the nearest spawn, which was readying another blast of breath. "Fight . . ." The rest of his words were lost as the manticore roared louder than before, the sound piercing him and making him so dizzy he nearly lost his grip.

Without warning, the manticore shifted its position, head thrown back so its mane fell across Dhamon, covering him like a blanket. The creature was angled nearly straight up, desperately trying to evade the acid spray, and Dhamon, Fiona, and Ragh threw all their efforts into simply holding on and not being sliced by the back spikes that were cutting into them. As it climbed, the manticore's wings beat at an odd angle, so ungainly that Ragh was surprised the creature could stay aloft. A keening came from the frantically beating wings, a shrill whistling that drowned out the wind and filled their senses, made them feel as if hundreds of heated needles were pricking at them.

"Hold on!" Dhamon yelled to Fiona, shaking his head to work it free of the mane so he could see.

Another roar, and Dhamon believed he'd heard nothing so deafening in his entire life. Not even the roar of the blue dragons on a battlefield matched this eruption. Gritting his teeth, he barely managed to sheathe his sword and with his free hand flailed about behind him until he grabbed a fistful of the Knight's tunic.

"Fiona, hang on!" *Don't become one more name to add to the list of dead comrades,* he thought.

As the painful noise continued, Dhamon sucked in a breath, his chest achingly tight. The sound became unbearable to a man whose hearing was so sharp. The multitude of stabbing needles felt like fiery daggers now, and at the same time, as they climbed upward, he felt as if his body was being pressed down by heavy stones.

"Can't breathe."

He was growing stupefied, as if he were drunk. He felt his blood pounding against his temples, and he was certain he would black out at any moment. He clamped his teeth down on his tongue, hoping to create a different pain that would keep him alert. He wound his hands tightly in the mane and in Fiona's tunic. *The sound is torturous,* he thought. *Does the creature mean to kill the spawn and us, too?*

"Stop!" he shouted to the manticore. "You'll kill us!" Then he bit down on his tongue again and tasted blood.

The sound was also brutal to the spawn. The two smaller spawn slammed their clawed hands over their ears in a futile effort to block out the noise. Dhamon twisted, and through a haze of pain spotted the largest spawn—the closest one—the one who offered the greatest threat. But the enemy as helpless, rather than dangerous. It contorted in the air, wings beating erratically, then abruptly it bucked and seized and plunged like a rock. It finally regained control at the very edge of Dhamon's vision. It hovered there for but an instant, then resumed its dive toward the New Sea until it disappeared from his sight.

"Stop it!" Dhamon tried again, jabbing his heels against the creature's sides. "Stop the noise or we'll die!" The manticore did not pay any attention to him.

Ragh had his chin tucked into his chest and his elbows squeezed against his sides, equally beleaguered, the sound and the pressures threatening to unseat him at any moment. Fiona, too, was fighting to stay conscious in the cacophonous onslaught.

The remaining two spawn had their mouths open, screaming in pain, Dhamon felt certain, though he couldn't hear them over the manticore's keening. Blood ran from one creature's nose and mouth, its eyes were wide and fixed, its wings were beating feebly now. A heartbeat later its wings stopped, and it joined the first in a swift plummet toward the water far below. The last spawn held on, its eyes narrowed, flitting between each of the passengers, lingering on Dhamon—who was the only one able to return its hate-filled glare.

Lips quivering in a snarl, the spawn dropped several feet below them, gaining some distance, only to swoop up suddenly on the other side. The spawn darted in, slashing at the manticore's wing, then retreated to a safe position again—all the while its mouth parted in a hideous, pained expression. Dhamon saw blood glistening in the moonlight, a long rent in the manticore's wing that looked ugly and raw. Still, their massive mount managed to beat its wings, keeping its odd position, its keening continuing unabated as it shifted ever so slightly to once more surprise the spawn by materializing in its path. Then the manticore roared, whipping its tail and flicking out its spikes to catch the spawn in the chest.

The spawn defiantly inhaled to fuel yet another gout of its caustic breath, but the spikes had caused mortal wounds, and the spawn burst in an explosion of its own acid. The manticore howled, as it bore the brunt of the blast. The acid ate away part of its mane and bubbled and hissed against the hide of its forelegs. The manticore had caught some of the deadly acid directly in the face and on the undersides of its wings, too.

Its wings slowed, the keening subsided. The pounding against Dhamon's temples stopped too, and he could breathe easily again. Dhamon released Fiona and felt around behind him to make sure she was OK. He saw she had dropped her sword.

"Fiona." Louder, "Fiona!"

"I'm all right." Dazedly, she placed both hands around Dhamon's waist.

Ragh was grumbling behind her, glancing down to make sure no more spawn were coming. He gingerly withdrew his claws from the manticore—they were covered in the creature's blood, he'd dug them in so deep.

The three spawn were but a token force from Shrentak, a city rife with spawn. At least Dhamon felt certain the spawn had come from Shrentak, no doubt sent to exact revenge for the trouble he had caused there. In that city, several days earlier, Dhamon, Ragh, and Dhamon's best friend Maldred had located an old sage whom they believed had the power to cure Dhamon's malady—the dragon scale embedded in his leg that haunted and tormented him. While the sage was indeed able to remove all the newer, smaller scales that had sprouted around the original scale, she'd done nothing to remove the large scale. In fact, she had disappeared, leaving him and Ragh alone in the catacombs beneath her tower. Maldred had become separated and lost.

Trying to find Maldred or leave, Dhamon and Ragh took a wrong turn and found themselves in the dungeons of the black dragon. Among the prisoners they freed were Fiona and Rig, two old comrades on a foolish quest of their own. During their struggle to leave the city, Dhamon had freed this manticore from a cage in the marketplace. They had left Maldred behind, fleeing to save their lives against overwhelming odds.

"Left Maldred behind," Dhamon muttered to himself. "Perhaps he's dead, too."

Dhamon guessed that despite the still-ferocious wind, it would take the manticore less than two hours to cross the New Sea and reach the coast of Abanasinia. He was right. It was dawn by the time they made it to the mountains. The creature landed clumsily along the edge of a trail, clawed feet scrabbling in earth made slick by the light rain coming down. Dhamon attempted to examine the manticore's wing, but the creature would have none of his indulgence. It licked the wound, then curled up as a dog might and quickly fell asleep. Ragh settled himself nearby and stared grumpily up at the clouds and the thin arcs of lightning that played overhead.

The landscape was as dismal as Dhamon's mood, the scrub grass dead and plastered against the ground, the scant trees leafless and wedged between rocks—everything brown and gray and chill. Fall had a firm grip on the place. He knew all of this country probably wasn't so depressing, that farther down the trail in either direction would be villages, and that quite a bit farther to the north would be larger towns. There would be fires burning. Pleasant conversation and warm food inside dry homes. There would be life.

"And I all I think about is death," Dhamon muttered to himself. He stood several yards away from the others, keeping a wary eye on Fiona. He saw that the skin of her sword arm was bubbled and scarred from the spawn's breath and that part of her hair was melted away. Her cheek and neck also had been hit by the acid, and Dhamon knew she would never look beautiful again. Yet she behaved as though in a trance, showing no awareness of her injuries.

"You're going back to Shrentak, aren't you, Dhamon?" the draconian asked after a long silence. His eyes continued to follow the flashes of lightning. "For your big friend Maldred?"

"Aye," Dhamon said, watching Fiona stretch out under a rocky overhang. The ground looked reasonably dry there. "As soon as possible I will go back. Maldred will trust I'll come looking for him." He paused. "If he's alive."

"You've still got Nura Bint-Drax to slay," Ragh added. "She might still be in the city."

"If she crosses my path."

Nura Bint-Drax, a naga and agent of the black dragon, had caused Dhamon all manner of problems in the past months. Ragh had been her slave, and she'd bled him countless times to create spawn and abominations. Ragh would be her slave still, had Dhamon not liberated him.

"I will make sure her path crosses ours, Dhamon Grimwulf. We will slay her together." The draconian studied him, waiting for a reply and receiving only silence.

The rain had plastered Dhamon's long, black hair against the sides of his face and made his tan skin gleam. He was striking and formidable look-ing, with intense black eyes that held mystery, a firm jaw, and a thin but muscular body that was draped in acid-ravaged clothes. Through a rent in his right pant leg, a large black scale was visible. It was shot through with a line of silver. All around it Dhamon's skin was pink, tender-looking. Ragh had been with Dhamon when the old sage removed the smaller scales. Dhamon was unconscious when the sage proudly told Ragh that she could remove the larger one, too, cure Dhamon completely—for a price. She said Ragh was the price, and the dracon-ian reacted violently, slaying her and hiding her corpse. When Dhamon woke up, the draconian told him that the old woman had given up and left.

The draconian was convincing. Dhamon believed him.

Ragh felt only mildly sorry about the lie. The draconian had come to . . . he mulled over the words, finding *like* too strong, but *tolerate* inade-quate . . . he had come to *accept* the company of the human. Ragh appreciated Dhamon's strength and drive. And he intended to keep him close by to aid in the matter of Nura Bint-Drax.

"She will cross our path, Dhamon Grimwulf," the draconian repeated his vow firmly. "I promise you that. And we will slay her." Then he lay down, and despite the rain fell quickly asleep.

Dhamon woke the draconian several hours later with a none-too-gentle nudge. "I was a fool to let us rest in the open." It was still raining, a spitting drizzle. He nudged the draconian again. "Move, and be fast about it."

Ragh lumbered to his feet, catching a glimpse of Dhamon's leg. A dozen new small scales already had sprouted around the larger one. "Dhamon . . ."

"Fast."

The draconian scowled to note that a puddle had deepened around him while he'd slept and that half of his body was now coated with mud. He began brushing at the dirt and mud, but Dhamon repeated the order and gestured toward the manticore, with a drenched and blank-faced Fiona already perched on its back. Then Dhamon nodded east toward the New Sea. Above it, specks of black hung like ink spatters in the dismal-looking sky.

The draconian squinted and shook his head. "You're thinking that's more spawn?" A growl grew from deep in his chest. "Could be birds. A flock of big ones." But there was that prickling at the back of his neck again.

"Aye, they're spawn." Dhamon headed toward the manticore. "From the look on your ugly face, I don't think I have to tell you."

"I'd rather face such a foe on solid ground."

Dhamon would have preferred to face the spawn on land too—*if* Maldred was at his side, and *if* Fiona had her sword and her wits about her. They might stand a chance, then—a small chance. When he spotted the spawn minutes ago his first thought had been to fly on the back of the manticore to safety in the closest town. But spawn wouldn't be deterred by a town, and their presence would only endanger the citizens there. No, the best chance was to lose them in the sky, evade a fight, something Dhamon found decidedly distasteful.

"We can't fight them in the air again from the back of that beast," Ragh continued.

Dhamon made a snorting sound and was quick to climb up and settle himself in front of Fiona. "I count nearly three dozen of them, my silvery friend. We've got one sword among us. They'll be here soon, so hurry if you want to join us—or stay here and face them alone on your solid, muddy ground."

For a brief moment Ragh considered hiding himself in some crevice, letting the spawn follow Dhamon—no doubt he was their intended target because of the havoc he had wrought in Shrentak. But the draconian didn't want to take the chance that some of the spawn would linger behind and find him alone—he didn't mind dying, but not yet, not with his revenge against Nura Bint-Drax unsated. Besides, Dhamon would be useful in the fight against Nura Bint-Drax—if they could out-fly these devil spawn.

Dhamon tapped the fingers of his right hand on the pommel of his sword and grabbed hold of the manticore's mane with his left. The creature spread its batlike wings.

Ragh was quick to lodge himself between a pair of back spines and dig his claws into the creature, as before. "I hope this beast has some more flying tricks."

"They're some distance behind us," Dhamon said, as the manticore bunched its leg muscles and vaulted into the air. "I'm hoping we can lose them in the clouds." He pointed toward a thick, dark bank high to the west. "Or we can get far enough away that they'll just give up and go home."

The wind was almost nonexistent over the East-walls, and the fine rain came down gentle and soothing. But it was also cool, and as they climbed and headed west, the temperature continued to drop. When Dhamon rode a blue dragon with the Dark Knights, his uniform was thick and designed to protect him from the extreme elements. The tattered clothes he wore now were thin and soaked. While he registered the cold, he was not bothered by it. Fiona, however, also wore tatters and shivered uncontrollably against him.

"What is happening to me?" Dhamon whispered. He knew by all logic he ought to be shivering too, uncomfortably cold—and thoroughly exhausted. He'd stood guard while the others had slept for several hours. He hadn't slept in nearly three days. Yet he was only mildly fatigued. Rather than feeling pleased about his surprising fortitude, he was worried and angered by it. In the past several hours he had watched as the small scales had again materialized around the large scale on his leg—all of the old sage's work apparently for naught. His thigh itched constantly, and he suspected more scales were forming.

"There is no cure. I should've never gone to Shrentak looking for one."

Black spawn wouldn't be chasing them if he'd stayed away from Sable's city. He wouldn't be stuck on the back of this wounded beast headed toward the white overlord's frigid land. Maldred would still be alive, safe, and planning some grand scheme to get riches for both of them. Rig and Fiona? Well, if Dhamon hadn't gone to Shrentak, they'd likely *both* be dead, victims of beatings and starvation in the dungeons.

He felt Fiona shiver again. Despite her madness, her courage was admirable—she didn't complain, not about the spawn, and certainly not about the cold.

But you're going to get even colder before the day is out, Dhamon thought. That was only a certainty, provided they could escape the spawn and eventually reach Southern Ergoth. The island continent— save one stretch of land on its western coast—was covered in ice and snow, courtesy of the white dragon overlord, and the winds that whipped across the land were intensely bitter. But they had to fly over the frigid island, or at very least over one of its glacier-filled bays in the south, to reach the Solamnic outpost on the western shore.

If they couldn't lose the spawn, they wouldn't have to worry about the cold, the ice, or anything any more.

The manticore roared as it climbed higher, and Dhamon could make out words.

"One chance," the manticore said.

They were the first words the creature had spoken since Dhamon had rescued it from the foul city of Shrentak, and as payment had agreed to carry them to Southern Ergoth. The manticore banked southwest, to where the clouds in the distance were the darkest. While the creature had fared well against the trio of spawn the night before, the manticore knew those coming now were too many to handle. The manticore roared again, loud and long and disturbing.

"The storm," Dhamon understood the creature to say. "We will lose them in the storm. Or we will lose ourselves."

For the better part of the day, the manticore somehow managed to keep a long lead on the spawn, and for a time Dhamon believed they might actually outdistance the vile things. But with the setting of the sun, the manticore tired, its sides heaving from its work. They'd passed over the road that ran between Solace and New Ports, only a few merchants on it this dreary day. Their course also took them over the Darken Wood and past Haven, then over Qualinesti, the ancient forest homeland of the elves. The scent of the rich loam was so strong it reached high enough to tease Dhamon's keen senses. They had nearly cleared the forest when a shout from Ragh let them know the spawn were gaining.

"There are *more* than three dozen!" the draconian yelled with as much volume as his whispery voice could summon. "The Black must hate you fiercely, Dhamon Grimwulf, to send a small army after you!"

The prickly sensation was stronger, and the draconian was certain now it was more of a link than a warning, an indication that spawn he had "fathered" were near. Some of those in the pack that was closing in on them must have been made with his blood and Nura Bint-Drax's heinous spell. The draconian reached a talon up to trace the thick scars on his neck and chest, where Nura had bled him to make the creatures.

"Dhamon! Urge this beast to go faster!" Ragh shouted, as he punched the manticore in the side in frustration. "I'll not fall to spawn! I must live to see Nura Bint-Drax dead!"

The manticore was struggling to go faster, sides heaving, and voicing what sounded almost like human gasps. The creature was steadily working its way closer to the thickest of the storm clouds. From the heavy scent of rain in the air, the increase in the wind, and the frequent rumblings of thunder, Dhamon could tell it was a considerable storm indeed. He had no real desire to fly into the midst of it—as a Dark Knight he had ridden a blue dragon, one that could summon a storm, and he knew from experience that it was far from pleasant to pass through a storm with lightning dancing all around.

For a moment he considered commanding the weary manticore to land so they could take their chances on the ground, as the draconian had suggested. Then the manticore finally cleared the forest and the shore and headed out over the sea. A short time later they were under the storm clouds, and the rain and wind were pounding them.

The rain felt like icy darts, driven by a wind stronger than that they'd flown through yesterday. The manticore was having trouble staying aloft. Dhamon shouted to Ragh, but the draconian couldn't hear him. Just as the manticore banked, Dhamon struggled to look behind him, but they were inside the clouds now, and all he could see was an angry mass of swirling gray and occasional bright flashes where lightning arced. When the thunder came, it boomed so loud it shook them, and the wind gusted so strongly the trio were nearly dislodged from the manticore's back. Dhamon desperately gripped the manticore's mane, and Fiona held onto him tighter than ever.

This is madness, he thought, again wondering if he should have stayed on the ground. At least the spawn were an enemy he could fight. This storm— a worse enemy as far as he was concerned—was battering them mercilessly, and they could do nothing to defend themselves.

Dhamon was uncertain how long they'd been in the midst of the clouds, minutes most likely, though it felt much longer. His fingers ached from holding onto the mane so tight, and with each breath he sucked in chill rain. Finally, the cold began to settle over him, seep into his bones, and he wondered how Fiona, even Ragh, could endure the same torture.

How long does the manticore intend to stay in the storm clouds? Dhamon wondered. The cloud bank had looked immense, and it seemed as if the storm could stretch all the way to Southern Ergoth. How long could the manticore keep flying in this foul weather?

As if in answer to his question, the manticore roared and wheeled, dropped, wings tucked close, slipping below the clouds for a look to the east. The creature wanted to see if the spawn had given up.

Dhamon tried to peer through the haze and rain and the whipping mane, leaning to look beyond the manticore's head. "By the memory of the Dark Queen," he cursed. There they still were, nearly a dozen spawn still coming, fighting their way through the abominable storm. Well, they'd lost at least some of their pursuers, he thought, until Ragh shouted a warning, and he felt a splash of acid on his back. Some of the accursed spawn had managed to work themselves above them and were attacking the manticore.

Twisting, Dhamon drew his sword just as the manticore spun about again. The rain came at Dhamon sideways, blinding him so all he saw were shifting masses of gray, flashes of lightning, and the streak of a spawn's black claw. The spawn's sibilant cry blended with the rush of the wind as it raked Dhamon's sword arm. At the same time it breathed a gout of acid almost straight in the manticore's face. The creature bucked and rolled but somehow kept its equilibrium, as it tried to dodge the spawn.

Flying alongside them, the spawn taunted Dhamon. Fragments of words were heard above the wailing chorus of the storm.

"Grab you," it said. "Take you."

Dhamon shuddered as he swung recklessly at the creature. He put all of his strength into the blows, as he was also fighting against the wind. He finally managed to connect, but it was a glancing blow. The spawn darted in and swooped back, clawing him and cackling. "Capture you."

"No!" Dhamon shouted. "You'll not take any of us!" If the spawn didn't mean to kill him, then it must plan to return him to Shrentak to face some obscene punishment or to be turned into a spawn—Nura Bint-Drax had tried to do that to him once before. "We'll die first!" Dhamon meant it. He was certain the scales on his leg were killing him slowly anyway.

"Take you!" another repeated, as spawn surrounded them.

A swirl of black moved in front of Dhamon, howling with the howling wind. Another swirl. Dhamon swung at one, as he felt the manticore jerk and thrash. He felt another splash of acid mixing with the beating rain, his tattered tunic dissolving and falling in shreds, his skin burning. The manticore shrieked in pain and struggled to keep its balance, stay aloft. Now he heard Ragh screaming. More splashes of acid.

The manticore roared, words Dhamon barely made out. "Blind. I am blind."

By all the gods of Krynn! Dhamon thought as one more blast of acid caught him and splashed over all of them and the manticore. He continued to swing wildly, so wildly that Fiona, hanging on to his belt, nearly lost her grip.

Behind Fiona, Ragh was flailing with one clawed hand, ineffectually batting at a particularly large spawn that was dogging him. Despite the gale, the spawn could maneuver—awkwardly—but its stinging breath was offset by the angle of pursuit and the storm's deluge.

"Solid ground!" Ragh muttered. "We should have stayed on the ground!" Then he felt a solid strike of acid wash over his back. The manticore felt it too. The creature's hide rippled and twitched, its tail was flung back to whip its spikes at a foe it couldn't see.

"Grab you!" a spawn above Dhamon shouted, the words mere whispers in the heinous storm. "Take you to the massster!"

Which would be Sable, Dhamon thought. We're nothing, insignificant, he told himself again. Nothing next to an overlord. What damage I did in Shrentak was nothing in the dragon's scheme of things. How could such a massive dragon be so petty as to command its forces to pursue us?

"I'm nothing!" he yelled as he drove his blade straight up, the effort nearly toppling him and Fiona.

The blade would have struck home, was aimed where the spawn's foul heart beat. But at that very moment, another spawn had managed to slice through one of the manticore's wings. The manticore gave a deadly cry and plummeted, as its passengers desperately tried to keep their grip.

"Grab the man!" one of the spawn shouted. The shout was repeated, other words mixed in. "Ordersss!" "Take the man!"

The cries were all whispers to Dhamon. His world became a swirling mass of gray, the sheet of punishing rain, the bludgeoning wind. Beneath him, the manticore made a heroic attempt to stop its fall, but its muscles worked futilely in an effort to beat its useless wings. The creature whipped its head frantically as it dropped, and the rain-slick mane slipped from Dhamon's fingers.

An instant later, Dhamon's sword slipped from his hand.

Spawn claws fumbled desperately to grab

Dhamon, but they only closed on air. Dhamon fell from the manticore's back, then Fiona and Ragh too, heartbeats later. The wind spun around him, the rain hammered him, Dhamon tried to right himself and grab onto . . . anything. A few spawn buzzed in close, clawed hands outstretched and reaching, but none could catch him as he twisted and plummeted.

"I'm sorry," Dhamon screamed, aiming the apology at Fiona. "Terribly sorry." Sorry for tricking her, months past, to get her and Rig to help him and Maldred free some ogre slaves. Sorry that he let her and Rig go off alone to Shrentak to try to save her doomed brother. Sorry she ended up in the black dragon's dungeons. Sorry that Rig was dead and that she would be joining him now.

To know me is to die, he thought. To. . . .

His musings ended as he slammed into the storm-tossed sea.

CHAPTER TWO
SHEEP'S CLOTHES

T he child sat on a low, moss-covered rock, bare feet grazing a stagnant puddle, toes lazily stirring circles on its surface. The insects were thick around her, a living fog that kept a respectful distance, not even a gnat daring to land upon this child.

She hummed softly, an old elven tune she'd heard months past and had taken a liking to, and the flies buzzed seemingly in harmony. Occasionally the shrill cry of a parrot intruded, and in the distance there was the snarl of a great cat and the noise of something large splashing in the river—but all these sounds accommodated the child's melody and pleased her. A smile tugged on the corners of her dainty mouth, and she tipped her head back to catch the late afternoon sun. Its rays were diffused by the swamp's thick canopy, but they were still intense enough to make the temperature hot and steamy—the way the child preferred it.

Finishing the tune, she glanced down at her

reflection, tinted a pale olive green by the wispy growths on the water. A cherubic face with wide, innocent eyes stared back, and soft, coppery curls moved about her shoulders, teased by a nonexistent breeze. She let out a deep breath, fluttering the ringlets that hung down over her forehead, then she kicked her feet, the littler plops summarily dismissing her reflection. She smoothed at her dress, which appeared to be made of fragile flower petals, and brushed at a spot of water on the hem. Then she spun around and eased herself down on the other side of the rock, giggling when the ferns that grew in profusion there tickled her legs.

"Enjoying yourself?"

"Maldred!" The child spat the name in a tone that was anything but childlike. "You've no reason to spy on me! Not here! Not in my domain! You should be well away from here and—"

"Your domain? You don't own this swamp." The speaker was a statuesque man with ropy muscles tanned from long hours in the sun. Despite his size, he moved as gracefully as a panther, making scarcely a sound as he approached. "You don't own me, either, Nura Bint-Drax. I'll go *where* I choose, and I'll watch *who* I choose."

She made an 'oohing' sound, with a sultry woman's voice, then punctuated it with a petulant little-girl pout. "You'll be *where* the master tells you to be, Maldred, and *when* he tells you to be there. It is he who pulls your strings, as you well know."

Maldred crossed his arms and stared down his hawkish nose at the child-woman. He opened his mouth as if to protest, then changed his mind and shook his head. He was sweating from the heat, his hair and clothes damp with moisture, and beads of sweat ran down his forehead and into his eyes and dotted the skin above his lip.

There was not a single drop of sweat on the child.

"Whereas I am his ally, Maldred, you are his slave," she added pointedly.

He continued to quietly regard her, laboring to appear stoic and unemotional but failing when his mouth turned downward in a sneer. No matter how hard he tried, Maldred couldn't hide his contempt for Nura Bint-Drax.

"The master *came* to me, asking for my help, Maldred. Sought me out above all others in this swamp." She thrust out her chin for emphasis, clearly trying to provoke him with her taunting. "O Crowned Prince of Blöten, you *crawled* to the master, *begging* for his help. That makes me strong and desirable, and that . . . that makes you—" she paused, letting the silence weigh heavy between them— "that makes you practically nothing, O Prince."

There was a sharp intake of breath, but still Maldred held his tongue.

The ageless child paced a tight circle around him, then returned to stand in front of him, her bright blue eyes slowly appraising him. "I'm surprised the master hasn't sent you on some menial errand," she persisted, eyes narrowing and small finger wagging. She pursed her lips and stepped closer, and he retreated to keep her at arm's length.

"Especially since you lost Dhamon Grimwulf in Shrentak. I'm surprised the master doesn't have you cleaning a cave or gathering food for his pets. In fact, I'm surprised he hasn't dismissed you entirely from his service."

Maldred's eyes flew wide, and he finally retaliated. "Dhamon was *with* me in Shrentak. I didn't lose him."

"You lost him to the mad old woman."

"The sage. I *led* him to the sage."

"Which wasn't part of the plan. You should have died for the affront of changing the plan. Helping him wasn't at all part of the plan." She placed her tiny fists firmly against her hips. "Because of your impudence, you lost Dhamon."

"I wouldn't have—"

". . . what? Wouldn't have lost him if the black dragon's minions hadn't interfered? Dhamon had released Sable's prisoners. There was bound to be a fight. Dhamon could have perished there, Maldred, and it would have been your fault. All your fault . . . losing him as you did. I thought you were going to keep such good track of him. I thought you were going to deliver him to the master. Isn't that what you agreed to do?"

"I did what I felt I needed to do," Maldred countered. "Besides, it was all part of the test, wasn't it? All part of pushing Dhamon to his very limits to see if he was the one."

She laughed lightly, the sound of crystal wind chimes tinkling in a breeze. Then the air shimmered and swirled around the child, as if the cloud of insects had all become fireflies performing at her behest. Her pale skin began to darken and take on the sheen of polished walnut, and she began to grow. Her stubby fingers became long and elegant, ending in pointed, manicured nails. Her legs grew shapely and sinewy, complimenting a lithe body that would attract attention in any city. Her face, though attractive, acquired a hardness and was crowned with a cap of short, inky hair that matched her flashing eyes. Her dress of pale flower petals became a worn, black leather tunic that had once belonged to Dhamon Grimwulf. She'd stolen the garment from him, along with his precious magical sword, when he encountered her in Ergothian whore-guise in the foothills of Blöten. She'd nearly killed him then, another one of her tests, but he successfully fought his way out of that trap.

And out of the next one.

"What you felt you *needed* to do . . . ?" She reached out a slender arm and poked Maldred in the chest with a finger. A spot of blood blossomed from where she'd pricked him with her sharp nail. "What you needed to do was bring him here to me. Do you fail at everything you attempt, O Prince?"

He stared blankly, not replying, eyes meeting hers balefully but seeing something in their darkness that made his skin crawl.

"Don't like this form, Maldred? It's human. I would have thought you'd find it pleasing. Or do you prefer my true one?" Her smile was definitely evil now, her eyes suddenly ice.

Maldred involuntarily shuddered as he watched the next transformation.

The seductive Ergothian's skin rippled like disturbed water, changing hue and texture, the smoothness becoming scales as large as coins. Her legs melded together into a tail as she towered above Maldred, and her body thickened. From the neck down she became a snake, one easily twenty feet long. Alternating bands of black and red scales glistened on her like wet jewels in the waning sunlight. Her head was not that of a snake, however, but that of the ageless child, and her copper-colored hair fanned away to form a hood. She raised herself up and leaned back on her coil, looking reproachfully at Maldred.

"Appropriate," he pronounced contemptuously. "You change forms the way a snake sheds skin." A pause. "And one form is no more preferable than the other."

Her eyes darkened and sparkled, and motes of blue light leaped from her face and danced in the air. "You, however, prefer this pretty human shell you've painted over your own ugly body, don't you? Humans are a lesser race, Prince, but I suppose even they are above your inferior race."

The motes of light grew brighter, sharper, becoming yellow, then white, then with a simple gesture from the child-snake, they sprang forward like darts to strike Maldred in the chest.

He recoiled from the impact, hands clutching where the light darts had embedded themselves. He doubled over, gasping, as a second volley struck. He was quick to raise his head, eyes that wished they were daggers aimed at her.

"You bitch!"

He would have continued to curse her, had her magic not taken hold. The light darts had burrowed under his skin and begun to chase away the spell that cast the handsome human form over his real body.

Maldred's muscles bulged, and his frame expanded, ripping his vest and pants until the clothes barely covered him. His chest became broader as he grew to a height of more than nine feet. His sun-bronzed skin changed to a bright sky-blue. His brow thickened above his eyes, his nose becoming larger and puglike. The short hair that had appeared meticulously trimmed turned snow-white and flared away from his face, a wild mane that fell well below his shoulders.

"There," the child-snake said smugly when the metamorphosis was complete. "I do like to gaze upon your true ogre-mage body, Prince. I despise you, and yet I gain greater pleasure from despising something as hideous as your ogre self." There was more silence between them before she added, "I wonder if the master also considers you hideous?"

Maldred's words came fast and angry. "Just which one *is* your master, Nura Bint-Drax? The Black, Sable? Or the one lurking behind us?" He spun and glanced at an ancient willow and the darkness beyond the veil of leaves that hung to the ground, hinting at a cave opening. After a moment he turned back to stare at her. "Or do you really think you can be loyal to several masters?"

She cackled. "My loyalties are certainly not to the overlord in Shrentak. I only pretend to serve that bloated wretch of a dragon—as that serves my *real* master's needs. I gain power and information from Sable. Magical incantations. The ability to create spawn . . ."

"And abominations."

A sly nod. "The things I learn from Sable make me more valuable to my real master. *Our* master."

"Serving two dragons is dangerous, Nura Bint-Drax."

"*Allying* myself with two dragons. And I choose to think it is wise."

It was Maldred's turn to nod, rubbing thoughtfully at his chin. "If Sable somehow wins, you have a place in this fiendish world. And if the dragon behind us wins . . ."

". . . I will have a place *at his side*. She rocked back on her coiled tail, smirking. "Whereas if Sable wins, you lose everything, and if the master wins, you're still nothing more than an ugly servant. No matter what happens, you have forever lost your dear friend Dhamon Grimwulf."

Maldred dropped his hands to his sides, clenching

and unclenching his fists. Dhamon had been as close as any brother to him.

"Does it pain you to betray him, O Prince?"

He would have struck her then with all the force in his massive ogre body, but he detected a rustling in the willow leaves behind him. Looking over his shoulder, he spotted a faint light emanating from beyond the cave mouth.

"So the master has awakened," Nura said simply. She slithered by Maldred and passed through the veil of foliage.

Maldred turned to follow, moved a hand to part the leaves, then paused momentarily. He closed his eyes and searched for the spark within his barrel-like blue chest. Searching . . . there! Wrapping his mind around the spark, he coaxed it to grow until a warmth more intense than this steamy heat rolled down his arms and legs, up his neck, until his skin tingled with magical energy. When he first learned the spell, there were also gestures and words, and it took some practice, but through the years this spell had become second-nature to him. Now all he had to do was concentrate. As the spark brightened, his ogre-mage body shuddered, and the skin began to purl. In the passing of a few heartbeats Maldred appeared to fold in upon himself, and his bright sky-blue skin returned to its sun-bronzed hue. The stark white flowing mane shed, to be replaced by short, blond hair that looked as though it had just been cut and combed. But Maldred's clothes still hung on his human frame in shreds, for his magic only affected his body—not what he wore.

The ogre in human guise retreated to the stagnant puddle and glanced at its surface, satisfied with what he saw. He knew he made a striking man, roguish and powerful looking, and just a bit noble from the set of his jaw. It was a form that turned the heads of women in practically every town and gave men pause about confronting him. It was a patchwork form he'd perfected, taking the best physical features from men who visited Blöten to deal with his father—he'd borrowed the brow of a brigand-king, the build of a pit-fighter, and the eyes of a Kaolyn assassin, who almost a decade ago had been hired to slay an upstart ogre warlord who threatened his father's power-base. Maldred's complexion was that of a young pirate he'd spotted years back on the coast near Caermish, and his smile was from a spy in Wayfold, whom his father had dispatched after he outlived his usefulness. The walk and mannerisms were strictly his own. He had grown to appreciate his human image, to prefer it over his natural form, as indeed he had grown to prefer humans to ogres. Nura Bint-Drax only said what he knew in his heart of hearts; ogres were an ugly, brutish race.

"Nura's right." He frowned and shook his head, released the spell, and his massive blue form again replaced the attractive human one. "I'm not worthy of pretending to be a human."

Then Maldred glanced over his shoulder, seeing the willow leaves that covered the cave entrance rippling from the force of the dragon's breath. A moment later, he brushed aside the veil and entered.

The light inside the cave came from the dragon's eyes—large, catlike, and dull yellow, eyes made murky in part because of a thick film covering them. The dragon, like all dragons, was immense, and not all of the beast was visible because of the dense shadows of the cave, but Maldred could easily make out its massive head and part of its huge neck. The dragon was black, yet it wasn't a *black* dragon. Its form was sleeker, head longer and wider, its color flat, not glossy, and the spikes of the thorny ridge that ran from just above its eyes and disappeared in the shadows along its neck were long and thin. It was not quite like any other dragon on Krynn. There was no scent about this one, though the cave carried the same strong, dank odor as the swamp. This dragon exuded tremendous power and radiated intense dragonfear. This latter had to be suppressed whenever Maldred and Nura Bint-Drax stood in its presence.

"Maaaaldred," the dragon said, drawing out the word in a throaty purr.

"Master."

The dragon looked tired and ancient to Maldred, though he knew that as far as dragons went, this one was actually quite young. Quite young but quite threatening, and Maldred hated the creature almost as much as he hated himself for working for it.

Its snout was vaguely horselike, and Nura Bint-Drax was coiled in front of its face, hands that she had formed, strangely attached to her snake-body, reaching up to gently tease the barbels that hung from the dragon's lower jaw.

"So you have decided to join us, O Prince," the child-snake cooed.

Maldred ignored Nura Bint-Drax but respectfully bowed to the dragon, then set his feet wide. A rumbling raced through the stone floor as the dragon spoke. The words were long and sonorous, and Maldred found himself having to concentrate to understand them.

"The human. Tell me about the precious human."

"Yes, master," Nura was quick to answer the dragon. "I will tell you about the human Dhamon

Grimwulf. As I have already reported, Maldred allowed him to escape from Shrentak a few days past—on the back of a manticore . . ."

The dragon snarled, the sound rocking the cave.

"But I am remedying the situation," she continued merrily. "I dispatched spawn, master. I ordered them to follow Dhamon and his companions and to capture him."

The rumbling grew. Maldred clenched his teeth.

"The spawn will bring him here to us, master," Nura continued. "Dhamon's companions will, of course, be killed, but they are of no consequence. One is an addle-brained Solamnic Knight, the other a worn-out, wingless sivak. I told the spawn to make sure that Dhamon was kept safe but to take their pleasure with the other two."

The rumbling softened, and Nura swayed in front of the dragon, obviously pleased with herself and considering the dragon's rumbling to be praise. Then the rumbling abruptly stopped, and the dragon raised a lip, revealing sharp, misty-gray teeth and a charcoal black tongue.

"The precious human is gone."

"My spawn will bring him back, master. I promise."

"Your spawn are dead, Nura Bint-Drax." The dragon blinked, and a veil of fog appeared in the cave mouth. "Watch." Within a few seconds images materialized in the fog—the manticore and its riders, and the three spawn that initially pursued them.

"Dead."

"I sent more spawn," Nura quickly cut in. "I sent more to be certain Dhamon Grimwulf would be captured. The second force was more formidable— larger in number and stronger, more resourceful— the manticore could not best them all."

"No? I tell you most of those spawn are dead, too." The magical vision in the fog now shifted to show what remained of Nura's formidable force—eight bedraggled spawn flying erratically back toward the swamp, a horrendous storm raging all around them.

"And Dhamon?" Maldred asked in a whisper. "Is he dead, too?"

The dragon growled, and the cave shook once more. If there were words buried in the growl, Maldred could not discern them.

When the rumbling subsided, Maldred met the dragon's gaze. "If Dhamon Grimwulf lives, he will come back to Shrentak. He left me there, and the bond of friendship is too great between us. He will not allow himself to abandon me. He will be back soon, looking for me."

The dragon blinked, and in response the veil of fog disappeared. "My magic does not reveal the precise location of Dhamon Grimwulf and his companions. However, it does give me a sense of where he is headed, and it is not to Shrentak."

"Alive," Maldred breathed in relief. "Dhamon is still alive."

"Tell me, master," Nura quickly cut in. "Tell me where Dhamon Grimwulf is going, and I will send another force of spawn. Within days, I swear to you, Dhamon will be in this very cave and—"

The dragon growled more angrily then, the sound echoing off the stone of the cave and the vibrations threatening to crush Nura and Maldred to the floor. Dust and bits of rock fell from the ceiling, and a crack appeared in the floor. When the tremors finally ended, the dragon reached a shadow-gray talon to its head, scratching at the row of scales along its jawline. One the size of a plate fell to the floor, and this scale the dragon nudged toward Maldred. A pale green glow spread from the talon to cover the scale. The glow became cloudlike, obscuring the talon and scale, then after several moments winked out. The scale sparkled darkly with its own magical energy.

"You say the bond of friendship is strong between you," the dragon said to Maldred. "Prove it. Take this scale and find Dhamon Grimwulf. When you break the scale, you and he will be brought magically to me."

Maldred bent and picked up the scale. The edges of it were sharp and hot, slicing and burning his fingers. He hid the pain and held the scale in front of him, seeing his broad ogre face reflected in its surface. The scale was thin and hard, yet he knew he was strong enough to break it when the time came.

"As you wish," he told the dragon.

"Do not tarry," the dragon continued. "Sable's swamp grows a little larger with each passing day. If you do not wish the swamp to swallow up your beloved ogre lands and your father, you'd do well to find Dhamon quickly. And make no mistakes this time."

"He will be yours soon," Maldred vowed. With one more nod to the dragon and a brief look of triumph at the snake-child, he whirled and left the cave.

Behind him, Maldred heard the dragon say, "I also have an errand for you, Nura Bint-Drax."

CHAPTER THREE
THE SINKING LAND

T he sea embraced Dhamon Grimwulf. Dark and turbulent, the water filled his lungs, and a wave rose up like a giant fist to pound him under the surface. In that instant—when everything was black and overpowering—he achieved a sudden lucidity. He realized that it would be easy to stop fighting. Just let the ocean pull him in deeper, suck in another few gulps of water, sink into oblivion with Rig—with Jasper, Raph, Shaon, and the others—people who had considered him a trusted comrade and who had died in his presence. This was his opportunity to join them. Perhaps his *duty* to join them.

He would suffer no more pain from the accursed scale, no more torment from the dragons that dominated Krynn and vanquished all hope. No more pain from losing friends, no more deaths on his hands. The scale on his leg was killing him anyway, each bout with it was worse than the one before. *Give up*, he told himself. Everyone dies sooner or later. Just take the easy way, and die now. He started to relax and surrender, felt an odd chill overtake him, then an uncomfortable pressure against his ears.

The water was doing its job, suffocating him. But as the pain increased, some part of him began to fight back.

Save Fiona and Ragh, he thought. Think of someone else for a change.

At the very last moment, when he felt his consciousness slipping away, he railed against the storm and the sea. He frantically kicked his feet, drove his arms down to his sides, and propelled himself upward. The scale would kill him soon enough, he knew, but he couldn't die today. He had comrades to save and important things he still must do.

His head broke the surface. He coughed to clear his lungs. The taste of the saltwater was strong and sickening. Battered by the wind-whipped waves, he strained to see through the foam and the rain, all the while fighting to gulp precious air. The water was nearly as dark as the sky, but flashes of lightning occasionally turned it green-gray.

"Fiona!" he screamed. "Ragh!" He prayed to the vanished gods that his companions were by some miracle alive, that he hadn't brought death to two more friends. "Fiona!"

The only response was an echoing boom of thunder and the mournful wailing of the wind. Dhamon bellowed again and again, between the times when he was washed under by the waves. It was a continuous battle to keep his head and shoulders above water, to peer through breaks in the swells, to see something . . . anything.

"Fio . . ." Dhamon's voice trailed off. He felt certain

he'd heard something. He taxed his senses, determined to pick up faint sounds through the crashing of the waves and booming thunder. The noise was loud, the sea cold and bruising.

There! He did hear something. A voice? Concentrating, Dhamon closed his eyes. Was it a hissing? By the Dark Queen's heads! Were there spawn still searching for him?

"Find the man!"

"Lisssten! I hear him. The man isss shouting!"

"Mussst find the man!"

"Heard him!"

"Filthy spawn," Dhamon muttered. "Pitiful, damnable creatures."

"Man! Where isss the man?"

He briefly entertained the notion of taunting the spawn, purposefully trying to lure them closer and taking one or two of them with him to a sweet death beneath the waves. In the end he didn't want to give the black dragon's forces the satisfaction.

How long Dhamon bobbed about in the sea, gulping air when he could, trying to remain hidden from the spawn . . . he couldn't say. Finally he could hear no more hisses, and he guessed the spawn had given up and flown back to Shrentak.

His arms and legs felt impossibly heavy from the effort of treading water, and it was becoming increasingly difficult to keep his sore eyes open with the constant pelting of saltwater. Still, he refused to be defeated, and he forced himself to resume swimming.

More sounds! Fiona? Or had the damn spawn returned? Had Ragh survived?

Dhamon held his breath to listen and once more tried to sort through the storm's cacophony to define what he had just heard. Not words. A flapping noise, but not wings. The groan of wood? A ship? Yes, there was repeated creaking, shouted orders—a few nautical terms he remembered Rig using. The creaking grew louder, then ended in a sharp snap! There was a muted splash of something hitting the water, then screams and more shouted orders.

"What? Help!" Dhamon shouted. Was it truly a ship? It had to be! They were men's shouts, panicked men, and he didn't detect any spawn hisses. The groaning persisted. Timbers protesting the storm! How big a ship? Could the men on deck see him floundering in the water?

"Help! Help!" he yelled, the words bitter and foreign to him. He waved one arm wildly. "Over here! Help! Help us!"

No response.

"Over here!" His shouts faded as he ran out of breath. "Here!"

Still nothing.

The groaning of the ship became fainter, then vanished entirely. The frenzied orders of the sailors became whispers, drifting off into nothingness. Long minutes passed, and Dhamon finally stopped shouting. He was certain the ship had sailed away, and he was equally certain Fiona was dead. Though she was a formidable warrior, the sea was a brutal, unfamiliar foe.

He struck out in the direction he thought the ship had gone, though he couldn't be sure his strokes were actually making any progress. After several minutes something brushed against him, and he instinctively reached for it, hoping it was wooden debris fallen loose from the ship that would help him stay afloat. Instead, his fingers closed on scaly flesh.

"Ragh?"

The draconian coughed a reply and thrust something at him.

"Fiona!" Dhamon said. "By all of the gods of . . ."

"She's alive," Ragh returned, gulping air before sinking, then rising slowly again. "Barely. I can't hold her up anymore."

"How is she?" Dhamon felt her face. She was breathing irregularly, and a flash of lightning revealed a deep, swollen cut on her forehead and bad scarring from the spawn's acid.

"She's tough, for a human," Ragh said. "Not the type to give up. I held onto her all the way down, never let her go. But the fall knocked her unconscious." Ragh went under again.

Dhamon cupped the back of Fiona's head, doing his best to keep her mouth and nose above the waves. He put his arm around her and pulled her away from Ragh.

He could tell that the draconian was struggling worse than him. His ungainly body was not made for swimming.

"Probably good for her she's unconscious. Won't feel anything. We're going to die here anyway, you realize," the draconian gasped, surfacing again. "We will die, and Nura Bint-Drax will go on living."

"I heard a ship!" Dhamon shouted.

Ragh sank below the waves again, and this time it took him much longer to push his way back up. "I heard it, too. Can't see it, though, and it can't see us."

"It can't have gone too far!" Dhamon insisted. He grabbed Ragh with his free hand and used his great strength to swim and keep them all afloat. He blinked to clear his eyes, trying to see something other than night-dark water. "Ragh, if we can get to the ship, together we might be able do something to attract its attention. . . ."

A wave slammed the draconian hard against him. "No ship could survive this!" Another wave crashed against them, loosening Dhamon's grip. The draconian sank again.

"We're not giving up!" Dhamon said. He started tugging Fiona toward what he guessed was a northerly direction. If at all possible he would find the ship.

"Ragh! Follow us!" He saw the draconian break the surface again and begin to swim, struggling to catch up.

Long minutes passed. Dhamon strained to hear the creaking of the masts and the bark of sailors, and he prayed that he might spot some trace of the ship when the lightning next arced overhead. "By all the gods of Krynn," he breathed, finally spotting the ship, or rather a part of it. A section of the vessel floated on a wave in front of him, jagged-looking as though it had been dashed against a reef. The ship had been wrecked.

He struck out for the wooden section, just as the water rose like a mountain beneath him and another fist-like wave surged above him and pushed Fiona and him under the sea. Fighting to the surface, he flailed about with his free hand, grabbing onto the edge of the wooden section before it could float out of range and pulling Fiona and him toward it. He strained to raise her up out of the water and lay her across the makeshift raft. Then he scanned the violent waves in search of the draconian.

"Ragh!"

The thunder boomed, and the wind offered a shrill retort.

Exhausted, Dhamon called out only a few more times before he pulled himself partially onto the wood, his hips and legs still dangling in the water. He didn't want to risk capsizing the thing by climbing on board, so he wedged his fingers into a crack between two boards and held on. When the lightning next flashed he saw that the draconian had somehow found the raft, too, and was holding fast to the opposite side.

"Solid ground, Dhamon," Ragh muttered weakly. "I told you we should have fought the spawn on the ground."

The draconian said something else, but Dhamon didn't try to make out the words. He closed his eyes and despite the chaos that surrounded him, he gave in to his fatigue. The world faded to gray, and he drifted between sleep and wakefulness, his aching fingers clinging to the wood. He regained full awareness just as a large wave pushed the raft onto a sandy shore.

The storm had finally ended. Stars winked down from between gaps in the thinning clouds. The wind was still strong, but nothing compared to what it had been earlier. From the color of the sky, Dhamon could tell dawn wasn't terribly far away.

Ragh crawled on his hands and knees until he was farther up on the beach. Finally satisfied he was beyond the wash of the tide, the draconian lay down on his side and retched, then flopped onto his back. "Drowning wouldn't've hurt as much as this," he said. One clawed hand held his side. "Solid ground, Dhamon Grimwulf."

Dhamon managed to push himself to his feet, then bent down and grabbed Fiona and carried her to the draconian. He set her down, carefully prodding the wound on her head. It was probably infected, but at the moment he had nothing to treat it with. He carefully felt her ribs and stomach, satisfying himself that there were no more serious injuries.

"Wonder where we are," Ragh said.

"Certainly not where we were headed," Dhamon answered.

"So this isn't Southern Ergoth."

"It isn't the Qualinesti forest either." Dhamon turned to gaze out to sea, wondering if any of the sailors from the ship had made it through the storm.

The draconian propped himself up on his elbows. "You have no idea where we are, do you?"

Dhamon brushed the sand off what was left of his trousers and studied the beach. Coarse white sand littered with pea-size pebbles stretched as far to the north and south as he could see. To the west was a high, rocky ridge. He could see no trees, no sign of other people, not even a hint of wildlife, no other wreckage washed up from the ship. Dhamon took a few steps away from Ragh and Fiona and shook out his arms.

"Dhamon!" Ragh called. "Where do you think you're going?"

Dhamon shrugged. "For a start, I'm going to try to find out where we are, see if I can find a stream, some source of drinkable water. I'll be along after a while. Keep an eye on her, won't you? If she wakes up, don't let her go anywhere."

The cool air had dried Dhamon by the time he crested the ridge and discovered a wide trail on the other side. The trail paralleled the ridge, running almost straight north until it curved west at the edge of his vision. From its width and the shallow ruts, he could tell wagons used to travel this way, but that was some time ago, as the path was covered with scabrous grass and seedlings. He knelt to examine the ground more closely, wishing it was daylight so he could see better. Maybe he could spot some footprints.

He guessed it was more than a few years since a wagon came this way. He stood and stretched and worked a kink out of his neck. He should still be tired, after their strenuous ordeal. He should want to rest with Fiona and Ragh, should ache from the battering he'd taken. Instead he felt curiously strong, as if he'd just arisen from a full night's sleep.

He scanned the horizon, visible now in the dim light of predawn. There were no signs of anything except a few long-dead trees. The distant cawing of a crow gave him a little hope—there was *some* life here . . . wherever here was.

"Not in Southern Ergoth. No snow. Not cold enough. Not in Qualinesti." Dhamon had been to the latter land, and he knew it to be lush and stirring with growth no matter what time of the year. "We can't be *far* from Southern Ergoth," he told himself.

He started down the trail to the north, first at a walk, then at a loping run. It felt good to stretch out, the running freed his mind. As long minutes passed, then an hour or more, the sky lightened further, but he still saw no signs of people. The trail had become overgrown with scrub grass.

When he heard another crow, he spun to the west, picking up two birds gliding to land somewhere behind a ridge of rocks. He noticed other ridges and wondered if they had been engineered by men rather than nature. They looked a little too uniform. Deciding to take a closer look, he jogged toward the next ridge, only to stop in his tracks before he'd crossed a quarter of a mile.

The pain started with a brief hot stab in his right

leg, which quickly became pulsing waves radiating outward from the scale. It raced up into his chest and down his arms until no part of him was spared. Within moments, he felt as if he were being boiled alive. The intense heat brought him to his knees, and he opened his mouth to scream, but no sound came out. He pitched forward, oblivious to the sharp rocks biting into his face and bare chest.

The piercing cold waves started next. His teeth chattering, he shivered involuntarily and curled into a ball. Wracked with agony, he feared he would pass out at any moment. Normally he welcomed the sleep forced on him by the dragon scale, but not this time, not when he was lost in an unknown land and too far away from Ragh and Fiona. Digging his fingernails into his palms, he focused on staying awake and riding out the alternating icy and fiery jolts. Over and over he reminded himself why he needed to stay alive.

There were things he had to do before he died, he knew. He had to deliver Fiona to the safekeeping of the Solamnic Knights, and he had to find Maldred. Dhamon felt certain his friend was still alive in Shrentak or being held prisoner somewhere in the surrounding swamp. He owed it to Maldred to find him and get him out of there.

Above all, there was the matter of Rikali and his child. He pictured the half-elf the last time he had seen her, slight and pale-skinned and very pregnant. He'd traveled with her for many months, enjoying her company but unwilling to make a deeper commitment. They'd parted ways for a time—Dhamon's decision—and when she came back into his life, it was on the arm of a young husband who thought the child she carried was his. However, Rikali confessed to Dhamon that he was the real father. Somehow he knew she was telling the truth. Dhamon couldn't let the dragon scale defeat him until he found Rikali and saw his child, made sure they had enough wealth to keep them safe in this dragon-infested world.

After a long time, the intense heat receded, and the numbing cold became a faint memory. This painful episode had lasted, he guessed, a half hour; that was the longest yet. The episode left him weak and nauseous, and he lay still for several minutes until he could catch his breath. Slowly he got back up on his feet.

"In the name of the Dark Queen!" he cursed. He glanced down at his right leg. It was completely covered in new, small scales emanating from the large one. His chest tightened—how long did he have left before the damnable dragon-magic consumed him?

He balled his fist and slammed it against the large scale. He tried to cover up the scales with his trouser leg, but the material was so tattered it scarcely covered anything. He continued trudging toward the ridge. He hadn't a single coin, but maybe he could persuade someone to give him some clothes when he found the nearest town— provided the townsfolk didn't run from him in terror, thinking him a monster.

"Clothes and water," he said aloud. Fiona and Ragh must be thirsty and hungry too.

He reached the first ridge and, finding nothing there, continued to the next. In the distance now he could see signs of civilization. Dhamon turned and retraced his steps to the beach.

It was early morning before he returned to Ragh and Fiona. The draconian stared at the scale-covered leg and opened his mouth to say something. A sharp look from Dhamon cut him off.

Fiona had regained consciousness and was absently twirling her fingers in her hair. There was no hint that she realized that Dhamon had saved her life or that he had been gone for hours. Dhamon passed by Ragh and joined her warily.

He inspected the unsightly purple welt on her forehead. "How are you feeling?"

She frowned. "Hungry."

Dhamon knew she was feeling other things, too. She had to be feeling pain, judging by the bruises on her arms and by the way she favored her left side.

"I found a town, Fiona. It's some miles to the west. Do you feel up to a long walk?"

For the first time since leaving Shrentak she looked at him as though she heard him and brightened. He wrapped his fingers around her wrist and gave a gentle tug. "Let's go, shall we? There's bound to be some food and water there."

Dhamon led her over the ridge and down the trail. Ragh followed at a short distance. It was past noon by the time Dhamon brought them to the place from where he'd seen the town. Clumps of weeds tumbled across a hardscrabble expanse. It was bleak and chilly in this strange desert. Autumn had settled deeply over the land. The ground was cut here and there by narrow, rocky ridges pocked by shallow, bowl-shaped depressions. The dust in the air settled in Dhamon's mouth and aggravated his thirst.

"Ugly," Ragh observed, spitting out some of the grit. "This is an ugly place."

There wasn't a trail leading to the town that Dhamon could see, and as they walked, he looked for any tracks. Outside of prints from a single wild pig, all he discovered was a nest of beetles and a coarse dirt that blew across the ground.

Fiona fell back, keeping even with Ragh.

"How did he get them?" the draconian asked in a conspiratorial whisper.

"All those scales?" Fiona did nothing to keep her voice low. "The large one came from Malystryx, the red dragon overlord."

"But it's black scale, not a red one."

"It was stuck on the chest of one of her Dark Knight agents, whom Dhamon bested. As the Knight died, he pulled the scale free and shoved it against Dhamon's leg, where it became embedded. Somehow she controlled the Dark Knight through the scale. Dhamon became Malys's puppet, too, until a shadow dragon, working in concert with a silver dragon, broke her control."

"But it's . . ."

"Black," Fiona finished. "The scale turned mirror-black in the process. Probably because the shadow dragon used its black blood for the spell to free him."

Ragh suppressed a shudder.

Dhamon stopped, turned, and faced them. "It was just a few months later that all the pain began, if you must know. It was some months after that when the smaller scales began sprouting. To tell you the truth, I think they're killing me."

The draconian stared at the back of Dhamon's leg. The small scales were mostly black too, but a few were cerulean blue and the shade of smoke. He spied a few more that had cropped up around the ankle of Dhamon's other leg.

"Dhamon . . . Those scales . . ."

"Aren't your worry." Dhamon pointed toward the horizon. "Not too many miles to the town. A couple of hours' walk at best. We'll get there by early afternoon, find an inn."

"What are you going to buy dinner with?" the draconian asked testily, as he thumped his stomach. "Certainly not with your charm." Ragh's gaze again dropped to the scales on Dhamon's legs.

"Someone will feed us," Dhamon promised.

"When we get to that town," Ragh said, "I'd better not go in with you two."

"Good idea."

"Maybe you shouldn't either," the draconian added, glancing at the scales again.

A crow sprang up from behind them, something dangling from its beak. Fiona went back for a closer look, then waved Dhamon and Ragh away.

"A skeleton," she told them. Then she resumed her march to the town.

Dhamon paused to inspect the skeleton, though. The man had been dead for weeks, he guessed, most of his flesh picked clean by the crows. There wasn't enough there to show how the man died. However, he could tell the man hadn't been poor and that he was slight in build, likely either an elf or a half-elf. Though his tunic had been ripped by the birds, Dhamon knew it had been expensive material, with polished metal buttons and braid trim. He looked for a sword or dagger but didn't even find sheaths. The boots had been fine polished leather, now pitted by the blowing grit. The heavy coin pouch that hung from the skeleton's side and the silver chain that dangled around its neck quickly found their way into Dhamon's pocket.

"That'll buy dinner," Ragh said appreciatively. The draconian dallied a moment to see if anything else valuable had been missed.

"Hopefully it will buy us a way out of this place and passage to Southern Ergoth." Dhamon started west again.

When Dhamon caught up with Fiona minutes later, she was waist-deep in silt and struggling to get out. She stood in the middle of a depression.

"The ground disappeared!" she sputtered angrily, reaching a hand to Dhamon.

He stepped forward to take her hand but found the ground opening up beneath him as well. He thrashed about, trying to grab something to hold onto, but his frantic motions only served to send him down faster.

"Quicksand!" he cursed. This unusual quicksand didn't feel wet and gritty. It was dry and powdery, and in the span of a few seconds Dhamon stood up to his chest in it, and was somehow being pulled farther down. He told himself not to panic, to relax and try to swim out of the stuff. He looked anxiously at Fiona, who was up to her shoulders now, trying desperately to extricate herself, and getting nowhere but deeper into the muck.

Dhamon tried to relax, and this seemed to slow his descent somewhat. "Ragh!" The dirt spilled over his shoulders now and was starting to creep up his neck. Despite his great strength, he could not pull himself out. "Ragh, get over here now!"

The draconian hurried up to them but cautiously kept his distance. His darting eyes took in Dhamon and Fiona's predicament. He cautiously crept closer to Dhamon, clawed foot outstretched and tentatively testing the ground with each step.

"Her first!" Dhamon said. "Save Fiona first!"

Ragh shook his head and stretched a hand out to Dhamon.

"Save her first, Ragh!"

The draconian snarled and moved over toward Fiona, still worried about the firmness of the terrain. Laying down on his stomach, he reached his arm toward her. "I save her first, Dhamon, if you will swear to help me slay Nura Bint-Drax!"

"Aye," Dhamon quickly agreed, anger flashing in his eyes. "I swear."

The silty quicksand had reached Fiona's jaw, and she had to tilt her head back to breathe.

"Pull your arm up, Fiona," Ragh instructed. "It's the only way I can help you! Be quick!"

At last Fiona managed to raise her arms. Half of her face was covered with the gritty dirt, which spilled into her mouth. She stretched her arms toward Ragh. The draconian grabbed her wrists and pulled her toward him until she was on solid ground.

Fiona spat and spat. "Thank you, sivak," she said.

Ragh turned his attention to Dhamon. His scaly hands clasped Dhamon's and began to pull. "You swore," Ragh reminded him.

"Aye." Dhamon said, as he crawled away from the silty hole, then turned around to watch as it whirled in agitation. "I swore. I will help you slay Nura Bint-Drax."

"Before those scales consume you."

As they watched from a safe vantage point, the depression grew deeper and the dirt swirled in its bottom like a whirlpool.

"What in the name of the Abyss is that thing?" Dhamon asked.

"Sinkholes," Ragh answered. The draconian indicated a few more within their line of sight. "Look there." As they watched one sinkhole shuddered and during the next few minutes filled itself up, then overflowed, spewing gravel and leaving behind one of the narrow ridges that dotted the land. "Means there're some underground cavities beneath this land, maybe caverns or rivers. The spaces expand, and there isn't enough support for the ground on top. So the land collapses in sinkholes."

"But that one filled itself up," Fiona said, cautiously gazing at the expanse of land they had yet to cross to reach the town.

"Probably means the caverns underneath are filling up. Strange. I'd say this whole area is unstable."

This time the draconian took the lead, eyes trained on the ground and looking for any disturbance in the soil. Their pace slowed considerably, as they circled around a half-dozen sinkholes that were churning or erupting. They reached the edge of town just as the sun was touching the horizon.

"I think I'll go into town with you two after all," Ragh announced, casting a last look at a large sinkhole forming only several yards away from them. "I'll take my chance with the local folks instead of the landscape. Maybe they won't mind our scales too much."

CHAPTER FOUR
COLD DESPAIR

his isn't a good sign." The draconian pointed toward the main street. The straggly clumps of brown grass looked sad and thin, like the hair on a balding man's head "Not good at all."

Shutters banged in the wind, and curtains fluttered in open windows. Signs proclaiming a cobbler and a blacksmith were weathered and nearly impossible to read. Other signs, farther down the street, were bleached beyond recognition and hung crookedly, rhythmically thumping against posts.

Not a single building looked well maintained. The roof of the closest business, a cooper judging by the rotted and split barrels out front, was caved in. Paint on overhangs and trim was cracked and peeling and resembled dried fish scales. Flower boxes sprouted weeds, and everything was pitted by the windblown grit, which seemed a permanent feature of the area.

Dhamon pointed to a lopsided well off to the side of an equally tilting one-story building.

"You're wrong, Ragh. There is something good about this place. At least I don't think you'll have to worry about the local folks' reaction to our scales."

"I didn't think you were capable of making a joke, Dhamon."

"I'm not."

Dhamon and Fiona headed to the well. The leaning building was precariously poised over a recently formed sinkhole. The ring of stones around the well was on the verge of crumbling from age and lack of repair, and as Dhamon rested his hand on a stone, it fell and he nearly lost his balance. It was oddly cold near the well.

He noticed that Fiona was shivering, but she refused to complain about it. She hadn't said more than a dozen words to him in the past few hours—though she had talked with Ragh. Her silent treatment of him was unnerving, and he considered trying to draw her out.

His thirst took precedence. "Hope the water's as cold as the air," he mused. He could smell the water far below, fresh and inviting, and he eagerly snatched up the rope and bucket. "I'll bet you're thirsty, Fiona."

Fiona reached for the bucket, her eyes first glimmering hopefully, then her lip curling downward as she saw the bucket had no bottom. She tossed it aside and it came off the frayed rope.

"I'll find a bucket," Dhamon told her. "Bound to be something in this town that will—"

Fiona spun, heading toward the closest shop.

"All right," Dhamon said. "You go find a bucket then."

Ragh took her place at the well. "I'd crawl down there for something to drink if I was certain the stones wouldn't give way." The draconian leaned over the edge and looked down hungrily. His knee brushed a stone, and several shifted. "I think a strong wind might blow this over." He looked up and met Dhamon's gaze. "There can't have been anyone around here for years."

"Aye, that's for certain." Dhamon indicated the sinkhole behind the leaning building. "The people obviously left when the land became unstable."

"Maybe." The draconian wore an uncertain expression. "Did you take a good look at the front entrance to the inn over there?"

Dhamon pushed away from the well, sending a stone to the water below. He returned to the main street. The inn the draconian mentioned was a few buildings down and at one time must have been quite impressive. There once had been three storys to it, though half of the top floor was gone. The building was a mix of wood and stone, with the stone painted dark green, but only flecks of the color remained. A broken bench on the sprawling porch was inlaid with bits of shells and bronze beads. The sign, lying split in two on the steps, proclaimed it the ENCHANTED EMERALD HOSTEL. Trousers flapped on the steps, the belt snagged in a crack which kept them from being blown away. The matching shirt was caught under the bench. There were shoes, too, and a pipe. A tobacco pouch was sticking out of one pocket. It was as if someone just had taken off their clothes, laid them out, and walked away. As Dhamon and Ragh looked around, the breeze whipped cold around them, and their breath feathered away from their faces. Then the wind warmed slightly, leaving them with an apprehensive feeling.

"Maybe it wasn't the sinkholes that made people leave," the draconian said, as he tested the steps and warily climbed up.

Dhamon peered up the street, where more garments were strewn against buildings and steps and overturned carts—wherever the wind had left them. "Maybe it was something else. Let's take a quick look around, get some of that water and some supplies, and then get out of here."

"You show intelligence for a human. I don't want to stay here any longer than necessary, either." The draconian gingerly prodded the door open and poked his head inside. "First I'm going to see if this town has a name, try to figure out where we are. There must be some maps around a place like this. With luck I'll find one. Then we can look for a way out of here and be on our way—after Nura Bint-Drax."

Dhamon watched Ragh ease inside the building, the old door banging shut behind the draconian, then he followed the street a little farther, looking for a tavern. He hoped to find mugs for water, and perhaps some bottles of spirits to ward off the autumn chill. Along the way, he glanced at the discarded, dirt-pitted clothing along the street. His route took him past a baker's. The loaves of bread behind the window looked like bricks resting on a bed of grit. There was evidence some insects had feasted on the loaves but no sign of rats or birds. Peering into the shadows, he spotted interior counters filled with long-hardened treats, as well as a faded dress and apron, slippers and a hat that were spread out on the floor in the center of the room. Nearby was a child's dress, a doll, and what looked like the collar of a dog.

"No people. No animals." Dhamon moved to the next building, one that in years past had been gaily painted with strange symbols. He traced one of the symbols with his finger. He'd seen something like it before, perhaps in an arcane tome shown to him by his friend Maldred. Remnants of a bead curtain clicked in the doorway, and the scent of something not unpleasant wafted from inside. Thinking this might have been a sorcerer's place, and therefore a place that held information about the strange town, he momentarily forgot his thirst and hunger and his caution. He pushed aside the beads and went inside.

◇ ◇ ◇ ◇ ◇ ◇ ◇

Fiona was inside a farmer's store and had propped the door open to let in more light. Goods were neatly displayed on shelves that lined three walls of the room. At first glance she didn't see any buckets, but she did spot a large salt-glazed pitcher that she was quick to snatch up. She brushed away a cobweb and blew the dust off a section of countertop, placed the pitcher on it, then proceeded to fill up a leather bag she had pilfered. On the shelf closest to her was a small set of tarnished silverware, and these she added to her collection.

"Dhamon should be doing this—stealing—not me," she muttered darkly. "He's the thief. A liar and a thief. Just like his ogre friend Maldred. Liar. Liar. Liar."

She gave the shelves a closer inspection. There were various-sized nails, hammers, and an entire rack devoted to building tools. There were lengths of rope, one of which she selected to replace the rotting one at the well, and there were a half-dozen lanterns and a large glass jar of oil. She made a note to return and fill a couple of the lanterns so they'd have some light when the sun completely disappeared—which would be very soon, judging by the sparse orange light fading from the shop.

Bolts of cloth were arranged near the floor, none of them appealing to her. They appeared common and were covered with dirt and webs. She spotted a pair of hunting knives, and these were quick to find their way onto her belt. They would do until she was fortunate enough to stumble upon a long sword. There didn't seem to be a real weapon or shield in here, however. She would have to look for an armorer's after she drank her fill.

Shovels, hoes, and rakes were leaned neatly behind the counter and against the center of the back wall. There were bins labeled "beans," "wheat," and "rye," on which insects had feasted. One barrel contained a mass of tiny onion starters, so hard and shriveled nowadays they could pass for marbles.

Looking behind the counter, Fiona shivered when a cold gust of wind rushed into the shop. After a moment, the air warmed a little. In the growing shadows she stared at a pair of trousers, a black tunic, and a smock, laid flat on the floor with shoes at the end of gathered cuffs. A brimmed hat sat about a foot above the collar, and at the end of a sleeve was a quill. It looked like the shopkeeper, departing on some mysterious errand, had carefully taken off his clothes and left them behind.

Underneath the countertop was a coin jar, practically filled with steel pieces. Fiona reached for the jar, then hesitated. "I am a Solamnic Knight," she said. "In the name of Vinus Solamnus, what am I doing?" Her fingers fluttered hesitantly above the jar. "If only Rig was here, he'd—"

"But I *am* here."

She whirled around, looking for the voice. "Rig!" Her heart leaped in delight. "I knew you'd find me! I just . . . where are you?"

She didn't see anyone; she was all alone in the shop.

"I am in the back room. Behind the curtain. I have missed you very much, Fiona."

She hastily dropped her leather bag, pushed the curtain aside, and rushed into the darkness.

❖ ❖ ❖ ❖ ❖ ❖ ❖

"No sorcerer's dwelling." Dhamon was standing in the center of a small room. At least it wasn't the kind of room that had been decorated by any sorcerer he was familiar with. The walls were covered with garishly dyed animal skins, more of the cryptic symbols he'd seen on the outside of the building—brighter than those on the outside, because the sun hadn't bleached them. Several narrow shelves held the skulls of small animals and crystal bowls with layers of colored sand. The place had at the same time a barbaric and gaudy look. There were jars filled with dried substances, pressed flowers and herbs, small bells with painted symbols on them, collections of bead and feather-festooned sticks. By the way they were arranged, it looked as though this had been a shop and all the oddities were for sale. There was an impressive tapestry, showing a quartet of rearing pegasi over the body of a two-headed bear. And there was the intriguing smell that had lured him in here. It emanated from a tray filled with bulbous roots—all of them apparently fresh and without any of the dust that covered everything else.

"Sorcery, yes, but not from one of Palin's ilk. Maybe those roots are edible, but I'm not *that* hungry."

A search revealed tinder and steel, and Dhamon

lit an ornate lamp filled with a heady, musky oil. His head spun from the oppressive scent, making him feel intoxicated, and he made a move to douse the lantern but stopped himself when the light spread and bathed the place in a warm glow. He spied more curiosities, including a few preserved animals—a coiled exotic snake, a curly tailed lizard, and a hedgehog with six legs, but he couldn't find a single scrap of parchment that would give him a clue to their location.

Curtains and beads hung from a beam that stretched across the back of the room, perhaps separating the little shop from the owner's living quarters. He might find documents there.

When he ventured behind the beads, he found a much larger room with a silt-covered table no higher than his knees. He brushed away the dust and set the lantern on the table, frowning to see his disheveled state reflected in the surface. The table was fashioned of polished walnut and inlaid with silver—a real showpiece. Spaced around it were overstuffed pillows, all coated with dust and the husks of insects. In the center of the table was a pile of fingerbones and petrified chicken feet, painted wooden cubes, and a cup containing dried green leaves.

Scarves and ribbons hung from the ceiling, and there were rows of shelves holding tiny preserved animals, monkey skulls, crystal sculptures of insects, jars of sand and powders, and fragile-looking scrolls. Dhamon's eyes settled on the latter. Maybe there's a map here after all, he thought.

He reached for the thickest scroll, his hand brushing a carved bear the size of a plum. It was one of many carved animals, ranging in size from a small cherry to a large apple, that dangled on strings from the upper shelves. Colorful wedges of glass also dangled and caught the light from the lantern and sent whirling patterns around the room. Watching them made him dizzy.

Not a sorcerer at all. A fortune teller's place, he decided, with a measure of disappointment. One long gone from this town. Stuffing the thick scroll under his arm and reaching for the others, his gaze fell on the largest pillow. A purple robe shot through with metallic threads lay across it. Bracelets lay nearby, earrings too, and an elaborate hat of some sort. There were thin wooden cards spilled at the end of a sleeve. On two of the other pillows were strewn more abandoned clothes.

"Customers long gone, too. We should do our best to be long gone from here," he muttered to himself anxiously.

❖ ❖ ❖ ❖ ❖ ❖ ❖

"Rig! Rig! I can't find you. It's so dark in here." Some sane part of Fiona knew Rig couldn't possibly be anywhere in this place, knew she should leave and get Dhamon. That part of her was overwhelmed by the madness that had taken root. "Rig! It's so hard to see in here. Come outside with me. It's too dark in here. And it's cold. It's very, very cold."

"Cold as the grave."

"What did you say, Rig?" She glanced behind her, where the curtains fluttered, and considered retreating to the shop to get one of those lanterns. Perhaps Rig was hiding, hurt, scarred by the spawn and draconians that they had battled in Shrentak. Maybe he didn't want her to see him with scars and deformities. It didn't matter to her what he looked like. She loved him.

"It doesn't matter if you're scarred," she cooed, her fingers touching her own acid-blemished face. "I will always love you."

She paused and listened, then repeated. "I can't see you, Rig. What did you say?"

"I said I am here, my lovely lady, waiting for you. I have missed you so very much."

"I've missed you, too, and—"

A swirl of black separated from the shadows. Spinning like a small whirlwind, the black swirl produced no breeze, but it exuded a sudden wave of intense cold.

"Rig!" Fiona stared at the shifting mass, trying to see behind it and find Rig, warn him of the mysterious whirlwind. "Rig! Be careful, my darling, I—"

"Dear Fiona, I have been praying you would come to me." The voice was Rig's, but she realized in horror it emanated from the black swirl.

"Rig?" Fiona stared in disbelief. "Y-y-you can't be Rig. You're not . . ."

Suddenly the room lightened and all the shadows were banished as from the center of the swirl burst an eerie, yellow glow. As Fiona watched, the swirl became black flames licking at the air, then changed into spiraling smoke. The wisps stopped spinning and wove themselves into a human form. The eerie glow at the center of the form receded but did not disappear completely. Although by some gift of magic Fiona hoped to see Rig, what she saw instead was a duplicate of herself.

"I have waited a long time," the Fiona-image said, still adopting Rig's voice. "It has been nearly a year since someone has passed this way."

Fiona took a step back. "I-I-I don't understand. What's happening? Rig? Where's Rig? What . . . ?"

She turned to flee, but the Fiona-image shot out a hand to grab her wrist.

Fiona screamed, for the mirror-Fiona felt as cold as the coldest ice. "Let go of me!"

"But, dear Fiona, I truly have been waiting for you." The Fiona-image twirled her around, its fingers digging deep into her flesh and drawing blood, its white-hot pinpricks of eyes boring into her.

With her free hand Fiona drew one of the knives at her belt and plunged it into the chest of her double. The blade sank in, but there was no blood, and the creature seemed unaffected.

"So long since real people have been here," the duplicate Fiona said. The Fiona-image no longer boasted Rig's voice, but used one that was low, musical, and inhuman. It glanced at the knife protruding from its chest and smiled mischievously.

"Y-y-you sounded like Rig," Fiona stammered. "You tricked me, made me think . . . what are you, anyway?"

"Your mind gave my voice its sound, sweet Fiona." The duplicate-Fiona opened its mouth wide, and where its teeth should be there were instead motes of sparkling light.

"You sounded like Rig, and you look like me, and . . ."

"I look like my victims, Fiona. It is what I do, what all of my kind do."

"After you kill me," she stated, "my clothes will lie empty, too."

The duplicate-Fiona shook its head, hair trailing away from its head like tendrils of red-tinged smoke. "True, my brethren and I killed all the people who lived here, so greedy were we then. And foolish. We thinned the population too much, and so we do not kill very often now. We only feed.

It has been so long since I fed. This island, so few come here anymore, Fiona. We must protect our cattle now and allow the herd to multiply."

The color drained from Fiona's face. "Are you some kind of vampire then?" She'd heard legends of such grisly undead. "By the breath of Vinus Solamnus, are you—?"

"Not vampires," the Fiona-image chuckled. "We are products of Chaos."

The Fiona-image studied the female Knight, glowing eyes caressing her form, delving into her mind and trying unsuccessfully to make sense of its latest victim. "You are most interesting . . . Fiona. Your memory is turbulent, names and faces changing places incessantly. Yet this Rig is the name most important to you. This man seems to be the center of everything." The Fiona-image paused, then resumed speaking in the mariner's unmistakeable voice. "You are clearer and better focused when thinking of Rig, but the rest of your thoughts are warring and imprecise. They wax and wane like the sea."

"You're a creature of Chaos? The god?"

"A *spawn* of Chaos, born in the deepest Abyss. I am death and power, and I am now all alone in this town. My brethren left after we fed too much on the people here. We fed on them all, and their babies and pets and those who came looking for them. When no one was left, my brethren moved on, but I stayed. I feed now on those few who from time to time happen to pass by."

"You killed . . . everybody in this town!"

"That was a long time ago. We fed on their memories, and when they had no more memories they had no futures. They became nothing years and years and years ago," the creature replied in Rig's voice. "They ceased to exist."

"Worse than murder."

"They left their trappings behind. Pathetic clothing and belongings to mark their brief existence."

"Filthy undead!" Fiona struggled against the grip of her evil image, but her body would not respond. She tried to grab her other knife, but her fingers would no longer cooperate.

"I am death and power," the Fiona-image repeated in Rig's voice. "I am hunger, and I must be sated." The Fiona-image leaned forward, eyes blinding, lips parting, motes of light sparkling.

"No," the true Fiona said defiantly. "You'll not succeed!" But she felt powerless, already defeated. "Please, no."

The mirror-image of Fiona gently cupped the female Knight's head in its hands, leaned closer, and kissed her.

◇ ◇ ◇ ◇ ◇ ◇ ◇

The air suddenly had turned cold, and Dhamon could see his frosted breath. He dropped the scrolls he'd been examining and wheeled around, seeing nothing alarming but hearing something that he at first thought sounded oddly like the coo of a morning dove. He listened more closely, realizing it was the soft and distant laughter of a woman. He knew the woman's voice.

Feril? Was it Feril? His eyes flew wide and his pulse quickened. Feril was the first and only woman he had truly loved, a Kagonesti from Southern Ergoth who had been one of the few who survived the curse of his companionship. She had sensibly left him long ago. He'd not seen Feril for some time, but his love for her was still strong.

"Feril." The word was a hopeful whisper.

The laughter turned into brittle giggles, the voice changing, metamorphosing, but still achingly familiar as Feril. In his excitement he didn't notice that the room was growing ever cooler as the voice rippling with laughter drifted closer.

"Feril?" Please by all the vanished gods let it be her, he thought.

The giggle persisted, but now he understood a few words—*Dhamon, lover, hold me, miss you.* No, he was wrong, it was not Feril, he had been tricked. But it was someone else he loved.

"Riki?" It could be her. The voice was thin and pleasant and sounded somewhat elven.

Lover. Lover. Lover, Dhamon heard.

"Riki." He was certain now that it was the half-elf. Relief flooded his emotions. He needed to talk to Riki, had desperately wanted to talk so he could set some things straight, make sure she was all right and well cared for. Had she delivered the child yet? Was it all right? *His child!* No. She couldn't have, he thought, not yet. The time was too soon. It would be soon, several days maybe, a week, no more than a month.

Lover. Lover. Lover.

Yes, Riki often had called him that, when they were together. Lover.

"Riki, where are you? Riki, it's me, Dhamon! I'm in here, Riki!" After he called her name, however, he chastised himself. Though the half-elf—even after she'd married—had followed Dhamon numerous times, she could *not* have followed him through the Qualinesti Forest and across the sea to here. . . wherever here was. It simply was not possible. Or was it?

The laughter and lyrical words were definitely Riki's.

"Impossible."

"Nothing's impossible, Dhamon. I am here, and I have missed you so. Have you missed me, too?"

The voice and the laughter swelled in volume, and the air grew colder still. Cold like at the well and on the steps to the inn where he'd left Ragh. Cold as harshest winter.

All at once Dhamon sensed a presence within the cold, and in that instant the laughter changed again, taking on a manly tone that at first sounded similar to Maldred, then quickly became dark and menacing and completely unfamiliar. Inhuman. Dhamon knew the voice was meant to scare him. Instead, it only served to anger him. The voice was not Feril, and it was not Rikali.

His hand instinctively dropped to his side, his fingers folding around air. The sword! He'd dropped it in the sea during the storm.

How could he be so stupid as to forget he was weaponless? Was he affected by the drugged oil in the lamp? Was that making him hallucinate? They were all weaponless. Where were Ragh and Fiona?

"Fiona!" Where was she? A moment's concentration, and he remembered that the Solamnic Knight had wandered away from him at the well when she went off in search of a bucket. And Ragh! The draconian was at the abandoned inn.

In a strange town with no signs of life, why had he allowed his two companions to go off on their own? It wasn't safe, especially with the whole area cursed by sinkholes. It wasn't like him to be so inattentive and careless. A former Dark Knight, he usually knew to keep his command together. What in the Dark Queen's memory was wrong with him? Was he under some kind of spell?

"Fiona! Ragh!"

"It was *my* doing, Dhamon Grimwulf. With only a suggestion, I lured your companions away from you. Separated, you are far easier to deal with."

Dhamon turned, looking for the voice, and somehow not expecting to see a person. A spawn perhaps. The spirit of the fortune teller who once owned this shop. Some magical creature. There! A shadow spilled out from under the table, running across the floor, pooling like oil a few feet away. Smoky tendrils rose from it, twisting and thickening, and finally forming an image that vaguely looked like the lizardmen that had populated the black dragon's swamp. But unlike the lizardmen, this image had glowing yellow-white eyes and misshappen horns sprouting from the top of its head. Dhamon doubted that was the creature's true form, but it was sufficiently hideous to unsettle even him.

The creature opened its crocodilian snout, and a thin tendril-tongue whipped out and struck at the air inches from his face. When Dhamon didn't flinch, the tendril retreated into a mouth that was shimmering and changing and receding to mold a human visage. In a few moments, the creature took on the aspects of Feril, the Kagonesti elf, then a pregnant Rikali, then Maldred, and finally the slain mariner Rig.

"Who or what are you?" Dhamon demanded, uncowed.

"A creature of Chaos," the thing replied evenly, its breath creating snow that twinkled and fell, melting in the pool of black that remained on the floor coursing around its feet.

"Undead."

"Perhaps," the creature said in Rig's voice, liking the rich accent of the dead Ergothian. "Undead, living, I have known no other existence. The people of this town called me a Chaos wight."

"All the townspeople you killed."

"Your companion . . ." The Rig-creature paused, head cocking as if searching for the right words, wispy tongue snaking out of its mouth and circling its lips. "Your woman companion . . . Fiona . . . she accused me of the same. In fact, she—"

Dhamon sprang away from the creature, leaping toward the wall and tugging down a narrow shelf. Monkey skulls and vials of sand thumped against the floor. A lunge toward the creature and he swung the wooden shelf like a sword, snarling unsurprisedly to note it passed through the Rig-image as if nothing was there.

"Demon!" Dhamon cried, as he swung the shelf again and again, the force of his blow sending the scarves and curtains billowing and the ribbons flying, with no damage to the Chaos wight.

"Fool," the creature returned. It thrust out an arm, smacking heavily into Dhamon's chest and sending him back several feet.

The hand had certainly felt solid enough—and freezing cold. Dhamon stepped forward woozily and tried to swing the shelf into the wight's arm. The creature laughed as the shelf passed through it.

"You do not have the ability to hurt me."

Dhamon dropped the shelf and threw his hands up, fingers closing tight around the wight's neck. The creature's open mouth was wide and black like a cave, laughter echoing deep inside. Dhamon squeezed harder and for a brief moment thought he was actually causing harm to the other-worldly creature. He felt the wight shudder, but it was only to effect another appearance change.

"I told you that you cannot hurt me. You have no

magic." This time it took on the visage of Dhamon, speaking in his voice.

Dhamon shifted around, keeping even with his double. His eyes scanned the shelves and walls, looking for a weapon. You say I can't harm you, he thought, but that could be false.

"No, it's true, Dhamon Grimwulf. Your thoughts are open to me," the Dhamon-image said. "You can inflict no pain."

Then if you can read my mind, let's see if you can predict this. Dropping his hands, Dhamon balled both fists and drove them into his double's stomach. His hands went right through the creature and out the other side. It felt as if he'd plunged his arms into an icy mountain stream, and when he pulled them back close he noticed they were bright pink from the cold. He continued to spar with his double, hurling various objects at it. Dancing toward one wall, Dhamon scooped up animal skulls and threw them. He tried vials of the sand and powder, bound sticks, anything he could reach and grab and throw.

The creature followed him into the other room of the shop, where Dhamon continued to pelt it with objects—more skulls, bells, the strong-smelling roots. Those roots actually gave it pause, though no real damage was done.

Magic, Dhamon thought. *The roots are magic.*

"Yes. Only magic can hurt me. And I tell you this only because you do not have any magic about you."

Likely there's nothing magical in this entire town.

"Nothing that can hurt me. Years past I destroyed those things that could bring me pain."

Dhamon yanked another shelf off the wall and swung it with as much force as he could manage. There were times he had wished for death—when the scale on his leg gave him so much misery he couldn't bear the torment—but he couldn't let this petty creation of Chaos kill him here and now. There was Riki and his child and Maldred to find. There was Fiona to take care of. The wight had mentioned Fiona. Had the thing killed the female Knight?

"I did little enough to the troubled woman," the duplicate-Dhamon said. "She is physically un-harmed."

Again Dhamon swung the shelf at his mirror image, again and again in a maddened flurry of blows destroying the shop.

"I did little to the scarred beast that goes by three names."

Dhamon's wild strokes continued, all ineffectual.

"Three names. Draconian, sivak, and Ragh. The beast thinks very highly of you, human—and that seems to trouble it."

Despite the chill exuded by his opponent, Dhamon was sweating from the exertion. His rain of blows slowed. There has to be a weakness! his mind screamed.

"I, too, think highly of you. You have not given up, though deep down you understand you cannot defeat me. Deep down you know I cannot be easily dismissed. You glance about for weapons, you scheme. Your mind does not stop. Impressive."

"I don't intend to stop! You'll not slay me!" This time when Dhamon swung, the shelf flew from his sweaty fingers and impacted against a wall. More monkey skulls and jars clattered to the floor.

"I have no wish to slay you."

Dhamon stepped back, chest heaving, eyes narrowed and locked onto the intense pinpoints of light that served as his duplicate's eyes. "If you don't want to kill me, then what's this about?"

"If I slay you, Dhamon Grimwulf, you will be gone forever—like all the people in this town. I made that mistake once. If I only feed on you, there may come a day when you will pass through this town again, and I will feed once more." The Dhamon-double raised a hand, flesh becoming black and wispy, finger-tendrils leading away and touching Dhamon's chest.

Dhamon felt utter despair. He had no desire to put up any further fight. He felt helpless, hopeless, and at the thing's mercy.

"Give in to me," the Dhamon-wight said. "Give in completely."

Dhamon relaxed and felt the finger-tendrils skittering across his chest. Still, some part of him rebelled against surrender, abject defeat. *I can't give in*, he told himself.

"You cannot win, Dhamon Grimwulf."

Dhamon dropped to his knees. *I can't give in.*

"As strong as you are, you cannot best me."

A tear slid down Dhamon's face and his hands shook. *Fight it!*

"I must possess you, as I possess this town, but I will take from you only what I took from your companions." The creature's wispy black fingers feathered across Dhamon's brow.

Don't let it win! Fight it with everything!

The creature's fingers continued to dance, then suddenly the hands drew back, and the creature tipped its chin up and roared. The Dhamon-form melted like butter. In the span of a heartbeat the wight took on the image of a lizardlike creature with thorny antlers.

"Don't fight me!" it raged. "You cannot win! You only postpone my feeding, Dhamon. You cannot put it off forever!"

Dhamon took a deep breath and shakily got to his feet. He was trembling from the effects of the creature's spell and from the cold the thing generated. It took considerable effort just to speak.

"The red dragon couldn't defeat me," Dhamon said, fully aware that the creature was reading his thoughts and learning about his confrontation with Malys and about the scale on his leg. "Neither will a lesser, petty creature such as you defeat me. Whatever it is you're trying to do to my mind, I won't let you!"

The creature retreated, floating above the floor and scrutinizing Dhamon as it had no previous victim. "Your mind is strong, human, and, to my astonishment, I admit I find myself unable to steal a part of it . . . at this moment."

"I *can* win," Dhamon pronounced. "I might not be able to hurt you, but I can keep you from hurting me."

The wight laughed cruelly, and its eyes grew brighter. "I will not *let* you win. Give me what I want, Dhamon. Drop your defenses and make this easy and painless for both of us."

Dhamon defiantly shook his head.

"If you don't give in to me," the wight said, each word deliberate and drawn out, "I will slay the ones you call Ragh and Fiona."

Dhamon sucked in a breath.

"You know I can and will do this, as they are not as formidable as you. I will suck their minds dry and for spite leave you all alone in this nameless place. When our paths cross again, I will once more attack you. Again and again I will come after your mind until I wear you down and succeed. You cannot hold me off forever. Give in to me if you want your companions to live."

The silence was tense for several minutes.

"Nothing," the creature repeated. "You can do nothing about it. Nothing, if you want your companions, your *friends*, to live."

"What . . . what exactly do you want from me?"

The lips of the lizard-image parted, revealing glowing yellow teeth and a snakelike tongue that slowly unrolled and slithered toward Dhamon.

"One memory," the wight said. "That is all I require. I feed on the memories of the living. I'll take only one from you. This time." The tongue snaked around Dhamon's neck and tugged him closer. Wispy fingers reached up and caressed Dhamon's temples. "Just one, then you and your companions may leave this town. But if our paths again cross, I'll take another memory. And another. Yet never all of them."

For a few moments more, Dhamon resisted.

"Death for your friends," the wight reminded. "Or one memory."

Dhamon took a deep breath, closed his eyes, and the creature entered his mind.

CHAPTER FIVE
STOLEN YOUTH

One hundred and twelve Knights were camped in a field of sage grass and wild-flowers between the town of Hartford and the Vingaard River. Dhamon knew how many Knights there were exactly because he'd counted them three times. He lay on his stomach just beyond the edge of a small copse of trees, hidden by the grass, intently watching the men. His little brother was at his side, currently napping out of boredom.

Dhamon was anything but bored, however. He'd never been more excited in all of his young life.

He'd seen Knights before, a few Solamnics who passed through town from time to time on their way to somewhere else; most likely they were headed toward Solanthus to the south, where he'd heard there was a big outpost or fort or something. He'd certainly been impressed by the Solamnics and by the quartet of Legion of Steel Knights that was in Hartford two or three years past for a special ceremony involving one of their officers. What young man wouldn't be captivated by uniformed, armed and armored men riding massive war-horses? He'd had older friends who'd gone off to join the Solamnics. One of his close friends, Trenken Hagenson, was now a Knight and due back for a visit late this fall or early winter.

These particular Knights—Knights of Takhisis, the townsfolk called them in whispers—were impressive, and they boasted such numbers! They stirred intense emotions in the locals—fear, wonder, loathing, admiration. What Dhamon felt was awe. There was a quality about these Dark Knights that he hadn't noticed in Knights from the other Orders. They were proud, powerful, supremely confident— Dhamon could feel their confidence all the way out here in his hiding place. What men these Knights were! If only Trenken could have seen them, he would have chosen this Order instead of the Solamnics. Each of the Dark Knights moved with strength and grace, shoulders thrown back and chest thrust out. There was not the slightest hint of fatigue or weakness, despite the fact they'd been up since before daybreak marching, drilling and practicing their swordsmanship. Dhamon knew all this, as he'd been here since shortly after dawn watching them.

Most of the time he'd been lying in the tall grass, as he was now, but when his neck and legs got sore, he edged back to the comfort of a willow tree and splashed himself with water from the creek. Then he stood behind the tree and spied on them through the veil of leaves as he snacked on the peaches he'd brought along. His brother had been sent to look for him, to scold him, and to bring him home to do chores. Dhamon explained he had more important things to do than shear sheep today; he had Knights to watch. His brother protested but quickly realized if he stayed here with Dhamon he could avoid his chores, too. If anyone got in trouble, it would be older brother Dhamon.

Dhamon was studying the Knight Field Commander now, his polished plate armor shining in the late afternoon sun. The man's face glistened with sweat, and when he took off his helmet, Dhamon could see that his short hair was plastered against the sides of his head. It was the height of summer, the temperature was fierce, and the cloudless sky suggested no rain in the offing. Dhamon suspected the commander and all of his charges were miserable from the heat. The few not in armor had large wet circles under their sleeves. It was amazing that not one of the Knights had passed out.

Dhamon himself was uncomfortably hot, though he had the shade from the trees and the nearby creek to cool him off. He shrugged out of his shirt and carefully folded it, scowling to see he'd dirtied it from lying on the ground. He made a note to clean it in the creek before he returned home so he wouldn't get in trouble.

The commander was barking more orders now. Dhamon could hear some of them. He was selecting men for another round of sword practice. After a glance at his brother to make sure he was still sound asleep, Dhamon crawled forward, determined to get a much closer look at his new heroes.

Six men were doffing their armor, taking it off piece by piece, laying it all on the ground though following some solemn ceremony. Bare-chested, they evinced gleaming muscles, and their leggings were soaked with sweat. They were paired by twos, all with long swords and shields that reflected the sun and made Dhamon squint when he stared at them.

A clap of the field commander's hands and half the men assumed a defensive position. The other three began to strike blows against the defenders' shields. It was like a dance, only better—Dhamon had seen plenty of dances during Hartford's various festivals—but their movements were precise and in unison, the blows leveled in concert. A drum started beating, and the sword swings kept time. Dhamon imagined himself one of the Knights, practicing, practicing, until he was strong enough for battle. The drum's cadence quickened, and the swings became bolder, still in unison as if choreographed by the commander. Then with one loud *boom!* the drum stopped and the men jumped to attention. The commander gestured to the first pair. Their swords flashed in the sun and clanged against each other, sounding crisp as bells. Dhamon was mesmerized.

For long minutes the two men met each other blow for blow, neither backing down as the other four men circled to watch. Neither appeared to tire. One man was clearly larger, and Dhamon thought he might have the advantage because of his height, but the smaller man proved faster, pivoting and slashing, bringing the shield up to deflect his opponent's thrusts. Dhamon was so engrossed in the mock combat that he didn't see the Knight commander step away from the circle and take a wide path through the wildflowers to steal up behind him.

The commander cleared his throat as Dhamon sprang to his feet, the color draining from his face, his mouth falling wide.

"You're too young to be a spy," the field

commander began curtly, "and you're not dressed properly for it. Nor do you carry any weapons."

Dhamon cast a worried glance back toward where his brother was sleeping, where he'd left his shirt. He wanted to say something intelligent to the commander, but his mouth had turned instantly dry, and his voice would not cooperate.

"So I'd guess you're from nearby Hartford."

Dhamon nervously nodded. Another glance over his shoulder. His brother was still sleeping, hidden and unawares.

"You've some muscles, young man." The commander squeezed Dhamon's arms. "So you're no stranger to hard work. A farmer, probably, eh?"

Another nod.

"Hopefully not a mute one."

"N-n-no Sir." Dhamon finally managed to stammer. "I was just . . . just . . . watching."

The field commander regarded him for several moments. Swords continued to clang in the background. "Watching?"

"Y-y-yes Sir." A moment more and he swallowed his nervousness. "Yes, Commander. I was watching your Knights."

The faintest smile appeared on the commander's face, adding to the age lines around his mouth. He looked old to Dhamon, this close up. The hair at his temples was gray, and the thin mustache over his lip had white streaks in it. The man's expression was hard, the steel-blue eyes adding to his sternness. His skin was weathered from the sun. His hands were calloused, and there was a thick, ropy scar on his forearm that Dhamon suspected came from a wound suffered in a great battle.

"And after this *watching*, just what do you think of my Knights. . . ?"

Dhamon waited for the commander to add *boy*, as his father's friends often did, and as did the storekeepers in town, the men to whom he delivered wool and other crops. *Just what do you think of my Knights, boy?* But the commander didn't call him boy, and Dhamon realized he was asking his name.

"Dhamon Grimwulf, Sir. And, yes, I'm from Hartford. My father owns a small farm there. We raise sheep mainly."

"My Knights. . . . ?"

Dhamon swallowed hard, meeting the commander's gaze. He threw his shoulders back and puffed out his chest, as he'd seen the Dark Knights do. "Your Knights are most impressive, Commander. I have been watching them, be-because I would like to join them. I want to become a Dark Knight, too."

Dhamon surprised himself. Certainly he admired the Knights and fancied himself becoming one. *Fancied*. It was a boyish fantasy, he told himself. Nothing more.

"There is nothing more I want, Sir, than to be a Dark Knight." But it was more than a fantasy, he realized. It was what he *really* wanted to be, a Knight, not a farmer—and he wanted to be a Knight of Takhisis, not a member of the Legion of Steel or Knights of Solamnia.

"Interesting," the commander replied. His gaze shifted to a spot by the willow tree. Dhamon's brother had awakened and was trying to crouch behind the veil of leaves. "Does he, too, want to be a Knight?" When the commander pointed to the younger Grimwulf, Dhamon's brother made a squeaking noise and spun on his heels, vaulted over the creek and disappeared from sight. The slight smile grew wider on the Knight's lined face.

"No, Sir," Dhamon answered. "Just me. That's my younger brother."

"How old are you, Dhamon Grimwulf?" The smile vanished, replaced by an intensely probing expression that chased the breath from Dhamon's lungs.

"Thirteen. Thirteen last week, Sir."

"You look older than a mere thirteen."

Dhamon could have lied, said sixteen or seventeen. He could easily pass for older, as he was as tall as his friends who were that age. But he was afraid to lie to this man. Those eyes could pierce any falsehood and exact a terrible retribution.

"Thirteen. That's a little too young," the commander said mildly, "for my unit. Though there are some who accept squires of your age. Years past our Order accepted boys at the age of twelve, but, as I said, that was years past. Now we look to young men who are sixteen, or older."

Dhamon set his jaw. "I do want to be a Dark Knight, Sir."

The commander slapped him on the shoulder. "That's why you've been watching us all day, Dhamon?" Behind them, the sparring stopped, and the men looked over to where he stood, visible to them from a distance. The field commander raised a hand for the next two men to begin their round. "Lying in the grass and studying my men since the sun came up?"

Dhamon tried to hide his surprise that the man knew he'd been here that long. And he had tried to keep so quiet! "Yes, Sir. I have been watching your Knights all day."

"Get your shirt, young Dhamon Grimwulf, and come visit with me and my men."

Heart hammering wildly in his chest, Dhamon

retrieved his shirt, donning it and brushing at the dirt stains as he ran as fast as his legs would carry him toward the camp. He combed his hair with his fingers and tried to look every bit as proud and confident as the bemused Knights who assembled to meet him.

"This is Dhamon Grimwulf of Hartland," the commander said, introducing him to a half-dozen men sharpening and polishing their swords. "He wants to be a Dark Knight."

Only one of the Knights extended his hand and nodded a greeting.

"And perhaps he will be one of us one day," the commander continued. "In a few years. Frendal, show him around the camp, let him help set up a few tents, handle your sword. But make sure you send him home before sunset. I don't want him getting into trouble with his family on our account."

Perhaps he will be a Knight one day. Dhamon was instantly crestfallen, though he hid his disappointment. One day. Why not now?

Frendal, he learned, was the second-in-command of the force. Originally from Winterholm in Coastlund, he had joined the Dark Knights a dozen years earlier when he was seventeen. He'd spent the first few years stationed in the Northern Wastes and in Nightlund. Now a courier had brought an important message, and Frendal's unit was returning to Nightlund. Frendal would reveal nothing else about their mission to Dhamon, though he regaled him with tales of battles against goblins.

"Can you fight?" Frendal asked teasingly as he passed his sword to Dhamon for inspection.

Dhamon held the sword almost reverently, finding it heavier than it looked. He admired the detail on the pommel and the crosspiece.

"It was a gift from my mother," Frendal said. "She was a Dark Knight, too."

"I've never had the opportunity to fight," Dhamon admitted, "but I *could* fight. I know I could." He stepped back and imitated a few of the sparring moves he'd seen practiced by the Knights. "I learn quickly."

Frendal's eyes twinkled. "I believe you do."

The day ended all too abruptly for Dhamon, and by sunset he was back home and helping his mother set the table. His brother had told the family that he was hobnobbing with the Dark Knights, and it was the sole topic of dinner conversation.

His father was angry about it. "The Dark Knights are evil and despicable," he said, finger wagging and eyes narrowed onto Dhamon. "They're vile men who wage war against the righteous. If you've a desire to be a Knight, we'll look into that next spring or more likely the spring after next. When I take the older ewes to the markets north of Solanthus, we'll inquire about the likelihood of your joining the Solamnic Knights. Mind you, it's a hard life, and dangerous, and if you pass the training you could be sent halfway across the world. But the Solamnics would be a damn far sight better than the Dark Knights. Though I'd rather see you spend your life working this farm, I'll not deter you. There is much to be said for service." The elder Grimwulf took several forkfuls of potatoes. "But you've a few years to think about all of this. You might change your mind."

But he wasn't punished or forbidden. Unlike some of Dhamon's friends, he knew his father wouldn't force him to be a farmer or a goatherd. He wouldn't be obligated to work this farm when he grew older. His father was a staunch advocate of free will and following one's heart, as he'd left home at a relatively early age to do what he pleased, so Dhamon knew his life's ambition would be his own . . . in just a few short years.

"The Dark Knights . . ."

"—are not for you," his father quickly cut in, "and you're not to go out there again. Everyone in town has the sense to stay away from whatever it is the Knights are doing out there."

Practicing, Dhamon wanted to say. Drilling and practicing and waiting for another courier before they left for Nightlund. But he said nothing. He finished his meal in silence and nodded politely as his father detailed tomorrow's chores.

Dhamon got up before the sun the next day, finishing the bulk of his work before he again found himself between Hartford and the Vingaard River, lying in the grass and observing the Knights. He slipped back home to finish his duties shortly before noon. Then he artfully eluded his younger brother and returned to the field again before dinner. He told his father he was going to a friend's, and he didn't consider it entirely a lie. The commander and Frendal had been friendly enough to him. If his father discovered his ruse, he would be punished, but any punishment would be worth the chance to spend more time with these Knights.

How many more days would they stay here? he wondered, hoping the courier was coming from some great distance and wouldn't arrive for perhaps a few more weeks. He saw nothing despicable or evil about these Knights, and they certainly weren't vile in their attitude towards him. They were exceedingly clever men, he thought, noting their routine. Their tents were pitched in straight rows, but each row offset the next, so to the undiscerning eye it would appear the tents were haphazardly scattered. There was a pattern to the patrols, but it had taken Dhamon two days of studying the pattern and scratching notes in the dirt to figure it out, and he knew no enemy would decipher it without doing the same.

He felt he couldn't approach them again, unless invited. Twice he caught Frendal looking toward the willow, and he suspected the Knight might have spotted him, in spite of his precautions and silence.

Let them figure out I'm here, he thought, that I'm interested. The more Dhamon thought about it, the more he knew he wanted to join the Order. He didn't want to wait until next spring or the spring after that to become a Solamnic Knight. He no longer wanted to become a Solamnic anyway.

The drumming started again, and again the men lined up to spar. This time the attackers were using a variety of weapons—spears, flails, maces, even some crude and unusual-looking hatchets and polearms, perhaps of goblin make.

"Maybe they're going to fight a hobgoblin army and they want to practice how to defend against their weapons," he mused. "Glorious!" The thought of such a battle ignited a passion in him that he hadn't known existed. He felt his face flush. Frendal had said they were heading deep into Nightlund, and it was common knowledge that there were goblins, hobgoblins, ogres, and trolls there. "Maybe Frendal will tell me what they're planning if I sneak up and catch his eye . . . ."

That hope died in a sharp breeze that swelled up out of nowhere, cutting the heat and flattening the grass. The shadows stretched to their limits and whipped about in the growing wind.

"What in . . ."

A heartbeat later his question was answered. A shadow cut across the setting sun, and Dhamon felt his throat constrict. He could scarcely catch his breath, and there was a rushing sound in his ears. It was a dragon coming in from the northwest, and the mere sight of it caused Dhamon to shake uncontrollably. He didn't know at the time that dragons wore an aura of fear the way a soldier wears a uniform. A dragon can cause entire towns to flee in terror. A dragon can also control its fear-magic, as the one landing was doing now, so the Dark Knights could stand unaffected in its imperious presence.

Yet Dhamon continued to shiver, and tears spilled from his eyes. He parted the grass so he could see what was going on. He was amazed and frightened all in the same instant, so frightened he couldn't budge, though his mind told him he should, ordered his legs to run as fast as they could to take him as far away from here as possible. Dhamon slammed his mouth shut to keep his teeth from clattering, and his fingers nervously worked into the dirt.

The dragon was blue. In the sunlight its color looked like the surface of a wind-tossed lake, scales shimmering a vibrant hue and appearing to be constantly in motion. The creature tucked its wings to its sides and thumped its tail against the ground once, the force sending two nearby Knights to their knees. Its huge equine-shaped head was all planes and angles yet somehow beautifully elegant. Its eyes were catlike slits of brightest yellow inside black orbs, filled with cunning and intelligence.

One rider sat on the dragon, dressed in a full suit of plate armor and wearing a heavily lined wool cloak that was out of place in the summer weather.

As the rider slid from the dragon's back, he was quick to remove the cloak and helmet. Dhamon guessed the man was in his early twenties—so young, and riding a dragon! He passed a trio of bound scroll tubes to the Knight Commander. Dhamon noted that the dragon tipped its head to the commander—a dragon offering a human a measure of respect!

"I *will* be a Dark Knight," Dhamon whispered to himself, "and someday I will ride a dragon, too."

He'd heard tales of the Knights of Takhisis dragonriders, and all his life he'd heard about the dragons of Krynn, but never had he actually seen one. This grand creature yielded to these men—to these Knights. He recalled that his father said he'd seen a dragon once, a bronze one when he was a young man traveling with friends in the Vingaard Mountains just north of Brasdel. His father said he'd never been more frightened, yet he somehow couldn't run away. He simply watched with fascination as the creature rode the air currents above the highest mountains, searching for . . . something, he could tell.

"Seeing your first dragon, son, is something you will never, ever forget," he said. And Dhamon knew he wouldn't forget, he'd lock away this time in his memory and tell his own children about what he'd witnessed, someday.

The commander and the courier talked for several minutes. Straining to hear what was said, Dhamon picked out mention of Nightlund and Throtl. He heard clearly that the men would break camp at dawn. Eventually the courier left, the great blue dragon knocking the Knights to their knees with the force it created as its wings beat to carry it high into the darkening sky. Dhamon watched the dragon depart, still trembling, still crying from fright, more determined than ever now to join these men.

The dragon circled the camp once, then banked to the north, wings spread wide and gliding with the wind. Dhamon's eyes never left the dragon until it became a speck of ink in the sky and then disappeared entirely from view. He imagined it was heading to the northern desert. He'd heard blue dragons relished the sand and heat. He was able to pick himself up from the ground then, as the trembling finally subsided. He washed in the creek, discovering that he'd soiled himself in his fear. He returned home a few hours after the sun had set, climbing through the window and into the small bedroom he shared with his brother.

He would never be a Solamnic Knight like his friend Trenken Hagenson. He would become a Dark Knight! And he wasn't about to wait another year for it to happen. Silent as a cat, he gathered a few changes of clothes in a canvas sack and thrust two steel pieces he'd saved into his pocket. He wanted to tell his brother good-bye, but he didn't dare wake him—then risk having his parents wake, too. They'd only stop him, or try to. He crept into the kitchen, looking for some peaches—he'd skipped dinner watching the Knights, and his stomach was rumbling. One last look around the home, which held mostly pleasant memories, then he quietly closed the door behind him.

Dhamon hadn't made it much past the tool shed when he sensed he was being watched. He stopped but kept his eyes trained north.

"Don't stop me, father. I have to do this. You know this life isn't for me. I will never be a farmer."

There was the crunch of boots over the dry earth,

the sound of hands smoothing at clothes, the clearing of his father's throat. His father stood only a few feet behind him. "Dhamon, the Dark Knights are despicable," he repeated. "You're a *good* son, and you'll be a *good* man. This path you want to head down, it's not for you."

"The Dark Knights aren't evil. I've been watching them, father. They are admirable, honorable men." Dhamon turned. In the twilight, with the stars just starting to appear, his father's face was indistinct, but he could sense that it was etched with sadness and concern.

"I have to choose my own path, father, like you did. And I want to do this now. No. I have to do this."

Dhamon was going to say other things; that his father might succeed in stopping him now, but maybe not the next time and certainly could not hold him here forever. That he had no desire to be a Solamnic Knight come next spring or the spring after that. He wanted to go with the Knights now. But Dhamon didn't say anything else, he simply watched as his father drew his hands up to the back of his neck and unfastened the clasp of a chain.

"I was only a year older than you when I went off on my own," his father said, the resignation heavy in his voice, "and your mother would cry if she knew I was letting you go now. But I wager if I stop you now, I'll only be keeping you here for a little while longer. Still, I've a hope you'll see this all as a foolish notion and come back sooner or later."

He held the chain in one palm. Dhamon's father had worn the chain every day of every year. Dhamon had never seen him take it off, until now. "My father gave this to me the day I left home." The chain was silver, sparkling faintly, and from it dangled an old gold coin with worn edges. Dhamon moved closer. There was a man's profile on the coin, bearded and with an unusual-looking helmet topped by a dangling plume from which hung a "1". The man's eye was a tiny, bluish diamond.

"Ours is a very old family, Dhamon," his father said. "We trace our roots to Istar. More than eight hundred years before the Cataclysm, Istarians traded throughout the world. Our ancestors were said to have been among the richest merchants, owning a grand fleet and commanding shares in every caravan that crossed the interior."

Dhamon nodded, remembering some of the stories his father had told and retold after dinner on special occasions.

"These merchants set aside their work during the Third Dragon War and took up weapons. Then they took up shovels and began to help people rebuild and prosper. One of our ancestors, Haralin Grimwulf, chose to aid the dwarves."

"I remember the story," Dhamon said. He shifted his weight from foot to foot, wanting to leave before his father managed to say something that would change his mind and make him stay.

"It was shortly after the war that the dwarves of Thorbardin were granted rights to mine in the Garnet Mountains. This was said to be the very first coin minted from there." His father pointed to the "1" and to the diamond. "This is an extremely special coin. No other exists just like it, not even in the great storehouses in Palanthas."

Worth a great deal because it was gold and set with a diamond, Dhamon knew, worth more if indeed it was so ancient and singular—certainly worth enough to buy his father a large farm and livestock. A true relic, a true family legacy.

"This coin was given by the dwarves to Haralin—for his help in the Third Dragon War and for working with them as they established the garnet mine. It has been passed down through the centuries from father to son. And now I'm giving it to you." He placed it around Dhamon's neck and tucked the coin under the V of his shirt. "Go to your Dark Knights, son. I've every confidence you'll eventually learn you've no place with them and that you'll either come home or find some other grand adventure. When you settle down, and when you raise your own family—though you may be very far from here—give this coin to your own first son and tell him of our Istar roots."

His father's eyes were watery, but he did not cry.

"I will pass this on to my first son," Dhamon vowed, "but I *will* find a place with the Dark Knights, father." And I will ride the dragons, he added to himself. "You will be proud of me." Then, gladdened that his father hadn't stopped him, he turned and sprinted away so his father wouldn't see his own tears. He didn't stop running until he reached the Knights' camp.

◇ ◇ ◇ ◇ ◇ ◇ ◇

"Dhamon Grimwulf," the field commander cried when he spotted him approaching beyond the last row of tents.

The sky was caught between night and morning, those hazy few moments when the world appears indecisive about whether to go on. There's a silence then, the animals seeming to hold their breath in anticipation. Then the line of rosy pink touches the far horizon, the birds start singing, and Krynn announces yes, there will be another day.

"I am going to be a Dark Knight," Dhamon stated. His shoulders were square, his chin thrust out, his eyes filled with a fierce determination. He expected the field commander to repeat that he was too young, to send him back home, but that didn't happen.

"Help Frendal with his tent," the commander returned jauntily. "We'll be leaving soon for Nightlund. We're going to join up with another unit. You will have much to learn along the way, young Grimwulf. And if you pass the tests . . . ." There was a pause, and the commander looked Dhamon over carefully.

"I will pass all of your tests, Sir."

"Then I will be the first to welcome you into the fold."

◇ ◇ ◇ ◇ ◇ ◇ ◇

There were times when Dhamon swore he was too tired to sleep. There was no part of him that didn't ache; his arms especially ached—from carrying supplies and practicing with a sword. His fingers were so calloused they bled for days, and just when he thought they'd started to heal he was given a new weapon to learn and heavier packs to carry, and they'd start bleeding all over again. He never entertained the notion of quitting, though the field commander had asked him if he cared to quit on more than one occasion. Each night he tugged the ancient coin from beneath his shirt, ran his thumb around the edge, and wondered what his family was doing.

Dhamon had expected the training to be rigorous, but he also expected some amount of glamor and excitement—and of course battles. All around him the men sparred and sharpened their weapons, polished their armor and talked about the ogres they expected to fight in Nightlund. Dhamon was left out of most conversations, though Frendal seemed to make it a point to chat with him once in a while. Once he even asked Dhamon about the old coin, and Dhamon welcomed the opportunity to regale him with the tale of the ancient Istarian merchant who'd been rewarded by the dwarves. But mostly Dhamon kept to himself and watched and waited, and in the quiet time when he had a break, he often practiced alone with a borrowed weapon.

One day they were nearing the Nightlund border, camping in a farm field, when Frendal assigned Dhamon a sparring partner. Dhamon performed poorly the first few sessions but quickly mastered swings and defensive poses and began to develop maneuvers of his own. Before the week was out he had won a match against a seasoned Knight. His real training started then, more intense than he could have imagined. His hands bled worse than ever, and his evenings were filled with studies by candlelight. He was tasked with committing to memory the precepts of the Order, the chain of command, and the storied history of the Dark Knights.

When they finally joined up with a second unit— across a Vingaard tributary and well into Nightlund now— he was tested first by Frendal, then the field commander, and finally put through an examination by a gaunt-looking Knight who wore robes rather than plate armor and whose facial features could have placed him anywhere between the age of forty and sixty.

"So young," the gaunt Knight commented, "to want to follow our ways."

Dhamon respectfully nodded, unsure if he was supposed to address the man directly.

"Frendal tells me you are exceptional with a sword and that you can recite the names and dates as well as any Knight here."

Another nod.

"When were the Dark Knights born?"

"In the year 352," Dhamon began, "when Ariakan, son of the Dragon Highlord Ariakas and the sea goddess Zeboim, was captured by the Knights of Solamnia."

"And in the Summer of Chaos . . . ?"

"The year 383. Ariakan directed his Knights to invade Ansalon. They took more territory in one month than all the dragonarmies had managed to conquer during the War of the Lance."

The stranger smiled and cupped his hands in front of Dhamon, mumbled words in a long-lost tongue. Magic! The stranger's palms took on a pale blue glow that quickly darkened and rose to form a sphere that hovered between their heads.

"You know the dates and the names and the conquests, young man. Yet to you I sense they are merely words. There is no real feeling behind them."

Dhamon opened his mouth to protest, but the stranger's curious expression cut him off.

"I will change that, young man. I will add feeling and understanding to your history lessons." With a gesture the sphere sparkled and became translucent. Then it moved forward, enveloped Dhamon's head and seemed to disappear.

◇ ◇ ◇ ◇ ◇ ◇ ◇

Dhamon was no longer in the farm field. He was in Neraka, in the midst of an impressive force of draconians and on his way to the Dark Queen's temple. Solamnic Knights came upon them, and the fighting began. He could smell the blood in the air, the wails of the dying filled his ears, and the carnage was everywhere. Dhamon was able to cut down five of the Solamnics before he was subdued . . . as Ariakan had slain five before he was captured.

Dhamon was in Ariakan's place!

Wounded and defeated, Dhamon was dragged to the High Clerist's Tower and imprisoned, just as Ariakan had been. It wasn't long before the Solamnics became impressed by his courage and intelligence and considered him a valuable captive indeed.

Through the magic-induced vision Dhamon watched himself as Ariakan scrutinize the Solamnics and pretend to be "rehabilitated." He claimed to be their friend and asked to study with them, but when the time was right, he would leave, armed with the knowledge to start his own Order.

Dhamon suddenly felt cold. Chilled to the bone, he wrapped his arms around his chest in a futile effort to warm himself. His legs stung from the biting wintery wind and from trudging so high into the mountains that ringed the Dark Queen's glorious city. Hungry and frostbitten, Dhamon saw himself as Ariakan wandering lost, praying to his mother Zeboim for help. That help was granted in the form of a trail of sea shells. The shells led him to a deep cavern where he rested and recovered and witnessed a manifestation of Takhisis—who gave him her blessing for the Knighthood.

◇ ◇ ◇ ◇ ◇ ◇ ◇

He wanted to see more—much more! But there was a soft, popping sound, and Dhamon reluctantly shook off the magic-induced dream and awoke. He was still chilled, despite it being summer, and his legs were still sore.

"Now, young man, you begin to have some feeling for our history," the gaunt Knight said.

Dhamon clenched his hands and said yes, and saying yes he felt something sharp bite into his palm. It was a sea shell—one he kept for many years as a remembrance of his first evening at the side of the Dark Knight priest.

There were many more nights when he experienced other magical dream-visions of himself as Ariakan. Through these visions the priest allowed him to relive the history of the Knighthood and the establishment of the Blood Oath and the Code.

"I want nothing more than to be a Dark Knight," Dhamon told the priest one evening. "Not a squire, not a camp worker. More than anything I want to be a Dark Knight."

That evening the priest—who had never in all this time given Dhamon his name—offered a smile that was both warm and unsettling. "Young man, you *are* a Dark Knight."

Dhamon was given a sword that very evening, a fine one with a crosspiece that looked like dragon talons. He was fitted for armor, given a night-black tabard and cloak, and sworn into the Order.

"Dhamon Grimwulf, you are the edge of a blade," Frendal intoned. "Wielded by our field commander, the blade will sweep into the heart of Nightlund and slay our enemies."

"The edge of a formidable blade," Dhamon said with great pride.

"You embrace our Knighthood and leave

behind your common past," Frendal continued.

"Yes, I leave it all behind," Dhamon agreed.

Frendal reached to Dhamon's neck, to the chain and ancient coin that hung there. He ground his boot heel into the soft Nightlund soil and dug a hole. "Behind forever," Frendal said as he dropped the family relic into the earth and covered it up.

Dhamon stomped the covering earth flat. "Behind forever," he said.

When they marched the next day into battle against a tribe of ogres, Dhamon thought only fleetingly about the valuable family heirloom and experienced only the slightest regret that it would never be passed to another Grimwulf.

◇ ◇ ◇ ◇ ◇ ◇ ◇

"Your memories are rich, Dhamon Grimwulf."

Dhamon wiped at his eyes. He was inside the abandoned fortune teller's shop again, and the Chaos wight was inches away, its eyes burning brighter than ever.

"That was a most wondrous memory," the creature said. The undead thing loomed in its lizardlike form, its thorny antlers bigger and more intricate than before. "Your mind is far more complex than the draconian's, much healthier than the woman's."

"Fiona! If you've done anything—"

"I told you I did not physically harm her. I took only a few scattered memories from the woman, confusing and nonsensical, none so delicious and sustaining as yours."

The creature hovered inches above the floor, looking much darker and forbidding now. Dhamon sensed it had gained power from whatever it claimed to have taken from him.

"So delicious, I must have another memory from you. Only one more." The wight glided toward Dhamon, long fingers growing longer, like vipers readying themselves to strike.

"Our agreement!" Dhamon recalled. "Our agreement was one memory, and you said you would let us leave this town."

"Perhaps, but can you prove I have taken anything from you yet? I've taken nothing. You owe me a memory."

"I very much doubt that, demon!"

"Delicious memories," the wight repeated in Rig's voice, then the voice became Feril's, Riki's, and finally it was Fiona's. "I must have one more memory. One more, and you may go."

Ghostlike, the viper fingers came at him, thrusting themselves inside his head. Dhamon tried to shift away, but the wight followed him, eyes glowing and maw opening. Its tongue snaked out and wrapped itself around Dhamon's neck to hold him.

"One more memory, I said. Then you may leave."

Dhamon fought the wight with all of his willpower. "I shouldn't've let you inside my mind the first time," he cursed. "I shouldn't've believed you."

"Believe me," the wight cooed. "Just one more memory."

"No!" Dhamon threw all his effort into one thought which might keep the Chaos creature at bay. He'd done something before to stall it, he knew. He felt an odd sensation, and a ripple passed down his back, as if he'd been chilled by a blast of wintry air. "No!" What he felt was the Chaos wight invading his mind.

A myriad of memories coursed through Dhamon,

childhoods of the people who used to live in this town, flashes of happiness from young lovers, losses of dear friends, strange incidents, too—memories of dogs and parrots and other creatures once kept as pets by the citizens here. The wight had killed them all, drained all their memories. For an instant, he sensed Fiona, perhaps touching a memory the wight had stolen from her. The Fiona-memory was eerie and disturbing. "Madness," Dhamon whispered. He'd encountered a part of Fiona's madness.

His eyes flew open! Her madness—that was the key. Her madness had weakened the creature, warped its mind.

"I am not weak," the Chaos wight argued. "Nothing has weakened me."

But Dhamon knew otherwise, wrapping his thoughts around Fiona and the hint of her madness, concentrating on that idea.

"Stop!" the creature keened.

Dhamon didn't stop. He only increased his efforts.

Suddenly the Chaos wight's hands withdrew from him, and the undead creature floated to the ceiling, pinprick eyes glaring down at Dhamon. "You think you have won!" it taunted.

"Aye, beast, I have won. You'll take no more memories from us, and you'll not threaten my companions again."

"Pass this way again and . . ."

"And I'll win again," Dhamon said as he backed out of the shop. It was dusk, and when he looked down the street he saw Ragh and Fiona walking toward him. The Solamnic Knight had a pitcher in her hand, and Ragh was carrying two large mugs. They'd finally managed to obtain water from the well, and under the draconian's arm was a rolled up sheet of parchment.

"Let's get out of here!" Ragh called when he spotted Dhamon.

"Immediately," Dhamon replied.

"You've not won." He heard those words as a whisper carried on a chill gust of wind. "You've lost something very precious, Dhamon Grimwulf: your family and a piece of your history."

Dhamon shook his head. He'd lost nothing that he could discern. He'd never had a family.

CHAPTER SIX
BEV'S OAR

hey call this dismal patch of dirt Nostar. A big island, as far as islands go, but a pretty big nothing as far as I'm concerned." Ragh walked between Dhamon and Fiona, a battered map held between his clawed hands. The scroll he'd retrieved from the inn had yellowed edges that flaked off when his scaly fingers brushed against them. "I've been just about everywhere on Krynn— and I visited here at least on three occasions. The last time was . . . oh, I guess forty or fifty years ago. Not long enough, if you ask me."

When neither of his companions commented, he continued, "I didn't recognize it at first. Nostar wasn't like this then. Not that this island was ever anything special, but it didn't try to make you a permanent part of the landscape by pulling you down into a sinkhole. There was grass most places, a lot more trees, and some hills here and there." The last he said wistfully, gazing out over the relatively flat ground scarred by sinkholes and piles of rocks. He shook his head. "I certainly remember a lot more green."

Using a craggy, gray rock formation dubbed the Three Brothers, to the west, and the sea to the east, they had decided to follow what the map showed as a road running toward a sizeable mining settlement. The map suggested the road was substantial, but what remained of the road was almost completely overgrown by the scabrous brown grass, and there were a few places where sinkholes had destroyed entire sections of it. They could see wagon ruts where some wagons had gone around the sinkholes.

"That's a good sign," Ragh said. "Means there's somebody other than us still alive on this gods-forsaken rock."

The map showed that Nostar stretched roughly sixty miles from east to west and forty north to south. There were only a dozen town names indicated on the map, and these were clustered around the northern and eastern part of the island—all but two of them set back a couple of miles from the coast. Of the two towns perched directly on the shore, they decided to head to the closest one, a place called Bev's Oar, a mile or so north of the eerily deserted mining settlement.

Studying the map, Dhamon saw that the interior of the island was practically devoid of notation, save for one egg-shaped lake and two scrawled words that had been added in a different hand than the map maker's—Hobgoblin Village. He raised an eyebrow.

"That's why there were never many towns on Nostar and why the ones that are here are small," Ragh said. "Most of the population is goblins and hobgoblins, bugbears, and their kin. Or it used to be anyway, last time I happened by. Not many humans and elves, and they always stayed near the coasts, fishing and mining. From what I remember, the goblins left the humans pretty much alone." Ragh rubbed at his chin. "Of course, things could've changed."

"Things *have* changed," Dhamon said flatly. "Consider that nameless place we just came from."

"It's got a name. Slad's," Ragh said. "According to the map it's called Slad's Corners."

"It's called empty now. Let's hope Bev's Oar has a decent population and at least a few ships in port. I want to book passage to Southern Ergoth as quickly as possible." Dhamon had noticed more scales sprouting since they'd left the vacant town, a scattering on his left leg—which Ragh and Fiona also noticed—and a dozen more on his stomach. He feared he had little time left to atone for the mistakes in his life. He intended to take Fiona to the Solamnic stronghold, find Maldred, make sure Riki and his child were safe. Thinking about it all quickened his pulse. "My guess is we have another seven or eight miles to cover before we reach Bev's Oar and . . ."

Ragh was quick to point out their map predated the war in the Abyss, when new land masses rose from the earth. "The island might be bigger now, so it might be twice as many miles to this Bev's Oar. Maybe more. That's assuming Bev's Oar didn't break off into the sea. And it's a long way after that to Southern Ergoth," the draconian mused. "Of course, there's no telling, really, the size of this damn place and just how far we have to go."

Dhamon groaned. "It doesn't matter how big it is, let's get going."

Nostar was south of Southern Ergoth by more

than eighty miles according to Ragh's map. It was about half that distance to Enstar, an island twice this one's size. They might stop over in Enstar, but "too far to swim," Fiona said absently.

Dhamon gave her a sideways glance. Sometimes he couldn't tell whether she was listening or not. There was always a fixed, dazed expression on her face. Her words now were tinged with anger. "I'm not going to swim forty miles *or* eighty miles, Dhamon, and I don't know why you keep harping on Southern Ergoth. You do need to find us a ship, Dhamon, so you can take me to the New Sea. Rig and I are to be married soon on the coast across from Schallsea Island."

She made an exasperated sound, but for an instant her eyes had sparkled with life, before her face resumed its disturbing blank expression. Though tired and hungry, she resumed their trek toward Bev's Oar, while Dhamon and Ragh purposefully fell back.

"You'll not be allowed at the wedding ceremony, Dhamon," she called over her shoulder, "causing all this bother."

Dhamon ached inside for what Fiona had become, a mockery of her old self, and he wondered why the Chaos wight couldn't have stolen the memories of Rig away from her. It might have made her a little easier to deal with. How much of Fiona's madness has found its way inside me? he thought. And what did the wight rob me of? He shook off his unanswerable thoughts, pointing to Ragh's map.

"Somehow we must find passage on a ship at Bev's Oar. But we'll need to get some warm clothes, first. At least Fiona and I need warmer clothes."

"I can feel the bite of winter, too," Ragh said.

Dhamon's finger drifted a little to the west on the map. "That river's not too far off our course, maybe fifteen, twenty minutes at the most. We can store up on water. And I could do with a bath." He hated the thought of delaying the journey to Bev's Oar, but Dhamon was worried about how he looked. The scales were bad enough—the scales *and* the filth made him look truly monstrous, he thought. He needed to clean up.

The river turned out to be a narrow creek no more than half a foot deep, but the water was clear and cold. Dhamon scrubbed himself raw, while Fiona stoically went downstream for privacy.

"You've got even more scales now, I see," Ragh said, nodding at Dhamon's legs. His right leg was solid scales, shining slickly from the water. The left was spattered with them.

Dhamon didn't reply. He didn't try to cover them any more—there wasn't enough material left in his tattered clothes. He avoided the draconian's accusing gaze and stared instead at the water. The man staring back had a hard look to him, dark eyes hiding all manner of mysteries. He had a handsome face, with high cheekbones and a firm jaw, but he was gaunt from lack of food, and his uneven beard and tangled mass of hair made him look like a brigand.

"Fiona!" Dhamon heard her sloshing along the creek. "May I have one of those knives?"

The Solamnic Knight looked up without recognition. She had cleaned up nicely, though her face looked raw with scars, and the cut on her forehead was still swollen and ugly.

"A knife, please?"

In a move so fast it surprised him, Fiona drew one of the knives from her belt and thrust it forward, its tip hovering in front of Dhamon's stomach. "Will this knife do?" Her eyes were vacant, her voice ice. She inched the blade forward until its tip pressed into his flesh. Her free hand drifted down to the second knife. "Or do you want to borrow two?"

He didn't reply and he didn't retreat. He just stared into her eyes, hoping to connect with sanity.

"Just why do you want to have one of these knives, Dhamon? Do you want to use my own weapons against me?" She tugged the second knife free, but held it at her side. "Or maybe you want to—"

"Cut his hair with it." Ragh grabbed the threatening knife. He'd moved up behind her silently. He passed the knife pommel first to Dhamon, who after a moment backed away.

"Oh. Cut his hair." Fiona turned and knelt at the edge of the creek. She transferred her remaining knife to her right hand and speared a crawfish on the pebble-lined bottom. She worried the blade at its shell, pulled out the flesh, and stuffed it into her mouth.

Looking at her, Dhamon felt more pity than anger. He quickly shaved and cut the tangles from his air. Though his hair was uneven and hung to just above his shoulders, he looked more presentable. Sticking the knife in his belt, and acknowledging Fiona's glare for doing so, he led his two companions back to what was left of the road. He didn't stop for rest or speak again until, an hour later, the silhouette of a town came into view.

It was a mining colony at the road's end, just as indicated on Ragh's map. The mining town was empty, and they quickly bypassed it for fear there might be another Chaos wight haunting the place. They continued to follow faded wagon tracks until just before sunset when they camped in the open away from a fresh cluster of sinkholes. The sunset was the only dash of color on the land, painting the ground a pale orange and making the edges of the low-hanging clouds look like liquid gold. They drank in the beautiful sight without speaking. Fiona and Ragh settled in for the evening when the last of the color faded.

Dhamon sat watch all during the night, listening to the soft snores of the draconian and the surf washing against the nearby beach. He stared out into the darkness as he felt the heat begin to radiate from the large scale on his leg. Clamping his teeth shut and swallowing a scream, he dug his fingers into the earth and endured another painful episode without waking the others. It was a night of excruciating agony.

All the while he thought of Riki and his child— his need to see them before he died, needing to know that they were all right. There was Maldred to consider, too, and other things to atone for if there was time. Before the torment sent him spiraling into unconsciousness, he prayed to the vanished gods that he had enough days to set things right.

◇ ◇ ◇ ◇ ◇ ◇ ◇

There was a cemetery on the outskirts of Bev's Oar, most of the graves marked by wooden planks the color of the earth. Rows of markers stood as straight as soldiers' ranks, the ground hard-packed and forbidding with silt blown across it by the wind.

"Graves are old," Ragh stated.

"Most of them," Dhamon said. He pointed far to his left, where two more recent graves told them someone was still alive in town to do the burying. Dhamon reached into his pocket and felt the coins he'd taken from the skeleton. He tugged a few out, the light catching them and glinting. "We'll get something to eat in the town, get some clothes, a passage." Get off this rock and be about my business—fast, he added to himself.

Dhamon inhaled deep—his keen senses picking up the smell of the earth, the rotting wooden grave markers, and the faint scent of bread baking, cinnamon. He pointed down a path to the row buildings about a half mile away. "Just through this graveyard and—"

"Wonder who's buried here?" Fiona had wandered away and was staring at the marker on the grave that seemed to be one of the most recent. Dhamon and Ragh joined her. The marker was a polished plank of walnut that looked like it was once the back of a chair, and carved on it were the words: DIED AFTER THE SUN WENT DOWN.

A chill raced down Dhamon's spine, and suddenly the smell of the bread wasn't quite as tempting. He looked at the other markers. The oldest were the hardest to read, the sea air and the years weathering them badly. However, they had the most information on them—names and dates: MAVELLE COLLING, BELOVED WIFE AND SISTER; WILGAN G. THRUPP, DIED OF THE SWEATING SICKNESS; BOLD BOLIVIR, TREASURED HUSBAND AND SON; ANN-MARIE, CHERISHED GRANDMOTHER; and more. Graves that appeared less than two or three decades old lacked any detail. There were no names, no real dates. One said: TALL MAN. Another: OLD WOMAN. Some said: DIED TODAY, though 'today' had to have been a year or more ago judging by the condition of the packed earth.

LITTLE BOY, RED-HAIRED MAN, FISHING MAN, THIN
ELF, ONE-EARED GOBLIN, WOMAN IN APRON, LOVELY
YOUNG GIRL, TAVERN OWNER, and the like.

"What in the levels of the Abyss?" Dhamon
breathed. "What kind of a weird cemetery is this?"

Ragh was tracing the more informational message on a very old, chipped stone. "Beven Wilthup-
Colling, Proud Founder of Bev's Oar. Born in the
summer of the Year of the Storms, Died at age sixty
in the Year of the Great Turtles."

"I'm done sightseeing at this cemetery," Fiona
said. "All this death is depressing. Death surrounds
you, Dhamon. Let's go into the village."

Dhamon grabbed her arm. "Aye, Fiona, we're
going into that village. But this cemetery has given
me a bad sense about the place. You and Ragh
shouldn't go in until after I've made sure it's safe."

"Dhamon the hero," she said tonelessly.

"I'm no hero," he said.

"No, I guess you're not. A hero would have
saved Jasper and Shaon."

Dhamon snarled, thrusting Fiona at Ragh. "Keep
her here until I get back."

"Who were Jasper and Shaon?" Ragh asked.

The dwarf Jasper was a very good friend,
Dhamon thought. I almost killed him but it wasn't
my fault, the red dragon controlled me. I couldn't
save him later on at the Window to the Stars. Fiona
knows. She knows the list. Jasper—one more name
on the list of people who died because they adven-
tured with me.

Shaon . . . A dragon I once rode killed her.

"Who were Jasper and Shaon?"

"The two of you stay here until I come back,"
Dhamon said tersely. He wasn't about to add Fiona
to the list, or the draconian for that matter.

"And if you don't come back?" Ragh asked.

Dhamon hurried down the path toward Bev's Oar.

He sighed with relief when he was beyond the graveyard and at the edge of town. The first few buildings he saw were relatively new and well-maintained, with brightly painted eaves and shutters and dried flowers arranged in pots outside the doors. Signs hung above businesses, the pictures on them showing a tavern, fishmonger, inn, and weaver. So far, so good. Things looked normal.

"Thank the Dark Queen's memory," he breathed. "People."

He wasn't sure what he'd expected to see, but part of him didn't expect the dozen or so men and women who strolled along a cobblestone street that served as the main thoroughfare—he could hear the indistinct click-clack of their heels, an altogether welcome sound. A dog yipped as it playfully chased a lanky young man around a corner and down a side street. A matronly woman clucking at a child at her side carried a basket filled with bread. Dhamon took a few steps down the street, his own heels clacking on the cobblestones—indeed a comfortable sound, he told himself, after all they'd been through. He considered waving to get Ragh's attention, have them both hurry into town right now, but he didn't know how the people would react to his scales. If they didn't accept him, they wouldn't accept the draconian. He had to check things out a little more.

Just a block or two more, he thought. So far no one had pointed at him and shouted in fear. Just one more block . . . Dhamon stopped in his tracks. While the buildings on this end of town were well-constructed and kept up, those down the first side street appeared thrown crazily together. A few were made of the hulls of ships, one even had a mast sticking out of its roof. Another was fashioned of vegetable crates stacked six or seven feet high, with a sail lashed over the top to keep out the rain. Next to that was a small dwelling made of woven sticks and fronds, looking like a hut one might find in a jungle.

Curious and alarmed, he continued on, spotting a residence built out of stones—as well as any dwarf could construct it. Next to it, however, was a mound of earth with a small door set into it and a ship's porthole carved into the side to serve as the window.

There were homes that looked like they were made of the remains of torn-down buildings. There were a half-dozen lean-tos, inside of which two hobgoblins sat eating charred rodents. They quietly regarded Dhamon for a few moments, then one gave him a wide grin and a welcome nod.

"Hobgoblins," he muttered. No wonder no one was pointing at him.

With each step he took, a part of Dhamon told him to go back to Ragh and Fiona and find another town as a safe haven. But finding another town would take time. He touched a scale that had just recently appeared on his wrist. He didn't have much time.

A trio of elves were patching the thatch on a narrow, two-story building. Across the street from the elves, a goblin watched and offered suggestions in broken Common. After a moment, Dhamon realized the elves were following the goblin's advice.

"Something to eat," he said to himself. "Clothes, passage. That's all we want. Not much. Then we'll get off this damnable rock as fast as possible." He needed some herbs, too, for Fiona's wound, but the wound was far from life-threatening, and he wondered if it was better to let the Knights on Southern Ergoth tend to her rather than waste another moment here. "Where's the docks?" Dhamon mused. He'd go just a little farther, explore down some more side streets to the north. If there was a fishmonger, there had to be at least fishing boats— and all it would take to get them to Southern Ergoth was a big fishing boat and someone who knew how to captain it. Anything that will float, he told himself. "There has to be—"

"Good morning!"

Dhamon whirled to see a gawky looking human with a mop of dirt-brown hair and a reed-thin mustache. The human was wearing a pressed white tunic with an insignia over his right breast, and he had a long red sash around his waist that caught the faint breeze and flapped at his knees. At his side was a hobgoblin wearing a ship's flag for a cape.

"Good morning to you!" the man repeated, extending his hand.

"And to you," Dhamon cautiously replied, his unease multiplying as he studied the pair.

The hobgoblin wearing the odd cape grinned wide, and a line of drool spilled over its lower lip and stretched to the ground.

"You're a stranger to Bev's Oar." This came from the man. The man glanced casually at Dhamon's scale-covered legs, then, dismissing them, met Dhamon's gaze.

Obviously I'm a stranger, Dhamon thought. "Aye," he said, finally shaking hands with the man and noting his firm grip. "I am new to this part of Nostar."

The hobgoblin grinned wider still and nudged the gawky man.

"Oh, yes. Excuse my manners. Welcome to our humble town!" The man patted Dhamon on the shoulder. "Always happy to see a new face. You're lookin' pretty tired. Must have traveled quite some distance to get here."

Obviously. "The storm the other night," Dhamon began in an effort to appear friendly. "I was washed ashore and—"

"Took the roof off the bait shop. That was quite a row, wasn't it . . . Mister . . . ?"

"Grimwulf."

The man frowned, worrying at a button on his tunic. "What a . . . grim name."

Dhamon hadn't yet decided whether to mention he had companions. "Listen, I—"

"Bet you're hungry, too. You could do with some sleep and some new clothes. Definitely some food. Definitely some clothes. Looks like you haven't eaten in days. So thin. We'll fix you up . . . Mister Grimwulf. In Bev's Oar we take good care of folks."

"There be no strangers here." This curious remark came from the hobgoblin.

Dhamon looked back and forth between the two. "Then if there are no strangers, who—"

The gawky man beamed. "I am the lord mayor of Bev's Oar. This is my assistant."

The hobgoblin nodded, more drool spilling over his lip and pooling at his toes.

"Assistant." Dhamon's face clouded.

The mayor caught his expression and sadly shook his head. "My *very able* assistant. The folks in Bev's Oar have no prejudice . . . Mr. Grimwulf." He pointed to the scales on Dhamon's leg. "We accept everyone, including you." His point made, he again raised his eyes level with Dhamon's. "Now about gettin' you some food and clothes."

Dhamon took a chance. "I have two companions waiting just outside of town."

"Well, hurry and fetch them. I doubt the inn will be servin' breakfast for too much longer."

CHAPTER SEVEN
NAMELESS FACES

T he inn owner would take none of Dhamon's coins for the feast she provided. The portly woman simply beamed at them and placed heaping plates of eggs, goat cheese, and warm bread on their table. She was also quick to fill their mugs with steaming cider.

Fiona dug in without question, eating so quickly she barely chewed her food. Ragh, too, ate ravenously, pausing for breath only when he'd finished his first plate. Dhamon, however, warily picked at the meal, eyeing the inn owner and the lord mayor and his hobgoblin assistant. The last two were seated a few tables away, engrossed in whispered conversation. Dhamon wanted to feel comfortable in this town that supposedly welcomed everyone, told himself he *should* feel comfortable. Ragh and Fiona obviously did. But he couldn't wholly relax and dismiss every apprehension. People just weren't this friendly, he knew from experience. Hobgoblins didn't easily mingle with humans and accept into their midst strangers covered in scales. Better that they get some clothes and be on their way to the docks and to Southern Ergoth.

"It doesn't feel right here," Dhamon whispered to Ragh.

"Too thin, you are!" the woman scolded Dhamon as she shuffled back to the table. "You need to put some more flesh on those bones of yours." She spooned more eggs onto his plate and shook the spoon at him for emphasis. "You look hungry. You should eat my good cooking more often."

Dhamon politely nodded.

"Mayor says," she continued, "you were washed ashore during the storm the other night. We've folks here from storms past, but the three of you don't look like any sailors I ever saw."

Dhamon stirred the eggs. "Thank you for the food, ma'am."

"Least I can do," she answered, shrugging her shoulders after he offered no further conversation. "We take care of folks around here."

With a full mouth, Ragh also mumbled his gratitude, and the woman affectionately patted him on the back.

Dhamon ate about half of what had been set before him, all the while watching the woman, the mayor, and the hobgoblin. The woman had not batted an eye at the wingless draconian and only gave the conspicuous scales on Dhamon's legs and wrists passing notice.

"Ragh . . ."

The draconian looked up and brushed at the crumbs on his lips.

"Does any of this bother you, Ragh?"

The draconian tipped his head. "That I've drawn no more attention than the two of you?"

"Aye."

"It's a nice change," he said. "Maybe I'll let it bother me when I'm done eating."

Dhamon turned his full attention to the lord mayor. He concentrated, his acute hearing picking up voices through the clink of forks against plates. "They are talking about us," he whispered to Ragh.

"Why shouldn't they be?" The draconian chuckled and raised his mug. The inn owner bustled over and refilled it, then topped off Dhamon's and Fiona's glasses for good measure. She retreated to the kitchen.

"They are speculating about where we come from, who we are, what we know about the world, and . . ."

"Why wouldn't they? This is a small town. Dhamon, eat."

Dhamon barely touched the rest of his food, pushing the plate away when the eggs were cold. When Fiona and Ragh finally ate their fill, Dhamon stood and dropped a steel piece on the table, not wanting to feel too indebted to the woman. He was about to direct Ragh and Fiona north to where he knew the docks were but was steered out the door in the opposite direction by the lord mayor. His hobgoblin assistant lingered behind, devouring more breakfast.

"I said we'd do something about those threadbare clothes of yours," the mayor said. "This way, Dhamon Grimwulf. Your lovely companion also needs new clothes. Is she your wife?"

Fiona shook her head. "We're not even friends any longer. I am to be married soon, to an Ergothian."

"Ergothian? What's that?"

"A man from a land far from here," she breathed.

"You must teach me all about Ergoth," the mayor said. "In fact . . ."

Dhamon shut out the rest of the lord mayor's conversation. He glanced over his shoulder. The inn owner was standing in the doorway watching them, a smile still plastered on her fleshy face. She waved to Ragh. There were a few dozen townsfolk moving on the street, their heels click-clacking, a few of them looking his way. Their clothes marked the majority of them as commoners, but they all appeared clean and healthy and in good spirits. A stoop-shouldered vendor, dressed a little better than most, was setting up a small cart on the corner and was hanging up thick strips of meat, spiced pork from the smell of it. There were other smells, too, floating in the crisp air—cinnamon bread and other goods from the bakery, fish, probably lying on the docks from fishing boat hauls, musky perfume from a woman who passed near them. He could still taste the eggs and goat cheese that heavily coated his teeth.

"How many people live in Bev's Oar?" Dhamon interrupted the lord mayor's conversation with Fiona.

"Don't know," the mayor said, as he led them to a freshly trimmed birch-paneled building. A spool of thread and crossed needles were displayed on a sign that hung above the door. "But there'll be three more if you decide to stay. I'd like to learn about this 'Ergoth.' "

Ragh brushed by them and planted himself on the porch, keeping in the shade of an overhang and studying the passersby. Though most of them glanced his way, not a single one balked or stared. "All right, it's bothering me now," he murmured to Dhamon. "Without prejudice is one thing. Without curiosity . . ."

"Stay on guard," Dhamon warned quietly, as he

followed Fiona inside the small shop. "We won't be staying much longer," he said loudly to the lord mayor. "We need to leave for Southern Ergoth as soon as possible. Perhaps with the evening tide."

The Lord Mayor frowned. "I hope we can change your mind. It's refreshing, us getting visitors like you."

The shop was larger than it appeared, but most of it was taken up with shelves. There were racks in the center, all of them holding either finished garments or folded pieces of material, and cloaks hung from hooks in the ceiling. The aisles were small, and the place felt cramped. There was a musty smell and a tinge of oil coming from a small jug next to a row of scissors. A few spiderwebs clung to the corners, dotted with the husks of dead insects. The shop was orderly but dingy.

Fiona almost smiled as the seamstress held up dresses and tunics that might fit her.

"You are . . . ?" the woman prompted.

"Fiona. I am a Solamnic Knight."

The woman proceeded to fuss over Fiona, helping her into a long, umber skirt and sand-colored shirt. Though plain, the garments were well-made and a welcome change from the sweat-stained and ripped clothing the Knight had been wearing. The woman wrapped a serviceable tunic and leggings in a sheet of canvas and handed these to Fiona, too.

"We really can't stay," Dhamon repeated to the lord mayor. "You've got a very nice town, though, and one I'm certain under other circumstances we'd be happy to call home for a time. But there are pressing matters. . . ."

"At least stay the night. We'll escort you to the docks and put you on a ship in the morning, if you haven't changed your mind." The lord mayor held up a tunic next to Dhamon, finding it far too short. "You can tell us all about the storm and where you came from. Your families and friends. What's going on elsewhere in the world. We haven't had news in some time. As I said, few strangers visit."

"And as *I* said, we're in a hurry."

The seamstress fussed over Dhamon now, supplying him with a pair of gray trousers that were a little worn at the knees and a white tunic that hung on his lean frame and also evidenced some wear. She paid no heed to the scales on his leg as she turned up the trouser legs into cuffs so they wouldn't drag on the ground. Satisfied with his appearance, she draped a thin, wool cloak over his arm "for evenings when the fall wind sets in." Then she fitted him with a finely tooled leather belt, into which Dhamon was quick to slide his knife. She handed him a second tunic, then stepped away and resumed her ministering to Fiona.

"Nasty sore on your pretty head, Fiona." She handed the Knight a ribbon for her hair.

"How much for all of these clothes?" Dhamon cut in.

"How much? Why ever would I charge you for them?"

"We can't accept charity," Dhamon said tersely, as he eyed a shelf with winter cloaks. "How much for the heavy cloaks?" Free food. Free clothes. No, something was wrong here; something that made his skin itch. "I must insist on paying for . . ."

The seamstress ignored him. "We'll make sure the lord mayor gets that sore tended to . . . Fiona." The woman brushed the curls away from the Solamnic Knight's forehead. "Nasty scar on your cheek, too. Hair a mess. All this from being washed ashore in that terrible storm?"

"It's from a spawn," Fiona said. "They breathe acid."

Dhamon cleared his throat. "I've got coins."

The seamstress turned back to Dhamon, bumping into a rack. She was quick to steady it. "No one pays me for these clothes!" Then she was waving for the lord mayor and—as if she was in charge—directing him to take Fiona to the town's healer at once. "Don't need to be losing anyone else," she muttered, as she nudged them out the door.

Dhamon turned to squarely face her. "Losing people?" he began. "What do you mean? We came through the cemetery. There were no names on . . ."

She gave him a surprised look, then made her clucking sound, and with a smile shut the door in his face.

◇ ◇ ◇ ◇ ◇ ◇ ◇

The healer looked scarcely older than a boy to Dhamon, yet he seemed to know what he was doing. He selected dried herbs and roots, many of which Dhamon was familiar with, ground them together, and created a paste that he liberally smeared on Fiona's forehead. As he worked, he pawed the hair away from his own face, revealing the slightly pointed ears of a half-elf, Qualinesti from the looks of him. Dhamon immediately thought of Riki and his child again. He decided there would be no more unsettling stops in this peculiar town. They would hop aboard a ship leaving with the evening tide, or even sooner if possible.

Dhamon watched as the half-elf created a different mixture to treat the acid scars on Fiona's cheek, though he told her sadly they'd never completely disappear. Then he insisted on trimming her hair.

Dhamon cleared his throat to get the half-elf's attention. "I suppose you don't want to be paid."

"Oh, I'll gladly take your coins, sir."

Finally, Dhamon thought. Someone in this town who acts normal. Dhamon quickly passed him two steel pieces, considerably more than his services were worth, then glanced out the shop window at an elderly couple strolling by arm in arm. He shook his head as two goblins scurried into view. A second later a human boy and girl and another goblin came gleefully chasing after them.

"What's wrong with these people?" he whispered to Ragh. "Is there some madness infecting them? Goblins playing with human children. Some of the merchants won't accept money. Hobgoblins walk around freely here, apparently hold public office, and—"

"Dhamon." Fiona stepped to his side. "You were partnered with a blue dragon when you were a Dark Knight. If I recall, you recently counted a kobold named Fetch as a trusted companion. Your best friend Maldred is a lying, scheming, blue-skinned ogre mage, and now you associate with a sivak." She nodded to the draconian standing in the doorway "You're looking through far too many windows," she continued. "You should be looking in mirrors instead."

"Perhaps you're right."

The healer gave Fiona a small clay jar and instructed her to rub more of the mixture on her wound in the morning. She thanked him and stepped out of the shop into the bright afternoon sunshine.

"Yes, thank you for your help," Dhamon added. He searched the half-elf's eyes for some answer to the riddle of the town.

The half-elf looked puzzled at Dhamon's expression.

"Your name?" Dhamon asked innocently. "How long have you lived here?"

The half-elf drew his features together in consternation, his face looking painfully pinched. "Name? I don't know. I guess I don't have one. No. Come to think of it, I've never had a name. Do you have a name?"

Now that was definitely strange. Dhamon thought about the graveyard and decided to risk a question, although he wasn't sure he wanted to know the answer. "Do the other people in town have names?"

The youth gave him a pensive look, as the silence between them grew thick. "Now that you mention it," he said after a few moments, "no."

Fiona and Ragh had moved on and were standing in the center of the street talking to the lord mayor's assistant. Dhamon gestured to the draconian and started toward the docks. *Come! Now!* he mouthed.

The draconian grabbed Fiona's wrist, and the two hurried to catch up.

The hobgoblin kept pace with the trio, arguing with them. "You cannot leave," he insisted. "The lord mayor will convince you to stay. Give him a chance to talk you into it."

"We're in a hurry," Dhamon said to the hobgoblin. "We're leaving—now." This last comment was directed as much to Ragh and Fiona.

The hobgoblin muttered a curse and trundled away in the opposite direction.

◇ ◇ ◇ ◇ ◇ ◇ ◇

"I don't see any ships." Ragh was standing at the end of the largest dock, which groaned in protest under his weight. "I don't even see a rowboat."

But there were fishermen. Three sat at the end of a long, narrow pier, poles in the water and eyes on painted cork bobbers.

Dhamon paced along the bank, keeping Ragh in sight. Fiona lagged behind, gathering small shells and putting them in the pocket of her skirt. Her task was difficult, as she refused to set down her bundle of new clothes.

"Not a single ship," Dhamon spat.

There wasn't even the outline of a ship out in the crystal blue harbor. Dhamon supposed all the fishing boats might still be out for the day, too far away for him to see, not due in until sundown. Perhaps the town, being so small, didn't attract sailing ships. But . . . He stomped off down the bank and up the narrow pier toward the three fishermen, who looked up in unison as he approached. He didn't want to waste time searching for another coastal town on Nostar. That could take days. Perhaps these fishermen knew someone with a boat.

They were young, human, perhaps not yet twenty, clothes worn but clean, faces clean-shaven, hair tied back. Perhaps all three were brothers. They had a similarity in their faces, their eyes all golden brown, their builds roughly the same.

"Excuse me," Dhamon began. "My friends and I need to find passage on a ship. A fishing boat would do." He jiggled the coin pouch so they could hear the steel clinking.

Two of the young men shrugged, but the one in the middle sat his pole down and rose to his feet. He brushed his hands on his breeches and looked to the shore. "All the ships are gone. Broken up and made into houses," he explained.

Dhamon instantly remembered the buildings made out of ship hulls. "All of them?"

" 'Bout soon as they come in, the townsfolk come out and break 'em up."

"And the sailors just let them?"

The young man paused in thought. "The sailors don't have no choice in the matter, I'd say. 'Course, the sailors don't object for long. They stay in town. Got nowhere else to go, I'd say. Some of 'em even live in their old ships."

Dhamon felt his face grow warm, anger, frustration and fear building and a dozen questions forming. He didn't know what to ask first, but the young man helped him out.

"See, folks who come to Bev's Oar . . . they don't ever leave."

"Well, we're leaving," Dhamon told him. "Ragh and Fiona and I are leaving now."

"I don't think so, sir. Word is all over town about you three. You have names, and that makes you real important. Glad to have you join us. I understand you're gonna teach all of us about the world."

"We're not joining you." Dhamon swung around and raced toward the bank, feet slapping loudly on the planks. "Ragh!" he shouted. "Fiona!"

The draconian and female Knight looked up, then both turned in the other direction, facing the town, their attention was caught by the throng of people suddenly materializing, the lord mayor and his assistant in the lead.

"By the memory of the Dark Queen!" Dhamon cursed.

He vaulted from the dock and onto the sand just as the press of townsfolk swarmed around his two companions. The Knight was tall, towering over some of the townspeople, but in a few moments Dhamon couldn't see her head. They'd managed to overwhelm her by their sheer numbers.

The draconian resisted, pulling away from people and roughly tossing them to the ground. Dhamon reached the crowd. He was loath to draw a knife, as he'd seen not a single weapon since he'd arrived. "Damn me for bringing us here!" he swore, as he forced his way into the mass and found Fiona unconscious and in the arms of the lord mayor's assistant. She'd obviously put up a fight, as the two nearest townsfolk were sporting broken lips and noses, but even she couldn't stand up to their numbers. They'd hurt her. Blood ran from a high cut on her arm, soaking the sleeve of her new shirt. The once-friendly townsfolk had become a mob, and he felt the hammering of their fists on his back.

"You must stay!" someone called to him. "You must teach us."

He shrugged off the blows and grabbed Fiona from the hobgoblin, who started to claw at him in protest. Cradling her to his chest with one arm, he dropped his free hand and tugged loose his knife.

"Get back!" Dhamon shouted, swinging the knife. "All of you mad people, get . . ."

The mob swelled in number and pressed closer, and the hobgoblin dropped to a crouch and sank its teeth into Dhamon's side. Dhamon shifted his grip on the handle and drove the blade down but only managed to nick the hobgoblin's shoulder. He raised the weapon again but found no room to maneuver now. The air was hot from the crush of bodies, filled with sweat and blood and the buzzing of voices. From somewhere, Dhamon heard the draconian calling to him.

There seemed at least fifty or sixty people. Perhaps the entire town had turned out. Dhamon noticed the portly inn owner who'd fed them so pleasantly just this morning, the seamstress who had clothed them, the healer who had nursed Fiona's wounds. This was the only one who seemed to be holding back. He finally spotted Ragh, feverishly clawing at people. Dhamon didn't want to kill any of these unarmed people, but he wasn't about to let them capture and imprison him either. He certainly wasn't about to stay in this damnable town of nameless faces.

Fists pounding against his back, booted feet kicking at his legs, he wormed an arm free and thrust the knife forward and down, into the stomach of the lord mayor's assistant. "I said everyone get back!" The hobgoblin fell to his knees. Dhamon tugged the knife free and stabbed now at a man with tired, sunken eyes. Hands fumbled against his, fingers pulling his fingers open. Someone grabbed his knife.

"Don't kill him! He can't teach us if you kill him!"

"Is the girl all right? Someone tell me if the girl's all right!"

"Don't use the knife! Don't hurt them!"

"Let us go!" Dhamon shouted. He fell forward, struck across the back of his knees with a board. Before he could regain his footing, he was pushed across Fiona. He felt the weight of bodies piling on him, and though his strength was formidable, it somehow wasn't enough to fight all these people.

He heard Ragh snarl, heard the harsh breathing of those closest to him, heard a familiar voice.

"Dhamon Grimwulf!" the lord mayor shouted. "Stop fighting us! We don't want to hurt you! We just want you to stay!"

Dhamon tried to reply, but his face was shoved against the sand, his chest crushing into Fiona. The smell of her blood and the other scents—sweat, perfume, fear—was overwhelming. He thought of Riki and his child, reached down deep inside him to summon all his strength for the child he desperately needed to see.

For a moment he felt hope, felt his arms pushing off, giving Fiona space and lifting the people on top of him. But even his muscles couldn't sustain such tremendous weight. He collapsed on top of Fiona, the air rushing from his lungs.

◇ ◇ ◇ ◇ ◇ ◇ ◇

When he woke it was night and his head was pounding terribly. Starlight spilled through a narrow, high window. He was alone in a cell. Fiona and Ragh were in a cell across from him. Fiona's arm was bandaged, and there was more of the paste on her face and along her neck. She sat on her bundle of clothes, unmoving, but her eyes were dully open.

"How is he?" Dhamon asked her, indicating Ragh.

"Alive. Sleeping."

Dhamon could see that Ragh's chest was laced with cuts, his leg bandaged in two places. The draconian's breath was ragged.

At first Dhamon was surprised that he'd been out so many hours. Checking his injuries, his fingers felt fresh scales beneath his clothes. His left leg was almost entirely covered now. Some had formed on his arms. He was slightly feverish and suspected he'd suffered another minor bout with the scale— the real reason he'd been out so long.

"A jail," Dhamon said bitterly. "They threw us in the town jail."

"Only to convince you to stay," came a familiar and unwelcome voice. The sound of the lord mayor's voice was followed by the scrape of flint and steel, as a torch was lit. The mayor carried the torch down the stunted hallway and stood between the two cells. "We want you to stay. You have to teach us things."

Dhamon gripped the bars and tugged, testing them. With time, he thought he might be able pull them loose.

"You have names, Dhamon Grimwulf," the lord mayor said. "We have none. No families. Few memories. We forget how to do things. We forget our friends. We need you to teach us."

"Chaos wights," Dhamon spat. "Damnable Chaos wights. It's like an epidemic."

The mayor cocked his head. "I would like to read, I think. I have several books. I expect you know how to read and can teach me. Maybe we'll make you my new assistant." He paused. "You killed the old one," he said ruefully.

Dhamon rattled the bars angrily. He wanted the lord mayor to leave so he could begin to break the bars and slip out. "You can't make us stay in this accursed town. None of you should stay, either. There's undead here, remnants from the war in the Abyss. They're called Chaos wights, and they're robbing your memories."

"You must be speaking of the shadow men," the lord mayor said in a hushed voice.

"Yes, the shadow men. They're Chaos wights."

"Glowing eyes."

"Yes," Dhamon said. "Let us out of here and—"

"The shadow men will be coming here soon.

They always come at night with the cold." The Lord Mayor placed himself directly in front of Dhamon and held the torch close. "I will see about getting you some good dinner, Dhamon Grimwulf. Maybe while I'm gone the shadow men will come and visit. They'll convince you to stay in Bev's Oar. They convince everyone, you know."

"Probably by making people forget they've got somewhere better to be," Ragh said, waking up and joining in. "Stealing their memories until there's nothing left, drinking their intelligence like damn vampires."

"The shadow men have never hurt anyone." The lord mayor faced the draconian and spoke to Ragh now. "The only thing the shadow men will take are your names. They will convince you to stay in Bev's Oar. Then starting in the morning, you will teach us about the world, and you will teach me how to read my books. Now, I will see about getting you some dinner." He took the torch with him when he left, leaving the hallway and the cells to the starlight.

"By the Dark Queen's heads," Dhamon groaned. "The wight told me his kind steal memories."

"I'd say there are more than one of 'em in this town," Ragh said.

"The people can't remember their names. They can't remember to charge for their goods and services."

What by all that's sacred did the wight take from me? he thought. Nothing important, surely, I have no holes in my memory. I'm certain I fought the wight off before it could do real harm. But these people apparently aren't able to fight them off.

"We've got to get out of here."

Fiona stood, hands on her hips. "No, we've got

to help these people. Make them realize if they fight back . . ."

"Impossible." The draconian's eyes glowed faintly red in the darkness. "They won't believe you. They don't have enough intelligence left in their thick skulls to believe you—to believe any of us. All they want is for you and me and Dhamon to stay, to teach them. Except when the wights find us maybe they won't leave us with anything worth teaching."

Dhamon gripped the bars tighter and pulled, feeling a slight sense of movement. The bars were imbedded in a hardened clay floor and ceiling. It wouldn't take him too long if he could muster his strength. "I won't lie down and die," he said, working on the bars. "I have things to do. We're getting out of here."

Ragh growled from deep in his chest and also grabbed the bars of his cell. Muscles bunching, the draconian strained to budge them. "It's worth trying."

The hallway door creaked open, torchlight spilling in.

"Maybe I can help."

"Maldred!"

"Dhamon, my friend, how do you manage to find yourself in such hopeless predicaments?" Maldred ducked his head to pass through the doorframe, the torchlight revealing he was in his true ogre form. His wide, blue shoulders were a tight fit in the hallway, and the top of his white-maned head brushed the ceiling. Despite his ragged clothes, he was a welcome sight. The torch was small in his large fist.

"But . . . how, how did you get out of Shrentak, and how did you find us here?" an astonished Dhamon asked.

"I have magic, remember?"

Dhamon glanced at Ragh, who shrugged. Fiona's eyes were narrowed, but she said nothing. Maldred passed Dhamon the torch, then knelt on the ground, fingers spread wide over the hardened clay. His long white hair fell over his shoulders and down his arms and hid his face. The torchlight danced across his form, exaggerating his massive muscles and the thick veins that stood out.

"What are you doing?" This question came from Ragh.

"Magic. Will you keep it down?" Maldred started humming softly, a tune with no identifiable melody or predictable rhythm. As it quickened, his fingers burrowed in the softening clay. Ripples spread outward from his hands, the clay becoming like mud.

Dhamon found he could more easily move the bars. Ragh's also gave way a little.

"A little more," Dhamon coaxed.

"Trying," Maldred replied, as he interrupted his humming. "Odd," he added. "It's getting cold in here."

The magic humming resumed. Dhamon dropped his torch and worked faster with both hands. The cold meant the presence of wights. Eyes darting, he looked in the shadows for glowing, undead eyes. His breath feathered away from his face as he wrenched the wall of bars loose.

"The shadow men are coming," Ragh growled.

"Aye," Dhamon said, stepping to the other cell and helping the draconian work on those bars. With one final heave, the two loosened the bars enough so Ragh and Fiona could squeeze out.

Fiona clutched the bundle of clothes to her chest. Breath misting in front of her, she fixed her eyes on Maldred.

"Liar. Liar. Liar," she said.

Dhamon shivered to feel the air growing colder still. "Mal, we've got to get out of here now. There are . . ." He swallowed his words as he glanced to the far end of the hallway where three distinct shadows had separated and formed manlike images. Their eyes glowed eerily, and their insubstantial hands reached out at them, claws elongating like slithering serpents.

"By my father!" Maldred boomed. "What are those strange creatures?"

"Around here, they call them shadow men," Ragh answered.

"Foul undead," Dhamon spat. "Wights! And we've got nothing to fight them with!"

Maldred reached for his sword, and the shadows cackled.

"That won't work," Dhamon said. He started backing his companions toward the door at the other end of the hallway.

"Maybe this will work." Maldred pulled something out from under his ragged tunic, cradling it in front of him so the others couldn't see. "I'll get us all out of here," he said. He focused his magical and physical energy, gripped the dragon scale hard, and snapped it in two.

"Liar. Liar. Liar," Fiona repeated venomously, as a swirling gray mist rose up around them and transported them out of the jail.

Chapter Eight
Shadows
of the Past

Dhamon was confronted by a vast emptiness, unending black stretching in all directions. There was nothing to hint at shapes or shadows, but he felt as if he was moving, his feet dangling yet touching nothing. He held his arms up, then stretched them out in front of him and to his sides, his fingers feeling only warm, humid air.

It was a startling change from the cool breeze that had wafted into his jail cell and comforted him until it turned into the frightening, cold currents of the Chaos wights.

He tried to call for Maldred but sucked in a fetid taste and scent. He couldn't hear himself, couldn't even hear the beating of his own heart. The taste and scent increased.

It was all magic, he knew, and he should have asked, when Maldred cast his spell, that they all be spirited away to Southern Ergoth, to the far coast where the Solamnic outpost stood. But Maldred had acted too fast. Dhamon hadn't had a chance to tell him where they were going, so now where was he taking them? Perhaps the Qualinesti Forest, perhaps the eastern shore of Nostar. Certainly not back to the ogre lands.

Dhamon was more curious than worried, as any magic created by Maldred was bound to be a positive enchantment. He called out to Fiona, however, on the chance she might be able to hear him, to reassure her that everything was all right and that she had no cause for alarm. He received no reply.

He continued to float in the nothingness, noting that he was feeling increasingly fatigued—either because quite a bit of time was passing or more likely because Maldred's spell was somehow sapping his energy. Perhaps Maldred was drawing on his energy.

"Maldred," he tried to call again. This time at least he heard himself.

A change occurred in the air. The temperature grew warmer still and the fetid smell much stronger. There were variations in the blackness now, suggestions of blues and grays and faint images that resembled shields, as though rows of knights were standing on each other's shoulders, three or four men high. He shivered, though it was warm, not cold.

"Maldred?"

"Here, Dhamon."

"Where are we?"

"My spell's taken us far away from that jail."

Dhamon heard strange sounds: a rough, constant 'shushing,' the flutter of something like leaves blown in the wind, the muted cry of a shrike, and the throaty cry of a burrowing owl.

"Mal, where?"

It was still night, wherever they were. They were

no longer near the sea; there was not a trace of salt-tinged air. However, Dhamon thought he detected the sulfurous scent of a blacksmith's shop, and now he could sense the draconian and the familiar presences of Fiona and of Maldred. The rank smell overpowered everything, however.

"Where have you taken us?"

"Someplace safe."

Dhamon blinked as the wall of shields began to move, as though the unseen knights were taking two steps forward and then back, repeatedly, keeping rhythm with the shushing. Before he could bring this to Maldred's attention, the shield-wall slid out of sight, replaced by thick gray patterns intersected by strands of green so dark they looked black. He stopped shivering.

Concentrating, Dhamon stared until he could focus. He discerned that he was inside a cave. The dark patterns were shadows created by outcroppings and recesses in the stone, the green was moss-covered vines that hung down to the ground and were disturbed by a gentle breeze that was stirring. Leaves continued to rustle, from just beyond where the cave mouth must lie. He turned slowly, finding the silhouettes of Fiona and Ragh only a few yards away. He also saw Maldred, who was speaking softly in words he couldn't understand, no doubt casting another spell. A moment later a globe of light appeared in Maldred's hand, and as it grew he tossed it toward the ceiling, where it hovered.

The cave was immense, and the light didn't penetrate the deepest darkness.

"Liar. Liar. Liar," Fiona hissed as she locked eyes with Maldred. The Solamnic Knight, standing next to the draconian, squeezed her bundled clothes against her chest and glared back and forth between Dhamon and Maldred. "The both of you are liars."

Dhamon looked at his old friend. "Mal," he said, "I was planning to come rescue you. Why, if we hadn't gotten ourselves stranded on that accursed island of Nostar, Ragh and I would've finished taking Fiona to Southern Ergoth and then come back looking for you. In fact, if you wouldn't mind casting another one of those quick spells and taking us to Southern—"

A sharp intake of breath—Fiona's. A raspy curse from Ragh. The shivering began again, as Dhamon whirled to stare, deep into the cave, toward a soft, yellow glow. The eyes of a dragon! Its massive scales shifted, making a strange hissing.

"Sable!" Dhamon's heart thundered in his chest. He snarled in fury and glanced anxiously about for a weapon. "Next time, Mal, see if you can find a place safer than Sable's lair!" He grabbed Fiona and Ragh, pulling them backward, toward where he judged by the slight breeze the cave's mouth would be.

"Move," he whispered to them. "Fast." Although astonished and confused by where they had landed, Dhamon's companions didn't hesitate, shuffling along with him. Fiona's hand drifted to reach for her non-existent sword.

"I once was Sable's servant," Ragh whispered. "She might remember my usefulness and let me live. But I fear you and Fiona . . ."

Draped in shadows, which blanketed much of its massive body, the dragon did not move or speak. It merely regarded them silently. The impression it gave was of a giant cat studying with mild interest an insignificant group of trespassing mice.

"Mal, you'd better turn around and follow us

slowly," Dhamon cautioned. "Fiona and I don't have a single sword between us, so we can't . . . Mal? Mal?"

Maldred hadn't retreated an inch or drawn his sword, Dhamon realized. In fact, the big man was slowly moving *toward* the dragon, arms spread wide as if in supplication.

Dhamon sucked in a breath. "By all that's . . ."

"Liar. Liar. Liar," Fiona chanted behind Dhamon.

"I . . . I think she's right," whispered Ragh. "Dhamon, I think your ogre friend has betrayed us."

"Betrayed?" Dhamon sounded incredulous. "Brought us here on purpose?" The possibility was too crazy, he quickly dismissed it from his mind, shaking his head. "No. He couldn't have. Maldred *wouldn't*." Not of his own accord, anyway, Dhamon thought.

Perhaps Sable had captured Maldred in Shrentak, bewitched the ogre-mage, and demanded that Maldred bring Dhamon here. It was the only sane explanation. If so, if Ragh was mistaken, then why was his friend so casually approaching the dragon?

Behind Dhamon, Ragh spoke up again. "Wait, I used to serve Sable. That's not Sable," he said in a hushed voice. "Now that I can see it better, that's not even a black dragon."

"Maldred," Dhamon said firmly, hoping to reach a part of his friend the dragon couldn't influence. "Leave with us. Back out now." If the dragon by some chance lets us.

"You're safe here, my friend," Maldred said, sounding less than confident of his own words. "I promise, you're all safe. The dragon won't hurt you."

Bathed in pale ochre light from the dragon's

eyes, Maldred, standing directly in front of the beast's massive snout, bowed stiffly at the waist. "I brought Dhamon here, master. Just as I told you I would."

Master? "Move, Fiona! Ragh!"

Fiona dug in her heels. "I am a Solamnic Knight," she said defiantly. "I should fight this dragon. It's not honorable to run."

Dhamon cringed. "Not without a sword!"

"Don't be in such a hurry." The sultry voice was not Fiona's, and it came from somewhere behind them all. "You're not going anywhere, Dhamon Grimwulf. Not you. Not the witless Knight. Not the worn-out sivak. The three of you are flies caught in a web, and I think you'll discover my master's the biggest spider of your dreams."

Recognizing the voice, Dhamon spun around in disbelief, meeting the eyes of Nura Bint-Drax in her snake-woman form. She effectively blocked their retreat, rising up on her tail in the middle of the cave mouth and swaying hypnotically, her scales glimmering. Her magic, more than her intimidating form, held Fiona and Ragh in place.

"None of you are going anywhere until my master permits it," Nura hissed. "*If* he permits it."

No chance at redemption, Dhamon thought. No chance to . . .

"Dhamon!" The big man, still in front of the dragon, motioned to him. "Come! Join us, Dhamon!"

Join you? By the Dark Queen's heads, this can't be happening! This can't be real!

Dhamon tried to convince himself that this wasn't happening, but he knew it was.

He'd felt the sensation of dragonfear, and now, looking back and forth from the cave entrance to its depths, he could see the naga swaying and see the eerie yellow of the dragon's eyes. He could see his traitorous friend, Maldred, in front of the dragon, waiting.

"Ragh," Dhamon whispered. Out of the corner of his eye, he saw the draconian shudder as though trying to break the spell of the naga. "Ragh," he said louder.

"I-I hear you." The familiar hoarse whisper sounded as though it was straining for power. "Have you some great plan for getting us out of this?"

From the cave's recesses, Maldred called again to Dhamon.

"Well, I have a plan," Ragh growled. "I plan on us dying, and I prefer to let the dragon kill me. That'll be quicker than whatever that snake-thing plans to do, is my guess."

"It's Nura Bint-Drax, Ragh."

"Whoever it is, it is ugly."

"It's Nura Bint-Drax." You know her, Dhamon thought. Since the moment I met you, Ragh, you have been obsessed with killing her. She cut off your wings, bled you to make spawn and abominations. You hate her. "You have seen her in other forms, but you must recognize her."

"I have never seen her. I would certainly remember her if I had see her before."

"The Chaos wight," Dhamon muttered. The Chaos wight had stripped the memory of Nura Bint-Drax from Ragh. That must be it. What memory did the damn wight steal from me?

"Dhamon!" Maldred called again.

It doesn't matter what the wight stole from me, Dhamon thought. Nothing's going to matter if we don't get out of here alive. But his legs didn't feel like cooperating. In the few moments he'd let his mind wander, the dragonfear had seeped into his bones.

At the same time, the naga moved closer.

The odd, heady smell of her perfumed oil mingled with the foul scent of the swamp. Dhamon felt weak, dizzy, ready to quit. I should've let the sea take me in that storm, he thought. This dragon wouldn't get the satisfaction of killing me now. I'll never see my child.

"Fight the dragonfear," he hissed, as much to himself as to Ragh and Fiona, "and the naga's magic. Don't give in. Put up a fight!"

He focused on his anger, a technique he employed when he used to ride a blue dragon and had to deal with its suppressed aura. He focused on the dragonfear. In a blind rage he lurched away from Ragh and Fiona, rushing toward Maldred.

"Ragh," he called over his shoulder. "It was Nura Bint-Drax who took your wings!"

Dhamon hoped that revelation might arouse the draconian, but he didn't wait to see what happened. He grabbed the surprised Maldred, swiftly reached behind the ogre's back and tugged free the great two-handed sword that was always sheathed there.

"Dhamon, no!" Maldred made a grab for the sword, but Dhamon was on fire with anger. In a few strides Dhamon had put space between him and Maldred and the dragon, steeling himself against the ceaseless aura of fear and readying the sword for action.

The glowing dragon eyes didn't so much as flicker. The dragon neither spoke nor moved, except for the continual hissing of its scales.

"Dhamon, stop!"

Focusing on the dragon, Dhamon was taken

aback by Maldred's lunge. The ogre struck and knocked him aside. The sword clattered away.

"Dhamon!" The ogre, his voice defiant, held up his arm in a warning gesture. "You must listen to me, Dhamon!"

Dhamon kicked at him, tripping Maldred, and scrambled to regain the sword. "No, you listen to me, Mal! The dragon's got you under its control! This dragon—"

"This isn't Sable!" Maldred cried. "This dragon isn't interested in hurting you!"

Yes, Ragh said the dragon wasn't Sable.

It wasn't Sable, but the fetidness still heavy in his mouth, the sounds of the swamp that crept into the cave——all of that told him he was in the Black's realm. So if it wasn't Sable, what other dragon was in the overlord's swamp? Why was Maldred in its thrall?

He lowered the sword a little. "All right. I'm listening," he told Maldred. "Talk fast."

From behind him, he heard Nura Bint-Drax hiss as Ragh and Fiona shuffled deeper into the cave, resigned to their fate. So, his words hadn't aroused the draconian after all.

"I said I was listening, Mal."

"Dhamon," Maldred began. "I know I owe you the truth. The dragon isn't controlling me now—or ever for that matter. But I am . . . in league . . . with him. I brought you here at his request. I have my family to consider, my nation, and I . . ."

Dhamon's unblinking eyes narrowed and met the film-covered ones of the dragon. There was something familiar about the creature, especially its eyes, those odd-shaped slits. For an instant Dhamon saw himself reflected in them, but a different self—one who was a few years younger, one with wheat-blond hair, one who was righteous and undaunted, one who almost died, a red dragon scale embedded firmly in his thigh.

"The shadow dragon," he said.

Yes. It was the shadow dragon who once had healed him with his blood—and with the help of a silver dragon. The dragon's blood and magic broke Malys's mastery over him, but turned the large scale on his leg black, his hair black, colored his soul.

He felt a coldness in his heart. He peered closer at the shadow dragon.

Dhamon had changed since that fateful day, but what about this dragon? He was obviously older too, but that was strange. In the span of those few years the dragon shouldn't have aged much at all. Dragons lived for centuries upon centuries.

A rumble shook the stone and earth, and it took Dhamon a moment to understand that it was the dragon speaking for the first time.

"You remember . . . ?" the dragon said. "In the mountains far from here."

"Aye, dragon. Long miles away and short years ago." Dhamon would never forget. Not even the great sorcerer Palin Majere could cure the scale, but the shadow dragon had saved him that day on which Dhamon accidentally stumbled into his cave. The dragon could have killed him then, as he could certainly kill him now, but it had saved his life.

The shadow dragon was not only unaccountably older but larger now, considerably so. Dhamon could tell he must be nearly two hundred feet long. Why had he grown so large? And why did he look so old? What could have aged it? Magic?

"Aye, dragon. I remember," was all he said.

The stone floor vibrated again from the strength of the dragon's voice.

"Aye, you saved my life, dragon, and I admit that I owe you for that."

"You know this dragon?" Ragh said to Dhamon, as he furtively glanced over his shoulder at Nura Bint-Drax. "You know the dragon *and* the snake-woman? How can you . . . ?"

Dhamon silenced the draconian and concentrated on the rumbling sounds to make out the dragon's deep and drawn-out words. Not only older and bigger, the dragon looked weary, Dhamon thought. Old and worn-out, though he should be neither.

"You wish to collect on my debt to you?" Did Dhamon understand the shadow dragon correctly? Had he manipulated Maldred to bring Dhamon here? Debt or no debt, he didn't have time to help the dragon. The scales were burning him out. He had to aid Fiona, find Rikali and his child.

"What do you want?" What could a dragon possibly want from a man?

Once more he made an effort to sort through the rumble for the words.

"Kill Sable," the shadow dragon said. "I want you to kill the Black who rules this swamp."

"No!" Dhamon felt the color drain from his face. "That isn't possible!" In fact, this was all *impossible*—being brought here by his friend Maldred, standing before an old, decrepit dragon who was young and vibrant just a few years ago, having Nura Bint-Drax lurking behind him as a giant snake, being urged to slay an overlord. "One man cannot stand against a dragon," Dhamon said, "let alone stand against an overlord. No. Dragon, I honor the fact that you saved my life, but I won't even attempt such a foolish thing."

"I saved you from the Red *only* so you would

serve me now." The dragon dug a claw into the cave floor, making an excruciating noise. "I saved others, too, tried to mold them to my purpose, but you are the most promising. You are the one."

Nura hissed, as Maldred tugged his sword out of the distracted Dhamon's grip.

"I don't understand your part in this," Dhamon said to Maldred bitterly. "You can damn well try to explain it to me later, after we get out of here. Which I intend to do now." He made a move to leave, but Maldred's hand closed firmly on his arm.

"You can't go, Dhamon," Maldred said. "Not yet. You must agree to kill Sable first."

"You're as mad as Fiona!" Dhamon shook off the big man. "Kill an overlord? No man—no army— can kill an overlord. Why does this shadow dragon even want Sable dead?"

"To claim Sable's realm," the shadow dragon said in a low rumble. The cave darkened for an instant, as the shadow dragon closed his eyes. When he opened them again, the yellow glow seemed to be aimed directly at Dhamon. A lip curled upward, revealing shadow-gray teeth. The dragon's tongue snaked out teasingly.

"You *can* kill Sable. You are the one." This was spoken by Nura Bint-Drax, who had slithered up behind Dhamon. "I have tested you, Dhamon, and I know the deeds you are capable of performing."

Dhamon turned to stare up into her cold snake-child face.

"Maldred was testing you, too. He pulled your strings more cleverly than me. "

"I had no choice," Maldred cut in, as Dhamon furiously wheeled to face the ogre-mage.

"*Tested* me?"

"Sable . . . the Black . . . everyday the swamp

grows larger. You know what is happening. You've seen it happening. Eventually the swamp is going to swallow all of the ogre lands, my homeland, Dhamon—unless something is done to stop the overlord."

"This is all about Blöde? This is about the stinking mountains and your father's damnable kingdom? I thought you despised your father."

"My people's land. And . . . I fear for my father's safety, if the overlord succeeds."

"This is all about this swamp?"

A nod.

"What in the world do you expect of me? Me! If you and your ugly relatives want the Black dead, you can damn well go to war against the dragon yourself. I want no part of it."

Maldred shook his head sadly. "My people are not the greatest of warriors. Not anymore. We need someone who is fearless, someone who has extraordinary reserves of strength and resolve—"

"You've been *testing* me?"

"To make sure you are the one," Nura interjected.

"And these tests . . . "

"My sisters and I," she said amusedly. The naga was referring to a group of cutthroat women who tried to kill Dhamon and Maldred in the Blöde foothills. "Giant spiders. The Legion of Steel who tried to hang you. All of that and more. It was all our doing, all part of the test. You should be proud, human. You passed every test . . . so far."

The veins stood out like cords on Dhamon's neck. Hands clenched, he seethed with rage, staring bitterly at Maldred. "Friend." Dhamon spat the word. "I called you friend, Maldred! I considered you as close as a brother. As much as one man can love another, Mal, I loved you. I risked my life for yours a dozen times over, and . . ."

"Dhamon . . . ."

"You manipulated me? Deceived me! For your damnable ogre race?" The words were hard and fast, daggers hurled at the big man.

Maldred tried to say something, but Dhamon didn't give him a chance. "I'm done with the dragons, *ogre*. And I'm done with you. I never want to see you or your friends again." Dhamon's throat grew dry, as the air constricted around him. He fought for breath.

"Nura," Maldred cautioned. "Let him alone."

The naga slid forward and twisted her tail around Dhamon's legs, coiling herself as she squeezed his throat. Her eyes glowed faintly green. The glow spread down her body, melting into Dhamon and fixing him to the spot. The glow spread to Ragh and Fiona.

The naga, wrapped completely around Dhamon, turned to face the shadow dragon. The eyes of the dragon closed momentarily. After another suffocating squeeze, the naga uncoiled and retreated. "He is the one, master," she said silkily, "but he seems unwilling to participate."

The shadow dragon lowered his head, barbels spreading on the floor as he stretched his neck forward. His dry breath struck Dhamon like a strong desert wind, but it carried no scent.

"I am the one to make him willing." The dragon extended a charcoal gray talon, drawing it down Dhamon's pant leg and parting the material as though it was thin parchment. The large black scale—and all of the lesser scales—gleamed darkly in the light reflected by the dragon's eyes. "The scales grow because of my magic, human. The scales pain you because of my magic. They're killing you."

The dragon glanced at Nura, and the naga retreated farther so that Dhamon could now breathe easier.

"I promise to stop the scales and the pain," the dragon continued, "if you slay Sable. I will provide the cure you so desperately seek. I will let you live, and I will make you wholly human again, without any further interference from me."

Dhamon felt his limbs tingle as he regained control of them. Over his shoulder he saw that Ragh and Fiona also had been restored to normality.

Dhamon stayed silent for several minutes. *A cure?* While the shadow dragon probably told the truth, Dhamon wondered if there was any cure for the accursed scale. He would die soon enough, for the scales were multiplying like an unchecked rash. But he couldn't agree to try to kill Sable. That would be a suicide faster than any death from the scales.

He glanced at the Solamnic. She was staring wide-eyed at the dragon, but her thoughts couldn't be fathomed. He looked at Ragh, who characteristically shrugged. It was up to him, Ragh was saying. The damn draconian couldn't even remember his vendetta against the naga. Wights! What else had they stolen from Ragh?

Dhamon glared at Maldred. "You know that it is not within one man's power to slay a dragon."

The shadow dragon's voice vibrated. "You will have help. My servants Maldred and Nura are both magically powerful. Your friends called Fiona and . . ."

"Ragh," Nura supplied. She seemed puzzled and offended the draconian had not recognized her. "Wingless Ragh and the Solamnic Knight Fiona."

"And you, human," rumbled the dragon. "You have powers you have yet to discover."

Rot! But Dhamon felt he had no choice but to agree. Later, away from the shadow dragon's cave, he could hope for an opportunity to escape from Maldred and the naga—or kill them both. Later, he, Fiona, and Ragh might have a chance. But now . . .

"All right," Dhamon said solemnly. "I'll go after Sable for you. And if by some twist of fate I win, you'll grant me this cure."

The dragon raised his lip in approximation of a smile. "Of course," he rumbled. "I will cure you, and I will grant you more than a cure." The creature lifted his head, staring toward the entrance of the cave, where a wall of mist was forming. "I will grant you the safety and well-being of your family."

An image appeared on the mist, of a torchlit village in a dry land. Scrub grass and stunted trees grew along a road. A snort from the dragon, and the scene shifted to the interior of a small building. A silvery-haired half-elf was propped up on a weathered bed.

"Riki," Dhamon said with emotion that surprised him, falling to his knees.

Riki was covered in furs and attended by three human women, one of them wiping the sweat from her forehead and trying to calm her.

"Pigs, but this hurts!" Dhamon heard the half-elf's familiar curse. "Where's Varek?"

"Outside," one of them answered. "We'll call him in soon. After the child comes."

Riki tossed her head back and moaned.

The image shifted again, pulling away from the village. Beyond the meager treeline was a crude military encampment that circled a large bonfire. Dozens of hobgoblins milled around. A particularly large one sat on a wooden crate, sharpening his spear.

The cry of a baby cut across the encampment, and the magical image wavered. The mist in the cave disappeared.

"The hobgoblins are my pawns," the dragon said in his rumbling voice. "They'll leave the newborn baby—and the half-elf and her husband—alive, if you do my bidding."

Dhamon stared the dragon. "I said I'd go after Sable," he said through clenched teeth. "I keep my word."

"I know you will," the shadow dragon returned. "Nura, will you give them some special weapons with which to slay Sable?"

The naga slithered away, reappearing minutes later no longer as a snake but in her Ergothian guise. Dhamon's old tunic was belted around her. In one hand she carried an elegant long sword, one Dhamon once had turned over a fortune in gems to obtain. He had bought it from the ogre chieftain, Maldred's father, who claimed it once had belonged to Tanis Half-Elven. The naga stole it from Dhamon during one of her tests. It was supposed to have hidden magical powers. Rather than handing the sword to Dhamon, Nura gave it to Fiona, who stared at her reflection in the polished blade.

In her other hand the naga carried an impressive polearm with an axe edge that caught the light from the dragon's eyes. A few years past, a bronze dragon had presented this weapon to Dhamon to aid him in his struggles against the overlords. A magical artifact, the glaive cut through metal armor. Dhamon had nearly killed Goldmoon with the glaive, back when he was under Malys's control. He'd wanted no part of it thereafter. Dhamon had tossed it aside, and Rig was quick to claim the magical glaive. The mariner had loved exquisite weapons. The glaive, too, had disappeared during Dhamon's tests.

Now Nura thrust the glaive at him, nodding when he reluctantly accepted the magical weapon. The dragon meanwhile plucked a small scale off its body and passed it to Maldred. "When the deed is finished," the dragon said, "use this to return here."

"What about him?" Nura asked the dragon, indicating Ragh.

"I don't need anything," the draconian snorted quickly, before the dragon could say anything. "I go where Dhamon goes, and I have my own special . . . resources."

Maldred tucked the scale under his tunic and motioned for Dhamon and his companions to follow Nura Bint-Drax.

"What if Sable kills us?" Dhamon thought to ask the shadow dragon before leaving the cave.

"You should make sure Sable does not," came the low-rumbling reply. "But . . . for trying I will spare your child. Only the child, however."

"You'd better make sure you're successful, Dhamon Grimwulf," Nura hissed.

Dhamon took one last glance at the shadow dragon, trying to read the obscure meaning in his film-covered eyes. Then he walked out behind the others.

"I hope you know we'll get ourselves killed going up against Sable," Ragh muttered, as they stepped out of the cave into the night-drenched swamp.

"Everyone dies," Fiona said indifferently. She sheathed the sword in her belt and reached for Dhamon, slipping into the crook of his arm and staring admiringly up at the glaive's blade. It caught the moonlight that spilled in through a gap in the branches. She smiled warmly. "It is good to be together again. I've missed you so very much, Rig."

CHAPTER NINE
THE SKIN OF SHRENTAK

D hamon stood on a rise bordering the eastern
edge of the sprawling city ruled by the black
dragon overlord Sable. Fiona leaned against
him, staring up at his sweat-streaked face. Below
them, a mist covered the streets, cloaking some of
its filth and decay. Its rising tendrils helped to
soften the appearance of the crumbling towers that
reached like gnarled fingers into a pale, gray-
orange sky.

Dhamon tried to look past the ugly surface of the
place—seeing men and women shuffling about, as
they walked about in any other city on Krynn.
There was joy here, somewhere. He heard a child
laugh, a man offering a pleasant greeting, a dog
barking excitedly. People eked out a living, loved
each other, raised families just as they did in Palanthas or Winterholm or Solanthus. Just like any city.
Except this city belonged to Sable, the black dragon
overlord, and it lay smack in the middle of a swamp
teeming with spawn, giant crocodiles, and all

manner of other horrors. While some of the frightful denizens of this place crawled beneath the streets, others walked freely around the city.

He noted a pair of spawn trudging past a woodworker's shop, dragging the carcass of something large covered in hide. A dozen or so spawn milled about on corners and under building overhangs in the merchant's quarter. There were a number of conspicuous abominations, grotesqueries mixed from draconian blood, dragon magic, the husks of elves and dwarves, and perhaps even kender. These were not as sleek as their spawn brothers and had corrupt bodies—extra limbs, misshapen wings, snakelike tails, and more. Dhamon believed he was turning into such an abomination, and he believed that when the transformation was complete his human brain would be displaced by . . . some otherworldly intelligence. The new being would be loyal to its creator, the shadow dragon.

As Dhamon continued to observe the city, he saw a sivak draconian leap from a blackened spire and spread its wings, lazily circling the center of the city before diving and losing itself in a tangled of ruined buildings and swirling mist.

The city stank of the swamp, of human waste and rotting corpses. The scent of evening meals cooking was faint amid the foulness. They'd eaten very little since leaving the lair of the shadow dragon. He knew Fiona and Ragh were hungry—he could care less about the welfare of Maldred and Nura Bint-Drax. Perhaps he could find something reasonably edible at an inn. It was important Fiona and Ragh keep their strength for whatever challenge was to come.

He listened to screams and growls from the creatures kept in pens for display and sale in the central marketplace. It was there that he'd wreaked so much havoc when he freed Fiona and other prisoners from below the city and in the process also released the marketplace menagerie. All that seemed like a lifetime ago.

He also heard soft music emanating from a building he suspected—judging by the trio of men stumbling out—was a tavern. It was a pleasant tune, carried by a flute and some sort of horn, which in one moment sounded like the sad cry of a sea bird and in the next subtly angry as it gained tempo.

Dhamon stood staring at the buildings and the spawn and abominations and listening to the unusual tune and thinking at least he had discovered one iota of beauty beneath Shrentak's ugly skin. All of a sudden the music ended, and he let out a deep breath he hadn't realized he'd been holding.

"Are we going into that city, Rig?" Fiona tugged gently on Dhamon's arm. "It looks strangely familiar. I think I'd rather stop somewhere else."

"So would I," Dhamon answered sincerely. During the two-day journey here, Fiona frequently addressed him as Rig. He was certain it was because he carried the glaive that Rig used to wield. With Ragh's help, he tried repeatedly to convince her Rig was dead and that Dhamon looked nothing like the mariner. Fiona did have momentary bouts of sanity, recognizing Dhamon and making it clear she loathed him.

"I'd rather be tracking Riki and my child," Dhamon said more to himself. "I'd rather not be going back into Shrentak either."

"Ugly name for an ugly city," Ragh said.

Nura Bint-Drax chuckled. "I think Shrentak is beautiful."

She and Maldred were several paces behind them. They had been engrossed in some hushed conversation. All the way here Dhamon had looked for an opportunity to go against the naga and the ogre-mage, but they were always prepared, always watching him, and Nura had constantly threatened Fiona and Ragh, recognizing Dhamon's companions as a weakness to be exploited. The naga, like Dhamon, hadn't slept, and he was certain she was as exhausted as he was, but she had magically blanketed her reptilian form with the guise of a comely Ergothian and was somehow concealing her fatigue.

Maldred clearly looked exhausted, and he made no attempt to hide it. He had approached Dhamon several times, endlessly trying to explain his actions and rekindle their friendship. Each time Dhamon rebuked him. Maldred would be easier to overcome than the naga, Dhamon decided. Tired and feeling guilty, Maldred could be bested somewhere down a dark alley. Dhamon doubted murder was considered much of a crime in Shrentak. Defeating Nura Bint-Drax would be another matter. He'd have to create an opportunity, call on Ragh's help somehow. Dhamon and the draconian had been exchanging glances, and he hoped Fiona could be counted on when the time came.

"We will pass the rest of the night up here," the naga announced, as she stared into the setting sun. "We will wait until the morning to go into the city and look for Sable."

"I thought you served Sable, too," Dhamon said. "Don't you know where she is?"

She ignored him and made a show of stretching and studying a trio of sivaks that rose in flight from the center of town. "We will wait, I say. In the morning, or perhaps the morning after that, we will go down into the city. It is up to me when we act, and I say, for the moment, we wait."

"Wait?" Dhamon made no effort to conceal his surprise.

"Yes. I want to make sure the overlord does not have too many minions about. We must determine the best time to strike."

"Well, I'm in a hurry. I'm not waiting." I'm dying, he thought, and I won't spend my last hours waiting on a whim. Before the naga could say or do anything, Dhamon grabbbed Fiona by the hand and hurried down the rise. Ragh followed quickly on their heels. If the naga wanted to dally, there must be a secret reason, Dhamon thought. Easier to deal with her later if he kept her unsettled and upset.

"Keep him in sight," Nura hissed to Maldred. The naga shoved the ogre-mage after them. "Don't lose him again—or you'll fast be a dead man! I've allies in the city who won't let him—or you— escape. He's your responsibility!"

Maldred glowered at her but said nothing, and in a few long strides he caught up to Dhamon. He drew his sword as a precaution, though he didn't dare use it against Dhamon—not if the shadow dragon's plan was to proceed. *You're a dead man, Maldred, if you don't keep track of him!* he heard Nura repeat inside his head.

"Dhamon, wait," Maldred pleaded. "Nura's right about this city. It's better that she finds out if Sable—"

"I can't defeat the damn dragon no matter when or where I strike," Dhamon said tersely. "Not with all of your help and magic. You know it, Maldred. It doesn't matter if the dragon has ten minions here or ten thousand."

"You *can* beat her," Maldred argued. "*We* can. We have to."

"To save the ogre lands," Dhamon snarled. "Right? To save your damnable people's dry patch of ground." He increased his pace. I need to save my child and Fiona before I save the ogre race. And before I die.

Dhamon wasn't sure where he was going, but he knew the naga could keep track of them, with or without Maldred. He sensed her rivalry with his onetime friend and would take advantage of it. A glance behind him showed her perched on the rise. He didn't slow until she was out of sight and he found himself amidst a throng of battered-looking men who were leaving a building site, heading home from the day's work. He listened to the clack of their heels against scattered bricks in the street, listened to their conversations about work and family, about how tired they all were, about the swamp they all hated. He clasped Fiona's hand to keep her close, and he scanned for alleyways, ones that were dark and empty where he could lure Maldred. So far the only ones he saw were in one fashion or another occupied. In one, two young women flanked an older man in a guard's uniform. He was happily pressing coins into their palms. In another, men were curled into balls, sleeping against walls and in doorways. In the next, a few men huddled against a precariously leaning building, thick fingers passing a heavy clay jug back and forth between them, as they pleasantly poisoned themselves.

Dhamon found himself envying them. He had poisoned himself often enough during the past months, drinking anything strong enough to help cloud his senses when the pain from the scale began. He'd numb himself after each episode, relishing the oblivion the alcohol granted, never minding the headache and gut-ache he had when he sobered, not caring that he was tearing up his insides. He was dying anyway.

But he'd had not a swallow since setting foot in Shrentak the last time—when he had sought the help of a mad old woman who tried to remove the scale, when bedlam erupted after he freed Fiona and the rest of the prisoners. He'd had no opportunity to drink since he'd fled from this city on the manticore's back. No chance on the Chaos wight's island. It was only now that he thought of how long it had been since he'd had a drink. Dhamon paused to stare at the huddled men and wondered at the taste of their particular poison. He thought about the steel pieces in the pouch at his waist and at how much potent alcohol that could buy.

"It'll only muddle your mind," Ragh whispered, perhaps reading his thoughts. "We need to be sharp, look for an opportunity to—"

"Aye, you're right." Dhamon testily turned away and kept to the middle of the street, still searching for an appropriate alley. "I am looking for an opportunity all right." Hearing him, Fiona sneered and suddenly disentangled herself from him, apparently looking at him with fresh eyes and realizing he was not Rig.

"I should be with Rig," the female Knight snapped, tilting her chin defiantly to the darkening sky. "I shouldn't be with you, Dhamon Grimwulf. I should be getting a new assignment from my Order. There is so much evil in this world to fight." She ran her fingers along the collar of her tunic. "My armor . . . . Where is Rig? Why are we here? What do you plan to do here, Dhamon?"

We're here to save my child, he answered to himself. "We're on an errand, Fiona," he said softly. "Remember, the shadow dragon sent us?"

She nodded, her eyes bright and her expression distant. "To slay the overlord. Sable's evil." The notion seemed to quiet her.

Dhamon led them deeper into the city, unconsciously heading toward the stunted tower where he'd found the old sage. Maldred fell back a little. Dhamon looked at the faces as he went. Most of them were sad and weary, most of the people were human. A few bore faint smiles suggesting they were dreaming of a life far from here. There were wizened ones with pale, watery eyes, men with weathered skin and vacuous looks. A lone, cheerful woman clutched a child to her breast.

"Riki," Dhamon whispered to himself. Did the half-elf and her young husband know that the village they were in was surrounded by the shadow dragon's hobgoblins? That Dhamon's child was endangered?

"Dhamon." Ragh had said his name several times before Dhamon heard and acknowledged him.

The draconian bobbed his head toward a row of buildings, their entrances and the walkway in front of them shadowed from the setting sun. "Do you think we ought to be strutting about so much in the open? Someone might recognize us." He indicated a pair of haggard-looking humans who'd been lagging behind them the past two blocks.

Dhamon kept an eye on the two, but they soon cut away and ducked into a leatherworker's shop. "Recognize us?" He stifled an uncharacteristic chuckle. The draconian was singular—a sivak without wings, and Dhamon flaunted a bunch of scales on his leg where the shadow dragon had sliced his trousers. There were even a few scales on his neck now, too, which he had tried unsuccessfully to tear free.

"It was dark, Ragh, when we escaped this place. I doubt anyone who's still alive got a good look at us."

Still, rather than take the chance, he accepted the draconian's advice. The shadows offered a better opportunity to get rid of Maldred, anyway. Dhamon glanced behind him again, seeing the ogre-mage eyeing them. There was no sign of Nura Bint-Drax in any of her guises. He guessed she could look like anyone she wanted and that she might very well be close by. Shuddering at the thought, he pressed on and ignored Ragh's and Fiona's questions about where precisely they were going. At the moment, Dhamon didn't really know.

◇ ◇ ◇ ◇ ◇ ◇ ◇

On the rise east of Shrentak, Nura Bint-Drax shrugged off her Ergothian form. Easing back on a comfortably thick coil, her coppery hair fanning away from her face in a graceful hood, she closed her eyes and pictured the shadow dragon. The last of the sun's rays warmed her face and struck her scales, setting them to glimmering, save for a shadowed patch near her tail. The scales looked like the small ones on Dhamon's leg, but there were only a handful—and they hadn't spread much since the day the shadow dragon stuck them there. The dragon's magic hadn't taken as firm a hold on the naga, who was naturally resistant to his spell, and so she expected that no more of his scales would grow. For this she was jealous of and embittered about Dhamon Grimwulf.

"You are the one, Dhamon," she hissed. "My master's champion."

The shadow dragon had fostered Nura's magical abilities. He'd sacrificed a bit of himself to engender her magical growth and to create a link between them so he could watch the world through her eyes. She had become an extension of him.

In return, she gave him her absolute loyalty. Inasmuch as she could revere anything, Nura did worship the shadow dragon.

"Master," she cooed. She let her mind drift to the cave several miles away from her resting place. The image of the shadow dragon hove into view, and around her she pictured the pleasant rankness of his lair. Nura inhaled deeply and held the scent as long as possible.

"Master," she exhaled. "Too early Dhamon Grimwulf has ventured into the city. Your puppet Maldred follows him. Yet everything is under my control."

In her mind the ground rumbled from the dragon's reply. She patiently waited until he was finished.

"No, I agree Dhamon is not yet ready to face Sable," she said. "Maldred and I dallied in the swamp and chose misleading trails, taking days, not hours to reach here. Despite the time we spent, he is not yet ready for the ultimate test. The scales have not spread fast and far enough—and yet he goes forward."

The dragon growled and sent ripples through the earth. Her mind picked out the words.

"Yes, master. I am confident your ogre-puppet will find a way to delay Dhamon until he is ready. Of course I will step in, if need be." Nura paused, her senses studying the shadow dragon, finding the great creature more alive with energy than she had ever seen him

"That time will be very soon," the dragon told her. "I can feel it. Dhamon rages against my magic, fights it with his mind, but his rage feeds his transformation. His body is not as strong as his mind, and I will win."

"Soon." Nura's thoughts caressed the dragon's, drawing strength from her master. Minds mingling, she could feel what the dragon felt. "Very soon," she purred.

Yes. Soon Dhamon would be ready to face the Black. Maybe it was a matter of hours, maybe a few days. She would guide him, and if he defeated the overlord, her master would have just what he wanted. And soon, she would rule at the shadow dragon's side.

"Show me the beginning, master," she urged. "Please, again, show me the beginning, the Chaos War and your birth. There is time. Dhamon is not yet ready, and the city streets are not yet dark." She intended to go down into Shrentak when all traces of the setting sun were gone. "It has been so long since you've told me the tale."

The shadow dragon relented and opened his mind, and Nura felt herself plunging into the Abyss. The images were a delirium to her. She felt practically smothered by the heat of the infernal realm. The noise of battle nearly deafened her. The sounds of lightning strikes always came first, brought on by the breaths of the swarm of blue dragons ridden by the Knights of Takhisis. Then sulfur filled the air, mixed with the sweet coppery scent of the blood of those who were falling and tumbling all around her. There were screams and shouted orders from the bravest of Knights, pitiful cries from the dying. The dragons roared, the caverns shook, and everywhere men and women perished by flames, swords, and magic.

"Glorious," she murmured.

The images were so real Nura felt blood spattering her face and felt her eyes water at the exquisite acridness of the Abyss. She flicked a tongue out, tasting the air and the blood, growing drunk on the glorious pandemonium.

"Show me more, master."

The war was waged, the battle grew grander and deadlier. In the vision Nura Bint-Drax moved easily through the many tunnels of the cavern, slithering over corpses and around dying dragons, seeing and touching everything and discovering something new that she had missed during her previous visions. As the images of war intensified, she seemed to merge with the the mass of combatants, skin tingling from the energy in the air from the blue dragons' lightning breaths.

In the center of everything was Chaos, a massive god-being known as the Father of All and Nothing. He batted dragons away with the back of his hand, his booming laughter sent chunks of the ceiling falling down atop Solamnic Knights and Knights of Takhisis, his very thoughts brought disaster to ranks of fighting men. Chaos called his own forces into play, forming out of his very essence smouldering dragons that crackled and hissed with fire. There were ghastly demon warriors and undead— frost wights and shadow wights.

There were also whirling dervishes of wild magic, and when they touched something there were unpredictable and catastrophic results. Nura also saw creatures that must be gremlins and odd, wide-eyed creatures called huldrefolk.

Through the smoke and horror, she witnessed again the birth of the shadow dragon.

Chaos's shadow was an ever-twisting giant thing, and when it grew wilder and more contorted, the Father of All and Nothing reached down and plucked it loose from the ground and gave it life of its own. It molded itself into a dragon form, but it retained the color of Chaos's shadow, and its scales darkly glistened with the light of the god's magic.

The newborn shadow dragon flew around the ceiling of the immense cavern, darting down to swipe at the blue dragons trying to close with Chaos. It gained strength with their deaths, absorbing their death-energy as it would absorb the energy of others in the coming dragonpurge—as it intended to absorb Sable's death energy when Dhamon Grimwulf slew the overlord. The few wounds it suffered healed quickly.

Dust and bits of rock rained down from the ceiling as the Father of All and Nothing bellowed his defiance at the puny creatures daring to challenge him. His shadow dragon minion continued to spread death and disaster.

When Chaos was again imprisoned in the Graygem, the shadow dragon escaped from the Abyss through a mysterious portal and found himself high in the mountains of Blöde.

"Thank you, master, for the vision," Nura Bint-Drax murmured rhapsodically.

When she first crossed the shadow dragon's path, he had healed her from a life-threatening injury she suffered fighting a hatchling black dragon. She had sworn allegiance to the shadow dragon, and he, in turn, often permitted her the vision of the Chaos War. The tale came more rarely now, despite her frequent requests. She intended to replay this version in her mind again soon—after she checked on that fool Maldred and on Dhamon's progress.

"You are right, master. Dhamon Grimwulf should be ready very soon." She slid from the rise and headed down toward the city, resuming her Ergothian guise as she moved. Above her the first stars were winking into view, and the beauty of the night sickened her, so it was with some joy that she entered the dismal, darkening streets of Shrentak and let the fetid redolence of Sable's city embrace her.

Chapter Ten
In Search of
the Overlord

Dhamon spied an empty alley off the same street where the old sage had lived. He had no way of knowing that she was dead, or that Ragh had killed her while he lay unconscious after suffering one of his worst scale episodes, and he had no intention of seeking her out again. But he knew that her stunted tower boasted secret ways of connecting with Shrentak's undercity of twisting corridors and fetid dungeons. Somewhere in the depths of the undercity was Sable's lair.

"There isn't anything down that alley, Dhamon." Fiona was following his eyes, staring in the same direction. "Nothing but dirt and garbage and rats."

Perhaps Maldred's corpse will feel at home there, Dhamon said to himself. I'll kill him slowly, not until he's given up a little useful information. He pointed to a tavern just south of the alley. "Hungry?"

"I suppose." She nodded, but continued to stare down the alley and dropped her fingers to the pommel of her long sword. "This sword talks to me, Dhamon."

"I know." The words hissed out between his teeth. The blade had "talked" to him, too, when he owned it months ago, taunting him with promises of cures for the scale on his leg. "That's all I need," Dhamon whispered to himself. "A mad woman with a weapon that talks to her." Not that he had much choice. He didn't want that sword, and Shrentak was not a place to leave Fiona weaponless.

Aloud, he said, "Pay no attention to what that damn sword says, Fiona. It lies."

"Like you and Maldred and everyone else."

Dhamon tugged her away from the alley and guided her inside the tavern. Ragh followed silently. Though the outside looked rundown, the interior was surprisingly clean and well kept, and the homey scents that hung in the air miraculously kept the foul odors of the city at bay. A fire burned at the back and, along with a dozen lanterns on the walls, made the place warm and cozy. The tables were all of a polished, dark wood, as was a bar that stretched nearly the entire length of the place. The furniture had some age to it, Dhamon noted. The ebonwood trees the pieces were carved from dated before Sable, when the land was a prairie rather than a spreading swamp. Dhamon doubted a single ebonwood tree grew in the great morass now.

A few patrons stared at Dhamon as he steered Fiona toward an empty table. After noting the oddity of his scales, they seemed to lose interest and resumed their eating and drinking. Ragh also drew stares, but the patrons looked away more quickly when he snarled ominously at them.

Dhamon put two steel pieces on the table, propped his glaive against the wall, and nodded to a serving girl. Smiling politely, she was quick to take the coins. The girl was plain looking, though she'd made an attempt to look pretty by daubing some color on her face, arranging her hair atop her head, and cinching the bodice of her dress tight. He guessed her to be in her mid- to late-thirties, though she lacked any wrinkle lines around her eyes and could have been ten years younger. Shrentak exacted a heavy toll on her citizens.

"I smell roast pig," Dhamon said.

"Yes. It's very good this evening. Three plates of it, I'll bring," she said. "And bread if you like."

"Aye. But bring four plates," Dhamon returned. "And ale all around, too." The steel pieces would more than cover the cost with a handful of coppers left over for the serving girl to take home.

The draconian shook his head after she'd moved away. "That alley just outside, Dhamon. We could have waited and ambushed Maldred there. You were thinking about it. I could read your mind."

"Aye," Dhamon admitted. "I was thinking about it. I'm still thinking about it."

"Its true Maldred has to be dealt with." Ragh mused in a conspiratorial whisper. "Him and that Nur . . . Nur . . . ."

"Nura Bint-Drax." Dhamon met the draconian's gaze, where there was still no hint of recollection about the snake-woman.

"We've got to kill the both of them, Dhamon, if we're to get out from under the shadow dragon's claw."

Dhamon nodded.

"Because we damn well can't do what that beast wants us to do. We can't go after Sable. It would be suicide."

"Aye, suicide." Dhamon sat silent. "But everyone

dies," he added after a moment. He'd willingly give up his life to save his child, make a stand against the overlord if that's what it took, but he didn't care to forfeit Fiona's and Ragh's lives, too.

The serving girl returned and set plates in front of all of them, leaving one at the empty chair. She was quick to disappear and come back with tall mugs of ale, nearly tipping over the one she sat in front of Dhamon. Her eyes wide and fixed on Dhamon's face, she gasped, mumbled an apology, and scampered back to the kitchen. Dhamon ran his thumbs around the lip of his mug and glanced down into its dark surface. His face was faintly reflected, and he noted a scale on his cheek that hadn't been there just minutes before, when they had entered the place.

When Dhamon looked up, he saw Fiona and Ragh staring at him.

The draconian swallowed hard and dropped his gaze to a whorl on the tabletop. "Going after the Black would be suicide, I repeat," Ragh raised his voice a notch. "You're not really thinking about it, are you? Going after the overlord?"

Dhamon resumed staring into the ale. He raised his fingers to his cheek. The skin around the scale was burning hot as though from a fever.

"You're strong, I'll grant you that, Dhamon, far stronger than me. And that weapon looks formidable. I'll admit the lady here is good with a sword, and she would be a strong warrior—that is if she came to her senses—but we can't take Sable."

"I know. Suicide."

"Suicide. But you're thinking about it anyway." After the draconian downed the contents of his mug, Ragh added. "I'll have no part in your suicide mission, Dhamon. I'm not sure why I came this far with you, why I didn't just slip off into the swamp after we left the shadow dragon's cave. Maldred and Nura were watching you, not me. I know you saved me from a spawn-held village, and maybe I feel I owe you for that, but whatever else you did, I don't . . ." Ragh's voice trailed off as he spotted Maldred coming in the door.

The tavern hushed. All eyes turned to watch the blue-skinned ogre-mage. Shrentak was known for odd denizens, but even here Maldred stood out. The ogre returned the stares. When the patrons started to look away, he glided catlike to Dhamon's table.

Without meeting Dhamon's glare, Maldred sat and hungrily dug into his meal. Fiona watched him between bites of her own dinner and began rocking back and forth, eyes narrowed to venomous slits. She reached for her mug, took a deep pull of ale, sputtered. She coughed to clear her throat and took another swallow. Around them, most of the other patrons returned to their conversations.

"You tried to make me hate Rig," Fiona spat, directing her words at Maldred. "You used magic on me and manipulated me."

The ogre-mage briefly interrupted his eating, looked up from his plate. "That was long months ago Lady Knight." Indeed Maldred had toyed with her affections when she and Rig kept company for a time with Dhamon and his little band of thieves. It had been a game to Maldred, and he had played it very well. Dhamon hadn't seemed to object.

"You are a thief," she continued.

He nodded.

"And you are a liar."

"And you are a definite liability, Lady Knight," Maldred replied grimly. He drank the ale in one swallow, then thumped the mug on the table to call for more.

Ragh caught Dhamon's attention and gestured to a nearby table. The men there seemed particularly interested in the blue-skinned ogre.

"Keep it down the two of you," Dhamon said to Fiona and Maldred. "Bad enough we look as we do. We don't need to draw any more attention." He made a move to push his plate away, then thought better of it. He needed to keep his strength up. He ate quickly, keeping his eyes on Maldred the entire time. Finished, Dhamon wrapped his fingers around the ale mug and pulled it close. He contemplated taking a drink, then decided not.

He leaned back in his chair. "Why does the shadow dragon want Sable dead? Really?" Dhamon said in a low voice to the ogre-mage.

Maldred steepled his fingers and answered in similarly hushed tones. "He told you. Two dragons of their size cannot exist without deadly rivalry in the same land. The shadow dragon covets this swamp and does not wish to go elsewhere." Maldred finished a second mug of ale. "Truthfully, I think he would be the better dragon for this country. He wouldn't meddle with the people who live here, wouldn't try to expand his territory and enlarge the swamp, would leave the ogre lands alone. He would be content with things the way they already are."

"Would he?" Dhamon said. "Just why does the shadow dragon need mortals to fight for him? He would stand a better chance against the Black than we would."

Maldred thought a moment. "A better chance, maybe, but he stays safe this way. And you, Dhamon, he feels you are some kind of anointed warrior. He believes you can sneak into the caverns and surprise and defeat Sable."

Dhamon gave a quiet laugh. "Surprise an overlord? I rode a dragon, ogre. Dragon's senses are incredible. You can't surprise them unless they're in a deep sleep, and not always then."

"Your senses are also acute," Maldred countered, "and you're stronger than any four or five men. I've seen what you're capable of."

"Sable will kill all of us, ogre."

"You don't know that for sure."

Dhamon took a drink then, feeling the ale warm his throat. He relished the sensation, which he had denied himself for too long. *But I will die soon to the scales anyway,* Dhamon thought, again touching the scale on his cheek. *So what difference does the method of my death make?* "I know what I know, ogre, but I'd try to fight Sable anyway if I knew for certain my child would be all right."

"The shadow dragon will keep his word, I promise you that. He'll leave Riki's family alone and call off the hobgoblins. I want to see her and the baby safe, too. And if by some chance you do win . . ." Maldred leaned back in the chair, which creaked in protest. "He'll cure you of the scales." A pause. "You need that cure, Dhamon, and you and I both know you need it soon."

Dhamon caught Maldred's stare, holding it for a long silence. Maldred finally looked away as the serving girl brought more ale.

Dhamon glanced at Ragh, who sat there stolidly, watching Maldred.

"Maldred lies. The shadow dragon lies," Fiona said to Dhamon.

"Aye, Fiona, the shadow dragon surely lies." Dhamon pushed away from the table and stood, tightly clenching the glaive's haft. "But I've got to try to save my child." Or die in the trying, he added silently.

Dhamon walked away from his companions. He heard Maldred rise behind him.

"Where do you think you're going?" There was a hint of threat in Maldred's voice.

"I'm going to see if I can find out where Sable is, ogre."

Instantly a mix of fear and irritation crossed Maldred's angular face. He strained to keep his angry voice down. "You can't, Dhamon. Not yet. Nura Bint-Drax will determine when the time is right. It's too soon, we've told you that."

"Well, the naga isn't here, is she? I don't remember the shadow dragon mentioning anything about timing. And I'm running out of time." He glanced around and noticed that many of the patrons had become interested in his and Maldred's conversation. "But don't worry. I'll not fight the Black without you at my side. Sable *will* kill me if I make the attempt. And I want to make sure you're there to die, too." If I don't choose to kill you first in the alley, he thought. When Dhamon reached for the door, Maldred dropped a hand on his shoulder.

"You're not going anywhere, Dhamon."

"No? And you're going to stop me here? With all these people watching?" Dhamon nodded to Ragh, who was intently regarding them. "Wait for me here, the two of you. I shouldn't be more than a few hours." He tossed his coin pouch to the draconian, frowned and nodded to Fiona.

Ragh understood. Dhamon was giving the draconian a chance to escape with the Solamnic as soon as Maldred left to follow Dhamon.

"Or do you want to step outside, ogre?" Dhamon

opened the door and immediately was greeted by the odors of the city street.

Maldred growled and let him go. The ogre-mage returned to the table, settling himself down with Fiona and Ragh and thumping his empty mug to summon the serving girl. His eyes were on the door, however, and he was clearly seething.

"Aren't you going to follow him?" Fiona asked.

Maldred shook his head. "Dhamon expects me to, but that wouldn't be a safe proposition right now. So I'll wait for him. You're here. That means he'll be back."

"Will he?" Ragh asked.

◇ ◇ ◇ ◇ ◇ ◇ ◇

Dhamon waited in the alley, expecting Maldred to follow him. He was trying to decide whether to kill the ogre here or later in the bowels of the city, where his corpse might go undiscovered for days. But the ogre didn't emerge from the tavern, and so after a while Dhamon cut across the street to the stunted tower of the old sage. Maldred had out-foxed him by staying behind.

"At the very least," Dhamon decided, "I'll find out if the overlord's home."

There were two spawn guards just beyond the stunted tower's entrance, and Dhamon made quick work of them. He was becoming an expert at fighting the vile creatures, and he knew to jump back after delivering a mortal blow, saving himself from the brunt of their death-throe acid blasts. The glaive was superbly balanced and lightweight, and gave him a good reach. But with every swing he pictured Goldmoon's face the time he tried to kill her. When this business was done, he'd get rid of the weapon once and for all. It had a magic that nobody could control.

There was only a little light in the corridor, this coming from a pair of guttering fat-soaked torches that had burned down to stubs. When he was last here, the light was reasonably bright and the air fresh. Now the staleness hung heavy and nested unpleasantly in his lungs, and a thick layer of grime coated the stone floor. Were he not in a hurry and had he not so many other things on his mind, Dhamon would have let the changes bother him, and he might have investigated matters. Now, though, he wanted only to find a way below, and within moments he located a narrow, winding stairway that took him far beneath the city streets.

The stale air turned increasingly foul. Dhamon smelled stagnant water, human waste, and decaying things he'd rather not think about. The corridors became darker the deeper he went, the torches spaced farther apart and many of them burned out. He knew the spawn could see well in the blackness and doubted they cared about providing light for the human prisoners who rotted in the cells he passed. Sable must have some human servants, though, Dhamon guessed, else no one would have bothered with providing any light.

Dhamon slipped down a corridor filled with waist-deep water. The water was cool, and the film that floated on top of it clung to his clothes. Some of the passages were vaguely familiar because of the animal sculptures that served as torch sconces. These had been burning magically before, when the old sage led him to her laboratory. Now the torches were all burned out, save one in each corridor, which gave off an offensive oily smoke—nothing magical about them any more.

A turn and the water deepened to his chest. Another turn and he was sloshing along in a near-river and most certainly lost. He'd let himself become too preoccupied with thoughts of his child and Riki. He hoped Maldred had managed to follow him, or Nura Bint-Drax. The naga had a knack for turning up.

"Damn." The floor dropped out from under him, and he had to swim now. It was difficult swimming while holding onto the glaive. There was no torch-light here, only scattered patches of luminous moss that clung to the ceiling and helped to guide him. He considered turning around but thought, Maybe that's what the water was intended to do, dissuade visitors. "I'm a drenched rat in a maze," he muttered. "I was a fool to think I could find the Black on my own."

Was it really as simple as Maldred said? The shadow dragon wanted the swamp and didn't want to fight Sable himself?

"It's all too simple," Dhamon decided as he turned down another watery corridor. He didn't doubt that the shadow dragon wanted the Black dead, but the reason had to be more convoluted than simply desiring the swamp. Things were never so simple as far as dragons were concerned. There had to be another explanation.

"But what?" Dhamon treaded water, finding himself at a juncture of two passageways. "Just what does the damn shadow dragon want? And why does he need me?"

He chose the branch that led off to the right and began swimming a little faster. He heard sibilant voices up ahead, two or three spawn. He could deal with them.

"Did you hear ssssomething?"

"Heard man talking."

"Where man?"

The spawn voices buzzed, sometimes in the common tongue, sometimes in their odd, hissing language.

"Where man?"

"Man supposssed to be here?"

"Where?"

"Here!" Dhamon shouted as he erupted from the water. He had swum quietly around a curve and entered a cavern, spotting the scaly threesome sitting on a ledge just above the water. He jumped up onto the ledge, swinging the glaive and sending the blade deep into the chest of the closest spawn.

The thing burst into acid before its companions could act, showering Dhamon with the caustic liquid, for he couldn't jump out of the way in time. Ignoring the pain, he pressed his attack, sweeping the polearm in a wide arc and cutting the second spawn in two. The weapon was indeed enchanted, but Dhamon's great strength gave it additional power.

"As strong as any four or five men," he recalled Maldred saying. He was at least as strong as that many men, all because of the shadow dragon.

And if the shadow dragon had planted its magic inside Dhamon a few years ago, as he had claimed, that meant there was indeed nothing simple behind what the dragon wanted. There had to be something intended beyond sending Dhamon after the Black. Just what in the many levels of the Abyss was the true scheme?

"What does the damn dragon want?" Dhamon shouted in frustration.

Hearing him, the last spawn scuttled fearfully backward. It inhaled and breathed, but Dhamon

ducked just in time and was hit by little of its hurt-
ful breath.

"I won't kill you," Dhamon promised, as he continued to stalk the frightened creature. "If you give
me some information." Now I am truly the liar, he
thought. I intend to kill you after you've told me
what I want to know.

"Man want what?" the spawn asked as it dodged
out of Dhamon's reach.

"I just want out of here. Take me up to the
street."

The spawn glared at him but nodded. "Take you
to ssstreet. Yesss."

"No." Dhamon inwardly cursed himself for
what he was about to say. In a heartbeat's time he'd
made his decision, changed his mind. "Take me to
Sable's lair." Perhaps, he guessed, the shadow
dragon seeks something hidden in the Black's lair.

The spawn vehemently shook its head and
exhaled noisily, but Dhamon hugged the cavern
wall and again was spared the acid breath. "Sssable
kill me if I do."

"I'll kill you if you don't," Dhamon shot back.
"Besides, Sable might actually reward you for
bringing me to her. I've caused the overlord all
manner of grief."

"Sssable kill *you* then," it said.

"Maybe. Now move."

They hadn't traveled more than a few minutes
before the passageway became wholly submerged
and very wide. Again Dhamon swam, following
the spawn, wondering if he was being led to the
overlord's lair or to someplace where a myriad of
spawn waited to pounce on him. Eerie sounds
came to him as he made his way through the
water—growls and groans from creatures that

clung to the sides of the rocky walls. The sounds grew, and so did Dhamon's unease as they broke the surface in the next foul-smelling chamber. He nearly dropped the glaive when his hands started trembling uncontrollably.

"Not much farther," the spawn told him. It raised a scaly claw and pointed to a shadowed alcove. "One more tunnel." It hesitated. "You go by ssself now?"

Despite the few patches of luminous moss, this cavern was all shadows, and it was too dark even to read the expression on the spawn's face. His unease, his trembling hands—it wasn't like him. *Dragonfear.* That was the only explanation. The spawn was indeed leading him to Sable—or to a lesser dragon serving the overlord.

"You go by ssself?"

"All right. I'll go alone."

The spawn sighed with relief and made a move to swim past Dhamon, heading back the way it had come. Though it was difficult to maneuver the blade in the water, Dhamon managed to sweep the glaive like a scythe to cut off the passing spawn's head. Then Dhamon dropped below the surface to avoid the acid blast.

"Convenient that you spawn leave no corpses," he muttered. Then he looked to the alcove, took a deep breath, and disappeared below the surface again.

There was no glowing moss here, and so he found his way by feeling along one side of the submerged tunnel. He continued pulling himself along until his lungs ached for air, and then he slowly rose, finding barely an inch between the surface of the water and the rocky ceiling. A few deep breaths and he was under again.

It seemed an interminable journey, and a heavy sense of dread settled in. He rose again minutes later when he noticed the water growing lighter in color. His head silently broke the surface in a chamber whose boundaries he couldn't discern. A great patch of the luminous moss illuminated enough parts of it, however, for Dhamon to guess he was in a dragon's lair. Giant crocodiles lounged on outcroppings. Other creatures he couldn't name clung to spires and ledges. There were things flying somewhere overhead—he could hear the flap of leather wings, but he couldn't see the creatures, and couldn't see the ceiling.

His teeth started chattering. Focusing his thoughts on holding onto his weapon, he managed to stave off the worse effects of the dragonfear.

It was Sable's lair. The Black was there, at the extreme end of where the pale light reached. Curled on a sandy stretch of ground, the overlord slept, coins and gems spilled all around it. The great dragon's breath was so strong it created a breeze in the cavern, and the sound of its slumber was a constant, sonorous rumble.

Dhamon had seen Sable once before—years ago at the Window to the Stars portal. All the overlords were there, when Malys tried to ascend to godhood and become the next Takhisis. The Black seemed more impressive here, alone, in her dark and malodorous realm. She was huge, eyes as large as boulders, scales thicker than the greatest plate armor. The tip of her tail was as big around as an ancient oak.

Dhamon could feel the power and the evil exuded by the dragon. Spellbound, he wanted to flee while at the same time he wanted to swim closer for a better look. He forcibly controlled his foolish impulse.

Did the shadow dragon desire the Black's wealth? Certainly the shadow dragon could obtain his own horde. So not wealth. Something magical? What?

Dhamon's eyes narrowed. He took a deep breath and dropped below the surface, just as Sable opened a massive eye. The overlord suspiciously scanned the chamber. Seeing nothing, she resumed her slumber.

◊ ◊ ◊ ◊ ◊ ◊ ◊

It was past midnight when Dhamon found his way back to the city streets. He was dripping—from sweat and the stagnant water of the tunnels—and the stench was overwhelming. He knew he must look a sight. His clothes were nearly burned off from the spawn's acid, his legs were covered with scales, arms dotted with them, and there were now a few on his face. He'd passed a mirror in the hallway of the stunted tower, saw the spreading scales on his legs, arms, and throat.

Fortunately there were only a few brave souls wandering the streets this late at night, and all of them—including a pair of spawn—gave him wide berth.

He was hopeful that somehow Ragh had gotten Fiona out of the city, and though hours ago he wished the draconian had managed to kill Maldred, now he hoped the ogre-mage was still alive. He was going to need him for his plan.

The tavern was still open, and peering through a window, he scowled to see Fiona and Ragh still sitting at their table. The Solamnic Knight had her arms folded on the table, her head nestled in them and was sleeping soundly despite the racket from the conversations and clinks of mugs. Ragh was wide awake, and was watching Maldred converse with the sultry Ergothian form of Nura Bint-Drax.

Dhamon muttered a string of curses and went inside.

Nura made a gagging sound and waved her delicate-looking hand in front of her face in a show of warding off Dhamon's stench. "Where have you been?"

Dhamon came closer, leaned over her shoulder, and whispered into her ear, "To see Sable."

Her eyes grew wide. She abruptly stood, nearly knocking him over. "You couldn't . . . ."

"Sable's all cozy in her lair. And she's got lots of . . . treasure."

"How did you . . . ?"

"Get in and out alive?" Dhamon lowered his voice when he noticed all the conversation around them had stopped. "Luck, I think," he said. "Sable was sleeping soundly, and I had the presence of mind to leave before she woke up."

Listening to him, Ragh nudged Fiona awake. The Solamnic rubbed at the sleep in her eyes.

"Ragh, Fiona, we're leaving now," said Dhamon, grabbing them and heading for the door.

"Thank you, Rig," Fiona said as she stepped outside.

Ragh was quick to follow her.

"It is too soon, Dhamon Grimwulf," Nura warned. "We need to make preparations and develop a plan. It is too soon to disturb Sable."

Dhamon slammed the door behind him and waited, waving away Ragh's questions. Within a few moments Maldred and Nura joined them on the street.

The Ergothian pulled herself up and thrust a finger at Dhamon's chest. "You are my master's tool, Dhamon Grimwulf," she said threateningly. "You'll follow my orders from here on out. I'll have no more of your—"

He jabbed a finger back at her. "I'll have no more of you." In a move that caught her completely off guard, Dhamon shouldered the glaive, took a step back and swung it at her. The blade whistled through the night air and sliced into where she'd been standing but a heartbeat before.

Nura was lightning fast. Narrowly dodging the blow, she stepped behind Maldred. "My master will slay you for your impudence!" she sputtered.

Dhamon circled round. "I think not," Dhamon said, taking another swing. Maldred drew his sword and held it defensively in front of him, unenthusiastically protecting the naga. Behind them, the Solamnic pulled her own long sword and began talking to it. Ragh backed up and assumed an aggressive stance.

"The master wouldn't dream of slaying me, Nura. I am the one, after all. His precious tool. He's been preparing me for the past few years, hasn't he? He planted the magic in me some time ago. As you said, you've been testing me. All that work . . . even a dragon wouldn't slay someone he's got so much effort invested in."

Nura's hands were working, fingers glowing and tracing patterns in the air. "You are the one," she said, "and I will force you to cooperate." Arcane words spilled from her lips, and the glow intensified.

"What about me, magic lady?" This came from Ragh, whom Nura had made the mistake of ignoring. The draconian slashed at the Ergothian's back, claws cutting through her tough skin. Nura shrieked with pain. Her spell was squandered in that moment, and the glow of the magic faded.

"Fool!" she cried. "All of you are fools! The master will never cure you now, Dhamon Grimwulf. He'll have the hobgoblins feast on your child!" She edged around Maldred, jockeying for advantage over Ragh and Dhamon.

Suddenly the Solamnic Knight brushed Dhamon aside and sprang forward, the tip of her sword aimed right at Nura's heart. She managed to prick her, as Nura dodged.

"You will cooperate! All of you!" Nura howled, as she reached behind and slipped her hand inside Maldred's shirt to retrieve the shadowy scale. She cracked it just as Fiona lunged again, disappearing and leaving the Solamnic Knight confused.

Dhamon heard the tavern door opening, and out of the corner of his eye he saw a half-dozen drunken men stumble out, intent on watching the fireworks. He paid them little attention, turning his anger on Maldred now. Fiona stepped on one side of the ogre-mage, and Ragh took the other.

"Let's take the monster once and for all," Fiona said.

"No, leave him alive," Dhamon said.

"Alive? Why? What are we doing, Dhamon?" the draconian sputtered.

Dhamon leveled the weapon at Maldred's chest. "The ogre is going to take us back to the shadow dragon."

The draconian raised his brow in puzzlement. "Not a good idea."

"The shadow dragon wants us to tackle Sable, because he's not powerful enough to do it himself. That must make us more powerful than the shadow dragon is, right? So we're going to attack the shadow dragon instead."

"Dhamon, you can't!" Maldred argued. "You—"

"Can't I? I'll find a way to make the damn dragon call off his hobgoblins and leave Riki alone. I'll make him cure me of these scales. The shadow dragon claims he's made me formidable? Well, let's see just how formidable I am! And you're going to take me there, Maldred. Right now, before the naga comes back . . ." Dhamon's words trailed off in a strangled cry.

He crumpled to his knees as the glaive fell from his hands. A second later he was writhing on the street, jabs of intense cold and incredible heat warring inside his body. "The scale," he gasped. One moment it was as though he was in the middle of a bonfire, the next as though he was adrift on a glacial lake. His muscles twitched wildly, and he shrugged off Fiona's attempt to comfort him.

Ragh looked with uncertainty between Dhamon and Maldred, then as the ogre-mage took a step forward, the draconian reached down and snapped up the abandoned glaive. He was unfamiliar with the weapon, but it gave him a reach that kept Maldred at bay.

"He's dying," Fiona said. She touched Dhamon's forehead, then pulled back in shock. "Rig's burning up! My beloved's dying."

More men came out of the tavern, all keeping a respectful distance and all watching curiously as they chattered. One started waving chaotically, and Ragh growled, noting the gesture was meant to attract a passing spawn guard.

"Wonderful," the draconian muttered. "Look down the street. We're going to have company."

Dimly Dhamon heard the insectlike buzz of the

tavern-goers, felt Fiona's fingers brushing the hair away from his face, felt the intense heat and cold.

"Rig is dying," she repeated. "Dying!"

Dhamon found himself agreeing with her. He was dying. The pain had never been so bad before. He found himself falling away into an emptiness.

Chapter Eleven
Shadow Keep

The grass was soft and cool, and Dhamon thrust his fingers into it until he could feel the damp earth beneath. So he wasn't dead, not yet. He was mildly saddened at this realization, as death would have solved all of his problems.

Death would have ended the pain from the scales.

If there was a place where spirits found peace, he would rather be there right now. It had been a long time since he'd known any real contentment.

Since he wasn't dead his problems persisted. He realized some time had passed since the episode in Shrentak, and though his eyes were closed, he could tell it was mid-day, probably, by the amount of light seeping through his eyelids.

He ached from the scales and found himself wishing for a big jug of that ale he'd drunk in the tavern last night. He couldn't remember when he'd hurt this much following an episode. It felt as if he'd sparred with a few dozen bakali.

His throat was dry, his tongue felt swollen, and he had trouble working up some saliva to swallow. He kept his eyes shut and his breathing shallow, deciding he ought to learn more about his surroundings before letting anyone know he was awake.

The breeze felt slightly warm against his face, and he picked up the faint, telltale odor of Ragh, like a blacksmith's shop. He could smell little else, save a trace of chicory and—something else— sheep. He himself still reeked from the water and sludge he'd waded and swum through to catch a glimpse of Sable.

So he was still in the swamp, he guessed, somewhere outside of Shrentak. He heard the striking song of a heron and the distant snap of a crocodile's jaws. There were no sounds of city life or of people. He could hear plenty of leaves rustling, and willow branches, as well. He was lying partially in shade, an effort on someone's part, probably Fiona, believing him to be Rig, to keep him out of the oppressive heat.

Opening his eyes just a crack, he spied sunlight streaming diffusely through a veil of leaves. Wider, and he spotted the draconian's scaly visage—Ragh bending over him.

"I wasn't sure you were going to make it," the draconian said flatly. "This was the worst time, so far. You haven't moved for hours. I was afraid I'd have to deal with the mad Knight and the blue-skinned ogre all by myself."

So the draconian hadn't killed Maldred yet. Too bad. Dhamon propped himself up on his elbows and rolled his head to work out a kink in his neck.

Ragh leaned closer. "How are you feeling?" There was genuine concern in the draconian's voice, and this distressed Dhamon.

"Fine," Dhamon said. Then truthfully: "More than a little sore. Did you get me out of the city? Where's Fiona?" And where's Maldred for that matter? he thought.

"Sore. You feel sore. But you feel all right otherwise?"

Dhamon frowned and raised his right hand to push Ragh away so he could stand up. He stopped and swallowed hard. The back of his right hand was entirely covered with scales, and there were pearl-sized scales on his wrist as well. He gaped at his arm, completely covered with scales the size of steel pieces. His left arm was the same, though the scales hadn't yet spread to his left hand. He touched the scales on his arm, and only when he pressed down hard did he register the slightest sensation.

"By the vanished gods." Dhamon jumped up, seeing Fiona and Maldred watching him warily from nearby. He moved away from them to the far side of a willow trunk. Ragh followed him.

He knew the scales were spreading, but this was all happening so fast. It seemed he might only have hours left before his transformation—into what?—was complete. He might not have time to confront the shadow dragon. Dhamon checked out the rest of his body. His legs were almost solid with scales— all the size of coins save for the large one on his thigh. There were also scales on his stomach and chest, and feeling around, he discovered several on his back.

"There's . . . more on your neck," Ragh told him.

Dhamon reached up and touched his neck, where the scales were like a choke collar spreading down to his shoulders. His fingers danced over his face, finding a few more on his cheek, one on his forehead. Had the shadow dragon out of vengeance sped up the foul magic? Had he learned that Dhamon balked at fighting the Black and was now circling back to the shadow dragon's lair?

He leaned against the tree, closed his eyes. A sense of hopelessness washed over him. He'd always prided himself on being strong. Alone in life. His only real family had been the Knights of Takhisis, and there was no coddling there. Strong, independent, fearless, and driven—those qualities had directed his life. At this moment, all of those qualities were of no use, all had forsaken him.

If Riki was here she would hold him, tell him everything was all right, that they would find him a cure for all his agony. She would be lying, but her words and warmth would be appreciated, as he had never appreciated them before, when she was actually with him. Palin—he was another one who would fuss over him, poke and prod and make some effort to remedy the situation, then fall to studying him like a specimen in his laboratory. Maldred . . . the friend Maldred had been . . . Maldred used to rage against the world with him. But none of those people were here now. He'd never appreciated them anyway. This crisis was his to face alone.

How long before my soul slips away?

Dhamon opened his eyes and scolded himself. He began to fight his anguish and substitute fury. The damn shadow dragon better speed up the magic even faster, Dhamon thought, better kill me quick before I reach him! Dhamon suspected he was beyond a cure now anyway, but he would force the dragon to spare Riki and his child—and then he would exact some measure of retribution.

The draconian fidgeted in front of him, wanting to say something but quiet behind the invisible barrier Dhamon had erected with his aloof, burning eyes.

"Leave me alone, Ragh."

The draconian stepped back a pace but continued to stand there, studying Dhamon. Finally he looked away when Dhamon's gaze became too uncomfortable. Ragh batted at a large insect that landed on his chest. Dhamon watched it fly away, only to be replaced by another.

He can feel the fly bites, Dhamon realized. He couldn't. Dhamon could feel the breeze blowing against only parts of his skin, not where the scales grew.

"How far are we from Shrentak?"

"Two miles I'd say, Dhamon, maybe three. We came here in a hurry when it was dark so it was hard to tell just how far we—"

"What about Maldred?"

Ragh folded his arms. "Maldred scooped you up after you fell unconscious in the street. Said we had to move quick and get out of the city before Nura came back with reinforcements. Fiona and I started to argue, but then . . ." The draconian shifted his weight. "Everything got quiet. I mean everything. Lights that were burning in windows started going out. The drunks disappeared. Not even a rat moved in the alley. Maldred said the naga had allies in the city and that it wouldn't be safe for us to stay. So we stopped arguing and followed him. To tell you the truth, I think Maldred helped you—all of us—out of a bad spot."

Dhamon rubbed his back against the trunk. There weren't so many scales on his back. He glanced down at the back of his right hand, opened and closed his fingers.

"They . . . the scales," Ragh began. "They started growing even faster, once you were unconscious, spreading like some dark rash. Maldred tried to work some magic to stop them. I think he managed to do something to at least slow them down. We didn't notice any more cropping up after dawn."

"Where's my glaive?"

The draconian glanced around. "Fiona has it. She grabbed it when you dropped it, and she hasn't let go of it since."

"I heard a crocodile a while ago. The river has to be near."

Ragh nodded. "A tributary. My nose'll lead us right to it."

"I can't smell the water."

"I can't imagine why not." There was a wry look on Ragh's scaly visage. He pointed to the northeast.

◇ ◇ ◇ ◇ ◇ ◇ ◇

Dhamon spent quite a while in the clean water. Not only did he want to scrub away the stink, he wanted time away from his companions' prying eyes. Doffing his tattered clothes, he discovered more scales—a few on the tops of his feet, under his arms. Each time he touched one he hadn't noticed before, he silently cursed the shadow dragon and the day he'd first met the mysterious creature. He scrubbed his clothes and found some humor in the notion that since he'd left the Knights of Takhisis he had a hard time keeping any of his garments intact for long. He didn't quit until enough of the smell was gone from his pants and tunic that he could live with himself. He put them on, climbed out of the river.

The soreness persisted in his limbs. If anything the pain had become worse, a dull throb that was echoed by a pounding in his head. While annoying, the pain would keep him alert and angry and feed his obsession with the shadow dragon.

"Rig!"

Fiona came scurrying toward him, holding the glaive over her shoulder, and smiling widely.

"I had a horrible dream, Rig. I dreamed you died in Shrentak." She thrust the glaive at Dhamon, then wrapped her arms around him, holding him close and pressing her face against his chest. Dhamon squirmed uncomfortably.

Behind her came Maldred, thick eyebrows raised and mouthing the word, "Rig?"

Dhamon wasn't sure why he did it, perhaps to unsettle the ogre-mage or perhaps because some of her madness had rubbed off on him through the wight, but now he returned Fiona's embrace, kissing her forehead. They held each other until Ragh began pacing around them. Dhamon slowly released the Knight.

"It was a horrible dream," Fiona repeated breathlessly. "I can't ever lose you, Rig. We shouldn't go back to that ghastly city."

"We're not going back to Shrentak, Fiona. I promise."

Maldred cleared his throat. "Think otherwise. Just take a look at yourself, all your scales. I know a secret way into the city, not a pleasant one, but our best bet now. We're going to have to try to defeat the Black if you ever want to be cured of those scales. The shadow dragon—"

"Is going to get an unpleasant surprise," Dhamon finished. "Now you're going to prove your friendship by taking me to him." I've a worthy weapon now, Dhamon thought, hefting the glaive over his shoulder. A fine magical one.

"Dhamon, listen to reason," Maldred persisted. "We're going to have to—"

Dhamon flung himself at the ogre-mage, dropping

the glaive, fingers spread wide. His nails dug into Maldred like claws, pulling him down, raking him. Before the surprised Maldred could react, Dhamon threw an elbow into his chest, knocking the wind from him. Then he continued his assault, driving a fist into his stomach, pushing him on the ground and slamming his fist into him repeatedly.

Dhamon had his hands around the ogre-mage's throat. Maldred's eyes bulged with fear.

The spittle flew from Dhamon's mouth. "You're going to lead us to the damn shadow dragon, and you're going to do it now."

"Dhamon . . ." the ogre-mage gasped. "I've got Blöde to think about."

"You'll have nothing to think about, *ogre*, if you don't cooperate. You'll be dead." Dhamon's eyes said he meant it, despite the good times they had shared, despite once thinking Maldred as dear as any brother, and despite the fact that the big thief had pulled him out of a bad scrape or two. "You won't be able to do anything for your damnable dry homeland if your corpse is rotting in this swamp."

Fiona had reclaimed the glaive. She eagerly joined in, swinging the big weapon around, leveling the axe-like blade of it straight at Maldred.

"Blue-skinned monster. You'll do what Rig wants, or I'll help him kill you."

Maldred looked between the two with darting eyes and finally nodded, pained resignation clear on his face. Dhamon let him up, and as he did so, he grabbed the ogre's two-handed sword away from him and passed it to Ragh.

"Bad enough you have magic," Dhamon told him. "You're not going to have a weapon, too. Ragh, if you hear him mumble or twitch his fingers, don't be afraid to poke him with that." He reached out and took the glaive back from Fiona. "Let's get going. Maldred's in a hurry to take us to the shadow dragon."

The female Knight smiled hopefully. "So you can be cured, Rig."

"Aye, so I can be cured." And so I can exact a promise that my child will be safe. Dhamon took her hand, as Maldred started off. The draconian followed right behind the ogre-mage, sword held out in front of him behind Maldred's back.

They traveled the rest of the day in relative silence. Fiona spoke only to Dhamon, addressing him as Rig the whole time. Her madness was getting worse too, Dhamon told himself. They stopped before sunset on the bank of an inviting fresh stream, and here, with Ragh hovering menacingly at his side, Maldred made another attempt to speak to Dhamon and convince him to turn around.

"The shadow dragon is very powerful, my friend."

"Aye," Dhamon admitted. He watched Fiona kneel at the stream and splash water on her face. "All dragons are. And I'm not your friend."

"I believe he would keep his word about curing you and . . ."

"I believe all dragons are duplicitous, and I think I should have never agreed to go on his foolish errand to begin with. I wasted precious time. I should have found a way that very night to attack him and to make him cure me and obtain a guarantee that he would leave Riki and my child alone."

"Dhamon . . ."

"You'll have to find your own remedy for Sable, ogre. Exchanging one dragon overlord for another is foolhardy. Idiocy. Oh, the shadow dragon might stop the spread of the swamp, but he very well could do something worse."

"It's never good to be under any dragon's claw," Ragh interjected.

Maldred hung his head. "Dhamon, my people are desperate. I had to take the chance to save them, and now you're taking that one hope away from me."

"Too bad." Dhamon looked at Fiona. She had the long sword out and was crazily whispering to it. "Long ago you taught me to look out only for myself, ogre. You were a very good teacher." He paused, eying the ogre-mage up and down. "To think I once considered you a good friend. Foolish of me." Dhamon wore a disgusted look. "How much farther to the lair, ogre?"

"An hour at best."

"Then let's move. I don't want to travel through the swamp in the dark." Dhamon looked back to the stream and saw that Fiona was gone.

❖ ❖ ❖ ❖ ❖ ❖ ❖

They searched for Fiona until it was too dark for them to see. Dhamon forced Maldred to create some magical light so they could look longer.

They knew she hadn't been hauled away by some furtive swamp-beast. There were no signs of a struggle near the stream. Her tracks indicated she'd simply strolled away into the undergrowth, but they stopped abruptly after several yards, as if she'd vanished in thin air. There was nothing to indicate she'd climbed a tree or retraced her steps, and there were no other tracks around hers.

They rested briefly that night but found no further clues even after the sun came up. When they called for her, they received no reply. Dhamon exerted his heightened senses, listening for her, listening for anything unusual. He tried to pick up her scent, he strained his eyes to catch a glimpse of her through the undergrowth.

At every juncture he cursed himself for not watching out for her more closely, for not keeping her safe, for not being able to rescue Rig in Shrentak.

It was past noon when Ragh, tugging on his tunic, spoke. "We're not going to find her, Dhamon. Fiona either doesn't want to be found, or something devoured her. In this place, I'd say it's probably the latter."

"No, we'll find her, my friend." Dhamon stopped. He'd not called Ragh "friend" before, but the draconian hadn't betrayed him, like Maldred. Ragh was the closest thing to a friend he had right now. "We have to find her, Ragh."

The draconian grabbed Dhamon's left wrist and forced him to look at his own hand. The entire back of Dhamon's left hand was covered with scales now, and tiny scales decorated most of his fingers, too.

"How much longer can you afford to tarry?"

Dhamon's limbs still ached fiercely. All of his worsening troubles could be blamed on the shadow dragon's heinous magic. "I don't know."

"Well, *my friend*, I know that if we don't continue after the shadow dragon soon, you won't be any good to Fiona—even if she's still alive. You won't be any good to the child you keep mentioning, and you certainly won't be any good to yourself. You're liable to end up looking like some misshapen spawn, and the first swordsman who comes across your path is going to try to cut you in two."

Dhamon felt oddly stronger today than yesterday, and his senses had become even more acute. He thrust the end of the glaive haft into the ground, looked around to make sure Maldred was in sight, then ran his hand through his sweat-damp hair. "All right. No more searching. For now. I find myself taking your advice, Ragh. Frequently I find myself taking your advice, my friend."

"I suppose that troubles you." Ragh gave him a rare lopsided grin. "I've been around a long time, Dhamon. I've got lots of advice to give, when I've a mind to give it. Now, let's go looking for this shadow dragon before I take some of my own advice and part company with you."

◊ ◊ ◊ ◊ ◊ ◊ ◊

Because they had ranged several miles in their search for Fiona, it took them until past dawn of the following day to backtrack and reach the large cave mouth concealed by willow leaves that Maldred identified as the shadow dragon's favorite lair. It didn't look especially familiar to Dhamon, but then he'd been there at night before. A quick search found old tracks—his, Ragh's, Fiona's, Maldred's. Yes, this was the place. But one set of tracks was more recent. They were smaller tracks, belonging to a child.

"The naga." Dhamon hurried inside. He headed straight toward the depths of the cave. "Ragh, keep a close watch on the ogre."

The cave was very dark and heavy with peculiar, fetid odors. Ragh came in behind Dhamon, prodding Maldred forward. "Some light," the draconian instructed, "and I know the gestures to that spell now, so don't try anything else."

Maldred cupped his hand and fluttered his fingers, mumbling a few fast words in an ancient language. A ball of glowing light appeared. The draconian held the great sword in one hand, cupped his other hand, and copied Maldred. Another glowing sphere appeared, hovering above their heads, following them.

"I've got a little magic in me, too, ogre. So watch yourself." Ragh hoped for a surprised reaction from Maldred, but he didn't get it.

"I taught a kobold that spell, Ragh. *A kobold.* It's easy magic."

Ragh poked him with the tip of the sword. "Move, *ogre.*"

They caught up with Dhamon, who was deeper in the cave where the air was still. "Nura got here first and warned the shadow dragon. Now we're both in a fix, Dhamon. You'll not get your cure, and the swamp will swallow my homeland."

Dhamon was peering into the recesses of the cave. "Maybe. But this cave goes on for quite a ways more than I first believed." He could detect no hint of the dragon, not the slightest stirring of air from its noxious breath, not the faintest glow from its filmy eyes. He couldn't smell the naga either— she had a distinctive musky odor he'd locked away in his memory. "Let's see how far it goes."

"It goes nowhere," Maldred said. He'd been here a few times before and thought he knew the full extent of the cave, but he allowed the draconian to prod him along.

The cave twisted and turned, heading deeper into the earth. The air grew cooler and more repulsive. They came upon a chamber filled with the skeletons of giant crocodiles, great lizards, and other beasts. Some were half-eaten and rotting, covered with a carpet of feasting insects, others were old, bleached bones.

The cave trail wound farther down, narrowing, and Dhamon still pressed on, though he realized the dragon could not possibly squeeze down here.

"Dhamon, this is pointless."

"Shut up, ogre."

"Stop calling me that."

Dhamon whirled. The light from the ball of light above Maldred threw shadows upward along the planes and angles of his wide, blue face. "That's what you are, isn't it, an ogre? That's why you betrayed me, because you're an ogre. Because you had to find a way to save your precious ogre lands. Well, ogre, as you said—it's pointless—and your lands aren't going to be saved, are they?" And neither will my child if I can't find the damn shadow dragon, he thought.

"I'm sorry."

"Maybe if you'd come to me as a friend, I would've helped you. Maybe I would've marched straight into Sable's lair, with whatever forces we could muster. Maybe I would've done that for the Maldred I thought I knew. But not for the ogre I can't stomach. Not for the ogre who put my child at risk and who is at least in part responsible for Fiona wandering somewhere blindly in this wretched swamp."

His tirade finished, Dhamon turned around and started retracing his steps. "You said this was the shadow dragon's favorite lair. Where are its other hiding holes?"

Maldred didn't answer until Ragh poked him sharply with the sword. "Nura led me to believe there are a few, but I've not been summoned to any others."

"So where would the dragon go?" Dhamon thought back to the cave high in the mountains where he first encountered the shadow dragon. Maybe there, but he hoped not. He'd stumbled into the cave by accident and had no way of finding it again.

"I don't know."

"Not good enough." This came from Ragh, who warily watched Dhamon.

Dhamon was feeling his way along a wall that was a mix of earth and stone. Ragh nudged Maldred closer, and the twin globes of light revealed a side passage.

"I thought I felt air blowing in." The passage was too narrow for the three of them, and after several feet yielded to a natural staircase that wound its way up into darkness. The dragon certainly couldn't have fit in here, Dhamon decided, but the naga might have. If she'd been this way, perhaps he should let the naga lead him to the dragon.

"Dhamon," Ragh cautioned.

"I know, but do you have a better idea at the moment?" Without waiting for an answer, Dhamon slipped into the passage and started up the stairs. The other two followed him, single file, with the draconian at the rear prodding Maldred. Dhamon's legs ached with each step and he felt a burning sensation on his back, which he suspected was more scales sprouting. "Damn all the dragons in the world." His head pounded.

The steps were worn away in several places, but a stream of water trickled down and disappeared in a wide crack. The light globes revealed handholds here and there and deteriorated carvings and etchings. Dhamon traced one with his finger. It looked like the image of some kind of draconian or perhaps a bakali, and there was a smaller bulbous-nosed creature flying above it. The other creatures were too faint to make out.

It was a tight squeeze at the very end. As Dhamon stepped out into a worked stone chamber, he felt the floor give way beneath him. Reflexes like lightning, he sprang forward, rolled, and stood up again just as Maldred forced himself through the entrance and lost his balance, throwing his arms out at the last minute to catch himself from falling through a widening gap. The ogre-mage looked down and saw jagged iron spikes a few feet below. He wormed his way past, as Ragh carefully stepped into the room, scraping his shoulders on the rocks.

The floor was tiled, alternating squares of slate and black-veined rose marble, with a thick layer of dust making them look fuzzy and out of focus. Dhamon prodded Maldred ahead of him with the butt of the glaive, finding two more places that gave way, with spikes at the bottom of each one's long drop.

"Why would Nura come up here?" Maldred wondered aloud. A quick gesture and a few words and he changed his light globe, making it larger and brighter. Behind him, Ragh did the same. Their light revealed a hexagonal room littered with benches and bookcases and a half-dozen shadowed alcoves.

Dhamon edged forward, careful to test each tile in the floor with the glaive. He found another loose one, but rather than collapsing into a pit of spikes, this one upon his touch produced a gout of hot, blue flame.

"A sorcerer's den," Dhamon spat. "A damn evil sorcerer if you want my guess."

Still, he turned and turned, eyeing the place.

Ragh shifted away from Maldred, keeping an eye on the ogre-mage. He was using the great sword to prod the stones, and he employed his extraordinary draconian senses to detect anything unusual. "Dhamon. I smell magic that is still alive."

"Alive?" Maldred gave the draconian a disbelieving look.

Ragh waved a claw toward a knickknack-littered table. "It's old magic but it still carries some energy. Some type of ward, I think."

Maldred raised an eyebrow and started to say something. Dhamon cut him off.

"Shut up. I don't trust you, *ogre*."

Maldred glowered.

"Let him cast his spell," said Ragh. "It can't hurt, and maybe it'll help."

Maldred resumed his mumbled spellcasting. There was a melody to his words, though a dissonant melody, and when the words quickened, glowing patterns appeared on a workbench, in the air in front of a high shelf, in a dozen places on the floor, and at various heights in the alcoves.

"Lots of wards," Ragh said.

"So what?" Dhamon demanded an explanation.

"Magical traps," Maldred explained. "Spells used to catch intruders—hurt them or kill them. Maybe they're too old. They haven't done anything so far, but I can't tell what they are supposed to do."

"Can you destroy their enchantment?" Ragh asked.

"I thought you had a little magic about you?" Maldred taunted. "Why don't you do it?"

"This wasn't in any spellbook I perused," Ragh returned testily.

"I'll bet you never looked at a single spellbook." Maldred started humming, and Dhamon moved close, ready to use the glaive if the big man tried anything suspicious. This magical tune was more complex and drawn out. After several minutes passed, the glowing symbols started to disappear. When Maldred was finished, all but three were gone, and these were high over alcoves.

"Can't break those for some reason," he murmured. The sweat was thick on his brow, showing the spell had taken considerable effort. "Stay away from those alcoves. I said I don't know what the wards do. Maybe they cause more of those blue flames. Maybe worse. Probably worse. I can't identify the magic."

"Because it's old," Ragh said.

"And thereby dangerous," Dhamon added. He'd lost a friend, a scraggly kobold named Fetch, to old magic—an enchanted pool that had belonged to Black Robe sorcerers some decades or centuries past. "I've wasted our time. Let's get—"

"Maybe not." Ragh forgot Maldred. The draconian had moved over and was engrossed in a collection of small objects on a shelf. He gathered them up in his free hand and set them on a table. He hunched over the table and blew, trying to clear away some of the dust, then he went back to the shelf, gathering more objects.

Dhamon pushed the ogre-mage forward, although the big thief was not eager to come close to the curious objects. "What did you find, Ragh?"

"This and that," Ragh said. "I don't know their names. Well, I'm sure a sorcerer would know what to call them. Things. I've found magical things." He started spreading them out. They were carved wooden figurines the size of a child's thumb, and all depicted a woman in flowing robes. "There's a word on the bottom of each one. 'Sabar.' It could be the carver's name. Could be the name of the woman. My fingers tingle, so I'd say they certainly do . . . something magical."

"Well, what?" Dhamon was losing patience. He was running out of time.

The draconian shrugged, looking around until he found a leather pouch. He put the figures in them. "I'll have to figure out what, later." He poked through the rest of the objects, which included an ivory hair ornament, a thick jade ring, which he slipped on his smallest claw, and a collection of a dozen round glass and ceramic globes.

"Okay, take all of those," Dhamon said. "Maybe they'll prove useful." He found another pouch and scooped a handful of dust into it for padding the objects in case they were fragile. "Put them in here, and be careful. I saw Palin with something like those glass beads once. If they're the same things I remember, they burst into fire when they strike something."

Ragh filled the pouch and passed it to Dhamon. "There might be some other things here, too, but I don't know how much time we should spend looking around. And Maldred . . ."

"Ogre!" Dhamon's hand shot out, but Maldred had slipped out of his reach. The ogre-mage stood at a narrow wardrobe, the door of which lay broken on the floor. Inside were musty clothes, but what was on top of the wardrobe intrigued him.

"Can you use a crystal?" Maldred asked. The draconian hurried over, too engrossed to pay attention to where he was walking. He nearly fell through the floor when a tile gave way. Maldred growled and pulled him onto firmer ground.

"Maybe I can figure out how to use it," Maldred said, stretching up to reach the crystal on top of the wardrobe. "I haven't seen one of these in quite a while. An old friend of mine, a healer in Blöten named Grim Kedar, used to have one." He pulled it down reverently and set it carefully on the table.

Dhamon had heard of crystal balls, in fact had seen Palin hunched over one once. This one was much smaller than Palin's, about the size of an orange, and it sat on a base that looked like a miniature jeweled crown. It was the jewels that caught his eye. Even through the cobwebs and dust they shimmered—rubies and jacinths, all set in gold. There was a word in silver filigree, where the base touched the ball—Sabar.

"Again—Sabar," Maldred said, reading it.

"Yes, O Sagacious One," whispered a deep, lyrical voice.

The voice caught them all off guard, and Maldred nearly knocked the ball off its pedestal in his astonishment. "Sabar?" he repeated.

"Yes, O Sagacious One."

He drew his face down to the crystal, seeing wisps of pale lavender weaving themselves into artful designs.

"What kind of a crystal ball is it?" Ragh pressed closer.

Maldred gave a shrug of his broad shoulders.

Dhamon leaned closer too, curious but also impatient to be on their way. He didn't know that the best crystal ball in the world would be of much use to him if he was going to fight the shadow dragon. He thought it would be more worthwhile to continue following Nura's tracks.

Maldred raised his face, then quickly dropped his gaze to the crystal again. "Crystal balls were fashioned by sorcerers long ago to do all sorts of things. Some supposedly looked to the future, but

Grim said that was only a fallacy. Some could be used to look to faraway places. Others might . . ." He looked up, this time deliberately catching Dhamon's stare. "Find lost things."

Dhamon thrust a finger at the crystal. "Use it," he demanded. "Make it find Fiona! Make it find my child. Make it find the shadow dragon!"

"If I can."

"You'd better succeed, ogre." The threat was heavy in Dhamon's voice.

Maldred sighed deeply and steepled his fingers in front of the ball. He closed his eyes and stretched out with his mind, touching the crystal without physically touching it, feeling its cool smoothness, hearing it sing softly with each brush against his skin. Then he felt the lavender wisps, breathing them and smelling their wildflower smell. Intoxicating. A woman appeared in the mists, dressed in robes of dark purple and wearing a tiara similar to that which served as the base of the crystal ball. She looked vaguely like the carvings, beautiful and exotic.

"Sabar," Maldred whispered.

"O Sagacious One, you call and I come to you." The woman bowed her head. "What may my humble self show you?"

Dhamon and Ragh watched in wonder. Maldred's knees trembled as the crystal drew energy from him to work its magic. The woman's complexion brightened as the ogre-mage grew weaker. Her eyes sparkled like perfectly cut emeralds.

"Sabar, show me . . . ." He first wanted to see Blöde, to check on his father's kingdom and the spreading swamp that threatened to consume his native land, but he knew that would have to wait. There would be time for that later, hopefully, when

Dhamon was preoccupied. "The shadow dragon," Maldred said. "The beast which laired in the cave below . . ."

". . . who was unaware of me in this chamber," the woman finished.

"Oh, yes," said Maldred, surprised at this information. "That dragon."

The woman twirled like a dancer, the dark purple of her robes flying out and resembling a spinning flower, stirring the lavender mist and filling the crystal with a swirling purple smoke. There was a flash of green, the winking of her eyes, then the smoke disappeared and a cavern materialized to fill the small globe.

Dhamon and Ragh spoke excitedly, but Maldred pushed their words to the background of his consciousness so he could concentrating on the magic in the globe. The crystal continued to sing to him, and he beseeched it to show him more.

The image in the ball changed, the view shifting inside the cavern, showing parts that were dark but vastly different than the opening of the cave. The stone here was orange and brown and dry. There was no hint of the moss and no standing water. Soon they could see a very large, shadowy dragon stretched out at the back of a high-domed chamber. The dragon's eyes flickered open, and Maldred urged the woman in the crystal ball to pull back. He couldn't risk the chance that the dragon might discover he was being spied on. Magical creatures might somehow be able to use the magic to see who was scrying them.

The image shifted again, showing the exterior of the cave, then showing the mountain in which the cave was nestled.

"Where is this lair?" Maldred asked.

The entire mountain range came into view, then a singular peak, a river tributary in the distance, and a row of spindly trees—distinctive features in the landscape.

"Throt," he said in a strangled voice. "The dragon must be in Throt."

"You can find this place?" Dhamon leaned closer to Maldred. He held onto the tabletop, gazing into the crystal, feeling his knees weaken. Throt was far from here, and he was certain his body would be completely covered with scales long before they reached this other lair. He was certain he would be dead, his soul gone.

"Yes." Maldred sagged on the table. The crystal was sapping his strength.

"And my child. Ask it about my child."

Maldred remembered the scrying pool of the Black Robes that had stolen Fetch's life, and he briefly wondered if this crystal ball would kill him.

"Dhamon's child," Maldred requested.

The woman in the crystal complied, eyes brightening and sapping more of Maldred's strength. She revealed the same village the shadow dragon had showed them on his wall of fog, but it was daylight this time, and there were humans milling about and tending to various ordinary chores. There were a few elves in the mix, and Dhamon spotted Varek, Riki's husband, talking to a young elven man.

"Riki and my child," Dhamon insisted.

Maldred gritted his teeth and asked the crystal again. His mind instantly propelled him through the lavender mist and inside a small building where the silvery-haired half-elf sat in a straight-backed chair, nursing an infant.

Dhamon gripped the table edge harder and stared, wanting to memorize every detail of the baby's face. The innocent he might never see. Unlike him, the child would have a family, a mother and father—even though Varek wasn't the true father.

"Are they safe? Where are the hobgoblins?"

Again Maldred passed this message and his strength to the crystal, and the vision moved to the outskirts of the village where the hobgoblins camped. There weren't quite as many of them, but this time Dhamon spotted three Dark Knights.

"The dragon might have been bluffing me," Dhamon said. He wasn't certain the dragon was allied with the Dark Knights. If that were true, the dragon could have deployed a legion of Knights against Sable, or at least he would have offered to lend a force to accompany Dhamon. "The hobgoblins are with the Dark Knights, not with the shadow dragon."

"So the shadow dragon was lying?" Ragh mused. "He couldn't really threaten your child?"

"Perhaps," Maldred said weakly. "Maybe they're not the dragon's forces, but maybe they have some agreement with the dragon for this dark purpose."

"But they're still alive," Dhamon said. "Riki and my child. Ask—where is this village?"

Maldred entreated the woman in the crystal ball. The village shrank, and now it was as though the watchers were flying above the village.

"This place is also in Throt," Maldred said after a few moments. The vision rose higher above the ground. "In Haltigoth, I think. Many, many miles from the shadow dragon's new lair." He made a move to push away from the table, but Dhamon held him in place, pressing a hand against the center of his back.

"One more thing," Dhamon said. "Ask the crystal ball about Fiona, too."

Maldred gasped, but relented, in part out of his own fondness for the Solamnic Knight. It was true he played a game with her, but he didn't care to see her die out of her madness. He fed the question to the woman in purple, who twirled again as the image changed. This time the lavender wisps paled, then turned white, swirling like clouds. The woman's eyes dimmed and flickered, and the globe showed nothing. "Dead," the ogre-mage said sadly. "Fiona must be dead."

Dhamon slammed his fist on the table, jarring the crystal ball. The spell was broken, Maldred kept the magical artifact from rolling off its crown pedestal.

"It's not your fault," Ragh told Dhamon.

"Sabar," Maldred whispered.

"O Sagacious One, we will meet again." The woman loomed large for just a moment, extended her hands beneficently, and Maldred felt instantly refreshed, all the energy taken from him restored in a rush. The crystal went clear.

"Dead," Dhamon muttered. Fiona, Rig, Fetch, Jasper, Shaon, Raph, and all those others with whom he had served in the Knights of Takhisis. Comrades all dead. Had he acted otherwise at important moments, he probably could have saved each one. To know me is to risk death, Dhamon thought.

But his child would not die, Dhamon wouldn't make any more mistakes.

"We're going to Throt," he announced. "Now. While I can still think. While I'm still in control."

He went through the wardrobe, searching the garments until he found a robe that would fit him, and a pair of leggings. He sliced off the robe so it would hang to just above his knees. The fates knew how sorcerers managed to move about in all this voluminous cloth. He dressed hurriedly and fashioned a bag out of a cloak he cut in two. This he tossed to Maldred.

"For that crystal ball," he said. "We're not leaving it here. We might need it again."

Maldred carefully placed the ball in the makeshift bag and tied it to his belt. He would have an opportunity after all to scry upon Blöde. "All right, Dhamon, we'll go to Throt. We'll do all we can . . . Dhamon!"

Dhamon was doubled over, clutching his stomach, retching. A moment more and he was on his knees, convulsed.

Ragh leveled the great sword at Maldred.

"Don't move. Don't move until Dhamon's up and moving again," the draconian said.

It was a brief episode this time but an agonizing one—long minutes during which Ragh and Maldred watched Dhamon writhe on the ground in pain. The ogre stood without moving all that time, the great sword pointed at his heart. Finally, a shaky Dhamon got to his feet. Without another word between the three of them, the trio carefully left the old sorcery chamber, threaded their way down the staircase and through the rank cavern, then stepped back out into the swamp.

CHAPTER TWELVE
TRAITORS AND
OTHER FRIENDS

iona sat on the bank of the stream, dangling her sword in the water. The sunlight caught the blade and created sparkling motes that rippled along the water's surface, mesmerizing her. The sword was superbly crafted, probably worth more coins than she'd ever possessed. Yet she was angry at the sword, for the magical weapon hadn't deigned to speak to her for several hours.

"Damn Dhamon Grimwulf," she said, looking up and noticing him talking with Ragh and Maldred. "Damn him for everything." She blew the gnats away, then turned the blade so she could observe her acid-scarred reflection in it.

"I look like a monster, every bit as awful as the three of them." She stared at her face, not noticing that the runes along the blade had begun to glow faintly blue. "Worse than a monster."

What you seek, the sword told her, breaking its long silence. The female Knight stood up, feeling the sword tug her away from the stream. *What you seek.*

She glanced once more at her companions—the traitorous ogre-mage, the wingless draconian, and Dhamon, who did not look so far removed from a black spawn himself now. "Monsters, the lot of them." Where was Rig? she wondered.

What you seek.

"Just what do I seek?" Fiona asked the sword.

The female Knight quietly left the clearing, the sword guiding her through a row of young cypress trees, then around a haze-covered bog. It led her almost a mile away. She paused to untangle herself from a vine and glanced over her shoulder. Her companions had evidently not yet noticed her absence.

"What do I seek?" she repeated dully.

Beauty and truth, it replied.

The sword brought her to the edge of a small clearing. There was a blanket of ferns in the center, and a young girl with coppery colored hair sat cross-legged there, her fingers teasing the fronds. The girl looked somehow familiar. Fiona thought she had seen her two or three times before, and in each instance bad things happened, but after all she was just a child, out here all alone, probably afraid, and she awakened Fiona's maternal instincts. The child beckoned Fiona closer.

What you seek.

"Who are you?" Fiona called.

"I am what you seek," the child said.

Fiona knelt next to her, and the little girl ran her hands over Fiona's face. The tiny fingers were warm, and they tingled pleasantly.

"Who are . . . ."

"Magic, Fiona," the child whispered. "I am magic."

Insects flitted around the child and the Solamnic Knight but didn't land on either of them. The child began to hum, a quick tune she interspersed with chirps and clicks. Then her fingers were tugging and pushing at Fiona's curls, tickling her eyelids, smoothing her tunic. When the tune ended, the child rose and motioned to the Knight to follow her.

Her sword sheathed, Fiona took the girl's hand and was led to a clear pond beyond the ferns. The child pointed. Fiona tilted her face for a better look.

"Oh! In the name of Vinus Solamnus!" She saw her own face reflected in the still waters, but this Fiona was unblemished, her eyes clear, and her hair looked freshly combed. She looked younger, too. Perfect. "I am beautiful."

"Of course you are beautiful. I made you so."

Odd, but the little girl didn't have a little girl's voice any longer.

"Rig will be happy to see me so beautiful," Fiona told her.

"Rig can't be happy," the child said flatly. "Rig is dead. Very dead."

Fiona stammered, shaking her head and saying that wasn't true, that Rig had been with her not too long ago.

"Dead. Dead. Dead," the child cooed in a sultry seductress's voice.

"No!" Fiona stepped away, heel catching in a root and falling down. The child stretched out her hands, grabbing her, fingers fluttering over Fiona's face again, magic boring in. This time the fingers didn't soothe. This time they gave her a horrible vision, replaying over and over the events of the night in Shrentak when Dhamon had rescued them from the prison cell beneath the city streets.

Again and again she watched Rig boost her up onto the manticore's back. An arm's length away from her, he was then cut down, his blood spattering her.

"No!" Fiona buried her face in her hands and sobbed. "Oh, please no."

"Dead. Dead. Dead." The child smiled evilly. "And the one who as much as killed him, Dhamon Grimwulf, will be coming to get you soon. Run, Fiona. If he finds you, he'll kill you, too. Run. Run. Run. You mustn't let Dhamon catch you. You must make certain that Dhamon, Maldred, and that wingless Ragh never see you again. Run!"

Nura Bint-Drax turned and ran playfully through the ferns, casting one last look over her shoulder at the Solamnic Knight. "Flee, beautiful Fiona! Rig is dead, and your enemies come for you!"

It was several minutes before Fiona regained some semblance of composure. Trembling, she tried to turn back to where she thought she'd left her companions. "I must tell them about the strange child and . . ."

"Fiona!" Maldred called.

The lying ogre.

"Fiona!"

Dhamon must be with him. Now Ragh was calling for her, too.

"Fiona! Where are you?" Maldred's voice again.

"Fiona!" shouted Dhamon.

"Oh, Rig," Fiona cried. "Rig, you are dead, and your murderer calls to me."

Relying on all the skills she'd learned in the Solamnic Knights, she turned and ran, managing to elude her pursuers until dark, when they finally stopped looking for her. When they resumed searching for her the next day, she was already farther away and successfully hid her tracks. She crept close to watch them from time to time, giggling at their foolishness but constantly moving when they neared again. She took great pains to cover her tracks so that even the expert tracker Dhamon wouldn't have a clue as to her whereabouts.

Finally the three enemies gave up. Finally they headed east.

"I'm safe," Fiona said to herself. As the little girl had been when Fiona found her in the clearing, the female Knight was all alone.

◇ ◇ ◇ ◇ ◇ ◇ ◇

The child sat on a mountainous rocky ledge, feet dangling over the side and legs idly kicking. She was a few hundred feet above a winding trail, looking down on a small merchant caravan and debating whether she should pay them a visit in her Ergothian seductress guise. There might be something inside one of their wagons that would please her master, and perhaps something that might also please her.

The shadow dragon lay deep inside the mountain, sleeping. He had been sleeping more than usual, his waking intervals shorter. Late yesterday afternoon, he spoke to her only briefly before he fell into one of his fitful slumbers that sent tremors through the chain. It was twilight now, and he still hadn't awoken.

She watched the wagons until they disappeared from sight, wondering if she had allowed an exotic, tasty morsel or an especially pretty bauble to elude her. She watched as the sky darkened and the stars slowly winked into view. Everything here in Throt was dry and boring. The craggy brown mountains looked like the spine of some massive, dead beast. The air smelled like . . . nothing. No hint of rain. Nura missed the damp and suffocating warmth of the swamp with its tang of rotting vegetation and assortment of hideous and beautiful beasts. There were birds here, but so little variety to them, all blacks and browns, all with the same annoying chirp. There were lizards—small ones with curly tails, but most of them the drab color of the mountains. Nothing tasty about them.

If Dhamon had not been so seditious, she and the shadow dragon would still be basking in the glorious swamp. If Maldred had been more trustworthy . . . if only she had anticipated that there would be a problem with that fool.

She brooded about Maldred until the sky lightened and the rocks shuddered beneath her. She jumped to her feet, ran to a wide slash in the mountain. Standing just inside of the opening, she shed her child image and slithered inside the dusty cave as the snake Nura Bint-Drax.

There was scant luster left on the dragon's scales, and he looked more gray than black.

"Master," she intoned. "I live to serve you." Nura Bint-Drax coiled low in front of the shadow dragon, not daring to move again until she felt the ground rumble in response. Then she raised herself high, resting back on her tail, hood flaring far back and eyes wide with pleasure. "Your plan is working? Tell me, master." Nura didn't try to conceal her excitement. "You expected all this. You anticipated it. It is all part of your plan to force Dhamon Grimwulf to slay Sable?"

The dragon shook his massive head, barbels thrumming across the floor. His breath quickened, and the breeze from it struck Nura hot in the face.

"Not exactly. I have discovered another way to produce the energy I need to live," the dragon said.

Nura Bint-Drax slithered back a respectful distance, able to see more of the beautiful shadow dragon from this safer vantage point. This cave was not so dark as the one in the swamp, and that was the only good thing about it as far as she was concerned. She could get a better view of the shadow dragon.

"Khellendros, called Skie by men," the shadow dragon began. "He once tried to craft a body for his love, Kitiara. Word among the dragons was he initially hoped to place her spirit in the body of a blue spawn. When that failed, he tried to rob Malys of her soul, intending to let Kitiara step into the body of the Red."

The snake-woman's eyes sparkled in fascination. "More, master. Tell me more." Such tales, known only by dragons, were what Nura lived for.

"Khellendros might have succeeded, had things fallen into place properly. But I will succeed with Dhamon Grimwulf. I will not make Khellendros's mistakes."

"I don't understand." Nura Bint-Drax furrowed her brow, thinking. Dhamon was supposed to kill Sable, so the shadow dragon, whose physical form was dying, could use his magic to transfer his spirit inside the Black's body.

"You forget, I can hear your thoughts," the dragon rumbled with a rare chuckle. The dragon stretched as much as was comfortable within the confines of the cave, drawing a talon out toward the naga and scratching at the stony floor. "No, that was never the intent, Nura Bint-Drax. Dhamon . . . and the others I was cultivating . . . the best specimen was going to house my spirit when this body deteriorated. Dhamon has proven the strongest. He has adapted best to my magic. He is the one."

"But Sable . . .?" The bewilderment was clear on her face.

"Sable was always just a means to an end. I intended to use the energy released from the over-lord's death to help power my spell. I am dying, Nura Bint-Drax. Living inside Dhamon's shell is my best recourse."

She gasped. "So it is Dhamon's body that will save you!"

"Yes."

"Your spirit will displace his."

The dragon gave a slight nod. "Energy from the god Chaos birthed me, and energy from the drag-ons' deaths in the Abyss nurtured me. Magic expended from the deaths during the dragonpurge strengthened me. And now . . ."

"I see. The energy from Sable's death will help you live in the body of Dhamon Grimwulf." Nura searched the dragon's visage and saw her reflection in its dull eyes. She hung her head ruefully. "I would have gladly housed your spirit, master," she said. "I would have gladly—"

"I know," the shadow dragon returned, "but you are more valuable, to me, and to this world. Dhamon can be sacrificed."

This pleased the naga, and she glided forward to caress the shadow dragon's jaw. "Tell me more, please," she entreated. "What are your plans? What should I do? What must we do to Dhamon Grimwulf?"

"At the moment, protect him."

The shadow dragon briefly closed his eyes, and

she feared he would fall into a deep sleep again, but he merely was taking pleasure from her ministrations. After a few moments his eyes again bathed the cave with their dull yellow glow.

"There is some interesting magic in the ogremage Maldred," the dragon said, "and in the weapons he and Dhamon carry. There is magic in the wingless sivak. The deaths of Maldred and the sivak should release the necessary energy, combined with the destruction of enchanted trinkets I have gathered since the Chaos War."

"Will that be enough?" Nura Bint-Drax asked skeptically.

"Not so much as the magic that beats in Sable's heart," the dragon quickly returned, its words sending more tremors through the rock. "But I only half-expected Dhamon to slay Sable. I had to buy time until his body was ready for my spirit. The magic will have to be enough. Meanwhile we will gather more to be certain."

"Oh, I see. How very clever, master. We will begin with the horde hidden away in the Knights of Neraka's stronghold in the Dargaard Mountains!" Nura had wondered why, when first they arrived in Throt, the shadow dragon had asked her to capture a Knight from those mountains and bring him to this cave.

"Yes. From that stronghold. The Knight has . . . told me of their vault."

"Will it be difficult to obtain, master?"

"Not for you, my Nura."

◇ ◇ ◇ ◇ ◇ ◇ ◇

They left the following evening, when dusk overtook Throt and before the stars came out in the sky. The dragon looked like a dark rain cloud moving swiftly with the wind. Nura rode on his back in her Ergothian female form. It wasn't her favorite guise, but at times it well suited her purpose, and the human arms and legs were useful in gripping the dragon's neck. It felt cold this high above the earth, and Nura endured no little measure of unaccustomed discomfort. She found herself wishing for the frail human trappings of furs.

It took them three days of travel, for when the sun rose each day the shadow dragon had to seek refuge from the light. Once they were fortunate to find a big enough cave. On the other days the shadow dragon used its magic to hollow out the earth at the base of hillsides, creating a makeshift lair more like a pit. Nura stood watch during the brightest daylight, encountering people only once—a band of scouts for a Dark Knight company. She dispatched them quickly, confident that the company would march elsewhere when the scouts failed to report.

Food was scarce, but Nura was able to use her magic to snare a half-dozen wild pigs. The shadow dragon ate these only at her urging, as he was so obsessed with his mission he thought little of his own needs.

On the third day, in the quiet hour before midnight when even the nightbirds and nocturnal beasts seem to melt away, they descended near the keep of the Knights of Takhisis.

The moonlight showed that the place was well guarded. Knights patrolled the barren, hardscrabble ground where the keep was wedged into the base of the Dargaards. A Dark Knight sorcerer was stationed on a crenelated portion between two archers, and there were certainly other guards whom they could not spot.

"You are right. It should not be difficult at all, master." Nura stood back from the keep, arranging her scant clothes and fussing with her hair—the way she'd seen human women do in every town she'd visited. When she was certain her looks would please the men, she nodded to the dragon. "Ready, master."

The naga gazed rapturously at the shadow dragon as her master drew a symbol in the ground with a shadowy talon. It was part of a spell it had learned from one of its first minions, a sorcerer who did not take to its scales as easily as Dhamon and who died when the dragon tried to force its magic. There were words to the enchantment, but the shadow dragon simply chanted them in its head, thought of Nura and their magical link, and slowly folded in on itself.

As the spell took effect, the dragon began to deflate, became flat, like a piece of cloth cut from the night sky. Then the strange cloth shaped itself and flowed like oil, running across the ground until it brushed Nura's heel.

As the spell finished, the dragon became Nura's shadow, moving alongside her unnoticed as she approached the gate. The guards stopped her, of course, but they were not overly alarmed, as she made it clear to them she was alone and carried no weapons. The mage on the parapet could find nothing untoward about her. The dragon's magic blocked the humans' pathetic attempts to scry beyond her Ergothian facade.

She was ushered in to see the commander, whose name she'd learned from the Knight of Neraka she'd caught days ago. She was announced as a comely gift from a local warlord. Her sexy appearance had been enhanced with a suggestive spell for good measure. She was taken to the commander's chambers. There she silently killed him, minutes after the door closed—and minutes after the shadow dragon wormed from the man's mind how to slip into the vaults below.

It was almost too easy. On another night, Nura might have tripped a glyph or other magical alarm just so she could have the fun of battling some of the keep's forces, but fun would have to wait for a more propitious time. Tonight it was important to get what they came for and leave without incident.

She gathered the pick of the lot, concentrating on those items that were small and concentrated in energy and felt to her touch to have the most arcane magic in them. Mostly these were rings and other bits of jewelry that she could fasten to herself. She found an exquisite leather backpack—itself cleverly enchanted—and filled it with magical goblets and daggers, one of which contained a spell that burned her fingers; collars and a stunted candle holder; boxes of incense and small vials filled with swirling multicolored oils. She and her shadow passed over items overly large or with too little enchantment to be of value.

They left without ceremony. Nura called upon a simple spell of her own to transport her and her shadow dozens of yards safely away from the keep. Nura was so giddy from her unusual escapade with the shadow dragon, that she vowed to find another such stronghold as soon as possible to share another shadow spell.

"And Dhamon Grimwulf thought he was such a good thief!" she exclaimed, as she climbed upon the shadow dragon's back and gripped his neck.

"Dhamon must be kept safe," the shadow dragon reminded her, as he leapt into the night sky and headed back to his new lair. "He is searching for us even now, Nura Bint-Drax. Find him first and make sure no harm comes to him. Indeed every day I feel more strongly that he is the one. He is my last chance."

CHAPTER THIRTEEN
REUNION IN BLOOD

"Do you really think this raft is going to hold all of us?" Ragh was helping to wrap twine around a dozen thin logs they'd lashed together, his stubby claws fumbling at the task. "I'm pretty heavy, and Maldred's . . ."

"Aye, I know. The ogre's no lightweight," Dhamon said. "No, I don't *know* that this raft will hold us. But all of us can't damn well swim. We have to try something."

Ragh gave him a skeptical look, remembering the incident at sea during the storm. "You're mad, my friend."

He helped push the makeshift vessel out onto the river and cautiously climbed aboard, setting his great sword carefully down in front of him. The raft didn't sink when Maldred and Dhamon joined him, but it rested low in the water, tilting precariously in whichever direction someone leaned. Ragh kept a claw on the sword's pommel so he could hold onto the weapon in case it started to slide off.

Ragh had suggested they walk to the coast, but Dhamon said travel across the overgrown land was impossibly slow, and he needed to get to Throt as quickly as possible. Ever since he'd given up on finding Fiona, and seen the vision of the shadow dragon in the crystal ball, Dhamon had pushed them to take risks. Not one of the three had slept a wink in the past twenty-four hours, but only Dhamon looked alive, alert.

"We could still march to the coast, take shortcuts and . . ." Ragh swallowed the rest of his words as the wind blew away the edges of Dhamon's hood. The draconian noticed the right side of Dhamon's face was almost completely covered in small, black scales, and only a patch on his neck was still flesh. Dhamon's hands were completely covered, too. The old sorcerer's garment he was wearing hid most of it from prying eyes.

"No, we're taking this raft." Dhamon stood grimly at the back, using the haft of the glaive to pole the raft along in the shallows. The draconian had to admit they were moving considerably faster than would have been possible if they were trudging through the thick grass.

Ragh looked to the east, his interest caught by a trio of lounging crocodiles and the cloud of flies that haloed them. "But this raft won't make it across the New Sea, you have to admit. It might not even make it *to* the New Sea."

"No, this raft won't, but a ferry will," Maldred interjected. "That's what you're counting on, isn't it, Dhamon? Finding a ferry along the coast?"

That was indeed Dhamon's plan, but he didn't bother to nod to the ogre-mage. He was scanning the river ahead, the thick foliage on both sides. He was thinking about the baby he had seen in Riki's arms in the crystal ball vision and wondering if it was a boy or a girl and if in some small way its looks favored him. He used to be good-looking, he mused, before these terrible scales began to spread. At least the child would have a family life with Riki and Varek, something Dhamon unfortunately had been deprived of, as far as he knew. Funny, he could remember almost nothing of his boyhood, couldn't recall his own mother and father—probably he was an orphan.

"If I can make it safe for them, the child will have a good home," he murmured.

"What did you say, Dhamon?"

"Nothing, ogre."

Maldred gave a great sigh, hung his head. Within a few moments, he was asleep.

Dhamon couldn't afford to rest. He wasn't hungry either, and his forced pace hadn't allowed his companions any time to eat. They could eat later. Perhaps he'd want food later, too. He didn't need much rest anymore, or much food. His senses were keen, his strength remarkable. It was amazing what little it took to sustain him.

Most of the time he felt stronger than ever, bristling with energy. By the same token, every inch of him dully ached! He was nauseated half the time, and the other half his head throbbed. His feet hurt always, as they were growing and straining the limits of his boots. Damn the shadow dragon! he cursed inwardly with each breath. Thankfully the sleeves were long on this old sorcerer's robe and helped to conceal his ugly form. When he came upon Riki and the child, he didn't want them to see what was happening to him. If only I see them while there is still something human about me, he thought.

He knew Ragh stole glances at him, as they followed the winding river under a waning sun. Dhamon was determined not to let the draconian know he was suffering from the shadow dragon's magic, so he spent his time looking at everything but his two passengers. The view of the Black's land was better from the river, and he imagined he might actually enjoy the journey were the circumstances different. The leaves of the cypress trees were a vivid emerald and decorated with colorful parrots, their long tails looking like ribbons tied to the branches. Though they were some distance away, he could see the fine detail on the birds, and hear their soft whistles. Their noise ebbed and flowed and at times added to the pounding in his head. He could make out the very edges and veins of the leaves, and hear their rustling, hear the little waves lapping against the raft, against the bank, hear unseen animals pattering through the brush, and by the sounds they made he guessed at what kinds of animals they were. He heard the snarl of a panther, the soft step of a deer, the growl of . . . something that wasn't a normal creature.

He pulled the glaive haft from the water and peered cautiously to his right. Not enough racket for a dragon, too much for a spawn or draconian. The creature growled again.

"What is it, Dhamon?" Ragh was staring to the right also, careful not to rock the raft and furious when Maldred woke up, leaned over, and nearly upset all of them.

Dhamon saw a branch move. It was inland from the river by better than three dozen yards. Probably nothing to be concerned with, but somehow he could see very well at that distance, even through tiny gaps in the dense foliage, and so he continued to stare. A large, scaly green hand shifted the branch. He made out the olive-hued torso of a lizard creature, a spear held in one of its clawed hands. A lizardman? No, he thought after more scrutiny. Too large, its scales were more pronounced. He couldn't see all of the beast, only tantalizing parts, but after a moment he was able to figure out just what it was.

"A bakali," he growled low. "A stinking bakali."

Bakali were an ancient race and at one time were thought extinct. Better for all concerned if all the bakali were dead, Dhamon thought. Though cunning, bakali were not especially bright, though they were strong and brutal, and they tended to serve whatever master offered the best rewards. There were small, scattered tribes of them in the Black's land, and Dhamon knew from encountering a hunting party a few years ago that at least some of them worked for Sable. This bakali was by itself, probably looking for something to eat. The way it was slinking, it was stalking something.

"Not my concern." He started poling the raft again, a little more slowly, watching the creature out of curiosity. Then he saw that it wasn't alone after all. There were at least three more bakali—a small force, nothing that could deter him. His heart skipped a beat a few moments later when his extraordinary vision revealed just what they were stalking.

"Ragh," Dhamon spoke softly, though he knew the bakali were unaware of the three of them on the raft, and certainly couldn't hear them at this distance. "There's Fiona."

This time Ragh's surprised reaction almost upset the raft. "The Solamnic? She's not dead?"

"Not yet," Dhamon commented drily, "but it looks like some big, ugly bakali are trying to change that." Although Dhamon, equally surprised to see the Knight, was glad Fiona was alive, he also felt resentful that she had reappeared now to delay his trip. "Damn it all." He was determined to keep her from ending up in the bakali's stomachs, however.

Had she managed to find their tracks and was following them for some reason? He hurriedly poled the raft toward the shore, indicating with a finger to his lips that the draconian and Maldred should keep quiet. He gestured toward the bakali, though he had lost sight of Fiona. He concentrated, trying to pick through the sounds of the swamp.

The sounds intensified. The ruckus from the birds and other unseen creatures grew eerily louder, though the animals apparently weren't coming closer. All of the sounds were becoming annoyingly indistinguishable to Dhamon's supersensitive ears.

"Ragh, stay here and watch the ogre. Keep your eyes open for trouble."

Ragh and Maldred obviously hadn't noticed a change in the sounds of the swamp. Ragh . . . Dhamon could hear the draconian's raspy breathing a little too clearly, could hear Ragh's heart beat, hear Maldred's too—it beat slower and louder than his own or Ragh's.

"You'll need help." The draconian spoke softly, Dhamon knew, but it sounded like a shout to his ears.

Dhamon shook his head. "Small stuff. I certainly can handle four bakali by myself." Even his own words sounded booming in his ears. "Watch the ogre, I say. We can't afford to let him get away and warn the shadow dragon." He tugged a corner of the raft onto the shore to anchor it, then, shouldering the glaive, he headed inland.

Matters swiftly grew worse as he disappeared through the trees and out of sight of the raft. The sounds of the morass quickly became overwhelming, practically deafening. The drone of the insects and chatter of the birds was almost vicious, the rustling of the leaves resounding. Dhamon staggered and dropped the glaive to throw his hands over his ears. It didn't help. A big cat snarled, the sound like a mighty roar. The river rolled by, sloshing thunderously against the bank wells. He slammed his teeth together and threw his head back. How could he help Fiona when he couldn't help himself? What by the names of all the vanished gods was happening to him now?

"Ragh," he gasped, wanting to tell the draconian to go after Fiona in his stead. Was he speaking loud enough? Could the draconian hear him? He shouted the draconian's name now, the single word like a dagger thrust into his ears. Parrots screeched overhead, adding to the agony. The chitter of the insects swelled impossibly, slender branches rubbed against each other and echoed brutally in his head.

He heard his heart pounding, thought he heard the blood rushing through his veins in rhythm with the river. His breath sounded like powerful gusts of wind.

"Quiet," he prayed. "Fiona. I have to help Fiona. Everything needs to be quiet." Amazingly, in the next breath the cacophony lessened, startling him. Athough still loud, it was no longer earsplitting, and he could think. Quiet. Please, please, make it quiet. Centering his thoughts on that one idea, he discovered that he could diminish some of the individual sounds—though it took some effort. He concentrated more intensely until all the noises lessened and became bearable.

His hearing restored, he retrieved the glaive and plodded forward. With each step he felt better. He listened for the hisses and growls of the bakali. He was able to pinpoint these noises, bringing them to the fore, then he heard something else—the hiss of steel, a sword being drawn, a feminine intake of breath. Peering through the giant blooms of lianas, Dhamon spotted Fiona in a fighting stance in a small, mossy clearing.

There was something different about her, he immediately thought. Something . . . her face! The acid scars were gone. The hair that had melted away had returned. That shouldn't be! Worry over that later, he told himself. Worry about the bakali now.

She was closing in defiantly on a towering bakali. The creature, looking like a cross between a man and a crocodile, with spiky ridges and armor-like hide, was easily eight feet tall. Slavering jaws clacked as it darted in, bone club held high.

Three others, armed with large bone clubs, were grouped on the side of the clearing closest to himself. Dhamon stepped out into the open, readied the glaive, and rushed at them.

Although the bakli seemed utterly reptilian with thick hides, they walked on two legs and had their own language like men. One of the three had a thicker brow, another's hide was brighter, looking the shade of trillium leaves, and the last had narrow shoulders and incongruously thick forearms. Otherwise they looked remarkably similar—ugly.

All of them had wicked-looking claws and narrowing eyes that locked fiercely onto Dhamon.

In a half-dozen long strides he reached the lead bakali, drew the glaive back and swung it hard in front of him. The creature snarled curses in its ancient tongue and raised its bone club high, but it never got the chance to use its primitive weapon. The axe-like blade of the glaive clove through the bakali's chest, practically cutting it in two. The two other creatures hesitated, then as Dhamon continued his charge, the smaller one turned and fled. Within a heartbeat, the laggard met the same fate as the first bakali.

Behind him, Dhamon could here the *thunk* of Fiona's sword against the hide of the biggest bakali. He paused and sniffed the air, smelling the blood leaking from the two he'd just slain and the one Fiona had obviously wounded. The smaller bakali was heading toward twin shaggybarks at the far end of the clearing, and Dhamon had to stop it before it could call for any others that might be nearby. This creature had a slightly different odor. Perhaps it was carrying an unguent or perhaps it was a female in cycle.

Just as Dhamon reached the shaggybarks the bakali jumped out between the two trees and hurled something at him. Three silvery shards flashed at him like shooting stars. Dhamon veered, but too late. All three found their mark, two in his stomach, one in his shoulder. They were metal barbs that dug through his sorcerer's robes and bit into his flesh.

As Dhamon darted around the largest tree, the bakali hurled three more of the metal barbs at him, striking with accuracy. Dhamon howled in pain as he raised both hands over his head, bringing the glaive down for a killing blow. The bakali had turned, but the blade clove its back before it could take more than a couple of steps.

Dhamon tugged the glaive free, seeing the bakali was mortally wounded, pathetically clawing at the ground in a useless attempt to escape. He ended its misery.

Then he loped back toward Fiona, who seemed to be losing ground in her fight. He smelled human blood now—hers, his own—and something else. It was a biting scent he couldn't identify, but one similar to that emanating from the small bakali.

He sniffed, and his pace involuntarily slowed, legs feeling suddenly heavy. Curiously, the constant ache in his limbs had lessened. He was starting to feel numb.

"Poison." Shouldering the glaive, Dhamon frantically plucked at the several metal barbs stuck in him. The odd smell was some sort of poison. He noted a residue of white paste on the sharp tips as he pulled them out, one by one, and tossed them away.

"Damn it all," he muttered. Dhamon forced himself to keep moving, though he felt overcome with sluggishness. He could tell his heart had slowed. He could call for Ragh again, though he knew the raft was probably too far away. "Damn the dragon and damn me." The poison made him groggy, but he guessed it wouldn't kill him.

A few steps more and he was at Fiona's side. He dazedly noted where the bakali had raked her left arm. Fiona barely nodded at him. She was faltering. Fatigue, he decided, or maybe more poison. Tired and wounded, she was losing her fight with the bakali.

Dhamon stepped between her and her foe and took a high grip on his weapon.

"Foul beast," he cursed. He thrust forward with the glaive, ramming the tip of the blade into the bakali's stomach. The lizard-creature swung back wildly, grazing him with its claws.

"Again," Dhamon told himself, summoning all his energy to swing a second time at the determined creature. This hit cut deeper and made the thing yowl. Worry spread across its reptilian visage. Glancing over its scaly shoulder, the bakali saw the fate of its companions.

The bakali chattered at Dhamon as it backed away, working hard to stay beyond the reach of the glaive. Dhamon couldn't understand what the beast was saying, probably in its native language. Probably it was pleading for its life. Dhamon could smell the stench of its fear. He could taste its fear. Shuddering at the disturbing sensation, Dhamon forced his heavy limbs to move just a little quicker so he could end this struggle.

"You ssshould hunt creatures with four legsss, not two," he told it. His words were slurred and his tongue thick, but he found his heart beating a little faster from the excitement. He heard Fiona creep up behind him, and he heard her take a deep breath just as he swung hard, putting all his strength behind this final blow. The blade parted the bakali's thick flesh like parchment, and the creature's black blood splattered Dhamon. A second swing took the creature's head off, and at that very moment Fiona acted. She thrust her enchanted blade deep into Dhamon's back.

Dhamon screamed at the shock and pain, dropping his weapon even as the female knight pulled her sword out of him for a second blow. He stumbled around, took a step back and tried to retrieve his weapon, but he wasn't fast enough. Fiona circled in the opposite direction, slashing at him from the side, the blade sliding between his ribs. Either of her blows would have killed a normal man, but Dhamon's extraordinary strength kept him on his feet. Fiona shouted her frustration. Her third swing had more thrust and caught him in the legs. He fell to his knees and flailed forward, trying to knock her sword away.

It was her madness that was causing this betrayal, he knew, and it was the poison in him that was keeping him from a proper counterattack.

"Fiona, it'sss me, Dhamon! Ssstop!"

His shout was slurred, although it would take more than volume to reach some part of her mind that might still be sane. Dhamon shouted again, more weakly. He barely managed to dodge beneath her next swing, and the next. "Ragh!" he cried. "Ragh!"

"Call for your wingless pet all you like," Fiona sneered. "I'll kill him, too."

Dhamon had stood up to draconians, spawn, dragons, and survived all of them. How could he die now, the victim of someone who, in his righteous days, he considered a friend? Move! he told himself. Get clear, talk some sense into her. Get the glaive. Get help. Help!

He felt the warm stickiness of his blood on his back and side, blood running down his leg. The coppery scent of it grew strong. He guessed her blade had broken his ribs. "Fiona," he pleaded. "It'sss me. Dhamon. Remember? Ssstop, or you'll kill me."

She bared her teeth but stayed her next blow. There was a tempest in her eyes—eyes seething out of control. He felt an uncharacteristic tug of fear at that look.

"It'sss me, Dhamon."

"Of course I know who you are!" Her words came fast and hard, like lightning and thunder from the storm inside her. "I know! The mighty Dhamon Grimwulf—failed Dark Knight, failed champion of Goldmoon. Failed. Failed. Failed. The only thing you're successful at is killing people. Killing your friends. By the memory of Vinus Solamnus, Dhamon, I will kill you!"

She darted in, and this time it took all his luck to stay out of her reach. He brought his arms up defensively, but hadn't the strength anymore to evade her blows. The blood he'd lost and the poison that was coursing through him were taking a heavy toll.

"Rig's dead, Dhamon," she said bitterly. Fiona lunged, her blade solidly striking his arm and sending a few scales flying. She was toying with him now—confident she had him and drawing out the end to her own satisfaction. "Rig's dead, and you killed him!"

Dhamon shook his head, somehow managed to fight his way to his feet. Dizzy, he nearly pitched forward but squared his shoulders and jumped back just in time. She'd have run him through with her fierce swing. He held a hand. "I didn't kill Rig, Fiona, I . . ."

"Liar!" She swung her long sword at waist-level now, piercing Dhamon's robes and drawing another line of blood. "Monster!" she howled, spying the scales on his stomach. "Spawn! You killed Rig as surely as if you'd plunged the blade in his heart. You took us—took him—from the dungeons, but you didn't do anything to save him."

"Fiona, listen . . ."

"We were abandoned in Shrentak, Rig and me. You didn't care what happened to us. Not you, not your lying ogre friend. You killed Rig, Dhamon Grimwulf, just like you killed everyone else who got too close to you." The female Knight lunged again, slashing at him, still toying with him, Dhamon knew. He didn't have the strength anymore.

He dropped to his knees.

"Praying, Dhamon?" Fiona taunted. "Are you praying to the gods to be saved?" She tossed back her head and laughed. "Well, the gods aren't in this accursed swamp, Dhamon. It's just you and me, and I'm not going to save you. I'm going to kill you."

Dhamon didn't fear death. At times he'd wished for it. But if he was dead he would never meet his child. He would never be able to help Rikali. *Ragh!* He opened his mouth, but nothing came out. *Help!* There was a sour taste on his tongue, which he recognized as the poison mixed with his blood.

"First it was Shaon," Fiona spat. She paced around him. "She was Rig's first love, you know. He told me all about her—someone I would have liked, I think. Oh, you'll say you didn't kill her, either, that you weren't responsible, but she died to the blue dragon you rode when you were a Knight of Takhisis, didn't she? Shaon wouldn't have died if you hadn't brought her into contact with that dragon."

It was getting difficult to hear Fiona, all he heard was a rushing noise, like a crashing wave filling his ears. Was it his blood pumping? His heart trying to beat? No, he heard his heart faltering. Did his child in some small way favor him?

"Next it was Goldmoon. Wait. You didn't kill her, did you, Dhamon? You only tried to—with that weapon over there, the one lying on the ground. You gave it to Rig, all red with Gold-moon's blood. Didn't want it anymore because it wasn't good enough? Not good enough at killing? Didn't want it because you weren't able to slay Goldmoon with it?"

With her foot, she nudged the haft of the glaive away from Dhamon. "Want to see if it's good enough now? Want to try to kill me with it? OK, pick it up."

Dhamon shook his head. He willed his fingers to reach for the weapon.

"Then it was Jasper. Sorry, you didn't thrust a blade into his heart either, did you? But you might as well have. He was with you—we all were with you—at the Window to the Stars. We were united against the overlords, intending to stop the new Takhisis from being born. Oh, we were very right-eous! Jasper died there, at the claws of a dragon, died because you led us all to that fateful spot." This time she nudged the haft against his leg. "Pick it up." She raised her voice, spitting each word. "And Fetch. From what Rig told me you killed the poor kobold, too. You forced him to use Black Robe magic until it sucked the life out of him. My beloved Rig had his life sucked away because of you too!"

All at once Fiona looked odd to Dhamon, hazy, like a chalk drawing running in the rain. All the edges were soft, her voice blurry. He couldn't hear his heart anymore, no birds or animals, no rushing in his ear. He sensed she was yelling from the expression on her face, but he heard only whis-pers—her voice and . . . Ragh's?

"Murderer. You killed Rig! You killed them all."

He caught a glimpse of something sparkling red, moving against the orange sky. It was his blood on the edge of Fiona's sword, and the blade was driving down again. Dhamon waited for oblivion.

"I tried to stop Maldred." Ragh's whispery-hoarse voice. "I tried to . . . Dhamon!"

Fiona's blade coming down. Chalk running in rain. Dhamon pitched onto his back and watched a streak of intense blue wash all the chalk away.

The streak was Maldred, though Dhamon was beyond knowing any reality. The ogre-mage hurtled over Dhamon and collided with Fiona, throwing the surprised Knight off-balance. His elbow slammed into her jaw. His fingers closed over the crosspiece of the sword and yanked it from her grip, then he tossed it beyond her reach.

Maldred looked to Ragh.

"She cut him pretty bad," the draconian answered. He leaned over Dhamon, palm pressed against a wound on his side, trying to stop the blood. "I thought you were trying to fool me, ogre, when you said you heard Dhamon calling for me. I thought you were just trying to get away."

Maldred didn't reply, but glanced at Fiona to make sure the Knight wasn't moving—he'd hit her soundly enough. "By my father, she did nearly kill him."

"Nearly?" Ragh shook his head. "Look at all this blood. I'd say she accomplished the task. He's dead, ogre. His body just doesn't know it yet. Look at all this blood."

The draconian's hands were covered, the ground was soaked, and Dhamon's robe was dark with blood. Maldred gingerly turned Dhamon over and saw the wound on his back.

"There's more blood on the ground than there is inside him," Ragh said, as he tried to stop the bleeding.

"What you're doing, it's not good enough," Maldred told the draconian. "Dhamon's a healer of sorts. He told me he was one time a battlefield medic with the Dark Knights. I picked up a few things from him, and from an ogre healer, Grim Kedar.

"Get me some moss, and hurry," Maldred continued. "Whatever you can find. Some roots—from three-leaved flowers, the purple and white ones that grow close to the ground. Make sure you don't break the roots. I need the sap that's in them."

Maldred ripped strips from Dhamon's robe, using them to staunch some of the bleeding. His eyes followed the draconian, who had scooped up the two-handed sword and the glaive, awkwardly carrying both while searching around the bases of small shaggybarks. "You'll make faster time without those," Maldred called. "I won't try to take them. I wouldn't need weapons to kill you." Then he turned back to Dhamon.

"I'm not a healer, dear friend," he said, knowing full well Dhamon couldn't hear him, "but I watched Grim often enough, and the old one taught me a few things. I'll try to save you. . . ."

The ogre-mage hummed from deep in his throat. There was no discernible pattern to the melody, nor did it sound pleasant or all that musical, but Maldred kept at it, concentrating on his humming, and all the while he continued to press on the wounds.

"Watch Fiona," the ogre-mage said, briefly interrupting his magic when Ragh returned with the moss and a couple of roots. "She's starting to come around. Sit on her if you have to. I can't deal with her and Dhamon both, and he's obviously the priority."

The draconian frowned, clearly not liking to be ordered around, but he thrust that irritation aside and complied. He didn't have to sit on Fiona. She was still groggy from colliding with Maldred, trying to raise herself up on her elbows and failing. She blinked and rolled her head from side to side, looking up at Ragh and moaning piteously.

"Did I kill Dhamon?" she asked.

Ragh looked over his shoulder at Maldred. "Maybe," he said. He shivered when her eyes brightened and she smiled.

"Ugly song," she commented.

Maldred's tune continued for a long time: until twilight, until he nearly lost his voice. "Dhamon should be dead, but . . ." he murmured at one point, his voice as raspy as the draconian's.

"But . . ." The draconian waited, glancing back and forth between Fiona, who had been permitted to sit up, and Dhamon, who still lay unconscious and pale. In Ragh's arms were cradled the glaive, the great sword, and Fiona's bloodied long sword, which he'd retrieved.

"But he's alive," Maldred returned. "He's a long way from healthy, though I think he's going to make it. He's lost too much blood, and a couple of ribs are broken. I'd like to get him to a real healer."

"We'll have to settle for getting him back to the raft right now," Ragh said. "I'd rather be on the river at night than around this part of the swamp." He prodded Fiona to her feet and nodded toward the river. "I wish I knew what to do with her."

Maldred snorted. "We'll take her along until Dhamon comes to and decides."

"Dhamon Grimwulf will kill me," Fiona spat, "as he kills everyone who gets close to him. As he'll kill both of you some day." Then she grudgingly struck off toward the river. She caught Ragh's cold look. "You'll agree it's too bad I didn't kill him."

"Yes, too bad," Ragh said softly. "Better that Dhamon die, than become a misshapen monster like me."

Fiona smiled.

"Move, Knight!" Ragh snapped, "and your weight damn well better not make the raft sink. I refuse to swim across the New Sea."

◊ ◊ ◊ ◊ ◊ ◊ ◊

The raft tipped dangerously with Fiona's added weight. Ragh tore strips from her tunic to tie her hands behind her, and he ordered Maldred to watch her. However, the ogre-mage had to pay more attention to Dhamon, who was feverish and delirious.

As Dhamon had done, Ragh used the haft of the glaive to pole them along the shallow side of the river. The moon showed the way and provided enough light for him to nervously watch his charges. "Why in honor of the Dark Queen's brood am I doing this?" he muttered. " I could be away, safe somewhere, away from the demented Knight and this treacherous ogre. Away from Dhamon, who might be better off dead."

Dhamon twitched, beads of sweat glistened on his forehead, which still showed mostly human skin. Underneath bandages dark with blood his scales gleamed. As Ragh watched him, he saw a small patch of skin on Dhamon's jaw darken and bubble. The area, about the size of a small coin, swelled and took on a dark sheen, became a scale.

"It's my fault," Ragh muttered. On their first expedition to Shrentak, he had gone into the city with Dhamon, to the old sage's laboratory. Dhamon had sought a cure from the old crone and fell unconscious during his suffering from the scale. Dhamon never realized the old crone's cure was working. While he was unconscious she had demanded as a price for the cure that Ragh stay with her as her dutiful pet. Ragh took offense and killed her, hiding her body when Dhamon woke up, telling Dhamon she'd given up and left.

He had prevented Dhamon from gaining that cure he desperately needed.

It was his fault Dhamon was looking less and less human every day. He told himself now he might have forced the sage to help. Killing her had been the easy way.

"His fever is breaking," Maldred turned to him and said.

"Maybe we should have let him die. Better that than to live as he is becoming," Ragh said, watching his friend twitch as if caught in some dream.

In fact, Dhamon was dreaming. He was dreaming of the storm in Fiona's eyes. He saw Rig trying to find his way through the storm. The dark-skinned mariner called Fiona's name, then Shaon's. Raph was there, too—a young kender who had died in Dhamon's company. Jasper too, and countless nameless faces—Solamnic Knights and soldiers he'd killed on battlefields when he wore the armor of a Knight of Takhisis.

The storm raged wilder, its darkness obscuring all the faces, the thunder drowning out Rig's cries for help. When the storm finally abated, an enormous cavern materialized, lit in places by streaks of lightning—not from a storm—from the mouths of blue dragons. The dragons flew along the ceiling, around rocky outcroppings and stalactites, swirling

closer to the Father of All and of Nothing. Chaos.
Dragons fell, some batted away by the god's hand.
Others rose up and swooped in to take their place.
Lightning continued to streak, sulfur filled the air,
and Chaos's shadow grew monstrous wings.

Chapter Fourteen
Ghosts in the City

Maldred pressed his back against the stone wall of the alley. It was dark, well past midnight, heading toward dawn. Though the fading moonlight didn't quite reveal his presence, nevertheless he stuck close to the wall, curling his fingers in the mortared gaps. The air was chilly, a big change from the humid swamp, and his breath blew away from his face in miniature clouds. He found himself shivering and wishing for boots and a heavy cloak. His bare feet uncomfortably registered the cold that had settled deep into the ground.

He stood there for several minutes, listening to the noises from the street beyond. He heard nothing unexpected—a sudden outburst of raucous laughter from a tavern that was just around the corner, the splash of something being tossed out a window, and the thunk of two pairs of boots against a wooden sidewalk. Two ogres, judging from the heavy footfalls, one perhaps drunk. Maldred waited, watching where the alley emptied onto the street, drumming his fingers.

"Why do we stay here? What is it we are waiting for?" That was the musical voice of Sabar, and Maldred turned to glance at his companion, registering the nuances of the shadows and locating her thin, purple-draped form.

Does she feel the cold? he wondered. She gave no outward sign that she was affected. Sabar seemed real, but he suspected she was just some pleasing manifestation of the crystal's enchantment. The cold wouldn't disturb her magic.

Ragh had protested when Maldred pulled out the crystal ball and coaxed Sabar to appear. Although the draconian was occupied poling the raft, he threatened to stop and toss the crystal into the river. Maldred somehow managed to convince the draconian that he might be able to use the crystal's magic to find a way of helping Dhamon. Ragh finally had backed off, with a warning:

"I'll be watching you closely, ogre."

"Are you watching for something?" Sabar asked the ogre-mage.

Maldred drew a finger to his lips. "Yes." A pause. "Well, no. Nothing in particular. I just . . ." His head snapped back as the bootsteps grew louder. The two ogres passed the alley entrance and continued on down the street.

"I am curious. Why did you wish to come here?" Sabar persisted. She put a hand on his arm, her fingers feeling like real, clammy flesh. "To this place . . . ."

"Blöten. The city's called Blöten. The capital of all the ogre territories." Maldred shrugged, edging toward the end of the alley. "I needed to see this place," he said after a few moments. "To see if anything's changed since I was last here."

He leaned out, peering north. The street was for the most part dark, for the most part lined with ramshackle buildings perhaps long abandoned. The moonlight showed rubble on the street. It was as if the city was falling down around its inhabitants. There was a light burning in one second-floor window, shabby curtains fluttering. A soft glow emanated from a window in a house on the next block.

The tavern was a few doors down. Light and coarse laughter spilled out, and something that passed for music. The two ogres were down the street, one weaving and gesturing. The drunk one had a wooden mug tied to his wrist so he wouldn't lose it.

"No place for a lady," Maldred mused.

"Yet I must always accompany you while you are inside the crystal," Sabar reminded him.

Inside the crystal. Were they really *inside* the vision, as she claimed? He shook his head, white mane of hair flying. It felt as if they were in Blöten. He felt the cold gravel beneath his feet, smelled the musky odor of ogres. It was all very convincing, but moments ago Maldred had been on the raft with Ragh, Fiona, and Dhamon. He'd asked Sabar to show him this city. He'd leaned close, trying to see better, and he let the crystal drink in his magical energy, hoping that might brighten the darkness of the image. It was night on the river and dark inside the crystal ball. Before he knew it he found himself in the Blöten alley, the mystical guide at his side. Sabar had to assure him more than once that he really wasn't in Blöten, that his body was still on the raft, fingers wrapped around the crystal.

"Only your mind is here, O Sagacious One,"

Sabar told Maldred again and again, "and I must accompany it on this journey."

"Then accompany me now to my father's palace," Maldred requested, touching the alley wall one last time. It certainly didn't feel like only his mind was here. His body was cold, as it always was in Blöten. "I need to speak with him."

They strolled by the tavern. Maldred glanced in, saw a dozen or so ogres around weathered tables. They were man-like, ranging in height from seven to nine feet, broad-shouldered and muscular, with wide noses, wide-set eyes, and bulging veins on thick necks. They were all Maldred's kin, yet not a single one looked quite like him. His hide was blue. Theirs ranged from tan or umber to a dusky yellow. Scars and warts decorated their arms and faces. One thing most of them had in common was broken or crooked teeth protruding over bulbous lips.

"These are your people," Sabar said.

Maldred nodded.

"And yet . . ."

"I look different from them," Maldred finished.

"Yes. You are . . . ."

"Blue. Yes, that's the obvious thing. And bigger."

"Is it the magic inside of you that gives you your blue color?"

Maldred shrugged. "I guess. Those few of my race who are sorcerers look something like me. Blue skin, white hair. We stand out, even among ogres." He gave a chuckle. "Though my old friend Grim Kedar is as pale as ivory, and there's magic about him, too, so it's not always true that ogre-mages are blue."

"You don't care much for your people, do you? Or your homeland?"

The questions caught him off guard. "Down this

way," he said, pointing, ignoring the questions, "and then west a very short distance. My father's palace is there."

They spotted only one other ogre out on the weathered wooden sidewalks, a hunchbacked youth with a shuffling gate. He was across the street from them, and glanced in their direction, hesitating for a moment, before continuing on his way.

"That one looks sad," Sabar noted.

Maldred walked faster. "Most of my people are unhappy." But it wasn't always that way, he added to himself. It wasn't that way until the great dragons settled in, and it got worse when the swamp of the Black started to swallow their land. A race of proud warriors and fearsome bullies, the ogres had been beaten down by forces beyond their power to understand or defeat.

They turned west. The buildings in this area were in somewhat better repair, and most of them appeared lived in. A thick candle burned in one window, voices drifted out of another. There was fresh paint on this street and less debris.

"Most of the wealthy live around here," Maldred said by way of explanation, "if you can call them that. They really don't have much." He nodded at the end of the street. "But you can indeed call my father wealthy."

The "palace" covered an entire block and was well kept compared to everything else they had seen. However, dead grass stretched up through cracks in a stone walkway and choked out what once had been spacious flower beds. There were two burly ogres standing on either side of a wrought-iron gate, and they snapped to attention when they spotted Maldred. He saw other guards inside the gate, clinging to the shadows. His father had increased security since his last visit.

"The hunchback we passed on the street and now these guards," Maldred said to Sabar. "If only my mind is here and my body is not, how can they see me?"

This time Sabar didn't answer readily. She had fallen a few steps behind as the guards, recognizing Maldred, opened the gate and motioned him through.

"The woman . . . ?" One of the guards asked.

"She's with me," Maldred reassured him.

He was nearly at the palace door when he heard one guard softly say, "I told you the chieftain's son prefers the company of humans."

Maldred rapped his fist hard against the wood and stood, waiting. There were heavy footsteps inside, the fumbling of a bolt. Moments later, Maldred and Sabar found themselves in a spacious dining room, seated in mismatched chairs at a massive oaken table.

"Your father is not expected to rise for a few hours," a serving girl explained, as she placed bread and mulled cider in front of them.

Maldred drank deep of the cider. He noticed Sabar didn't touch any of her food. "Wake him," he told the girl, after wiping his mouth. "I'll deal with the consequences."

There weren't any consequences, and this surprised Maldred. His father seemed genuinely pleased to see him, and he also seemed surprisingly old. The great Donnag, ruler of all of Blöde, always had a multitude of warts, spots, and wrinkles, but the lines around his eyes had deepened, the skin beneath his eyes sagged more, and there was a weariness to the ogre chieftain that seemed uncharacteristic. Maldred suppressed a shudder. He needed his father to be healthy and strong. He would have to rule Blöde if his father became too feeble or died.

Sabar was right, Maldred knew in his heart of hearts. He didn't care much for his people. He fit in better with humans than with his own kind. He liked the company of humans better, and he had no desire at this juncture in his life to become the ruler of Blöde. "That will be a sad day for me," he mused.

"What did you say, my son?"

Maldred shook his head. "I came here to see how you and Blöde were doing, Father. To see if the swamp had . . . ." Maldred paused as the ogre chieftain approached, placing a hand on his shoulder. The hand passed right through him.

"Trickery!" Donnag cried. He clapped his hands, and before Maldred could speak four heavily armed and armored ogres tromped into the room. "Deceit! We have been—"

"No, Father! It's really me." Maldred was as astonished as Donnag that there was no substance to his form. He could certainly touch things. Why couldn't he be touched? "Well, I'm not really here, physically. I'm in the Black's swamp and . . . ."

Another four guards joined the first quartet. The largest of them spouted orders and made a move to take Maldred into custody.

At the last moment, Donnag waved his men off.

There was something in Maldred's pleading tone that gave the chieftain pause.

"I found a magical crystal, Father, and through it my mind . . . ." Maldred looked to Sabar, but she'd disappeared. "Look, it's magic that brings me here."

Donnag seemed to accept this and gestured for half the ogre guards to leave. After a lengthy silence, the chieftain settled his bulk into a chair at the end of the table, one so opulent, though old and marred, it could have passed for a throne.

"Even on the rare occasions, Maldred, that you . . . physically . . . visit our city, you're not truly here. Your mind and dreams are always elsewhere. Always elsewhere."

"Don't say this to me now, Father. Right now I am . . . trying to help you and your wretched city. I am trying to stop the swamp and the Black. I am doing exactly what you asked me to do—no matter that it is costing me dearly."

Donnag nodded to the serving girl. "Something warm," he said, "and tasty." Then, he said to Maldred, "We know. We know that you have worked to hand your good friend Dhamon Grimwulf over to the naga so Dhamon could fight the Black and save our homeland. But you changed your mind, didn't you? We understand that you have put your human friend before your kith and kin—"

Maldred was on his feet, chair flying backward, hand clenched around his empty goblet. "I did not put Dhamon before you and your people, father. I betrayed him to the naga and her dragon master. I did everything a puppet was supposed to do." His shoulders slumped as he met Donnag's rheumy gaze. "Things didn't work out as planned."

Donnag nodded appreciatively. "Already some of Sable's creatures have come here. They watch us." He nervously fingered the gold rings threaded through his lower lip. "Not many, not often. They just make their presence known."

Maldred's eyes narrowed. "This presence . . . ."

"Spawn. Black ones. You know what kind of creatures they are. Our men have spotted a few on the rooftops, watching us."

"Where?"

A shrug, then, "Across from our palace, and in the Old Quarter. Some were seen a few days ago."

Not the Black's spawns, Maldred thought. Nura's or the shadow dragon's. He doubted the Black overlord would bother spying on a city of ogres. Perhaps the naga was looking for Dhamon, thinking Maldred would bring him here to see . . . .

"Grim Kedar's is in the Old Quarter," Maldred said, remembering. The naga knew a lot about Maldred and might suspect that Maldred would take Dhamon to the famed ogre healer. Indeed he had taken Dhamon to Grim Kedar once, but the ogre healer had not been able to help . . . though Maldred discovered later that Grim had been ordered not to help by his father, the ogre chieftain.

"Grim Kedar was in the Old Quarter," Donnag corrected ruefully. "Grim was very old, my son."

"Dead?" The word was a gasp wrenched from Maldred's throat. "Grim Kedar is dead?"

"He was accorded a fine service. I paid tribute to him. Many dignitaries said kind things. We truly miss him."

Maldred's hands clenched the edge of the table, his fingers digging in. "Dead!" The candles in the room made the tabletop gleam, and Maldred saw his wide face reflected. How could he see his image? How could he touch the smooth wood? How could he feel his breath quicken? "How did Grim Kedar die?"

"I told you, son. Grim was old. Had you been here, you could have spoken at the ceremony, too. Grim was very fond of you."

Maldred released the table, clenching and unclenching his hands. "I've got to go."

"So soon? You just got here."

"I tell you, I'm not truly here anyway," Maldred returned sharply. "I'm just some vision produced by a crystal ball a long, long way from here." He got up, walked past the guards. "I'll be back, Father. As soon as I'm able, I'll return here without the aid of the crystal ball. And I promise we'll find a way to stop the swamp."

Sabar walked beside him past the gate. He didn't acknowledge her, just kept walking. Keeping a brisk pace, he retraced his steps the way they'd come, turning after they'd passed the familiar tavern. It was still in the hazy time before dawn. The conversation with his father had apparently taken no time at all. Perhaps time was distorted inside the crystal. Perhaps other things were distorted, too.

"Maybe Grim really isn't dead," Maldred said hopefully.

The sky was a pale gray by the time the ogre-mage and Sabar reached the building that used to serve as the residence of Grim Kedar.

"The place looks the same," Maldred said to Sabar.

"It looks dirty," the magic-woman said.

The wooden facade was worn and cracked, like wrinkles on an old man's face, and the front window was shuttered. The door was closed. Still, Maldred hadn't expected it to be locked. Grim never locked the door.

Maldred's fingers brushed the latch. He turned and said to Sabar, "You say I'm not here physically, but how do I feel this metal? I ate my Father's food. I feel the cold. I can see my breath. I don't understand how this can happen."

"Your mind is strong," Sabar replied. "It permits you to feel things that weaker people might miss. You are fortunate to have so much magic inside of you."

"Yes," Maldred replied glumly. "I'm truly blessed to be what I am." He twisted the latch, broke the lock, and pushed the door open. "Wait a minute."

His gaze drifted up the front of the three-story building across from Grim Kedar's. He saw a shape, moving behind the only intact section of crenelated roof.

Can't quite tell what that is, he said to himself. Maldred remained still, hand still on the door, still observing the gliding shape. He felt Sabar's cool fingers against the back of his arm. "It looks like . . . ." His eyes narrowed as he darted inside the old healer's shop. "A spawn. A stinking spawn."

Sabar followed, closing the door behind them. Maldred held out his hand, muttered a string of ancient ogre words and caused a ball of light to glow on his palm.

"Grim!"

After several moments he tried again: "Grim Kedar!"

The interior of the shop was as neat as always. There were two tables and chairs where Grim's customers sat and drank his concoctions and sometimes gambled. Behind the counter was a finger-bone-curtained doorway that led into a room where the ogre healer used his herbs and magics on paying patients.

Maldred brushed aside the curtain, the bones clacking together behind him. Sabar slid in behind him.

"Grim! Grim Kedar!"

"He's not here." Sluggishly rising from a cot in the back room was as slight an ogre as Maldred had seen. He was eerily thin, with only a hint of muscles along his upper arms, and he was only seven feet tall when he stood. "My uncle's dead."

A child, Maldred decided.

The young ogre ran his long fingers through a mass of jet-black hair and fixed his watery red eyes on Maldred. "I know you," he stated. "Just because you're the chieftain's son doesn't mean you can barge right into . . . ."

Maldred retreated back into the shop, the bones clacking wildly behind him. He went straight to the far wall and to a teetering bookcase. Tossing his globe of light toward the ceiling, he ran his fingers across the book bindings, searching.

The bones clacked again. "Have some respect," the young ogre demanded. He hurried toward Maldred and made a move to pull the big ogre-mage's arm away, but his hands passed through the blue flesh. "What in the name of . . . ."

"It's magic," Maldred said as he angrily whirled. "I've plenty of magic inside me, it seems. Grim had magic, too. Healing magic, though apparently not enough to save himself. He's really dead, isn't he? No one else would be sleeping here if he was still alive."

The young ogre glared. "My uncle—"

"Was a good man," Maldred finished. "The best who lived in this godsforsaken city."

"I know," said the young ogre sadly. "He'd help anybody."

"He helped me on plenty of occasions," Maldred said.

The young ogre glanced at Sabar. She'd soundlessly passed through the curtains behind them. "He was known even to help humans," said the young ogre. "Said the gods created them too, and we shouldn't belittle them so."

"Grim was a good man," Maldred repeated.

"Even took a human in once, he did."

Maldred raised an eyebrow. "When?"

"It was a dirty little child he found wandering outside on the street. He took her in so no one would turn her into their slave. That was only a day or two before he died."

"The child . . . ?"

"Oh, she's long gone. Someone must've taken her right away after he was found dead. A pretty human child like that is worth a handful of coins."

Maldred felt his throat tightening. "A little girl, you say."

"Why, yes, and—"

"About this tall?" Maldred's hand dropped to his hip.

The ogre nodded.

"With hair the color of polished copper?"

"Yes."

"This little girl, did she have a name that you remember?"

The ogre shrugged. "I never bother remembering human names. I don't want to be around them long enough to worry about learning their names."

Maldred returned his attention to the bookcase, tugging out an especially ancient book on the topmost shelf. Paper flakes fell from the pages as he brought it to the counter. A motion, and the ball of light followed him to hover overhead.

"Did they bury Grim?"

The young ogre shook his head. "Burned him." He leaned over the counter, trying to see what Maldred was reading. "They burned him and the others who died the same day."

Maldred stared at the young ogre, inhaling sharply. "Others?"

"Six more. All died the same day. They said my uncle died because he was old, but I think it was some epidemic. Something that got him and the others all at once."

Maldred pressed for names. The young nephew of Grim Kedar could only remember two of the dead ones. They had been friends of the ogre-mage from his youth, and they were among those Grim Kedar trusted in the city.

"Nura Bint-Drax." Maldred muttered the name as a curse.

"Sorry?"

"The child who killed your uncle," Maldred said. "She also killed my friends. But she will pay."

Maldred ignored the young ogre as he continued to search through the book, finally finding the passage he sought and frowning as he memorized it. When he was certain he knew the incantation, he moved behind the counter and poked through jars and small boxes.

"You can't take any of those things. This is my shop now."

Maldred brushed by him, glancing down at Sabar. "You say we're not physically here. Then how can I keep these things? I might be able to use them to help Dhamon slow down the magic that's turning him into a spawn."

She took from him a collection of preserved leaves, tiny feathers, and a packet of coarse red powder. "My magic will keep them for you," Sabar said.

"We've got one more stop," he told her. "Across the street. That spawn I saw, I'm going to—"

The young ogre opened his mouth to say something else, but no words came out.

"Give me that crystal ball, ogre."

◇◇◇◇◇◇◇

In a flash Maldred found himself back sitting on the front of the raft. The first rays of the morning sun were stretching across the river, setting it to shimmer.

Ragh snatched away the crystal ball on a jeweled base, and thrust it into his pouch, tying the pouch to a belt he'd fashioned of a strip of cloth. The raft tipped precariously. Ragh shifted his balance and resumed poling with the glaive.

"I'll take care of the lady and the crystal for a while," Ragh said tersely.

"I wasn't finished!" Maldred fumed.

"You were at it plenty long," Ragh returned. "Too long. I shouldn't've let you use it in the first place. Not without Dhamon up and watching. How do I know what you're up to?" After a moment: "Did you find anything to help him?"

Maldred glowered at the draconian, debating whether to fight him. The draconian would be a formidable foe, but Maldred considered himself smarter and stronger and was certain he could best the creature. But to what end?

"I found something where I went," Maldred finally answered. In one meaty fist he held several feathers, leaves, and a small pouch of powder. "But we have to wait for Dhamon to regain consciousness. He has to accept the magic for the spell to work."

"He might never wake up," Ragh said sadly. "If he does, I'm not sure he'd accept any magic from you."

CHAPTER FIFTEEN
PASSAGE

Fiona sat uncomfortably on the shore of the New Sea, in the middle of a patch of sharp-smelling ferns. Her wrists were bound with a heavy strip of cloth from Dhamon's robe, with a sweat-stained gag in her mouth. The tip of her own sword prodded her from the back, whenever the female Knight moved a little too much.

Ragh held her weapon, and he was lying concealed in the taller ferns behind her. Dhamon stood wobbily a few yards behind them, effectively cloaked by late afternoon shadows and a veil of willow leaves. Maldred was with Dhamon, watching everything and remaining silent. The ogre-mage had been quiet and busy ever since Dhamon came to at about midnight, a little better than three days after Fiona had attacked him.

Dhamon still ached terribly from the scales, which covered him almost completely now. There were only three significant patches of human skin remaining—on the left side of his face, down his left side, and across the small of his back. Maldred had cast a spell on him, a particularly uncomfortable enchantment that he'd initially objected to out of distrust. Oddly, Ragh had sided with the ogremage, saying the spell might stop the spread of the scales. After a fashion, Dhamon relented, and not a single scale had sprouted since the spell. Neither had a single one disappeared.

Dhamon had abandoned his boots because of the scales on the tops of his feet and the thick gray skin tough as boiled leather covering the bottoms of his feet. He barely registered the rocky ground and exposed roots he trod on anymore.

The wound on his back was the worst, but Dhamon's ability to heal was remarkable, considering how deep Fiona had cut him with her sword. His back wound should have killed him, he knew. It would have instantly killed any normal man. And he hadn't completely recovered. The fever racing through him could be from that wound or the scales or even Maldred's spell. Whatever its source, the fever added to his misery.

His fever and the soaking heat threatened to pitch him to the marshy loam. He focused his efforts on remaining alert and leaned on the haft of the glaive for support.

Ragh cast him a worried look.

"I'm all right," Dhamon muttered. Surprisingly, he found some comfort in the draconian's concern. Odd that fate had put him in league with a sivak at this juncture in his life. When he belonged to the Knights of Takhisis they had relied on sivaks as spies and informants, but he never placed any amount of real trust in any of the creatures. Until meeting Ragh, he had loathed the lot of them. "Really, Ragh, I'm all right."

The draconian gave him a skeptical look, then returned his full attention to Fiona. He crawled forward to wipe the sweat off the Knight's face, then returned to his post behind her. Dhamon dragged his tattered sleeve down his left cheek, trying to wipe away the trickles of sweat, but this garment was soaked and did nothing to help matters. Thirsty again, he thought. I need more fresh water, maybe more rest. I need to stand on the shore and catch the breeze. Dhamon was not about to allow himself any of those luxuries, for of his three companions, the draconian was the only one he believed he could trust, the only one to his knowledge who had not betrayed him.

Fiona squirmed and tried to spit the gag out of her mouth. Ragh poked her with the tip of the sword again.

"Stay still, Knight," Ragh warned her with a growl. "Unless you want to—" With his free hand he parted the ferns. "Dhamon! Another boat. This one's turning to shore."

Dhamon shifted so he could peer through the leaves and watch the New Sea. The sea was black near the shore from dark algae growths that swirled like oil on the surface. Farther out the water was a brilliant blue, mirroring the color of the cloudless sky. The waves were a little choppy from a slight wind. Sunlight flashed on the surface.

A boat was indeed cutting toward them. It was small and with a single square, dirty-white sail, so, Dhamon guessed, it was a fishing boat. As it neared, he could smell the fish and chum. His sharp eyesight picked out nets gathered along the sides, a long gaff hook propped against the rail, and the open barrels of bait near spools of line.

"Got a nibble," Ragh said in a hushed voice.

"Don't be so certain yet," Dhamon returned. "Let's see how close it comes."

Dhamon knew that it must look like a trap. The Solamnic Knight sitting on the shore with her hands tied in front of her and a gag in her mouth. It screamed trap, especially given that she was in the Black's realm where all manner of malicious men and creatures held sway, none of whom would hesitate to use a beautiful victim to lure others into their savage clutches. *And now we take our place among those malicious creatures,* Dhamon sadly thought. *At the moment we are no different than Sable's minions.*

But what choice did he have, he reminded himself. Fiona would not willingly help them gain passage, and she had to be treated as a renegade. Fiona . . . *unblemished* Fiona. After he'd regained consciousness, he had asked her why she attacked him and also what unearthly force had healed the acid scars on her face and neck. To the first question she replied, "Seeking justice." To the second she said simply, "The sword healed me." Dhamon knew the sword was not capable of restoring her looks, so the mystery persisted.

Repeatedly he had pleaded with her to help them attract the attention of a ship. "Never, never, never," was her reply.

So she was helping unwillingly. He would not permit Maldred to don his human guise.

"No, let no one be deceived as I was," he bitterly told his onetime friend. "You are an ogre."

He or Ragh, with their scales, would scare away any passing ship, so they had settled on this plan, this obvious trap that might catch some chivalrous soul's attention.

They'd been waiting since dawn and finally had snared this small fishing boat.

Come closer, Dhamon willed it.

Three other ships had drifted near earlier, one a ferry and the other two piled with merchant crates. All wisely steered clear. Dhamon had considered swimming out and taking one over by force, but he was still too weak for such adventurousness.

This boat was coming closer still. He saw only four men on the deck. The man on the bow looked to be giving the orders. He had some years on him, his hair was a mix of black and gray, and his close-cropped beard showed white streaks, but the sun-weathered skin of his face didn't sag and his eyes were clear. He watched the Solamnic Knight, his jaw set firm.

"Aye, a man with some age to him, but not an old man. A chivalrous man too, from the look of him," Dhamon whispered.

The man certainly carried himself proudly, though Dhamon noticed he paced about the deck with a limp.

"C'mon," Dhamon urged. "Come and rescue the poor woman. That's it. Closer." He glanced at Ragh, hoping the draconian would keep in hiding until the last possible moment. This was a perfect boat, small enough to sail on their own. "Closer now."

Fiona wriggled against her bonds, and Ragh prodded her again. "Don't move," the draconian whispered. "Don't move or I'll cut you like you did Dhamon."

Long moments passed, the boat was close enough now for Dhamon to hear the captain without expending much effort. The captain directed his men to be wary, urging one to scan the trees and shallows, another to listen closely for any suspicious sounds.

"It's a trap, Eben," one of the men warned.

"Obviously," Dhamon muttered under his breath.

The captain nodded. "Probably," he said, drawing a long knife from his belt. "I doubt that whatever beasties tied her up and set her there just walked away. They're hiding."

"We should walk away, Eben. It's a trap."

The captain firmly shook his head. "I'll not let whatever foul creatures set that trap keep the girl. We'll get her free."

"We're fishermen, Eben," another cut in. "We're not warriors. We're not heroes."

"Heroes? Fishermen? We're men, aren't we?" the captain returned. "You can stay on the boat, the three of you cowards. I'll go in for the girl and take care of it m'self if I have to."

Chivalrous and foolish, Dhamon thought, and good for us that he is. "C'mon. Closer," he breathed.

One of the four fishermen was a half-elf, who was paying particular attention to the trees where Dhamon hid. Dhamon sucked in his breath and glanced at Maldred with narrowed eyes. The ogre-mage sighed and looked away. Dhamon still didn't trust him.

"I don't see anything, Eben." This was the half-elf, who continued to stare at the foliage. He snatched up the gaff hook. "That doesn't mean there's nothing there."

"Oh something's there, Keesh. I'm sure of it," the captain returned flatly. "Probably some lizardmen or bakali. There's enough of either of them around here. Maybe some slavers working for the Black—using one human as bait to catch more. Doesn't matter, though, let's get this wreck closer. Maybe whatever's there won't put up much of a fight. Maybe we can chase them off.

Let's get the girl and be away from this place."

They dropped sail and lowered anchor about forty feet out, at the edge of the blanket of black algae. Dhamon watched as the captain released a deep breath and gave a shake of his head, as if scolding himself for what he was about to do. Then he awkwardly heaved himself over the side, knife still in one hand. Two of his fellows elected to follow. But the one who'd objected so strongly to the risky endeavor hesitated a moment before announcing loudly what a big dose of stupidity this was and reluctantly joining them.

The fishermen cautiously sloshed toward Fiona, who was squirming vigorously despite Ragh's prodding. The half-elf was in the lead, still intensely scanning the ferns and trees. His eyes widened as he spotted a flash of silver—the sun caught the blade held by Ragh.

"There, Eben!" The half-elf pointed with the gaff hook. "Something in the ferns behind the woman."

At that moment Ragh exploded from his hiding spot, dashing by Fiona and purposefully knocking her over as he went, clawed feet tearing up the marshy ground. In a heartbeat he was in the water and plunging toward the half-elf, who was wading forward to meet him, twirling the gaff hook.

"There's no reason to kill them!" This was shouted by Maldred.

Dhamon glared. "Don't you move, ogre. Stay put until this is done." He snapped up the great sword in one hand and hefted the glaive in the other. Both were two-handed weapons, but despite his wounds he felt agile enough to wield them both.

"There's no reason to kill them," Maldred repeated.

I've no intention of doing so, Dhamon thought.

He pounded across the ground, rushing toward the fishermen.

"Monsters!" the half-elf shouted. "Two of them!"

Dhamon shuddered at being called a monster.

"A pair of draconians," the one named Eben cried. He waved his long knife in the air and rushed up to the half-elf's side. "Such creatures are dangerous, my friends. Worse than lizardmen. On your toes!"

Ragh brought the long sword up to parry the gaff hook, then gripped the pommel tight and twisted the weapon while bringing up a clawed foot and kicking the half-elf in the stomach. The half-elf fell back into the water, stunned and disarmed.

"Don't . . ." Dhamon started to admonish.

"I wasn't planning to kill them," Ragh answered as he ducked beneath the sweep of Eben's long, glittering knife, "though I think their intentions are otherwise."

When the fishermen saw Dhamon, registering his scaly appearance, one of them whirled and headed back toward the boat, nearly knocking over the half-elf in his rush.

"Captain!" Dhamon shouted, sweeping the glaive menacingly just above the water. "Drop your knife!" Dhamon gestured toward the other armed man. "You, too."

Both men hesitated.

"We could easily kill all of you," Dhamon threatened, "and I think you know it, but we'd prefer to let you live."

When the captain hesitated another moment, the half-elf made a move for the abandoned gaff hook. Ragh was quicker, grabbing the makeshift weapon and hurling it a few yards away. The half-elf didn't quit, pulling a knife from his belt.

"We won't hurt you, I say!" Dhamon continued.

"Damn draconians," the captain spat.

"That one's a spawn," the half-elf said, indicating Dhamon.

"Drop the knife, Keesh, William," Eben advised the fishermen. "We've no choice." He lowered his own knife. "My fault, men."

"We shouldn't've come in to shore," the half-elf said with angry eyes fixed on the captain. "You knew it was a trap. You're a fisherman now, remember? You're not a Knight anymore."

"I had no choice," Eben repeated.

"Drop the knives," Dhamon warned again. He pointed the great sword at the captain. "I'm in a considerable hurry, and I'll not ask politely again."

The older man shook his head. He thrust the knife in his belt. His two companions copied the move.

"Good enough," Dhamon said. "We'll not hurt you. I give you my word." He looked to see the retreating fisherman climbing on board the boat. "Keep that one from leaving, Captain."

"If you want to live," Ragh interjected.

"Spawn, giving their word?" the half-elf raised his upper lip in a sneer. "I think you'll kill us anyway. I think—"

"The woman," Eben said, hushing the half-elf with a wave of his hand. "What do you intend to do with the woman . . . ?"

"We intend to get help for her," Dhamon answered, "but it's a long story and too long to tell you."

Behind them, they heard the noise of a chain, the anchor being pulled up. Dhamon was angered that Eben had not ordered the man to stay.

"What we need is safe passage. That's all. Across

the New Sea and to the coast of Throt." Dhamon
nodded to Ragh, glancing at the fishing boat.

Ragh waved the long sword threateningly at the
half-elf, then brushed by him, sloshing toward the
boat. The frantic fisherman was fumbling with the
sail now and had managed to get it half-way raised
before the rigging became tangled.

"Passage for us. Then you're free to go about
your business."

"You'll not harm my crew."

It wasn't a question. "No, I'll not harm any of
you—if you cooperate."

Ragh was climbing up the side of the boat, as the
fisherman edged to the other side of the deck, knife
flashing. "Just passage, and perhaps some of whatever food and water you've on board."

"For the two of you?" Eben gestured to Fiona.
"And her?"

"Her name's Fiona. Aye, the two of us, Fiona,
and one more passenger." Dhamon glanced over
his shoulder. "Ogre! Bring Fiona, we've got a way
to Throt!"

◇ ◇ ◇ ◇ ◇ ◇ ◇

There was not much wind, and so they didn't
reach their destination until a little more than two
days later. It was twilight when they arrived, and
the pale purple sky, striped gray with bands of
clouds, took some of the harshness away from the
stark land of Throt. The grass of the uneven plains
that stretched before them was dry and brittle,
and the bushes that grew in clumps had shed
most of their leaves. There was a stand of pines
that looked a little out of place, the trees all relatively small. To the east, and running almost

straight north and south, was a jagged chain of mountains. The shadow dragon was there somewhere, if the magic in the crystal ball spoke true. The mountains were not particularly impressive or high or what Dhamon imagined a dragon would choose for its lair, but he had the impression they looked like the spikes on a dragon's back.

It won't be long now, Dhamon thought. The village near Haltigoth, where Riki and his child were waiting, couldn't be too far. If they pushed, they should reach it by sometime tomorrow. He was slightly familiar with Throt, having been in a few skirmishes in the country when he served in the Knights of Takhisis in years past. Admittedly he had not spent much time on the ground, as he was fighting from the back of a blue dragon named Gale, but between his memory and the crystal ball, he was hopeful they would find their way.

He had not hurt the fishermen, as he'd promised. It turned out Eben was a former Solamnic Knight who had left the order more than a decade ago when he was seriously injured during a skirmish with hobgoblins. The man still had a pronounced limp from the encounter. Dhamon considered leaving Fiona with him and telling him she was safe with the Solamnics, but he had the notion that the mad Knight might find a way to overpower the fishermen and come after him again. Better that he take Fiona into the village and leave her with Riki and Varek until the shadow dragon was dealt with. Then he'd return and take her to some Solamnic citadel, provided he had enough time left in his life.

"You had no right, Dhamon."

Maldred's harsh tone roused Dhamon from his musings. Dhamon gave a curt laugh. "What? No right to give up your big sword to the fishermen? Aye, ogre, I had every right."

Maldred's eyes became slits. "My father gave me that sword."

Dhamon waved to the captain of the fishing boat. The boat was pulling away from the rocky shore, aiming for the deeper waters of the New Sea. The grinning Captain Eben waved the sword.

"We needed to pay for our passage, pay for those fishermen's time and discomfort. We cost them a few days' work and no manner of worry. We ate their food and drank their water and spirits. They were all so nervous I don't think one of them slept the entire time we were on board. It was fortunate for us the sword was valuable."

Maldred snarled, his lower fangs protruding from bulbous lips. "Valuable? That sword was worth more than their entire boat, Dhamon, and you well know it. He could buy a large new boat with that prize, two or three in fact, and hire more men. Very charitable of you."

Dhamon couldn't help but smile.

"There was an enchantment about my sword. You could have given them that damn glaive— tainted with Goldmoon's blood. Or Fiona's sword. My father gave me that sword."

Dhamon turned away, looking at Fiona. The draconian was still wielding the Solamnic Knight's sword, keeping it trained on her.

"Take the gag out of her mouth, Ragh," Dhamon said.

"You want to hear more of her insane prattle?" The draconian shook his head. He stared into the wild eyes of the female Knight. "Don't worry, I'm not going to untie you," Ragh said. "I would never be so foolish as that. But I will take the gag out of your mouth—if you promise to keep quiet this time."

Fiona only glared at him.

"Swear."

She defiantly shook her head.

"No, the gag stays, Dhamon. Unless you want to watch her." Ragh was surprised that Dhamon didn't argue. "Remember when we took it off to let her eat on the boat. . . ." The draconian paused, cocked his head. He heard something. The gentle rustling of dried branches, a hushed and indistinct voice. He and Dhamon looked to the northeast, staring into the spreading twilight, searching for the source of the ominous noise.

CHAPTER SIXTEEN
THROTIAN
WELCOMING PARTY

Whoever they are," Ragh said, "I think they're hiding behind those pines.

"Whatever they are," Dhamon corrected. He stared at the trees, shutting out the soft voices of his companions and focusing on the distant noise. There was the rustling of bushes and the faint sound of pine branches rubbing against each other. And there were voices, at least four distinct ones that he could make out. "Whatever they are," he repeated. "They aren't human." They certainly didn't sound human to his extra-keen ears. They were talking in a guttural rasp he didn't recognize.

Ragh listened intently for a few minutes, cocking his head. "I agree—odd voices. Something I recognize there. A word: blessed. Another: Takhisis."

As the rustling persisted, a small shape darted out from behind the pine trees.

"I can make out at least six voices," Dhamon said. He pointed at the one running.

"Goblins." Ragh spat the word. The draconian

couldn't be entirely sure of the shape of the creature, which skittered behind a clump of scraggly bushes, but he finally recognized the language. He had spent enough time on Krynn to know goblin when he heard it spoken. "Big rats."

Ragh stood silent, watching Dhamon for some signal, glancing at Maldred and Fiona to make sure they weren't causing problems. The Solamnic Knight, struggling with the ties at her wrists, caught his gaze and stopped, shrugging.

"If there are only six of them, we could just ignore them," Ragh suggested.

"There's more than six," Maldred said. The ogre-mage had come up behind them and was looking at the pines, too. "You might not hear more than that, but goblins don't travel in such small numbers. There must be at least twice that many."

"It shouldn't be a problem, no matter the numbers." Dhamon propped the glaive over his right shoulder and gripped the great sword in his left hand. "I've found that goblins are little more than a nuisance. Oversized rats, just as Ragh said. And they die quickly."

The two days on the fishing boat had done wonders for his health. The serious wound caused by Fiona had nearly completely healed. The pain from the scales had abated somewhat, and his fever had broken early this afternoon. He felt alive and alert, and he found himself almost anticipating a fight to test his recovered strength—though goblins would not present much of a challenge.

"No, they shouldn't be a problem," Ragh agreed, "depending on just how many of them are out there."

"Doesn't matter how many, I said." Dhamon saw one of them clearly now, crouching among the leafless branches of a stunted shadberry bush. It was about three dozen yards away, and the fading light served to make it look especially grotesque. It was a small creature, not quite three feet tall, with a mottled red-brown hide dotted with warts. Its visage was flat, as if it had run into a stone wall, and its nose was far too broad for the rest of its face, its ears lopsided and irregularly pointed. Looking closely, Dhamon saw that its forehead sloped back a little, giving way to a coarse smattering of black-brown hair tufts on the top and sides of its head. Its large eyes for night-seeing were wide and fixed on Dhamon's.

"A damn nuisance, goblins," Dhamon hissed. "Worse than rats." He took a step in the direction of the shadberry and watched as three more scurried out from the pines and jumped in the clump of bushes. They were all carrying crude-looking short spears in their twisted hands. Their spindly arms hung down almost to their knees. They were foul, ugly creatures.

The goblins were chattering behind the bushes, and the words, sounding like snorts and grunts, reminded Dhamon of a pack of dogs arguing over a bone.

"What are they saying?" he asked Ragh.

"They're talking about us," the draconian returned. "Mostly about Maldred. They're worried about him. They know by his color he's an ogremage and can cast spells. They're frightened of magic." After a few moments: "They're puzzled by you, however. They think you're some sort of spawn or draconian, but they want to get a better look at you. And . . . they're wondering how many steel pieces Fiona might fetch."

"Let them worry and wonder. Then let them

die." Dhamon strode purposefully toward the clump of bushes. He tossed his hood back so the goblins could see his scaly face. "I'm wondering just how long it will take me to finish them off." A glance over his shoulder. "Ragh, watch Fiona and Maldred."

"There are a dozen," Ragh said, just as that many creatures came out of hiding, waving their spears and shouting. "There are a dozen of them that I can see."

The goblins spilled out from the bushes, though they didn't advance more than a few yards. They stank. A gust of wind drove the stench into his nostrils, and Dhamon had to work to keep from gagging.

They raised their dissonant voices to a shrill and annoying chorus. Dhamon loped toward them now, expecting them to run, half hoping some would stay and fight. To his surprise, the goblins all held their ground, shaking their spears at the air, the smallest one hopping and whooping.

"Suit yourself," he said, as he raised the glaive and swung. "Let's see how many of you I can kill with one pass." The blade fairly whistled as it swept forward, and only then did the goblins in its path leap back. Dhamon pulled the weapon around for another swipe, then stopped himself before he managed to cut any down. "Damn it all."

None of them were truly threatening him, he realized. None had darted in, not a one had lobbed a spear. They just hobbled around and hooted annoyingly.

Dhamon let out an exasperated sigh. Maldred's goodheartedness—the Maldred who once had been his friend and who, back then, seemed to revere all life—had perhaps finally rubbed off on him.

"Fight me!" he cursed. Dhamon couldn't bring himself to attack the foul little things unless they made a hostile move. They held their place, whooping louder.

"Wonderful," Dhamon grumbled. "Are you going to fight or just shout and dance?"

There came more noise, grunts and clicking sounds. The goblins continued to chatter as they formed a semicircle around him, their grunts and growls sounding almost rhythmic now, like a chant. The tallest of the lot, a bent old fellow with a dirty yellow hide and more than a dozen steel rings threaded through his lips, cheeks, and nose, was waving wildly toward the pines. Another was pointing behind Dhamon, to where Ragh and Fiona and Maldred waited.

From behind the pines came forty more goblins, all with spears, and half of them wearing pieces of leather they'd cobbled together into breastplates. One flaunted a helmet, human-sized, that had been hammered in places to keep it from falling down over the goblin's head. Two carried wooden shields garishly painted with the images of open-mouthed goblins. They were animated and snarling, though not one waved a spear menacingly in Dhamon's direction.

"Ragh!"

"Coming," the draconian said. He pointed the long sword at Fiona, then Maldred. "Both of you, move. Stay in front of me so I can watch you."

"What are they saying now?" Dhamon asked as Ragh and the others approached.

This time it was Maldred who answered. "Essentially they're welcoming you to Throt, save that they call it Goblin Home. They are honored by your presence. They apparently have decided that you and the wingless sivak are among Takhisis's greatest creations. They believe they are blessed by your presence. The chief argues that Ragh is the greater blessing, however, as you still have some flesh on you and might be part human."

"And you, ogre?"

"They believe I'm your slave, and Fiona is your property."

"Ragh?"

The draconian snorted. "Maldred's translating well enough."

"They talk a lot. Are they saying anything else worth knowing?"

Maldred paused, shifting his glance between the goblins and Dhamon while deciding how to answer. "They're asking how they can serve you— the 'perfect children' of their revered god."

The sky continued to darken along with Dhamon's mood, and he felt the ground tremble again beneath his feet—perhaps the precursor to an earthquake. "Perfect child of Takhisis. Ha. So everyone thinks I'm a monster," he said softly. And maybe everyone's right.

The goblin prattling stopped when Dhamon raised the glaive high, and as one the odd little creatures stood at some semblance of attention, breathing shallowly, eyes flitting between Dhamon and Ragh, faces all nervous. The stillness was broken by a wolf howling, and moments later by the screech of some night bird overhead. Again the ground trembled slightly, longer this time, before subsiding.

Ragh moved up alongside Dhamon, speaking in barely a whisper. "Use them, Dhamon. Put them on our side. Then we don't have to worry about them."

"Worry? I'm only worried about one thing."

"Yes, I know. Finding the shadow dragon," Ragh finished.

"All right. Let's see if they can help," Dhamon said. "Let's see if they can guide us to Haltigoth, that is, the village *near* Haltigoth where Riki and my child are." They'll be a welcome nuisance if they do that, he thought. They can help against the hobgoblins outside the village if need be. "We'll start now. The clouds are breaking and with the moon out it will be clear enough for travel."

Ragh was quick to relay Dhamon's commands to the ogres. When the draconian finished, several of the goblins grinned wide and bobbed their misshapen heads.

"They're quite happy to help us," Ragh told Dhamon, "though they say there are several human villages near Haltigoth. How will they know which is the right one? They fear they will displease you if they guess incorrectly."

"They should fear to displease me," Dhamon said, "although I'm counting on the woman in the crystal ball to tell us which village."

◇ ◇ ◇ ◇ ◇ ◇ ◇

They'd walked until after midnight, a forced march set by Dhamon that had the goblins running and gasping and clutching their bony sides. The ground was not helpful, for it was broken by tree stumps and jagged rocks, with sharp dips and slick slate that sent the goblins flying. Dhamon found nothing interesting about Throt. The land was primitive and something he would have preferred to avoid.

When the goblins began to fall too far behind and even Ragh, Fiona, and Maldred had trouble keeping up, Dhamon grudgingly stopped by a thin, twisting brook. The moon was high, clearly illuminating the dying vegetation all around them and setting the water to shimmering like molten silver. The goblins struggled to catch their breath. They kept a polite if not wary distance from Dhamon and his associates.

Dhamon had ascertained that none of the goblins knew the common tongue, so he could talk freely without fear of insulting or provoking his guides. "To be venerated by these things is uncomfortable," he confessed to the draconian.

It was clear Ragh didn't share that feeling. The draconian basked in the goblins' adoration and kept them busy bringing him water from the brook and plucking sweet apples that were still clinging to a nearby tree.

They'd removed the gag from Fiona's mouth but didn't untie her hands. The female Knight wouldn't accept fruit or water and refused all conversation.

"They think we are going to ransom her to someone in this village. They think she's royalty."

"Don't tell them anything different, Ragh."

"They want to know why you and I don't have wings."

Dhamon grimaced. "What did you tell them?"

The draconian offered him a grim smile. "I told them I honestly don't know where I lost mine," he said. "Likely in some great battle so many decades ago that I've forgotten."

"And me?"

"I told them your wings just haven't sprouted yet." The draconian instantly regretted the words when he saw the life go out of Dhamon's eyes. "About Sabar," he said, quickly changing the subject.

He gently removed the cloth bag from his waist and produced the crystal ball.

There were a collection of ooohs and ahhhs from the goblins, and a few inched forward uncomfortably close until Dhamon halted them with a look.

"Ogre," Dhamon said, calling to Maldred. "Use this crystal again, and see if you can find the village for us. I want to look in on Riki and the baby."

Maldred selected a flat, dusty patch of ground, spread his legs and rested the ball on its crown base between his knees. Using the ball was so much easier now, as his mind was already familiar with the magical pulse of the crystal. Soon the purple mists filled the globe, parting to form the image of Sabar.

"You seek me again, O Sagacious One," she purred to Maldred. "Are we to take another journey together? I would enjoy that."

Maldred quickly shook his head. "Show us the village, Sabar," he said evenly.

"Blöten?"

"No. The one from before that, the one inhabited by the half-elf and the babe."

"As you desire, O Sagacious One."

Sabar twirled within the confines of the crystal, gradually revealing the village. Dhamon motioned one old, yellow goblin forward. The creature leaned over the globe, finger extended and almost touching the glass, but clearly afraid.

"Ask him if . . ." Dhamon nudged Maldred, watching intently as the image shifted to show Riki sleeping with the babe at her breast, Varek lying curled at her side. "Ask him if he's seen this place."

The goblin's crude language sounded even worse in Maldred's deep voice. The ogre-mage spoke for several moments, pausing at intervals to let the goblin answer him. Finally Maldred looked up from the crystal. "The old goblin's name is Yagmurth Sharpteeth. He's their leader, and he says he knows where this village is. Apparently he and his people are quite familiar with it. They usually visit it in the late summer, raiding small fields for corn and potatoes, and in the spring they come again when sheep are born. They didn't visit it this summer, though, as a force of hobgoblins have been camped just outside of it for the past three or four months." A hint of a smile crept across Maldred's face. "The goblins hope the 'perfect children of their revered god' will lead them against their cousins, the hobgoblins, so they can crush their enemy and again raid the village for food."

Dhamon studied the goblin named Yagmurth. "Only if necessary will there be a fight with the hobgoblins. Tell him that. Fights take time, and I'm in no mood to waste time. There'll be a battle only if that's the last resort, for I'll do anything to make sure Riki and the child stay safe. But don't tell him that. In fact . . ." He felt the ground shaking again. "Maldred, ask the crystal ball . . ."

The ogre-mage was startled. Dhamon hadn't called him by his real name since they'd been transported from the Nostar cell to the shadow dragon's cave.

"Ask the crystal ball if a cure is still within my reach." Dhamon ran his hands across his stomach, feeling all the scales beneath the ragged robe. He touched the left side of his face to make sure there was still flesh there, and he waited impatiently while Maldred talked to Sabar. Dhamon visibly relaxed and breathed a great sigh of relief as he heard Sabar answer yes.

"But Sabar says you don't have much time left in

which to find a cure," Maldred explained. "You have to find the shadow dragon soon."

"Aye, Mal. I am well aware of that." The fever had suddenly returned, and the skin on his cheek was drenched with sweat, despite the chill of the fall night. His stomach felt was if it were on fire. Dhamon turned abruptly away, walking toward the brook. "Why don't you look in on your damnable dry mountains of Blöde while you're at it? Check in on your dear father."

Ragh snatched up the crystal ball. "You already did that, didn't you?" The draconian returned the ball to the pouch, trying it to his makeshift belt. "You don't need to use this anymore."

Dhamon shed his tattered robe, hearing more oohs and ahhs from the goblins following him as they admired his scales. He waded into the water, hoping its coolness would chase away his fever and put out the fire raging in his stomach. He left the glaive on the bank and growled when a goblin ventured close to touch the weapon.

"Get back!"

The creature didn't need a translation. The meaning in Dhamon's eyes was clear. The goblin scampered away to join his fellows, eight of them sitting high on the bank at a respectful distance. They all watched intently Dhamon's every move. When the ground trembled again, stronger than it had before, Dhamon saw the look on the goblins' crushed faces turn to horror. The trembling persisted and became more intense. Pebbles rolled down the bank and into the stream.

Dhamon jumped up, nearly losing his balance as the earth rumbled. Spears in hand, the goblins were chattering in fright, forming small groups and shouting.

"They're scared!" the draconian called to Dhamon.

"I don't need to speak their language to know that."

"They await our orders."

Dhamon shrugged on his robes and snatched up the glaive. He watched Fiona stumble as she tried to get up. "Cut her loose, Ragh. It'll help her keep her balance."

Ragh started to argue but thought better of it when the tremors became more pronounced. As the draconian headed toward the Solamnic Knight, a fissure appeared behind him and a half-dozen goblins were instantly swallowed by it. Before their hysterical fellows could attempt to rescue them, the ground beneath the sweet apple tree erupted in a geyser of dirt and rocks, sending the tree toppling down the bank and half the remaining goblins running in all directions.

Something began to rise from the ground where the tree had been.

"By my father!" Maldred cursed. "What in all the levels of the Abyss is that?"

The ogre-mage hadn't expected an answer, but he got one from the draconian.

"It's an umberhulk," Ragh groaned.

"A what?" Dhamon and Maldred asked practically in unison.

"A monster," Fiona hissed.

Climbing from an ever-bulging hole was a hideous creature, easily eight feet tall and nearly that wide around. It looked like a cross between a great ape and a crustacean, with long crablike pincers at the end of massive arms clacking loudly. It was the color of wet earth, of which it strongly smelled. A pair of jagged mandibles on either side of its cavernous mouth were dark as midnight. Its eyes—four in all, two pairs of them—were darker.

Legs as thick as tree trunks bent as the strange creature shook itself, scattering a shower of dirt. The umberhulk stamped with its great clawed feet, and the ground was set to trembling again.

The creature swiveled its head, mandibles moving, pincers clacking. Its mouth opened slowly, revealing an intense blackness. Teeth that looked like jagged roots were also blackest black, yet they gleamed weirdly. When the creature roared, it sounded like a dozen angry lions, an explosion of noise that filled the night and brought tears to the goblins' eyes.

"The eyes!" Ragh shouted. "Don't look at the umberhulk's eyes! There's magic in them!" The draconian repeated this order in the goblins' tongue. His eyes averted, he stumbled forward, leading with the long sword, but in a second the Solamnic Knight stepped in front of the draconian, cut him off and snatched the sword from his outstretched claws. Ignoring his exclamation, Fiona advanced on the beast, her blade gleaming in the light of the full moon.

The umberhulk held its arms out to its sides in a macabre, triumphant pose, then roared even louder and stamped forward to meet the female Knight.

"It was hunting the goblins," Maldred said in a low voice. The ogre-mage was sneaking looks at the umberhulk without meeting its gaze. "The vibrations in the earth mark its passing. It was burrowing like a gopher." The ogre-mage had his hands in the air, fingers splayed, and his palms were glowing with enchantment.

Dhamon hadn't given Maldred permission to cast any spell, but now was not the time to argue.

He dashed forward, trying to reach the umberhulk before Fiona.

Fiona got there first, staring up into the umberhulk's four dizzying eyes. "Madness," she pronounced, as she blinked and shook her head. "Beautiful eyes." Then for a moment she stood as though paralyzed, weaving back and forth as the umberhulk roared. "Madness," she repeated, somehow rallying her senses.

Nearly all of the goblins who had not fled either stood spellbound or were wandering aimlessly along the edge of the brook, as if they were caught in some mind-clouding magical spell. One wandered too close to the beast, too dazed to see a pincer-arm shoot out, too numb to feel the pincer close about its waist.

The umberhulk held the goblin high, then squeezed the little creature, nearly slicing it in two. Then the creature tossed back its head, opened its mouth, and swallowed it in one motion. The umberhulk reached to snatch another one.

"Monster!" Fiona howled, sounding like the Fiona of old, momentarily. As she drew back on her sword and brought it down hard, the blade bit into the chitinous shell of the thing's pincer-arm but did no significant damage. The female Knight, as if possessed, struck at the massive creature again and again. Ragh managed to maneuver behind them and join in, clawing at the umberhulk's back while kicking dazed goblins out of the creature's reach.

Another goblin dropped into the umberhulk's maw.

"We'll be at this all night!" Dhamon shouted, noting that neither Fiona nor the sivak seemed able to cause the umberhulk any real harm. "Its skin is as tough as plate armor!" He edged closer, narrowly avoiding a pincer and knocking it away with the butt of his glaive. With Ragh and Fiona so near, Dhamon couldn't risk sweeping the glaive in a wide arc. Instead, he raised it above his head and brought it down in a powerful chopping motion. He felt strangely eager for a good fight.

As the blade of the glaive sliced into the umberhulk's shoulder, its thick, green blood fountained into the air and rained down on them.

"It bleeds!" Fiona shouted. "If it can bleed, it can die!" She accelerated her efforts, some blows bouncing off the thing's armored hide, a few miraculously cutting into its arm just above the pincer. The runes along her blade glowed brightly blue, and its sharp edge sparkled in the moonlight. "I can kill it with this sword!"

She drew back for a thrust, just as the umberhulk turned with a speed unexpected for its size. A pincer-arm shot forward, clacking loudly. Fiona had fast reflexes and pulled away at the last instant, yet it snagged her clothes. She spun around behind the creature, pushed Ragh aside, and stepped up her frenzied attack.

"We're actually hurting the foul creature!" This was shouted by Ragh, who also managed to cut the creature and draw some repulsive-smelling blood.

Dhamon stepped in for a hard chop, this time cutting even deeper into the umberhulk's shoulder and wounding the creature so badly that one pincer-arm twitched, then hung limp. He drove his blade down again, this time with more force. The umberhulk screamed, a horrible sound, like stone scraping against stone. The ground rumbled, and cracks raced away from the umberhulk's clawed feet. Its legs churned, and it began to retreat down its huge hole.

"It's fleeing!" Ragh shouted in triumph. Still, he pressed his attack. "We're winning!"

"We can't let it escape!" Fiona cried angrily. "Don't let it go!"

"She's right!" Dhamon said, as he brought the glaive up again, swinging it down this time into the center of the creature's back. He bunched his arm muscles and yanked the blade free. "If it gets away, it can pop up anywhere for another chance at us!"

The ground rumbled louder, as the sinking umberhulk roared its defiance.

"Wait, it's not going anywhere." As Maldred finished his spell, a soft yellow glow poured from his palms onto the ground. Like a line of molten lightning it streaked to the umberhulk. "Out of the way! Move, Dhamon!"

Dhamon had to grab Fiona, for the Knight was continuing to lunge at the beast with rapid sword blows. Ragh jumped back just in time. The magical light struck its target, spiraled around the umberhulk, and took root in the ground.

"What's going to happen now?" Ragh said. "What kind of magic . . . ?" The rest of his words were swallowed by the furious upheaval of the earth.

As they watched, everywhere the light flowed the ground began to thicken, trapping the creature's legs and its one good pincer-arm in solid stone.

It shrieked its rage. Whipping its head about, its four eyes fixed on Ragh and magically befuddled him. The draconian's snout dropped open, and he started shuffling toward the screaming umberhulk and the still-hardening earth.

"Now, Dhamon!" Maldred shouted. "Finish it!"

Dhamon was in good position. Releasing Fiona, he swept the glaive at waist-level with all of his strength. The great blade parted the chitinous shell of the umberhulk. The creature howled, and the earth shook wildly. The stone earth in which he was embedded began to crack as the creature fought to break free.

Again Dhamon swung.

"It bleeds!" Fiona cried gleefully. "We can kill it! I can kill it!" She leaned in and landed a few more blows before the thing gave a tremendous shudder and stopped moving.

The earth quieted after a few moments. Dhamon stepped back and took a breath. It took several minutes for Ragh and the goblins to come to their senses and many minutes after that for the goblins who'd run away to straggle back.

Dhamon went over to the brook to clean the blood off himself and the glaive. Glancing up, he saw the draconian trying to take the sword away from Fiona.

"It talks to me!" she was shouting madly.

"Let her have it," Dhamon said, as he walked over to join them.

The draconian raised an eyebrow. "She nearly killed you, Dhamon. Are you as mad as she is to let her keep this weapon?"

Maybe, he thought. Aloud he said, "We'll rest here an hour, no more, then be on the move again."

◇ ◇ ◇ ◇ ◇ ◇ ◇

They pressed on until dawn, following the brook that widened into a stream as they proceeded north.

"Yagmurth says the village you want is just around that rise," Ragh told Dhamon. "They want to know if you're going to lead them into battle against their hobgoblin cousins. Because you slew the umberhulk, they think you can perform miracles."

Dhamon didn't answer at first. He was staring at his reflection in the water. I am a monster, he thought. The fire in his stomach had spread all over his body. For the past several miles it was all he could do to ignore the pain and plod onward.

"You're getting taller," Ragh said, glancing at Dhamon warily, then looking over at the Knight, who was still carrying her magic sword and talking to it. "You realize that, don't you? I'd say by a few inches at least."

The seams of Dhamon's ragged garments were stretched over his growing limbs. "Aye, Ragh, I know."

Dhamon continued to stare at his reflection. His face was different, too, and it took him a few moments to understand how different. His forehead was slightly higher, and a ridge was forming over his eyes. Like Ragh, Dhamon thought his neck was thicker, too, though he couldn't be sure. His ears were smaller, slightly, as though they were melding against the sides of his head.

"Maldred, ask Sabar if there's still enough time."

"Taller," Ragh commented quietly, "and more forgiving. You let Fiona keep the sword. You call the ogre-mage by name."

"There's time," Maldred replied after several minutes of silence, during which he consulted the magic-woman in the crystal. "But not much. She says to hurry."

I am hurrying. Dhamon ran his hand through his hair, a shiver racing down his spine when he saw his palms were dark gray like the bottoms of his feet. He stepped back from the stream and looked toward the village. "I need to make sure Riki and the child are safe." A moment later, "And I can't let them see me. Not until I've forced a cure from the damn shadow dragon. If I can find the dragon in time."

The old yellow goblin shuffled over, careful to keep a polite distance, waiting until Dhamon was done speaking before it began chattering to Ragh. The other goblins huddled together, watching the exchange between the draconian and their leader.

"Yagmurth asks again if you will lead them in battle against their hobgoblin cousins. He wants very much to fight." Ragh bent closer to the old goblin, waving a hand in front of his face to ward off the stink. He growled and snapped in the gutteral tongue until Yagmurth seemed happy.

The old goblin squared his shoulders, whipped about, and trundled back to his fellows. Fiona gave the whole bunch a look of loathing, then joined Dhamon and Ragh.

"What did you say to him?" Dhamon watched the goblins chatter happily among themselves, making whooping noises and raising their spears.

Ragh glanced over his shoulder, watching Maldred replace the crystal ball in the makeshift bag. The ogre-mage tied it to his waist. "I told them that I, the greatest of Takhisis's creations, would lead them into battle against their hobgoblin cousins." He lowered his voice. "If necessary. If we can't get Riki and her family out of town any other way. If the crystal is true, and the hobgoblins aren't there at the shadow dragon's behest, there might be some problems with a rescue operation."

"And what about me?"

"I told Yagmurth you had business elsewhere."

Dhamon shook his head. "No. I—"

". . . Have to get your cure before it's too late. Your child doesn't need a draconian—or spawn—

for a father. Save yourself, Dhamon, and I'll endeavor to save your woman and child."

"Ragh, I . . ."

"I will go with you, sivak." Fiona put her hand on the pommel of her sword. "I will go with you to help the half-elf Riki. That is an honorable cause." The Solamnic Knight's eyes were wide and staring, but the fiery madness seemed temporarily gone. "I will not help Dhamon find a cure, and I will not stay in the company of the ogre-liar, so I will go with you. That is what I should and will do."

She shrugged and wiped at a stain on her tunic, then looked up with a wild look in her eyes again. "But when Riki and her family are safe, I will track Dhamon—as high into the mountains as he chances to go." She turned from the draconian and locked eyes with Dhamon. "And then, Dhamon Grimwulf, we will finish this, you and I. You will pay for Rig's death—for the deaths of Shaon and Jasper and whomever else you betrayed. You will pay for everything."

CHAPTER SEVENTEEN
VISIONS AND
SHADOWS

Riki will be all right, Dhamon. They might not have to fight the hobgoblins to get her out. They might be able to slip in, take her, your child, and Varek too."

"Aye, maybe."

It was the first either of them had spoken since they'd left Ragh, Fiona, and the goblins, hours ago. They were making their way toward the mountain ridge. The wind was strong, cutting across the uneven plain, rustling the tall, dried grass and whipping up small rocks. The sky was cloudless and blue, making the brown landscape seem even more desolate and drab. The few trees that grew on the craggy ledges were thin and barren, save for a lone pine that stretched tall and defiant.

Dhamon lengthened his stride, keeping his eyes on the pine. He'd chosen a route that avoided the cluster of small settlements and farms between Haltigoth and the mountains, and one that roughly paralleled a merchant road to the south.

Maldred maintained his appearance as a blue-skinned ogre-mage. Earlier, Maldred had attempted to don his human guise when two men on horseback rode by, but Dhamon became angry and shouted at the ogre, so Maldred kept his true appearance. The sight of the ogre kept the men on horseback at a distance.

Dhamon didn't want to be reminded of Maldred as a human, the sun-bronzed friend who once shared many an adventure with him, but as they neared the shadows of the mountains, he realized, too, that he didn't want Maldred to look human because he, himself, didn't look human anymore. And unlike Maldred, he couldn't cast a spell to make himself look like a man again.

Did Sabar speak the truth? he thought. Was there still time to reach the shadow dragon and force the damnable creature to cure him?

He wondered if Maldred would betray him again, warn the shadow dragon somehow of their approach. Would he cut some new deal to save Blöten and the surrounding land? He wouldn't put it past the ogre-mage. Dhamon would have left Maldred behind with Ragh and Fiona, if he didn't think the ogre might be needed to find the shadow dragon and if he didn't need Maldred's crystal-ball scrying

"We had some good times," Maldred said.

"Aye," Dhamon admitted. "A few."

It was even cooler in the shadow of the mountains, and the coolness was a welcome antidote to the fever that consumed Dhamon. Dhamon found himself staring up at the mountains and wondering if perhaps the dragon had chosen its lair here wisely after all. The peaks were stark and imposing, like the dragon.

"Dhamon, we can wait here a moment, ask Sabar to look in on Riki, to see if the Knight and draconian have accomplished anything."

Dhamon shook his head. He didn't want to know that, not at this juncture anyway. They'd traveled too far to turn back now. He couldn't afford to be distracted either by Ragh's success or failure. Dhamon needed to concentrate on confronting the shadow dragon. He'd put his trust in Ragh, and that was that.

He suspected the ogre-mage had volunteered to use the crystal because it would afford him a moment of rest. Dhamon had been driving them pretty hard, and neither man had slept in nearly two days.

"Look in on the shadow dragon instead," Dhamon suggested. "Try to pinpoint the exact location of his cave. If you can't get us a good idea of where he is, we'll spend days wandering around here." And I don't have the time, Dhamon thought. Softly, he added, "Or maybe you prefer us to wander around. Maybe you don't want me to find the cave until it is too late. Maybe you want the shadow dragon to win." The fever hadn't lessened. If anything the fire in his stomach and across his back was more intense. Just walking was a chore.

While Maldred was summoning the image of Sabar into the crystal ball, Dhamon closed his eyes. He focused all his thoughts on the heat and pain, attempting to use his willpower to shut them down, but it didn't work.

Dhamon stared at the mountains. The dragon was somewhere up there, hidden in some massive cave. He gazed toward the south, where the peaks were the highest, then suddenly felt a spasm of fiery pain and almost buckled.

"Dhamon?"

"I'm fine," he said tersely. A few deep breaths and the worst of it passed, but his chest ached now. He tore his robe at the neck, then ripped it open down to his waist. Leaning on the glaive for support, he rubbed his chest and his ribs with his free hand. His left side was now covered with scales that burned to the touch. As his fingers moved over his abdomen, he felt another fiery jolt. There was a similar sensation low on his back, and he knew that more skin was disappearing.

How much of my skin remains? he wondered. There was a stream nearby. He wanted to look at his reflection, but perhaps it was better if he didn't know.

"Dhamon."

"I said I'm fine." He turned to face Maldred, seeing the ogre-mage seated on the hard ground, the crystal between his knees. Maldred stared at him with wide eyes. Dhamon reached up to feel his face. There was a slight popping sound, and he felt his jaw extend outward and the scales under his chin thicken. "Is there . . ."

"Time yet? A chance for your cure?" Maldred dropped his gaze to the purple-clad woman in the crystal ball. "Sabar says there is time—very little."

"Does she really say that?" Another streak of fire raced across his face. "Or are you just telling me what I want to hear? Are you playing some game?"

Maldred didn't look up. "I'm not lying to you, Dhamon. Not now. Not ever again." He ran one of his hands across the crystal globe's surface. "I know I made a mistake in allying myself with the shadow dragon, a very serious mistake. I was so frantic to save my people and my homeland that I took the first good opportunity that came along. You can damn me for my stupidity and desperation, but don't damn me for putting the ogre nation before one man. Even a friend."

"It was your father's idea. Wasn't it? For you to side with the naga and the shadow dragon?"

"Yes."

"And like the dutiful son you are, you bought into it."

"I thought at the time the idea had merit. I should have looked for another way. I well know that now. I should have asked your help. Instead I deceived my best friend and lost your friendship, and I've done my father and his kingdom no good. There might be no saving them now."

"There might be no saving any of us if these cursed dragons go unchecked," Dhamon said. "The shadow dragon . . . ."

Maldred turned his attention to the crystal, seeming to caress it, and in response the woman inside conjured up an image of a mountain range. One high peak melted away to show a great dark slash.

"O Sagacious One," she breathed. "This is the one you look for." Sabar twirled, her purple skirts sparkling and filling up the whole of the ball. When she stopped moving, the vision shifted again, this time showing the inside of a cave at the top of the peak.

Dhamon peered closer. The image flowed inside the mountain. The passage was wide and steep, angling downward and twisting like a serpent as Sabar took them deeper into the cave. Dhamon imagined it smelled dry and stale—it certainly looked that way. Dust and clay were everywhere. There were tiny, curly-tailed lizards on ledges, and several varieties of bats clung to the walls and gently beat their wings.

Sabar led them deeper, and what little light they saw was pale and tinted purplish-red. There was moisture on the wall, and a faint glimmer suggesting veins of silver. Then the wall disappeared and a great cavern loomed. It was lit by a dull yellow glow, and Dhamon knew this came from the eyes of the shadow dragon.

The great creature was curled almost like a cat, its tail wrapped tight against its body, the tip of the tail disappearing beneath its head. Dhamon wondered if Nura Bint-Drax had managed to reach her "master's" side here in this remote mountain. But he couldn't tell if there was anyone else inside the cave.

The shadow dragon was awake and seemed to be studying something, its scaly visage intent, its eyes unblinking and fixed on . . . something far-away.

"It sees us," Dhamon said.

"Not possible," Sabar replied.

"It sees us," Dhamon repeated.

Maldred slowly nodded. "I think you're right."

"You used the crystal too much, Mal. Somehow that damnable dragon knows we're coming, that we're nearby." As he spoke, the shadow dragon's eyes moved ever so slightly, narrowing, and its lip curled up viciously.

"In the name of my father!" Maldred clamped his hands around the crystal, blotting out the image of the dragon and instantly dismissing Sabar from view. "You're right, Dhamon, but I didn't think the dragon would see us so easily."

"Didn't you?"

"No. I said no more lies."

Dhamon gave him a withering look, then turned toward the far mountains. He wasn't sure exactly where the shadow dragon's lair was, but he knew from the crystal ball they couldn't be more than twenty or thirty miles away.

His steps were fast and determined. He had no intention of waiting for Maldred. In fact, he was mulling over the possibility of losing the ogre somewhere in the craggy peaks. Dhamon didn't for a moment believe Maldred's claim that there would be no more treachery. He didn't for a moment . . .

Dhamon stopped in mid-stride, feeling a tightening in his chest. The fire on his back grew hotter still, his fever was raging. He gasped for air, found his mouth and throat parched. No sound came out. He heard his heart hammering, and he heard a pounding—Maldred racing toward him. He heard the ogre-mage's labored breathing, heard the cool, dry wind that whipped around him. Then, as suddenly as the tightening sensation began, it abated, leaving only the heat.

"Dhamon . . ."

"I'm all right, I tell you!"

"You're not all right. Let me try the spell again. It slowed the scales earlier."

Dhamon brusquely dismissed this suggestion and resumed his brutal pace. With a sigh, Maldred followed as best he could.

"I believe we should head toward the north," Maldred said, catching up. He was staring up at the mountains, thinking he'd seen this place in Sabar's vision.

"Aye," Dhamon said. "To the north. And up."

Maldred said something else, but Dhamon pushed the words away and focused on the whistling of the mountain wind. He prayed the wind would blow colder still and abate some of the burning fever in his body, and at the same time he knew that nothing—save a cure, or death—would stop the pain and fever.

Miles passed. Dhamon put distance between himself and Maldred, who was not able to keep up the relentless pace. They began to ascend when Dhamon recognized a gnarled spire of rock, high up, that looked like a hawk's beak.

"Not too much farther," Dhamon muttered hopefully to himself. They continued to climb, continued north. Shards of rock constantly bit into Dhamon's feet. He almost welcomed the sensation, as the scaly pads on his feet were so thick he'd barely registered the roughness of the terrain. It felt good to feel something.

Dhamon paused here and there to check his bearings. During one such interval the ogre-mage trudged up from behind. Good. He wanted Maldred to make sure they were on the right course. And it was like the days of old, as if Maldred could read his mind.

"Dhamon, let's check our position again," the ogre-mage suggested.

A nod of agreement, and the ogre-mage gratefully sat down. He took several deep breaths and rubbed his thighs. "You're making fast time, Dhamon. You go too fast for me."

"I need to go fast. I'm in a hurry, remember?" The tone was more sharp than Dhamon had intended.

Maldred carefully pulled the crystal ball from the pouch. He set it on a tablelike section of rock, spread his fingers around the base, but before he could say anything the mountain suddenly trembled all around them with the force of a small earthquake. The crystal rolled off its crown perch and began to tumble down the slope.

"By the Dark Queen's heads! No!" Dhamon leaped for the crystal ball. "I have been a fool! You have caused the quake! You do mean to keep me from the dragon until it is too late! You did this!"

Dhamon's fingers closed on air as the crystal ball rolled down the slope. The mountain continued to shake, rock cracking and pebbles cascading.

Maldred had lost his footing and was flailing about for any foothold. His blue skin was soon lacerated from rocks, and his hands and arms were bloodied. The rocky outcropping above them broke off and smashed into him as it bounced down the slope.

"Look out, Dhamon!" Maldred managed to cry out in warning.

Stronger and more agile, Dhamon dodged the rockslide and managed to stay on his feet as he raced down the incline, trying recklessly to reach the crystal.

"It wasn't my doing!" Maldred shouted, his voice all but drowned out by the crumbling of the mountain range. "I swear it wasn't my magic!"

The tremor persisted for several minutes, during which time Dhamon reached a lower level and there discovered the shattered fragments of the magic crystal. Pathetically he pawed at a small piece of lavender cloth.

"By all the gods, no!" he screamed.

In anger and frustration, his fingers dug into the pouch at his side, pulling out two of the carved figurines Ragh had found in the sorcerer's laboratory back in the Black's swamp. He hurled them as high and as hard as he could. They struck the cliffs above, and there was a flash of bright red light and the crack of thunder. The mountain shook again, rock shards raining down the slopes.

Dhamon reached into the pouch again, intending to rid himself of all these accursed, unreliable magical items, but the ogre-mage came stumbling up behind him, and Maldred's big blue hand shot out and closed on Dhamon's wrist.

"Stop!" Maldred looked beaten, bruised, and bloodied. He was panting. "Dhamon, stop!"

Dhamon paused, eyes gleaming furiously.

"It wasn't my doing, honestly. The quake. I didn't—"

"I know. I believe you."

Maldred looked astonished. He released Dhamon. "I told you, no more deceit. I want to help save you, Dhamon. I need to save . . . something."

Now that he was calmer, Dhamon knew Maldred wouldn't have risked destroying the precious crystal ball. The enchanted item was far too precious for the thief who was also a sorcerer.

"I know. It was the shadow dragon," Dhamon said. He dropped the piece of lavender cloth in Maldred's palm. "He has great magic, I know, and I am certain he used it. Obviously he wants to keep me away. He fears me, Maldred."

The ogre-mage stared at the cloth, remembering Sabar draped in it, twirling in the lavender mist. Was the magic-woman shattered, too? Or was she entirely illusion?

His breath caught, and he turned to look Dhamon directly in the eyes. "No." The ogre-mage swallowed hard. "That's not entirely true. I have no doubt he caused the quake, but he doesn't want to keep you away. He *wants* you to find him. I know it. But he doesn't want you getting close until he's ready. He's delaying you. The scales on you, he wants the scales to . . ."

He's delaying me while my body becomes

more grotesque, Dhamon realized. "Yes, he's delaying me until it's too late. As punishment he's delaying me until I become a spawn or a draconian or some mad meld of the fiendish creatures. Until I've lost my mind and my soul and am no longer any threat."

"Let's get going, then," Maldred said, looking up the mountainside. "Let's not allow the shadow dragon to win."

Dhamon took the lead again. The quake had altered the face of the mountain, and Dhamon worried that the mouth of the cave had been erased.

They climbed for a few hours. Dhamon felt increasingly concerned that they were irretrievably lost. He thought of Riki and the child—and of Varek, too, who would have to act as the father of Dhamon's child. He wondered if they were all safe, and wondered if Riki ever thought of him, wondered if in some small way the child favored him. Wondered if . . .

You will never know those things, Dhamon Grimwulf.

His eyes flew wide, as these were not his words, but he heard them clearly inside of his head.

You will never see them . . . Riki, the baby . . . you will never let them see your scale-ridden self. You will never touch your child.

"No!" Dhamon shouted. "That's not true!" He screamed in rage, then he screamed again—this time in sudden, sharp pain. He felt as though flames had attacked every inch of his body, burning away his tattered clothes. He dropped the glaive, and his fingers ripped at his clothes, pulling them off and tossing them aside. His hands flew to his ears, trying to drown out the words that persisted.

You will never let them see that there's nothing

human about you anymore. You will never let them see the creature you have become.

"No, you damnable beast! I will see them!"

Maldred, close behind, shouted at Dhamon, but he couldn't hear anything except the words inside his head. He forced himself to walk, despite the agony and the taunts in his head. With each step he felt his bones crack and stretch, felt his skin burn away to be replaced by scales. He reached to his back, felt something growing.

Wings, the voice said. *Spawn have wings, Dhamon Grimwulf.*

His fingers registered a snout forming on his face. He opened his mouth to scream a protest, but his tongue felt thick and foreign.

There is no humanity left in you, Dhamon Grimwulf, and soon you will have no soul.

Dhamon reeled. He tried to imagine what he must look like. He turned around and saw Maldred gape, take a step back away from him. Even Maldred was shocked, afraid.

I have no intention of turning into one, no intention of sharing Ragh's existence. I still have my mind, he thought. *If for only a while longer. While I can yet think on my own, I can always take the glaive, end my life.*

Live. Come to me, the voice said.

He felt a slight tug, as though someone had taken his hand, but there was no one there, and the sensation was more of an urging than a physical pulling.

"By the Dark Queen's heads, you'll not win! I will kill myself before I become your spawn puppet!"

There was deep, sonorous laughter—loud and long and haunting. The laughter enveloped Dhamon, yet he knew it was coming from inside him. The laughter was all inside his mind. The shadow dragon was thoroughly inside his head, he realized, and it was attempting to control him and draw him near.

"The beast wants to see me lose my soul," he managed to gasp. "He wants to see the last of my humanity die."

He looked around. Maldred had disappeared. Fled. Betrayed him again.

In the next instant not only could Dhamon hear the dragon, he could see it clearly—a bloated mass of shadowy scales breathing and moving and flying toward him in his mind's eye. It was nearly as large as an overlord. Huge and terrifying, its image weakened his will. He felt his mind surrendering.

"I've got to fight it," he told himself. "Stay strong long enough to kill myself. Where's the glaive?"

All of a sudden Dhamon felt as if he were flying, the wind rushing beneath his leathery wings, his claws outstretched, his eyes scanning the ground below for . . . dragons. For magical energy. He had been mentally swept away from the mountainside and deposited . . . where? In a cavern? Hot and dry and smelling of sulfur. There was a blue dragon nearby, small and with a Dark Knight mounted on its back. Dhamon felt his wings pulling into his sides, felt himself diving. He realized the cavern was incredibly immense. The air was laced with the scent of lightning and blood, filled with shouts of battle and the cries of the dying. When he looked around he saw other blue dragons, all ridden by Knights.

"The Abyss? Am I witnessing the Chaos War through the shadow dragon's eyes? Is it forcing me to watch this catastrophe to stamp out my resistance?"

The blue dragon loomed in front of him. He

stretched out his claws, felt them sink into the young dragon's side. His claws began rending the creature, killing it quickly and sending the Knight-rider plummeting like a discarded doll. He felt a rush of excitement from the kill, felt a wash of energy pulse up through his claws and into his chest. Then he flew to another blue dragon. And another. And another.

Dhamon felt his mind slipping away.

Yet with each kill he felt renewed, stronger, infused with the life energy of the dying Blues. With each one that collapsed to the cavern floor, he felt an increasing power of pride—he knew that Chaos, the Father of All and of Nothing, would be pleased. He banked in the hot, parched air of the cavern, climbed to the ceiling and spotted the giant form of Chaos smiling at him.

This is the Abyss, Dhamon realized. This is indeed the Chaos War.

The great battle continued to play out before him, and when it was done, he—the shadow dragon—flew from the cavern, through a misty veil and out into the wilds of Krynn. He soared high and fast, hating the daylight, searching for darkness and finally finding it in a deep, dry cave high in ogre lands.

There he rested, cocooned by the blessed darkness. When he emerged from the dark, he joined the dragonpurge, feasting on the magical life energy of smaller, unwary dragons, all of whom swiftly died beneath his shadowy claws.

Come to me, Dhamon Grimwulf, the voice repeated. *Spawn. Pawn.*

The pull was stronger.

In his mind's eye Dhamon peered through the shadows now, saw a pale, dull-yellow light, spotted a young girl with coppery hair in the far recesses.

He saw Nura Bint-Drax through the shadow dragon's eyes.

"Let me see the beginning," Nura cooed. "Let me see your birth again, my master."

Dhamon witnessed the shadow dragon's creation, a shadow detached from the Father of All and of Nothing, watched him take part in the Chaos War and watched his activities through the dragonpurge and since. He watched the dragon's initial meeting with Dhamon and with others. He watched the shadow dragon spreading his scales.

Finally he saw the shadow dragon settling in the swamp, choosing the warmth and the heat pleasing to his form. He watched as the dragon's seeds grew, scales spreading, killing some of its hosts. But not Dhamon. Dhamon was the one.

My pawn, the voice purred. *My spawn.*

Dhamon furiously shook his head and closed his eyes. He knelt and fumbled about for his glaive. "I am too late for my cure," he told himself.

Live, the voice persisted.

"For just a while longer," Dhamon returned bitterly. "I intend to prevent you from doing this to anyone else. You will create no more spawn! I'll come to you, all right, you damnable beast, but on my own terms. Damn all dragons in the world!"

He thought he remembered the dragon telling him that his mind was more powerful than his body. He knew his body was very strong indeed.

"I'll use my mind to fight you. Leave me now," he said. His voice sounded strange, unfamiliar, deep and exotic. "Get out of my head!"

Dhamon concentrated all of his mental energy. He reached deep down inside, finding a spark he hadn't known existed, kindling and nourishing it.

It felt like pushing a boulder, but after what seemed like an eternity, the boulder began to budge.

He shoved the boulder down the side of the mountain, out of sight and out of mind, then sat back on a flat rock, took a deep breath, and opened his eyes. The shadow dragon was gone, but he knew precisely where to find the beast.

Maldred was suddenly back, at his side, eyes unblinking, but almost moist with tears.

"Aye, my old friend. It's too late for me," Dhamon said. His voice still seemed so strange to his own ears. "There will be no cure."

Maldred stammered something, but Dhamon waved the words away. He rose, discovering that he was very tall now and stood nearly eye-to-eye with the big ogre-mage.

"It's too late now, and I'm going to damn well make sure it's too late for the shadow dragon, too." He knew the shadow dragon would be waiting for him, that it wanted him to come—to gloat, to punish him, to finish his condemnation.

"Dhamon, I will help you. You can still try . . . ."

The mountain range rumbled again, smothering Maldred's pleading and forcing both of them to leap behind a huge boulder to avoid falling rocks. When the tremors died down, the face of the mountainside had changed again.

"The shadow dragon knows I'm coming," Dhamon said, when it was over, "and he wants me to come. He wants to punish me, wants revenge, and he wants to slay my mind and use my body as his puppet." He paused, staring up at the mountain with eyes that could now see tiny details in sharp focus. "But I want revenge, Maldred. So I'll come to him all right, and let my cure be damned."

◇ ◇ ◇ ◇ ◇ ◇ ◇

Nestled deep in the cave, the shadow dragon growled gently, nonetheless sending a ripple of tremors through the rock.

In her little girl guise, Nura Bint-Drax padded forward. "You are pleased, master?"

The dragon slowly nodded. "Dhamon Grimwulf comes. Before the day is out, he will find our lair. He is ready, Nura Bint-Drax. Finally ready."

"We are ready, too," Nura Bint-Drax said in her woman's voice. "And anxious." She busied herself gathering all the magical treasures they'd accumulated from Dark Knight storehouses and elsewhere, methodically placing them near to the shadow dragon and between its claws. "Very, very anxious."

Chapter Eighteen
Ragh's
Goblin Brigade

The goblins followed Ragh closely. Each bore an expectant look on his smashed-in face. Yagmurth was especially happy, his smile showing off yellowed, broken teeth. The draconian had to ward off the stench from his army, raising his head toward fresh air.

Fiona purposefully stood downwind. However, she was interested in Yagmurth, who seemed to carry himself with confidence and speak louder than the rest. The smallest goblins had the thinnest voices, and one scrawny, brown one sounded like a mewling cat. For the most part, the bigger the goblin, the more noise it made and the greater its stink.

The female Knight watched their expressions and listened to their craggy voices. She picked out occasional words in the common tongue—words that either didn't exist in the goblin language or were universal in all languages: "sivak," "Takhisis," "general."

"General?" she repeated to herself, cocking her head and noticing that the one who kept saying "General" was now watching her closely. "General . . . who?"

This goblin separated himself from the pack. He was nearly three feet tall, with a nose that reminded her of a turnip and skin the color of rust. His eyes seemed too large for his pug nose, and his hair fell in scattered patches of uneven lengths. There was a bone ring in the goblin's right ear, from which dangled two bluejay feathers and a clay bead.

She sucked in her breath in an effort not to chuckle at the strange-looking creature.

"General," the goblin said, followed by a string of nonsensical—to her—clicks and snarls. "General."

"Yes, General. Forgive me for speaking aloud. I had no intention of drawing your attention. Go away."

The little, strange-looking goblin didn't go away. In fact, he drew nearer. The goblin babbled animatedly, including the word "General" a few more times. The goblin's voice yipped excitedly, reminding her of a small and annoying dog. The goblin clearly wanted her to say something in response, but she raised her lip in a snarl to quiet the thing.

"Ragh!" Fiona called. "Your goblin friends are bothering me. Can't you do something with your 'army'?"

The draconian shouted in the goblin tongue for them all to quiet down.

Instantly, the old goblin named Yagmurth thumped the haft of his spear against the ground, calling all his fellows to attention. Then he gently thwacked the haft against Ragh's leg. When the draconian looked down, Yagmurth started chattering loudly.

"I know," Ragh answered in their guttural tongue. "You are waiting for me to lead you against the hobgoblins and their leader General Kruth. But I, the greatest of Takhisis's creations, believe there might be a better, slyer way of winning the day."

The draconian registered the disappointment on the goblins' faces. Yagmurth thumped the spear again.

"Perfect child," Yagmurth asked in the goblin tongue. "How is there a better way than battle?"

Ragh shrugged his shoulders. Years before he fell in with Dhamon, Ragh settled nearly all his problems by combat. There were a few exceptions. For example, he had learned if his problem was bigger and nastier than himself, it was wise to avoid a fight

"There are always alternatives to fighting," Ragh dissembled smoothly. "This is an opportunity that calls for stealth and intelligence—two things I'll bet you have plenty of, and two things I'm certain your hobgoblin enemies have never heard of."

The goblins swelled with pride. By the tone of their excited voices and expressions, even Fiona could tell they were won over by Ragh's flattery and listened to his plan. As he huddled with his army, Fiona, tired of their banter and their stink, stepped away from the crowd and held her own strategy session—with the sword.

"I seek revenge," she told it. "I seek . . . ."

The sword gave her the answer she sought.

"Fiona." The draconian stamped his foot. "Fiona!"

She looked up, frowning to note that the draconian had interrupted her dialogue with the sword. The draconian was watching her closely. In truth, Ragh remained half-afraid the female Knight, in her madness, might lash out at him or the goblins.

She twisted her head to look at Ragh, raising an eyebrow. "What?"

"We need your help."

The frown disappeared, replaced by an almost wistful expression, but her eyes looked distracted, flitting over Ragh and then shifting away, studying something in the distance that perhaps only she could see. "You need my help with your plan?"

He nodded.

"Oh, yes, you need me," Fiona agreed. "That's why I stayed with you, sivak. You need me because I look human. I'm the only one who can walk into that village and scout what's happening, see where Riki and Varek and Dhamon's baby are, how they are doing. I can see if they know that they're in serious danger if they stick around this place."

The draconian nodded again.

"I can see what the hobgoblins are up to. Yes, you need me."

Ragh loosely translated what she had said to Yagmurth, who'd skittered up to his side and was staring at the female Knight with curiosity and fear.

"That's the only reason I stayed with you. For the sake of Riki and Varek and the baby. Otherwise I'd be following Dhamon. Sooner or later I will make him pay, you know."

"Yes, yes. You'll make him pay," Ragh grumbled. The small army of goblins had gathered behind him, chattering in their thin voices, making their clicks and snarls. "But for the moment, Fiona . . ."

Yagmurth thumped his spear and waved for silence.

"You can count on me, Ragh," Fiona said, after the goblin chatter died down. She smiled wide then, but her smile looked odd, and her eyes remained unfocused.

Ragh instantly wondered if he really could count on her. "On the other hand, Fiona, maybe—"

"I like Riki enough," she continued brightly. "I'd like to help her. And her baby. I won't be having a baby of my own, sivak. I won't be getting married. Ever. I won't be having a family of my own. Now that Rig's dead ..."

"Maybe instead we should—"

"The village is just around that rise, right?" Fiona stepped away. "I can't see it from here." She sheathed her sword. "I'll go now," she announced, "for a baby I can't have."

She started north. Ragh quickly hurried after her, putting a clawed hand on her shoulder. "About Varek, Fiona. If you talk to Varek you probably shouldn't mention to him that—"

"That the baby isn't his?" She smiled more genuinely. "Of course the baby is Varek's. It can't be Dhamon's because Dhamon is going to die when I see him next. He'll pay for what he did to Rig. He will pay for everything, sooner or later, I swear."

Mad as a hare, Ragh thought. He cursed himself as he watched her go, digging his claws into his palms in silent frustration. "Damn, but I should have gone with Dhamon instead. Why by the number of the Dark Queen's heads did I volunteer to retrieve the half-elf and her family? Why?" He ground his heel into the packed earth. "Some part of me thinks I should've just disappeared into the swamp a long time ago—leaving Dhamon and Maldred and Fiona to their own foolishness. Disappeared . . . and . . . ." He scratched at his head. "Done what with myself?"

The old yellow goblin gently rapped his spear against the draconian's leg to get his attention. "Human slaves," Yagmurth sniffed. "They are so unreliable. It's better just to eat them—they're tasty when they're young—but I think this one'll do as you command."

The two stared across the Throt landscape. It reminded Ragh of a desert in its barrenness and severity. He could count the trees he saw on both hands, and he spied only a few birds. There were places on Krynn as desolate, he knew—he'd been to them. There were climates more hostile. This was certainly tolerable, but he didn't care for it.

"Don't like goblins," he muttered in his own speech, leaving Yagmurth scratching his head. "Don't like waiting for a crazed Solamnic Knight. Don't like not knowing about Dhamon. My friend Dhamon." He shook his scaly head at his predicament. "Why didn't I just disappear into the swamp?"

Ragh didn't budge from the spot until Fiona came back two hours later. Her breath was ragged, her face streaked with sweat and dirt. The sword she clung to was bloodied.

The draconian rushed to her, still wary of the sword she carried. "Fiona, what happened? Are you hurt? What did you—"

Yagmurth chattered and hopped between the pair, trying to make them speak in a language he could understand.

She gave the goblin a sneer and kicked Yagmurth away, brushing at a strand of hair. "The village is small from the looks of it. Very. I couldn't get in close, though. The hobgoblins belong to the Knights of Takhisis. I can tell from the emblems on their armor."

"Hobgoblins in armor? Wonderful."

"Leather and chain for the most part. It was wonderful to fight against an armored opponent again, after all this time—even if they were filthy hobgoblins. I stopped thinking about Rig for a few minutes when I was busy fighting. Everything seemed so clear." She paused to take a deep breath, her eyes wide and glittering.

"Battle suits you," Ragh said simply.

"I ran into three of them, hobgoblins, on the south end of the village. Sentries, obviously. They wouldn't let me pass into the village, and though I couldn't understand them I figured out the gist of the situation. The town was blockaded."

He pointed to her sword.

She shrugged. "I killed two of them, the third ran. I would have given chase, but thought I might find myself outnumbered. I came back to report to you."

A rare sane decision, Ragh thought. "Good. I worried."

She spat at the ground.

"They'll reinforce the south end of the village now, of course," he said.

"I suppose," she agreed. Suddenly the distracted look was back in her eyes. She turned back toward the village, but Ragh stepped in front of her, edging away from her sword.

"Let's not be hasty."

"I am a Solamnic Knight, sivak. My report to you is concluded. I will now go back to the village and slay whatever reinforcements they've gathered to the south."

The draconian groaned. Against his better judgment he put his arm around her protectively and tugged her away from the rise, to the west. "No, Fiona. They'll be expecting someone coming again from the south. We'll fool them, pick another direction."

"Another? OK. West. Let's charge in from the west." She gripped the pommel of the sword firmly. "Tell your little, stinky friends about the plan, and let's see if they can keep up."

Ragh was already telling Yagmurth and the others that had gathered around them. The draconian directed the goblin force to follow him and stay as quiet as possible. He could only pray that Fiona herself would stay quiet and not prove a liability. He had to rush to catch up to her, the two of them leading their ragtag army around to the west and a bit north, circling the village and using a copse of pine and oak trees as cover.

There were some hobgoblins just inside the treeline, and Ragh didn't notice them until it was too late. A pair of armored sentries sniffed the air suspiciously, scenting their approach. Though related in some ways to their small cousins, the hobgoblins bore little real resemblance to the smaller, uglier creatures. These sentries and soldiers were the size of men, and vaguely man-shaped in their limbs, with coarse brown-gray hair covering their bodies. Their faces looked batlike, ears large and pointed, snouts wet and snuffling, sharply pointed teeth, and constant drool spilling over swollen lips.

"Move!" Ragh barked. "Get them!"

Thrilled to be commanded by Takhisis's perfect child, the whooping, shouting goblins descended on the hobgoblins.

"Victory!" Yagmurth cried in Goblin. "Ours is victory!"

The goblins moved hungrily, stabbing hobgoblins right and left. They fought well, but several of them were also killed in the initial melee.

"Monsters!" Fiona shouted. "Foul things!" The Solamnic pushed her way through the ranks, drawing her sword and swinging it wildly until the blade whistled.

The impressed goblins folded in behind her, shouting encouragements. Fiona closed with a large hobgoblin. Small ones behind her jabbed at the hobgoblin's legs, yipping maniacally as the large hobgoblin found itself pressed from all around.

Ragh narrowly avoided a spear thrust from one hobgoblin and nearly tripped over Yagmurth. His hobgoblin foe jabbed his spear again, this time scraping Ragh's ribcage.

"I felt that!" Ragh grunted.

Smirking, the hobgoblin redoubled his effort.

All around him goblins and hobgoblins were shouting and fighting. A few feet away, Fiona was still squared off against her big hobgoblin. Just at that moment, she lunged in and sliced at the hobgoblin's hands, shearing off a few of its fingers. The hobgoblin howled and flailed wildly, trying to push Fiona back with a charge, but at the same time it was assailed by a flurry of goblins, stabbing at its legs with their short spears.

"The creature is mine!" Fiona yelled. She drew her lips into a tight line and delivered more blows. The first finished her opponent, but the press of goblins held the creature up with their incessant stabbing until one of her swings lopped its head off.

"Victory!" Yagmurth howled again. "Ours is victory!"

Ragh's opponent threw back his head and screamed a string of obscenities as he saw Fiona finish off his comrade. He screamed louder as the corpse was quickly swarmed by goblins.

Ragh's opponent was the last hobgoblin on his feet. "You're too far from the village," Ragh hissed. "Too far for anyone to hear your alarm." The draconian dropped beneath a spear thrust, then darted in so close the hobgoblin's long weapon was ineffective. Ragh stretched a hand up to the creature's throat, slashing wildly with his claws, tugging his opponent down, and biting down on the hobgoblin's neck.

"Foul monster!" Fiona shouted, as she waded in to help.

"Foul tasting," the draconian said as he spat out a chunk of hair-covered skin. "Filthy, flea-ridden beast." He stepped away as the hobgoblin fell backward. Fiona stabbed it to be certain it was dead, and the goblins swarmed over it, tearing it to bloody pieces.

"Yagmurth," Ragh said, pushing his way through the goblin throng.

The old goblin struggled to reach the draconian, tugging along with him a small goblin, possibly his son, whom he was scolding for taking part in the unseemly rending.

"Good job," Ragh said

The old goblin smiled and ran his leathery tongue over his teeth. "Some places goblins and hobgoblins are kin," Yagmurth said, "but not in Goblin Home. Here we are enemies." He expounded on the situation. Ragh missed a few of the words, ones stemming from a dialect he wasn't familiar with, but he learned that the majority of hobgoblin tribes in Throt had thrown their lot in with the Knights of Takhisis, serving as soldiers, as errand-runners, taking land from goblins once their allies at human behest.

"So the Knights of Takhisis want this town guarded by the hobgoblins for some reason," Ragh mused. Ragh brushed several goblins aside to stare at the homely visage of the hobgoblin he'd fought and killed. The draconian closed his eyes and shut out the awestruck murmurs of his goblin-followers and focused on his inner magic.

Moments passed before Ragh's form shimmered like molten silver. The draconian's legs and arms became thinner and longer, his fingers crooked like twigs, his chest broadened into a barrel shape. The silvery scales lost their shine and turned into a splotchy, reddish-brown hide. A moment more and that hide was covered with coarse, uneven hair. His ears grew long and pointed, his snout became broader and shorter, and his tail all but vanished. His eyes flashed, then became dull and wide-set.

Ragh, like all sivaks, was able to assume the form of any creature he killed. He did not employ this talent much. He greatly preferred his draconian body and was proud of the way his keen sivak eyes perceived the world. A hobgoblin had a disconcertingly narrow range of vision because of the close-set placement of its eyes.

Ragh flexed hobgoblin arm and leg muscles, finding them adequate but clumsy. The hands, especially, took some getting used to. The fingers were too long. He twisted his neck this way and that and rotated his shoulders, trying to feel comfortable.

"Wretched creature," the draconian observed. "Unfortunate, pathetic creature." But taking on the body of the hobgoblin could prove advantageous, Ragh explained to the amazed goblins.

"Perfect child of our revered god," Yagmurth said, bowing respectfully.

Ragh snorted in amusement. When he spoke to Yagmurth now, his voice was different—still hoarse but deeper and somewhat unpleasant to his pointy ears.

"You are most powerful and most wise, Ragh—greatest of Takhisis's creations," repeated Yagmurth.

"I am most . . . something," Ragh returned with a chuckle. "Here's what I intend to do."

"What did you tell him?" Fiona demanded when he had finished in the goblin tongue, and his army had ceased their chattering. "And just what did he say to you?"

"I told him I intend to stroll into the hobgoblin camp and see just how many are in their force and why the village is under guard. Then I'll lure some of the beasts out so you can bloody your sword some more."

"Acceptable," she pronounced after thinking for a moment. "Do not tarry long. We must make sure that Riki and her baby are safe, then I must go after Dhamon before his tracks are old. He must pay."

"Of course he must pay," Ragh muttered, shaking his hobgoblin head as he lumbered away, his goblin entourage falling in line behind him and trying to shush each other. "Follow me," he called over his shoulder, "and I'll show you where to hide and wait."

Fiona stared at the hobgoblin corpses and the bodies of eight goblins that had been left behind. She hurriedly covered them all up with fallen branches, then followed after the goblins. "Dhamon will pay," she said to herself.

❖ ❖ ❖ ❖ ❖ ❖ ❖

In less than an hour, Ragh encountered two more sentries and quietly dispatched them, making his way into the hobgoblin camp. There he learned that more than sixty hobgoblins were on duty. It was a small force but equal to the number of dwellers in the village. Sixty was certainly more than his ragtag two dozen goblins.

Too, Ragh learned, the people in the village boasted no real weapons. The hobgoblins had expropriated all their swords, spears, and bows. They left the villagers a few knives for cooking, but the village was unarmed, defenseless.

Engaging a tired and unsuspecting hobgoblin in conversation, Ragh drew out this intelligence, that the hobgoblin force had blockaded the village on the Knights of Takhisis's orders because most of the village residents were Solamnic or Legion of Steel sympathizers. Several locals had passed information to enemies of the Knights of Takhisis and had harbored spies in the past. The hobgoblins had been ordered to kill any Solamnics or Legion of Steel Knights they captured, as a warning to nearby villages.

Ragh recalled that Riki's husband had past ties to the Legion of Steel and guessed that might be why his young family was here. Varek probably kept up his old allegiances.

"I'll trick some of the hobgoblins into following me to this stand of trees," Ragh explained to the assembled goblin army. He repeated his comments in Common for Fiona. "I expect you and your people to ambush them, Yagmurth, but let Fiona, the human woman, tackle the biggest ones." He also said in Goblin but didn't translate into common tongue, "Let the woman-slave take on the most dangerous of the hobgoblins. That way you'll be safe. Her life is not as valuable as yours." He didn't have the heart to tell Yagmurth that Fiona was a better fighter than any dozen of them.

The draconian posing as a hobgoblin had stolen

a suit of armor that was a mix of chain and plate. During his spying expedition, Ragh had found the general of the hobgoblins and had tricked him into going behind a rise. There the draconian slew him and assumed his body. This bigger hobgoblin body was a little more pleasing to the draconian, for the general was in better shape than the sentry. However, he was saddled with slightly bowed legs on which he couldn't quite walk comfortably.

"Now the hobgoblins think I'm their general," Ragh told the goblins with a grin. "I'm not going to try anything so suspicious as ordering them all to leave. I'd wager some of them would contest me. But I'll order them to come out here with me in small groups that you can manage. Enough will follow my orders that we can decrease their number, I think."

"As we follow the orders of the greatest of Takhisis's creations," Yagmuth pronounced. "As we serve the perfect child."

◇ ◇ ◇ ◇ ◇ ◇ ◇

It took several hours but the plan worked brilliantly—so brilliantly that Ragh, disguised as the hobgoblin general, was able to lure every one of the hobgoblins out to the forest, in relay groups, until the entire force was vanquished, killed, or fled. Unfortunately, however, this tactic cost nearly a dozen goblin lives. Only fourteen of Yagmurth's people survived the sometimes chaotic fighting. Yagmurth himself survived and was eager to follow Ragh to any other battle he might suggest, but the draconian was able to dismiss the goblin leader and his dwindling army with a false promise to meet them in two days at the stream where they had first confronted the umberhulk. Sadly, as though he suspected the truth, Yagmurth shook Ragh's hands and left with the goblins.

Fiona had loved the fighting, and now she detested Ragh for sending the brave goblins away. "Liar. Liar. Liar," she muttered as she watched them retreat from view.

Ragh shook out his shoulders, shedding his hobgoblin form and returning to his wingless sivak shape.

"You lied to them, sivak."

"Yes, Fiona. I lied to them," the draconian admitted, "and I'll probably have to tell some more lies in order to get Riki and her baby and Varek away from here safely."

She tossed her head. "Yes, Riki and Varek and . . . the baby. That is my mission now."

"We'll go together," Ragh said tersely. As much as he would prefer to send her back alone—for the humans were bound to wonder at the disappearance of all the hobgoblins and the sudden, alarming presence of a draconian—he still couldn't bring himself to fully trust Fiona. Her eyes no longer flashed any semblance of sanity.

"Together, then," she reluctantly agreed. "Then I must hurry after Dhamon."

◊ ◊ ◊ ◊ ◊ ◊ ◊

Things didn't go well. The alarmed villagers had already prepared themselves for some crisis and started at the sight of Ragh strolling down their main street. The draconian was wounded by a badly tossed hobgoblin spear before he could shout anything to quell their fears. Now he was in the care of Riki, who had him seated on a chair inside her small house—the only chair she trusted to support his considerable weight—and she was bandaging the sivak. She smoothed ointment on his ribs where he had been gouged and blotted blood from his forearm and shoulder, where he had been pelted with rocks.

"Pigs, but they got you good, beastie!" the half-elf said. Riki fussed over the draconian, as Varek and Fiona looked on. "My new friends in this place didn't know you weren't no evil beastie. They were just tired of all the . . ."

"Hobgoblins," Ragh supplied.

"Hobgoblins and such that been keepin' us from goin' anywhere." She twisted a bandage around his shoulder, one that looked suspiciously like a baby diaper, and stepped back to admire her handiwork. "That should do you, Ragh."

The Solamnic had picked up the baby and was cradling it maternally. A baby boy with flashing dark eyes and wheat-blond hair. On the baby's leg was an odd-shaped birthmark. Fiona traced it with her finger. It looked vaguely like a scale and was hard to the touch. Her finger caressed the baby's face. The child's ears were gently rounded, giving no hint as to his mother's heritage. As far as Fiona could see there was no resemblance to Varek, only to Dhamon. She wondered if Varek had guessed the truth.

"I have to admit I'm surprised you're alive," Riki chattered away to the sivak. "You and Dhamon . . . and Maldred, too, I heard you say." She wagged a finger at him. "I figured you would all have been hanged months ago. I didn't mean to just leave you in that jail, but I had the babe to think about. And me and Varek."

Ragh recalled with a grunt. Riki had denounced

them to some Legion of Steel Knights months ago in a godsforsaken jail on the Plains of Dust. She'd done it to guarantee the safety of Varek and herself, and she'd done it apparently with no remorse.

"Don't get me wrong, beastie," Riki added, as she adjusted the bandages one last time. "I'm glad you didn't die. You're not a bad sort for a beastie. But I don't understand how you and your friends avoided that noose."

"The tale is a long one and for another time, Rikali," Ragh said wearily.

"I'll have quite a few such tales to tell my babe when he gets older," Riki returned merrily. "Tales about this village, too. Them horrid hobgoblins kept us all from goin' anywhere for quite a few months, and all because Varek and some of the others were workin' to help the Legion o' Steel. Doesn't pay to act good in this sad world."

The draconian nodded. She was right. It didn't pay to act good.

"What about the Solamnics?" Fiona cut in. She didn't look at Riki, she didn't raise her eyes from the baby's. "I understand there are Solamnic sympathizers in this village, too."

"Pigs, but there are!" Riki continued, slapping Ragh on the back to show that the job was done. "All manner of too-good-to-stomach folks here. I'm surprised I was gettin' along so well with them all—me and Varek and the babe." She paused and glanced around the one-room home. "Where's Dhamon? You don't know where he is?"

Fiona shook her head. "No, but I will find him. I will track him down, I promise you."

"Good," Riki said, not completely understanding. "She balled her thin hands and planted them on her hips. "You can tell him Varek and me have left here—we're not wasting time, waitin' for hob-goblins to come back. We're goin' right today. Going to . . ." The half-elf turned to her husband. "Where did you say we was goin', Varek?"

"Evansburgh, I think." He glanced around nerv-ously. It didn't look as if they had gotten very far with their packing. "Maybe not today, but we should leave soon, Riki. If . . . when . . . word gets to the Knights of Takhisis that their little monsters have been—"

"Slain," Fiona interjected

"Slain, yes, they'll send Knights instead of hob-goblins. Evansburgh's a larger place. Or maybe we'll go to Haltigoth and lose ourselves there." He rubbed his palms on his tunic. "I want my family to be safe. I'm loyal to the Legion, but this is no time for me to risk my life. I'll not make the same mistake and put Riki and our child in danger."

Riki glided over to Fiona and took the baby. "Tell Dhamon where we're probably goin'. Mal, too, OK? You'll tell them? I wouldn't mind seeing them again."

Fiona said nothing.

She turned back to Ragh. "You tell them, and tell them I'm real sorry I turned them over to those Legion o' Steel Knights a few months back. Did what I had to do, you understand." She cooed over the baby and gently blew at his forehead. "You tell them."

"I will tell them," Ragh said. It was, perhaps, another lie. Then he was at the door, looking out and grimacing to note a knot of curious villagers waiting outside.

Fiona brushed past him out into the bright sun-shine. "Yes, you tell Dhamon, sivak, but you'll have to speak quickly, for when I find him, he won't have long to live."

Riki raised an eyebrow, but Ragh had already raced past her, catching up with Fiona, whose sword was drawn, her knuckles white against the pommel, the blade clean and shining.

CHAPTER NINETEEN
INTO THE LAIR OF THE SHADOW DRAGON

His senses reeled. The smell of the mountains overwhelmed him—the very stone, the dirt and dust squeezed into the cracks, rotting pine needles from dead trees, the molted feathers of hawks that lined unseen nests. Goats had passed this way not too long ago, he could tell, and at least one wolf that was no doubt tracking them. There was the scent of some kind of carcass inside a crevice.

"A dead rabbit, maybe, hauled up high by an owl," Dhamon said. He thought he could smell the owl, too, amazed at the intensity of the musky scent. "It's eating the rabbit." Dhamon now could hear the owl and the scratching of its claws as it ripped the meat, the tugging sound of its beak as the flesh was pulled away.

He heard the breeze stir the pine needles, those clinging to stubborn little trees wedged in earth-filled cracks, and those that had fallen and were whirling across the rock face. He heard faint taps and after a moment realized they must be the hooves of the goats striking the rocks. How far away were they? He suspected they were a good distance. *Just how far can I hear?* A bird cried, a jay from the distinctive sound, and there was a sharp intake of breath that was louder than anything. This was accompanied by the repugnant odor of sweat and oil.

"Maldred. I wondered how long it would take you to catch up with me."

The ogre-mage's breath was irregular and deep. Maldred didn't say anything right away. He bent over, hands clamped on his knees, face a darker blue than normal from the exertion. Finally he stood and looked up to meet Dhamon's eyes.

With wide eyes the ogre studied Dhamon, then finally looked away, finding something on the mountainside in which to be interested.

"Aye, Mal, the dragon's magic is still changing me." Dhamon reached a hand up to the left side of his face. There was no human skin there now, only scales. There was no human skin left anywhere on him. "I've got a fire in my chest that's raging, and it's taking too much effort to keep the beast out of my head." He glanced up at the mountains. "I've never been afraid of dying, Mal. No man escapes that fate, so why fear it? But I wanted to see my child first. I wanted to say some things to Riki, apologize to her, and to Fiona too. . . ."

Maldred opened his mouth to say something, and then thought better of it.

Dhamon took off running again. He suspected there was an entrance to the dragon's lair nearby. He could feel the truth of that instinct as he increased his speed and as Maldred's scent fell behind.

The cave mouth was small as far as dragons were concerned, but effectively cloaked. It was difficult to spot at first. He doubted that it was easily noticed by those men or creatures traveling north from Throt to Gaardlund or Nightlund. Merchants and mercenaries would pass by, none the wiser. The climb was steep and treacherous—even for someone like himself. Further masking the entrance was an irregular overhang that cast a long shadow across a wide swath of broken, jagged rocks. Deep inside that shadow was the opening.

The low roof made a very tight squeeze for the shadow dragon, one that would probably cause it to shed a few scales from its back and belly. Perhaps it was an entrance the dragon rarely used but held in reserve, but because the dragon had known of the entrance, he had inadvertently communicated that information to Dhamon.

Dhamon didn't know that with a single spell the dragon could turn himself into a shadow—as thin as a sheet of parchment and flowing as smoothly as water. He didn't know that the shadow dragon could follow wherever the much smaller Nura Bint-Drax was able to go. Dhamon didn't know that the dragon actually preferred this way in and out of his lair because of its smallness and remoteness.

"Do you see it? A way in?" Maldred had caught up once more and was peering into the shadows and seeing nothing. He was shielding his eyes from the sun with one hand. The other hand was clenched around the haft of the glaive. Dhamon's hands had changed radically just in the past hour. Now they were claws, similar to Ragh's, but with longer curled talons that made grasping difficult. Dhamon didn't object when Maldred claimed the polearm that he had been forced to abandon. He didn't seem to care that the ogre-mage also carried the pouch with the magical miniature carvings, which Dhamon had discarded when he grew out of his clothes—or rather, burst out of them.

"The cave?" Maldred pressed. "Do you see it?"

"Aye," Dhamon said in a hush, his voice rich and strange. "There's a small entrance. It's our best way in, I believe. It looks too small for such a creature, but I sense the way is not unattended, as I had hoped it would be."

"There are guards?"

"Aye. Two, I think. That's all I sense in any event. And they're relatives of yours."

Indeed, the guards were a pair of overlarge ogres, crude, muscular brutes who stood outside the cave. They were reasonably attentive, however, considering their forsaken post. Great double-axe polearms were propped near them, each larger than the glaive. From the ogres' waists hung thick-bladed broadswords and long knives. One carried a crossbow. Strapped to their huge thighs were more knives, and lashed to their backs were long quivers filled with javelins.

"Walking armories," Dhamon mused. He knew he could take these two ogres—he could take a dozen now—but it might be a noisy fight and alert the shadow dragon.

Despite all the weapons, they weren't wearing armor, making them vulnerable. No shields were in evidence. Each displayed an odd tattoo splayed across his naked chest, and each wore a loincloth made of the hide of some large lizard.

Not a tattoo, Dhamon noted, after a moment. Scales, I think.

Yes, he was certain—they were small patches of scales.

"So the ogres're pawns of the dragon," Dhamon whispered. "Just like me." Would they eventually become spawn or abominations like himself? he wondered. He was still changing, becoming incredibly strong, he realized—he intended to make the shadow dragon regret that mistake, before his soul vacated this grotesque body. He shivered at the thought of what he must look like now. He glanced at Maldred. The ogre-mage looked quickly away.

"What do you see, Dhamon?" Maldred asked,

"As I told you, I see a pair of your ugly kinsmen guarding our way in." Dhamon quickly described them. "I don't believe they have seen us yet. We're too far away, and they seem very relaxed." Yet Dhamon was able to see them clearly with his extraordinary vision.

"There are two other ways in, the closest at least a mile from here," Dhamon said.

"Probably guarded by something else."

"Aye. Better guarded, I'd wager, if it's more accessible. Anyway, I don't want to waste more time searching. I count my life in minutes now, Mal." Dhamon paused, rubbing his chin. "You swear you have never been here? You don't know this lair?"

Maldred shook his head, his white mane of hair tangling around his shoulders. "I told you, Dhamon, no more lies. The dragon summoned me to his cave in the swamp, yes. I knew he had more than one lair. It is said all the dragons do, and Nura Bint-Drax bragged of those she had visited. But I've never been here."

"I wonder if Nura is here, too." Dhamon said. "The dragon favors her over you."

"No one favors me," Maldred said with a nod. "Maybe my father. Now about the two ogres . . . ."

"I suppose you'll insist they be spared, that all ogre life is sacred. Weeks ago I would have disagreed." But the changes taking place inside him and all the things that had happened to him had made Dhamon feel that life was a precious thing. "Even ogre life is sacred? Maybe you're right. I suppose I can lure them out and—"

Maldred shook his head again. "They are agents of the shadow dragon, as I was an agent. And you say they carry his scales."

The uncurable scales, Dhamon thought.

"If they carry his scales, there is no hope for them."

You don't want them turning into something like me, Dhamon thought. Did you know all along the dragon wasn't going to cure me?

"Tell me again about the cave opening, Dhamon, and where the ogres are."

As Dhamon described the cave and the ogres, Maldred knelt and carefully set the glaive down, thrusting his hands against the parched ground, fingers digging in. Soon the ogre-mage started humming, a tune Dhamon had heard a few times before. The melody was simple and haunting, and with it came a glow that ran down the ogre-mage's arms and swept over the ground surrounding him. The earth was instantly brightened and shone as though it was a mirror reflecting the sun.

Dhamon watched as the glow faded and the hard earth softened and began to ripple, like the surface of a pond disturbed by a gust of wind. The ripples were faint, but he could follow them with his eyes as, arrowlike, they flowed upward.

Maldred interrupted his humming to take a deep breath and lower his face until his chin was inches from the ground. He altered the tune to something new to Dhamon, slower and low-pitched, dissonant and distinctly unpleasant.

With his keen far-seeing, Dhamon watched the

cave entrance as the ripples approached, unnoticed, flowed around the ogres, and washed over the wall of the mountain behind them. The stone began to ripple and shimmer. The rock became liquid, and now the liquid rock washed out over the startled ogres, trapping and drowning them within moments, before they had a chance to cry out.

Dhamon almost felt sorry for the ogres, dying like that—smothered by magic. It wasn't an honorable way to kill them.

"It was quick," Maldred said, as if reading his thoughts, "and necessary. If they'd seen something . . . ."

"The shadow dragon might have seen it too, through their half-spawn eyes."

The ogre-mage nodded, creeping forward. "How far can you see inside?"

"Not far." After a moment, Dhamon added, "Not yet, anyway." He stepped closer and focused his keen senses on the dark mouth and its shadowy interior, concentrating on picking up any sound or movement. "There's nothing inside."

It took them only a few minutes to climb to the cave entrance, for Maldred used his earth magic to make the path easier. Several minutes more and they were inside, moving swiftly and silently despite their size. There was little light here, but Dhamon found that didn't inhibit his keen eyesight. Like all ogres, Maldred could differentiate objects in the dark by the heat they exuded, so he kept his eyes trained on Dhamon's back, following the fever that raged within.

The scent of ogres was strong inside, and Dhamon guessed the ones they'd felled had been stationed in the cave for quite some time. Others, too, he decided after a moment—the smell of ogre was everywhere. How many more? Were they elsewhere in this cave complex? Or were they far away on some nefarious errand for the shadow dragon?

They wound their way down a large, endlessly curving corridor. The ogre scent lessened. Soon the only ogre scent Dhamon could be sure of was Maldred's.

Twice Dhamon thought they were being followed. He heard something behind them, perhaps more of the dragon's sentries lurking in nooks he'd noticed and dismissed, but whatever was following stayed so far back, he couldn't make out its scent yet. He couldn't wait for it, he decided.

They plunged deeper into the mountain cave, with Dhamon watching Maldred warily over his shoulder.

Suddenly Dhamon felt the presence of the shadow dragon, a nudging at the back of his mind. The creature was trying to intrude on his consciousness again, but Dhamon managed to successfully repulse the dragon. He didn't think the dragon knew they were near, but he didn't want to take any chances.

"Faster," he muttered. "Mal, move."

He heard the ogre-mage's feet quicken, and Maldred's breath came quicker.

"Faster," Dhamon said again, louder, then cursed as he stumbled. His legs burned and felt cumbersome. He felt them growing again, becoming thicker and more muscular still. He felt his chest tightening again, his head beginning to throb. "By the Dark Queen's heads! How much longer will this torment go on?"

How much longer would his human spirit remain in this foreign body? Did he have time to find the dragon? Time to fight it? Time to learn if Riki and his child had been saved?

"How much time?" he whispered, as he found his footing again, resumed his grueling pace.

He heard Maldred's labored breathing loud behind him. The ogre-mage was having a difficult time keeping up.

"Not so fast," Maldred complained, as Dhamon rushed around a wide curve and headed down a steep incline. "I can't match you."

As much as Dhamon preferred to keep an eye on the duplicitous ogre-mage, he decided he couldn't afford to linger.

"Dhamon, slow down!"

It was possible, Dhamon supposed, that Maldred was telling the truth when he said he would never lie to him again. While Dhamon wanted to believe that, in honor of the close friendship they once shared, he couldn't allow himself that luxury, that wishful leap of faith. Not when he might have only minutes left.

The shadow dragon had worked his wiles against the ogre-mage once. Now, if Maldred was holding out hope of saving the ogre lands, the shadow dragon could again persuade him to turn against Dhamon.

"Dhamon, slow down."

"I can't." Dhamon didn't believe he had enough time left to slow down, nor could he bring himself to completely trust Maldred. So he practically ran now, as much as possible within the confines of the stony tunnels, fast outdistancing Maldred as he raced toward the chamber far below where he knew the shadow dragon laired.

One more turn, one more slope.

Dhamon guessed he was far below the surface now and heading still deeper underground. It was quite a bit cooler here, and the dry air and dust of the higher terrain was replaced by a dampness heavy with the scent of mold and guano. He looked to his right, eyes parting the darkness, and saw moisture beading up on the stone. A line of silver glistened there. Yes, he remembered that line of silver. He'd noted this during his brief link with the shadow dragon.

"Close," he said. "I'm getting close."

Just a brief distance.

"Indeed," came the unbidden reply. "You are very close."

From far to Dhamon's left emanated a dull, yellow glow. It quickly grew and brightened, the light bouncing off a mound of gem-encrusted objects, golden sculptures, and gilded weapons piled in front of the waiting shadow dragon. The light momentarily blinded Dhamon, he'd been so long surrounded by pitch black.

Dhamon felt relief, but also a reckless giddiness, a fear and hope that he might yet save his child. He also felt anger that his whole life had led to this point. Everything came down to this single moment, this confrontation with his nemesis.

Nura Bint-Drax, appearing as a child of five or six with coppery-colored hair, was there too, hovering close by the shadow dragon. Its claws were outstretched, almost supplicating, while the child Nura was in the midst of casting a spell.

Dhamon started toward her, then hesitated. Suddenly he felt a rumbling beneath his scaled feet. There were words in the rumbling, but he missed some.

"You are crafty," the shadow dragon purred. "My prized ogre minions did not bother to warn me of your approach, Dhamon Grimwulf. Did you kill them?"

"They are better off dead," Dhamon retorted.

The dragon curiously raised the ridge above one eye.

Dhamon edged forward, slowly, cautiously, keeping an eye on Nura and still keeping the shadow dragon mentally at bay. "I won't call myself Dhamon Grimwulf any longer. I stopped being Dhamon Grimwulf when the last of my flesh disappeared. Now I'm just some foul creature you've created to destroy. A spawn, though not so perfectly formed as the ones Sable birthed. I've no wings, dragon. Only stubs. Your creation is flawed. I'm an abomination."

The dragon roared, the sound harsh and metallic like a thousand clanging bells. Dhamon couldn't tell if the dragon was laughing or voicing its fury.

"But your flawed and ugly creation is strong," Dhamon continued, inching closer. "I intend to show you just how strong." Swiftly bunching the muscles in his legs, Dhamon leaped but didn't make it more than a few yards before he slammed into an invisible barrier. He suspected by the wide grin on Nura Bint-Drax's face that it had been erected by her spell. The wind knocked out of him, Dhamon could do nothing about Nura's next lightning-fast enchantment.

A huge, invisible fist slammed down on him from above, crushing him to the stone floor, pinning him there and forcing the air from his lungs.

"Hurry, master," Nura said nervously. "I cannot hold him long. He is indeed very strong, and he seems able to fight my greatest magic."

"I require only a little time, Nura Bint-Drax," the dragon rumbled in response. "Hold him still, and I shall vanquish his spirit."

"You can't hold me!" Dhamon shouted at the

naga, "and you can't defeat me." Dhamon pressed his clawed hands against the stone ground and drew on his hate as well as his strength to push himself against the force, which yielded only slightly. He redoubled his efforts. "I won't let you beat me, you damn snake!"

He heard the stone crack beneath his claws, heard Nura whispering encouragements to the dragon, heard the dragon speak in drawn-out syllables foreign to him, also heard the slapping of footsteps. Dhamon inhaled deeply, picking up the nearby scent of the ogre-mage. Even if he arrived in time, would Maldred help him, Dhamon wondered as he pushed harder against Nura's unseen force.

Could he help himself?

The dragon continued its strange recitation. The noise jarred against the leathery palms of Dhamon's clawed hands. He tried to understand the words, which were obviously part of a spell. Dhamon raised his head slightly and, turning it, managed to see the shadow dragon's massive eyes shimmering darkly. Motes of light gleamed in the centers like birthing stars. A moment more and the magical glitter spilled out like tears to coat the treasure nestled between the dragon's claws.

"Hurry, master," Nura urged. "I am still holding him!"

"No," Dhamon grunted, refusing to surrender. He made more headway against the force and finally managed to crawl to his knees. "You won't hold me."

He didn't know what the shadow dragon was trying to do, but it had to be dangerous enough to require outside magic—clearly the mound of magical treasures was powering the dragon's spell. Dhamon'd seen it done many times when in the company of Maldred and Palin and, once, when the red overlord, Malys, tried to use the eldritch energy of ancient artifacts to power her ascension to godhood.

"I can't let you win."

"The master will triumph." Now Nura spoke in her woman voice. "He will live forever, and I will live at his side."

Dhamon hadn't noticed her approach, but there she was, inches away—looking cherubic and innocent and cupping her hand as if she were holding him in her palm.

"You cannot best my master, Dhamon Grimwulf. You would do well to surrender and avoid the suffering. Oblivion would end all your pain."

"Never!" The strangled cry echoed off the cavern walls. "He will not rob me of my spirit and transform me into a damnable abomination! He will not!"

"You already are an abomination, Dhamon. It's a pity you can't see yourself. So much more impressive than your weak, human body, but an abomination!" Her face took on a peculiar softness. "Relax, Dhamon. Let your spirit find oblivion. Make it easy for us and yourself."

"I will die before I let that happen!"

Nura laughed, the sound of crystal windchimes. "An abomination! But, Dhamon Grimwulf, my master is merciful and won't let you die—not entirely. He will take over your body and displace your spirit, no matter how hard you fight."

She laughed again, soft and long, and when she stopped this time her eyes twinkled with a merry malice that made Dhamon involuntarily shudder.

He continued to push against the invisible field while searching inward. The furnace in his chest was fiery, and the heat stretched from his chest and stomach down to his arms and legs and feet. The heat beat out a pulse, and as Dhamon concentrated and searched inward, the pulse became a thunder in his ears.

He dug his claws into the stone. *Into* the stone, he realized. The force of his claws alone had split the rock.

"You feel it, don't you, Dhamon Grimwulf? You realize it finally? You know what my master is doing. What he would have done weeks ago, if your body had progressed faster, if you had accepted all the changes sooner. If you had managed to slay Sable . . ."

". . . which would have permitted the magical energy dissipated from the Black overlord's death to power the shadow dragon's spell." This came from Maldred. The ogre-mage was standing at the entrance to the chamber, warily watching the shadow dragon, and Nura as she hovered over Dhamon.

Maldred tried to look away, not wanting to stare at Dhamon's ultimate form, but he couldn't help but be fascinated. His gaze kept returning to his onetime friend—now a pathetic, misshapen creature, an abomination.

"Well, Prince," Nura purred, "I see Dhamon got away from you again. You're not very good at keeping your charge in check."

With a snarl, Maldred rushed forward, but he also struck an invisible wall. The child raised her hand, fingers sparkling like her eyes, mouth moving in unheard words. The magical glaive flew from Maldred's grasp, soaring through the air to land in the pile of treasure melting in front of the shadow dragon.

"Where did your precious sword go, Prince?

Your wonderful, magical greatsword? The one your father gave you? And Fiona—where is that blade? The sword I had specially crafted? I want all those magic weapons, and I want them now!"

Maldred beat his fists against the invisible barrier, tossed back his head, and howled his rage.

"Won't let the dragon win," Dhamon muttered to himself, still pushing, pushing.

"Oh, but you will. You have no choice, Dhamon," Nura said, returning her attention to Dhamon. She squatted next to him, outside the barrier. "Powered by the death of Sable, or powered by the magic in the treasures, it really doesn't matter. The master will soon have the energy to complete your body. The master will live."

"Fight it, Dhamon!" Maldred shouted. "Fight it with everything you've got!"

Nura leaned her face down close to Dhamon's, her warm breath seeping through the barrier. "Power the spell and displace your rebellious spirit . . . . and place his soul inside your beautiful, new scaly shell."

"No!" Dhamon screamed, straining his leg muscles.

"The master is dying, Dhamon Grimwulf," Nura persisted. "The Chaos energy that birthed and nurtured him is fading away, but he will be renewed, through you. He will live a long time, because I was right after all—you are the one."

"Never!" Dhamon pushed heroically, managed to get to his feet. He stood, woozy and weak. And still the invisible force pushed down on him, pinning him.

"You are beginning to understand, aren't you?" Nura's tone was almost sympathetic as she tipped her head back. "You understand it all?"

"Aye," Dhamon croaked. His voice sounded stranger and stranger. "I am the one, right? The only vessel your bloated master could find to change with his magic?"

Her smug expression wavered almost imperceptibly.

"The only one. What? How many others did he try? How many others did he manipulate, fail to create, destroy with his foul ambition?"

She gave him a curt nod. "Our tests proved you were the only one strong enough to handle the magic, Dhamon, thanks to the dragon magic already inside you."

Because of the blasted scale from the Red that had been thrust upon him a few years back. Dhamon understood. Because of the magic the shadow dragon and the silver dragon had used to break the Red's control. Oh yes, he had plenty of the accursed dragon magic inside of him.

Nura smiled as she watched him struggle under the pressure. "The master always said your mind was stronger than your body. I disagreed, though you are indeed perceptive and clever. It is a pity that your mind won't be yours any longer. A pity that all of that cleverness—"

Her words were swallowed by the shadow dragon's mighty roar, as the cavern trembled. The spell was completed, and the magical treasures became a mass of pale, colorful light before dwindling to nothing. The cavern burst with brightness, with the force of the new magic, and Dhamon felt a wave of energy surge through Nura's invisible wall, washing over him.

Chapter Twenty
Shadow Play

D hamon felt himself spiralling down into a suffocating darkness.

The heat centered in his chest spread all over his body and threatened to consume him.

"Mal?" Dhamon called out.

There was no answer—only the darkness and the swirling sounds and the great heat.

No part of him was spared. Daggers of fire jabbed into him from every direction. He felt pulled apart, stretched on a torturer's rack. His arms and legs were being torn from his torso, even as they were burning up with pain.

Dhamon gasped, sucking in as much air as his searing lungs would permit, trying to shut out some part of the acute pain and see . . . something . . . anything.

All he could detect was a break in the darkness that was jet black.

"What? Mal? Are you there, Mal?"

A throaty growl was the only reply.

"Strong!" Dhamon heard himself say aloud. "I am strong, Nura Bint-Drax!" The words followed the beating rhythm of his heart. "Nothing is stronger than me, you damn snake! I'll stop your magic!" But her spell was already done.

The pain and fever deepened, so extreme Dhamon expected—hoped—to perish before he could draw another breath. He screamed. His scream became a roar, then trailed off when the heat started to abate. He screamed again just to be sure he was still alive, then stole a deep breath and found the will to resist a little longer.

"The heat," he whispered. "It was cleansing me!" The heat was chasing all the weakness from his once-human body, leaving only power and force. "I will live, Nura Bint-Drax! And I will keep a promise I made to Ragh. I will see you dead."

His body was still changing, growing larger perhaps. He thrust a hand in front of his face but saw nothing except the darkness. He heard a popping sound and felt his chest broadening and swelling, but this time he felt no pain. Where was the pain and heat?

He didn't actually feel anything now, he realized with a start. An unwilling participant, he waited as he sensed his body double in size, then double again.

"Fiona!" Somewhere in the darkness Maldred was calling to the Solamnic Knight.

So Maldred was still here. Why was he calling Fiona? Was she here, too? Dhamon wondered. How did she get here, so far below the earth? The darkness was finally receding. The depths of the cave come into focus. He could see himself.

My eyes, Dhamon heard a voice inside his head say. *You are seeing with my eyes now, Dhamon*

Grimwulf, but soon you will see and sense nothing ever again.

The shadow dragon's consciousness was thoroughly embedded in his mind—two beings sharing one body. What vile magic could take away someone's soul? he thought.

"Ragh! Fiona! Hurry!" Again he heard Maldred's voice.

So the draconian *and* Fiona were here, somehow had managed to follow him. Had they gotten Riki and the baby away from the hobgoblins? Was his child safe? He tried to call out to them, but he couldn't work his voice. He wasn't even able to open his mouth.

"Fiona!" Maldred's voice echoed and echoed.

It didn't matter if they were here, Dhamon thought. They should leave. Maldred should tell them to flee while there was still time for them to save themselves. Again he tried to shout to them, warn them to run. He centered his thoughts on opening his great mouth and shouting for them to run away as fast as they possibly could.

What about the dragonfear? Dhamon wondered. They *should* be running away. The aura of dragonfear exuded by the shadow dragon should be repulsing them. But it wasn't, nor, come to think of it, had the dragonfear been present when he entered the chamber. In fact, he realized, he'd felt not even a twinge. Had the shadow dragon become so weak it couldn't generate its magic? Had it thrown everything into its spell to control Dhamon?

"That's Dhamon? Is that really Dhamon?" This was the draconian's familiar hoarse whisper. "By the first eggs! He's not turning into a spawn. He's turning into a dragon!"

All of a sudden Dhamon knew that was true. He

could sense his size—legs as thick as ancient, sturdy oaks, claws massive, talons long and deadly. The nubs on his shoulderblades were gone, replaced by wings that were tucked close to his sides, unable to stretch very far because Nura's magical barrier was still in place. His neck was long and serpentine, his head wide and his eyes large—now they saw everything with great clarity.

The shadow dragon turned its head, and Dhamon saw Maldred, fists still pounding against the invisible wall. Fiona slashed against it with her accursed sword, crying out something . . . something about being cheated? She screamed her ire, and this time Dhamon heard her clearly through the rumbling cavern and his forcefully beating heart.

"Damn you, dragon!" Fiona cried shrilly. "It's my destiny to kill Dhamon Grimwulf! Me! I want to make him pay for Rig! To pay for all of them!"

"Ragh! Help me with the barrier!" Maldred shouted as he pounded.

Curiously, Ragh did nothing. Instead he spoke so softly to the ogre-mage that Dhamon couldn't hear what was said—despite his dragon-sharp hearing. The ground was rumbling too loudly, Fiona was shouting wildly and Nura Bint-Drax was talking too, speaking more of her arcane words. Another spell!

She must be working to keep up her invisible barrier, Dhamon guessed, working to keep his companions from breaking through and saving him and fighting the shadow dragon.

If Nura was so intent on her spell, that meant the shadow dragon's magic was not yet final, that the monster did not yet have full control over Dhamon's dragon body.

And if you don't have full control, I might yet be able to stop you, Dhamon thought. *My companions and I will stop you.*

It is far too late for that, Dhamon Grimwulf, the shadow dragon mentally taunted him. *My enchantment is finished. I own this body now. I should have never sent you after Sable. I should have kept you close. I didn't need Sable's death energy after all. I just needed the magic from all of these wondrously enchanted items . . . and your inner magic. I needed you. Nura was right all along, Maldred too. You are the one I will live through.*

You lie, dragon. Your spell isn't done, but your puppet Nura is trying to buy you the little time you need to finish it, Dhamon raged. All those weeks he'd thought the shadow dragon was turning him into a simple spawn or abomination—baiting him, threatening the ultimate transformation if he didn't kill Sable, promising a cure if he did, throwing in a threat to Riki and Varek and Dhamon's child for good measure. All those weeks he was slowly being turned into a vessel for the dragon's essence, for a dragon crafted by the god Chaos.

"No!" Dhamon shouted, startling everyone by the roar that erupted from his dragon's mouth. "I will not let you win!"

He tried to say other words, but the shadow dragon came into his mind like a storm and overwhelmed his consciousness. In Dhamon's shrinking mind's eye he saw the image of Chaos pluck his god-shadow from the cavern floor in the Abyss and give it life and the form of a dragon. He saw it all again: the newly birthed dragon—the shadow dragon—slaying Knights of Takhisis and Solamnic Knights. The shadow dragon fighting and killing blue dragons and drinking in their energy.

As I killed all of them, I will kill your spirit. I will fly again in my new, perfect form, the shadow dragon hissed in Dhamon's mind. *I will banish your very soul.*

Dhamon felt his awareness slipping away, his life's blood spilling away. The dragon was winning. Everything around him dimmed—Nura's continued incantation, Fiona's shouts. He heard what sounded like thunder, perhaps the beating of the dragon-body's massive heart invading his body, then he heard nothing. He sensed a blackness, welcoming and frightening. His end beckoned, and he felt himself gradually drawn toward it.

❖ ❖ ❖ ❖ ❖ ❖ ❖

"You did it!" Ragh shouted. "You did it, ogre! The barrier's down!"

At Ragh's suggestion Maldred had grabbed some of the carved magical figurines in the pouch and lobbed them against the enchanted barrier. The explosion was small but enough to shatter Nura's spell, as well as collapse part of the cavern's ceiling.

Fiona rushed forward, dodging falling rocks.

"In the name of Vinus Solamnus!" she cried. "For the memory of my Rig!"

Ragh hesitated, eyes shifting from the Dhamon-dragon to the husk of the shadow dragon. Maldred was staring at Dhamon.

"By my father," the ogre-mage said in a low voice. "By all that's sacred. Just look at him, Ragh. Look at what he's become."

Dhamon in dragon form was not quite like any other dragon that had ever been seen on Krynn. His scales were black mirrors, reflecting the cavern and everyone in it. His scales were mostly shimmering silver. In a few places the scales were glossy.

The dragon-Dhamon was an impressive creature, not so large as the shadow dragon, yet far more elegant-looking. It was as if a great artist had sculpted the creature, stealing the best traits from Krynn's various dragons and creating a unique composite.

The shadow dragon had borrowed the shadowy black horns from a young Red he slew in the purge. The magnificent wings were from first Blue he killed in the Abyss. The claws were copied from a white dragon, webbed and deadly as a well-worked blade.

"Beautiful," Ragh admitted, staring wide-eyed at the Dhamon-dragon now. "He—it's a beautiful creature, to be sure. Incredible."

"Beautiful or not, it will die," Fiona hissed. She had edged close and now raised her sword and continued inching toward the dragon. The dragon was moving sluggishly. The spell was still working its last vestiges of magic. "Now is the time to strike! While the beautiful beast is still vulnerable."

"Nooooo!" Nura howled. The naga had been watching with pride, awestruck by the final transformation, but now she belatedly roused herself to action. "You'll not scratch my master's new body! You'll not hurt him, you wretched woman!"

Nura raced toward Fiona, changing as she went, becoming taller, her legs melding together to form her hideous snake-body, stretching twenty feet from the top of her head to her tail. Her coppery hair fanned away to form a hood.

Ragh simultaneously leaped into action. Dhamon can take care of himself against Fiona, he thought, but the naga is dangerous.

The draconian shot at the snake-woman.

At that very moment, the dead body of the shadow dragon gave a twitch.

Maldred noted it and stopped the incantation he had begun. He had to take a second look because he was so astonished—he had thought the shadow dragon dead.

"Ragh! Fiona!" Maldred boomed. "The shadow dragon controls both forms! We've got two dragons to deal with here, not one!"

The ogre-mage halted the one spell and thrust his fingers into his pouch, closing on the last figurine he had left. He ran forward, hurling the carving. Maldred had aimed it at the shadow dragon, but his aim was off. It struck the cave wall, sending chunks of rock flying and a piece of the ceiling crashing down. The vibrations threw Maldred to the ground.

In the haze of debris Maldred thought he'd actually struck his target, but then the dust and rocks settled, and the shadow dragon moved again, more noticeably this time.

The sleek, new dragon tried to move, but was still sluggish. It seemed the shadow dragon could not effectively power both bodies at the same time.

Dhamon opened his mouth and roared his rage.

The shadow dragon howled in return.

"Kill the shadow dragon! The shadow dragon!" Maldred shouted as he pushed himself to his feet. "Kill it and we might break the spell. We might save Dhamon!" He picked up the glaive, and madly charged toward the dragon to whom he owed his own debt of revenge.

The cavern rocked from all the energy—from Maldred's enchanted carvings, the shadow dragon's and Nura's spells, and the release of magic from the treasure horde.

The noise and constant quakes finally proved too much for Nura Bint-Drax. She spun one way, then the next, as if tortured by her choices. She whirled against unseen foes, stretched toward the shadow dragon, considered an enchantment, then dismissed it while thinking of another.

In her moment of indecision, Ragh's fingers closed around the hood of her snake-throat.

"Dhamon thinks I should know and hate you, snake-woman," the draconian spat. "Well, I do hate you, but I don't want to know something so foul as you." He squeezed, wrapping his legs against the sides of her snake body and holding on. "I just want you dead."

Yards away Fiona stood suddenly frozen, her own indecision mirroring her divided soul. Her Knight's honor bound her to attack the shadow dragon, but she desperately wanted to pursue her revenge against Dhamon.

"Where have you gone, Dhamon Grimwulf?" she screamed. "Where is my revenge?" A tear streaked her dust-covered face. "How do I know who I should fight?"

A part of her recognized the sparkle in the dragon's eyes, the sparkle of his dark, mysterious gaze. It was the same sparkle she'd noticed in the baby she held in her arms hours ago. Rig's eyes had been dark, too. Oh, how she missed the mariner.

"I will never have my own child," she said, lowering her sword slightly. "I will never have . . . ."

In that instant, Dhamon finally moved, creeping forward. He still felt as though his soul was plunging toward the darkness, but he fought against oblivion with the few ounces of humanity left in him.

I can't let you win, he told the shadow dragon.

Not just for Riki and his child's sake, but for Fiona and Ragh and Maldred, and for the countless others who had fallen and would fall to this reborn shadow dragon in the centuries it would roam the face of Krynn. *Perhaps this is my sole chance at redemption,* Dhamon thought, sending his thoughts to the shadow dragon. *To stop you from walking the face of this world.*

The shadow dragon fought back mentally, his strength divided between two forms.

In Dhamon's mind two dragons fought—one mirror-black scales and supple lines, the other a large, gray beast, sluggish and depleted, but nevertheless formidable.

The old one lashed out with a great taloned claw, slashing at the new dragon. "Surrender," the old one hissed. "You've no choice. And you only anger me by resisting."

The new dragon roared a word that sounded like "Never," a word that echoed in the confines of Dhamon's mind. The new dragon reached out with a claw, too, batting away the old creature, not hurting the shadow dragon, but keeping it at bay.

As Dhamon shook off his thick dazedness, his goal became increasingly clear.

You took on too much, Dhamon told the shadow dragon bitterly.

I will best your spirit, the shadow dragon returned. *Then I will best your companions.*

In Dhamon's mind the old dragon dove toward the mirrored one, both claws outstretched, mouth opened wide, showing rows of jagged, shadowy teeth. A serpentine tongue snaked out, whipping the air, then lashing at the snout of the new dragon.

Dhamon recoiled from the image in his mind.

You've no more magical items, dragon, he cursed vehemently. *There's nothing to power your dying spell.*

But I do, the shadow dragon instantly returned. *There's magic in the wingless sivak, and more in the ogre-mage. The naga, too. Their deaths will release the energy I need.*

Then the shadow dragon began to retreat back into his old body.

"There is time to vanquish your spirit later, Dhamon Grimwulf," the shadow dragon hissed. "First I must collect more of the necessary essence—starting with your friends."

So you don't have enough power yet to wipe out my humanity, Dhamon said. *There must be something about me that is too difficult to overcome. What?*

Why was the shadow dragon having so much trouble? Dhamon wondered. Could it be he carried a touch of Fiona's madness, bequeathed to Dhamon by the Chaos wight who had invaded his mind? The shadow dragon might not be able to cope with that unexpected fragment of madness lodged within the body he had been nurturing for his own ends.

Yes, that madness is the final barrier, the shadow dragon admitted. *But with more magic, I will defeat the madness. After your friends are dead, their energy will be mine. When they are gone, I will come again. And then you will be destroyed.*

❖ ❖ ❖ ❖ ❖ ❖

Maldred slashed with his claws at the bloated shadow dragon. He'd used magic to sharpen his claws, and now he began to slice through the dragon's scales and draw shadow-dark blood. "Killing this dragon is the key!" he cried exultantly. "I'm sure of it!"

The draconian struggled with the naga, his clawed fingers tightening around her neck. The Solamnic Knight was slowly backing away from Ragh and Dhamon, watching as though mesmerized as the shadow dragon came alive and raised a claw and batted Maldred away as though he was but a cornhusk doll.

The shadow dragon spread forward, dull yellow eyes locked on Ragh, its jaws opening.

"Rig is dead," Fiona murmured dully to herself. "Shaon and Raph and Jasper. All dead. Soon Ragh will be dead. And Maldred too. Everyone dead."

The shadow dragon hardly bothered to glance at the Solamnic Knight, as it closed on the draconian and the naga, its lips drawn back in a feral smile, showing its teeth.

The beast didn't even care about her, she thought. First it would finish Maldred. Then Ragh. Finally she would be the only one left alive . . . the only one . . . alone.

Fiona rushed forward, sword gleaming in the magical light that still swirled around the chamber. She brushed by Ragh and closed on the shadow dragon, swept her sword hard and wide, and bit into a thick, scaly plate on the dragon's stomach.

The shadow dragon wheeled on her, astonished to have been attacked by a lone human. His eyes narrowed on the magic weapon.

"Your sword," the shadow dragon cried. "I will have it now."

"Fiona!" Maldred shouted.

"I'll have the magic in your sword," the dragon repeated, "and I'll have you."

Fiona spat at the beast and pulled back, swinging her sword forward into the dragon's outstretched claw, digging into dragon flesh and causing a spurt of black blood.

"Come and get me, dragon!" she yelled.

"Fiona, get back!" Maldred shouted again. He had come up behind the dragon, where he touched his thumbs together and hurriedly tried a spell. His hands took on a faint green glow, and he stood and pointed his fingers like weapons at the shadow dragon.

Ragh finished his strangling of the naga and dropped her to the ground. He stumbled over her serpent-body, spun and shot for the shadow dragon.

At that moment, with the shadow dragon distracted by so many foes, Dhamon felt a surge of power. In his mind's eye the mirrored dragon had been chasing the evil dragon. Now the mirrored one breathed a black cloud that streamed toward the other.

Fiona thrust upward. Her enchanted blade dug deep into the staggered shadow dragon.

He had sacrificed too much energy to power the transference spell. He had used up all but the last of the god-magic that had birthed him in the Abyss.

Again Fiona thrust her sword, unknowingly buying Dhamon precious seconds to increase his mental battle and release his breath weapon. Buying Maldred time to enforce his spell. Buying Ragh time to close on the weary old dragon with his talons.

"Come and get me, dragon!" Fiona yelled again.

The mirrored dragon breathed again in Dhamon's mind—and suddenly that black breath materialized in the chamber beneath the mountains. The black, poisonous cloud raced away from Dhamon's maw to engulf the shadow dragon's head.

In the wink of an eye, the shadow dragon was finally purged from Dhamon's mind, and in that instant, Dhamon shook off all of his sluggishness.

The shadow dragon slammed a claw down on Fiona. He swung his head about, watching Maldred balefully. The ogre's spell sent globes of green fire at the creature.

Maldred with his green fire, Ragh with his mighty claws, Dhamon with his breath weapon. The three united to attack the beast.

It finally fell.

As Fiona had fallen.

❖ ❖ ❖ ❖ ❖ ❖ ❖

When they looked around, the naga had disappeared without a trace. Ragh had thought the frightful creature was dead, but Nura must have slithered off during the final battle—the demise of her beloved master. They didn't have the energy or the heart to follow after the child-snake-woman who had ensnared them all in her mad scheming.

They buried Fiona deep inside the dragon's cave, near where she'd valiantly made her last stand. Near her head, Maldred used his magic to turn the rock wall into liquid—for several moments—then he rammed her prized long sword into the stone. The once-enchanted sword would forever mark her honorable fate.

Maldred spread the enchantment over the earth and broken stones, sealing the spot into a smooth sheet of rock.

"I hope she's found Rig again," the draconian said when Maldred was finished. "I hope that if there is something beyond this world, a place where spirits go when their bodies are done . . . I hope she's there with Rig. That together they're at peace."

Dhamon didn't say anything. He closed his great dragon eyes and silently grieved—for Fiona and Rig, for Shaon and Raph and Jasper. For all the lives he'd touched and befouled. Minutes later, in eerie silence, he slipped from the chamber, taking the widest passage that climbed to the surface. Maldred and Ragh followed him.

They didn't speak until they emerged in the foothills. The sun was setting, painting the dry ground with a warm glow and setting Dhamon's scales aglow as if they were molten metal. Dhamon lay down, talons stretched to the horizon, wings tucked in close.

Ragh cautiously climbed up first, settling himself at the base of Dhamon's neck between two wicked-looking spines. Maldred waited, watching the sun sink lower, the glow start to fade. Then he perched himself behind Ragh, grasping one of Dhamon's spines and clenching his legs tight as the dragon spread his wings and effortlessly vaulted into the sky.

Flying came instinctively to him, and Dhamon wondered if it was seeded in him by the dragon-magic, or whether it was partly because of the years he flew on the back of the blue dragon Gale. The wind rushed above and beneath his wings, played across his head and caressed his back. He felt he should be troubled by his ruined humanity, but the power of this new form, the sensation of flying, kept his morose thoughts at bay.

Perhaps there was something wonderful and fated about becoming a dragon. Dhamon found himself enjoying the sensation of flying so high above the earth.

"Where are we going?" Ragh had to shout to be heard above the wind.

Dhamon's answer was to bank far to the south, to the edge of the mountain range. The sky was starting to grow dark by the time he landed, nodding for Maldred to get off.

The ogre-mage did so with some reluctance.

"I will miss you, Dhamon," Maldred said. "I will hope that fate sees to bring us together again, and I will hope that in the intervening time you find a way to forgive me."

Dhamon waited until the ogre-mage stepped away before spreading his wings. His legs propelled him skyward once more, and as he rose higher his neck craned back for a last glance at his onetime friend. The blue-skinned giant was gone. In his stead was again the bronze-hued man with a handsome, angular face and close-cropped, tawny hair. That was the old form that Dhamon knew and the one that seemed to suit Maldred the best.

"You're not dropping me off on some lonely peak," Ragh grumbled. Softer, but not so soft that Dhamon couldn't hear, he added, "Besides I've nowhere to go."

Their course took them slightly west now, then toward Haltigoth. Stars were winking into view by the time they landed. The draconian slipped from Dhamon's back, and Dhamon called upon a spell that came to him unbidden from mysterious depths.

Within the span of a few moments, the dragon that was Dhamon Grimwulf appeared to fold in upon himself, shrinking, then becoming flat, like a pool of oil. The oil glided silently to the draconian, attached itself, and moved with him as his shadow. Ragh hurried to the nearby village, skirted the stable, and passed beyond the closed merchant stalls. There was a small, stone building with a thatch roof. Dhamon's keen senses led them there.

Ragh crept toward a window at the back.

Riki and her husband sat at a wooden table. Riki cradled an infant—a boy with mysterious, dark eyes and wheat-blond hair. A boy, Dhamon decided, that he would check in on again over time to make sure his way in this world was safe and profitable.

"Seen enough?" Ragh whispered after several minutes. The draconian did not want to risk discovery.

Aye, the shadow answered. *I have seen well and enough.*

They left the village, flying again and cutting a course against a cold, fall wind. Dhamon headed north, where a dragon named Gale held sway. He wanted to see his old battle partner and see Gale's surprise. In the miles that stretched between Throt and Gale's lair perhaps he would figure out how to explain what had happened to him.

"What then?" Ragh asked. "After Gale?"

Dhamon wasn't certain. Perhaps they might journey to the Dragon Isles, certainly to somewhere he'd never been before. This new body, a new life, demanded new surroundings.

"They named the boy Evran," Ragh told him. "Riki said it was an old family name she wanted to honor. Sounds nice. For a human name."

Dhamon inwardly smiled. Evran was his middle name. Few but Riki knew that. The child did indeed favor him in some way.

Collections of the best of the DRAGONLANCE® saga

From *New York Times* best-selling authors Margaret Weis & Tracy Hickman.

THE ANNOTATED LEGENDS

**A striking new three-in-one hardcover collection
that complements *The Annotated Chronicles*.
Includes *Time of the Twins*, *War of the Twins*,
and *Test of the Twins*.**

For the first time, DRAGONLANCE saga co-creators Weis & Hickman
share their insights, inspirations, and memories of the writing of this
epic trilogy. Follow their thoughts as they craft a story of ambition,
pride, and sacrifice, told through the annals of time and
beyond the edge of the world.

THE WAR OF SOULS Boxed Set

**Copies of the *New York Times* best-selling War of Souls
trilogy paperbacks in a beautiful slipcover case.
Includes *Dragons of a Fallen Sun*, *Dragons of a Lost Star*,
and *Dragons of a Vanished Moon*.**

The gods have abandoned Krynn. An army of the dead marches
under the leadership of a strange and mystical warrior. A kender holds
the key to the vanishing of time. Through it all, an epic struggle
for the past and future unfolds.